Praise for *War Brides*

"Outstanding. . . . wonderfully warm. . . . Battle is a gifted writer whose novels deserve acclaim."
— *Baton Rouge Magazine*

"A superb old-fashioned novel."
— *Los Angeles Herald-Examiner*

"Arresting . . . [Battle has] a skillful touch."
— *The San Diego Union*

"A compelling novel . . . entirely riveting."
— *Richmond Times-Dispatch*

"The characters are memorable, the settings believable, and the reading effortless. *War Brides* is a book that will interest you up to the last page, the last paragraph, even the last line." — *South Bend Tribune*

"A good, old-fashioned read."
— *Charleston Evening Post*

"Satisfying and readable."
— *Anniston Star*

ABOUT THE AUTHOR

Lois Battle is the author of seven other novels including *The Florabama Ladies' Auxiliary & Sewing Circle, Bed and Breakfast, Storyville, A Habit of the Blood,* and *The Past is Another Country.* She lives in Beaufort, South Carolina.

WAR BRIDES

LOIS BATTLE

PENGUIN BOOKS

PENGUIN BOOKS
Published by the Penguin Group
Penguin Putnam Inc., 375 Hudson Street, New York, New York 10014, U.S.A.
Penguin Books Ltd, 27 Wrights Lane, London W8 5TZ, England
Penguin Books Australia Ltd, Ringwood, Victoria, Australia
Penguin Books Canada Ltd, 10 Alcorn Avenue, Toronto, Ontario, Canada M4V 3B2
Penguin Books (N.Z.) Ltd, 182–190 Wairau Road, Auckland 10, New Zealand
Penguin India, 210 Chiranjiv Tower, 43 Nehru Place, New Delhi 11009, India

Penguin Books Ltd, Registered Offices: Harmondsworth, Middlesex, England

First published in the United States of America by St. Martin's Press, 1982
Published in Penguin Books 1998

10 9 8 7 6 5 4 3 2

Grateful acknowledgment is made for permission to reprint excerpts from the following copyrighted works:
"Chickery-Chick"—Sidney Lippman & Sylvia Dee. Copyright © 1945 by Santly-Joy, Inc. Copyright renewed and assigned to Harry Von Tilzer Music Publishing Company (c/o The Welk Music Group, Santa Monica, CA 90401, for the U.S.A. only). All rights outside the U.S.A. controlled by Chappell & Co., Inc. (Intersong Music, Publisher). International copyright secured. All rights reserved. Used by permission.
"Long Ago (and Far Away)" by Jerome Kern and Ira Gershwin. Copyright © 1944 by T. B. Harms Company (c/o The Welk Music Group, Santa Monica, CA 90401). Copyright renewed. International copyright secured. All rights reserved. Used by permission.
"Open the Door, Richard"—Words by Dusty Fletcher and John Mason, music by Jack McVea and Dan Howell. © 1946, 1947 by Dutchess Music Corporation, New York, NY. Copyright renewed. Used by permission. All rights reserved.
"Some Enchanted Evening"—Richard Rodgers & Oscar Hammerstein. Copyright © 1949 by Richard Rodgers & Oscar Hammerstein. Copyright renewed, Williamson Music, Inc., owner of publication and allied rights for the Western Hemisphere and Japan. International copyright secured. All rights reserved. Used by permission.
Excerpts from "The Girl That I Marry" by Irving Berlin on page 196. © Copyright 1946 by Irving Berlin. © Copyright renewed. Reprinted by permission of Irving Berlin Music Corporation.
"(There'll Be Blue Birds Over) the White Cliffs of Dover." Copyright MCMXLI renewed by Shapiro, Bernstein & Co. Inc. International copyright secured. All rights reserved including public performance for profit. Used by permission.
"Wish Me Luck"—Phil James & Harry Parr Davis. Copyright © 1939 by Chappell Music Ltd. Copyright renewed, Chappell & Co., Inc., Publisher. International copyright secured. All rights reserved. Used by permission.

PUBLISHER'S NOTE
This is a work of fiction. Names, characters, places, and incidents either are the product of the author's imagination or are used fictitiously, and any resemblance to actual persons, living or dead, events, or locales is entirely coincidental.

THE LIBRARY OF CONGRESS HAS CATALOGUED THE HARDCOVER AS FOLLOWS:
Battle, Lois.
War brides.
I. Title.
ISBN 0-312-85557-5 (hc.)
ISBN 0 14 02.7643 2 (pbk.)
PS3552.A8325W3   813'.54   81–16732

Printed in the United States of America
Set in Garamond 3

To Doreen, my mother

"Entreat me not to leave thee,
Or to return from following after thee;
for whither thou goest, I will go; and
where thou lodgest, I will lodge:
Thy people shall be my people, and thy
God my God . . ."

> The Book of Ruth

"Sensual pleasure occupies a very small and fiery
place in the illimitable desert of love, glowing
so brightly that at first nothing else is to be
seen. Around this inconstant campfire is
danger, is the unknown. When we arise from a
short embrace or even a long night, comes
again the necessity of living near each other,
for each other."

> Colette, *La Vagabonde*

WAR
BRIDES

CHAPTER
I

DAWN MUELLER pulled the baby closer to her breast, gripped the ship's railing with her free hand, and looked around for her daughter. The child had been taken below by a friendly young woman just a few minutes before, but as Dawn scanned the unfamiliar deck she felt a twinge of anxiety. Everything that day had been such a mixup—the mad bustle of two hundred women and their children finding cabins, the streamers and flags waving, the shouted farewells from families and friends on the wharf, the band blaring patriotic tunes, the deafening horns signaling departure. And, then, the anticlimax as it was announced that sailing would be delayed.

After two hours of waiting, the Bon Voyage band had packed up and left. A clean-up crew loitered on the periphery of the wharf. Many of the passengers had gone below. Those who remained chatted quietly to each other, shushed irritable children or gestured to the remaining well-wishers on shore with improvised sign language. A group of women, who looked as though they might have smuggled some strong Australian beer on board to celebrate their departure, clustered in a semicircle and raised their voices in a familiar song.

> There'll be blue birds over
> The White Cliffs of Dover,
> Tomorrow, when this world is free . . .

An officer tipped his hat, and hurried on before she could ask if there was any more news about the departure. She noticed a beautiful woman in a powder-blue suit standing a little distance from her, quietly smoking a cigarette, and thought she might ask her for information. But there was an aloofness in the woman's manner that discouraged conversation. Squinting her eyes against the sun, Dawn searched the wharf for her family. She had signaled them to leave many times, but of course she knew they would stand there until midnight if necessary.

She saw her father button the vest of the old suit, now too large for his bony frame, and put his arm around her mother. Charlie wasn't given to gestures of affection in public, and she strained to see if her mother had started to cry. But Marge stood stoically by Charlie's side, her spectacled face lifted toward the bulk of the ship with the same quietly attentive expression she showed whenever her favorite priest was in the pulpit. Even Dawn's sister, Patsy, whose wiry body was rarely still for a minute, stood in silent vigil, the setting sun making a halo of her copper hair and shadowing her impish face.

The pressure in Dawn's breasts told her that she should take the baby below and nurse it, but she couldn't bear to leave the railing. It might be years before she would see her family again. Perhaps she never would. The possibility of a permanent separation made her heart contract. The old division of feeling—wanting to be with her husband, Zac, but hating to leave her loved ones—flooded through her. She reached into the bag that was slung over her shoulder, fumbled for a handkerchief, and pulled out one of the baby's clean nappies instead. Wadding it up, she blotted the tears that were streaming from her eyes.

> There'll be joy and laughter
> And peace ever after,
> Tomorrow, when this world is free . . .

The bright future the women were singing about was already here. The war was finally over. Blackouts, air-raid drills, ration coupons, queuing up for butter and eggs, sleepless nights worrying over men who were across the seas—all those horrors and deprivations were past. Yet she no longer felt any of the euphoria that had swept through them all on VJ Day and the months that followed. She had told her father she would be there to help the family pick up the pieces after it was over. Now she was leaving, and taking the beloved grandchil-

dren to go halfway 'round the world. The irony of leaving her homeland as an American war bride struck her; of all the people she knew,
she had been the least interested in the arrival of the Yanks.

THE NIGHT AFTER the papers announced that the Americans would
set up a base a few miles from their town, she had tucked her daughter
Faye into bed as usual and joined her family in the sitting room. As
she settled down by the fireplace and started to fold the clean clothes
from the wash basket, Charlie creased his evening paper with great
deliberation and set it aside. He got up, stretched his once-muscular
workingman's body, and cleared his throat. Patsy put down her book
and winked at Dawn: they were in for another harangue. Charlie
lectured in what Patsy called his "union meeting voice" for at least
ten minutes, poking the air with his pipe for emphasis. His message
was clear: if he caught either of his daughters misbehaving with
Yanks, he'd turn them out of the house. He addressed both of them,
but Patsy was the focus of his attention. She was only sixteen and
Charlie was sure she was still flighty enough to have her head turned
by a handsome stranger in uniform. Dawn was, after all, a widow with
a child and old enough to know better.

Patsy's foot began to tap impatiently on the worn carpet. Marge,
never missing a stitch of her knitting, glanced up over her spectacles,
tacitly admonishing her to pay attention. Patsy stilled the offending
foot. Marge never challenged her husband's authority or interrupted
his speeches, even when they were a trifle excessive in their rhetoric;
but her glances influenced her children's behavior more than his
bombastic preachments ever did. Charlie put his pipe back into his
mouth, drew on it thoughtfully, and nodded to his tiny audience.
Patsy heaved a sigh and shifted her weight in the old cane chair.

"Oh, Charlie, you make it sound as though all Yanks are Jack the
Rippers."

"They're men away from home. They've been fighting hard and
they've not seen any women in a long time. It's only human nature
that they should try to take advantage."

"Nobody's going to take advantage of me," she answered firmly.
"I'm not an infant, you know."

"I know you're a good girl, but . . ."

"But what?" Patsy challenged. "We all know there's been no man between seventeen and fifty around here for ages, but if I finally manage to see one, I promise I'm not going to act like a tart."

"Watch your language, young lady. Nobody said anything about tarts. Mind, I'm not saying you'd keep company with a chap because he'd get you a pair of stockings, but . . ." he paused, thinking of something that might inject a little levity into his warnings, "you're tuppence light in the crumpet when it comes to dancing and you might not look at a man's character if he could teach you a new jitterbug step."

"Oh, come on, mate," she cried impatiently, wounded pride not allowing her to acknowledge the twinkle in her father's eyes.

"The Yanks have a lot of money," he continued soberly. "And they won't mind throwing it around. They'll have luxuries we haven't seen in a long time, and probably couldn't afford if we did. They'll be out for a good time."

"I wish you'd stop talking about them as though they were an army of occupation. They're the Allies, after all."

"They might be the bloody Allies now, but they didn't come into the bloody war until our boys had been fighting for over two years."

"Oh, let's not go into *that* again," Patsy groaned.

Marge took off her glasses, rubbed the indentations at the side of her nose, and placed her knitting in the work basket. "I think it's time we all had our cup of tea," she interjected in her calm, eternal peacemaker voice. "Besides, it's time for the news reports."

"That means I've missed my dance program," Patsy wailed as she looked at the grandfather clock on the mantelpiece. "Just because I had to hear another Moral Lesson for Wayward Girls."

"I'll have no more of your lip tonight, Miss Priss," Charlie barked. He stoked the fire and searched around for a simple order that would restore his sense of authority. "You'd best not be troubling about Mr. Glenn Miller until you've gone out to the shed and brought in more wood for the fire. Dawn will put the kettle on, and I'll go in and see if the youngster's dropped off."

Patsy grudgingly rose to her feet as he left the room. Dawn went into the kitchen and lit the gas. When she returned with the tray of tea and scones, they were huddled around the ancient wireless. The announcer's voice droned over the continual static. ". . . and inflicted heavy casualties during the first few hours of the advance. General MacArthur was quoted as saying . . ."

Dawn poured the tea and passed the cups around, her hand shaking slightly. A feeling of great weariness came over her. Would it never be over? The war dominated their lives so completely that it was impossible to remember what life had been like before its great shadow had cast them into continual gloom. At the beginning there had been good-natured sacrifice, expectation of speedy victories, plans for what would happen "afterwards." Her young husband, Ian, had enlisted immediately and looked forward to his service in the Air Force as a great but temporary adventure. And she had felt more pride than fear when he and her brother, Kevin, had been shipped to North Africa. When Ian kissed her goodbye, he had patted her belly, which was just beginning to swell with her first pregnancy, and told her that she should look around for a house they might move into when he returned. She packed up the scraps of furniture from their little flat, moved back in with her parents, and struggled through the last months of pregnancy without him. She kept her spirits up by looking at property, and planned their future home right down to the color of the bedroom curtains. Even when his letters stopped coming shortly after Faye was born, she stubbornly assured herself that his silence was due to some snarl-up in the overseas mail. Then the official letter arrived:

Dear Madam:

In confirmation of the notification sent to you by the Australian Air Board, it is my painful duty to confirm the death of your husband, Ian Farrell, No. AUS/16785, Aircraft Pilot Royal Australian Air Force of No. 148 Squadron, who was killed at 12.35 P.M. on the 5th October in Kabrit, Middle East.

The Air Council desire me, in conveying this information, to express their sympathy and deep regret at your husband's death in the service of the Empire.

I am, dear Madam, your obedient servant.

Just six weeks after she'd received the news, a similar letter had come announcing her brother's death.

As the announcer concluded the report of the day's events and started into a list of local men missing in action, Charlie got up from his rocking chair, rested his arms on the mantelpiece, and stared at the photo of his son, so vibrantly full of life in his white cricketer's outfit. Charlie's eyes were vacant; his teeth ground on the stem of his pipe.

Dawn had thought Marge would be the one who would take the news the hardest. But Marge, whether out of a need to remain the calm center of the group of souls she considered her responsibility, or because of a philosophy that encompassed disaster and death, seemed to come to terms with the staggering loss. Except for the fact that she now rose every morning to go to Mass and sometimes moved her lips in silent prayer or a conversation with her departed son, her behavior was outwardly unchanged. But Charlie could not share his wife's belief in a divine providence. He began to lose weight. His moods, which had always been volatile, now swung from violent thrashing rages to quiescent, brooding mournfulness. The double bereavement threw Dawn into a numb shock for several months. Then she began to function in an efficient but anesthetized fashion, crushing all emotion beneath the daily tasks of washing, cooking, cleaning, caring for Faye and doing volunteer work at the military hospital.

"No one we know tonight," Patsy said when the announcer had finished the list.

"We may not know them, but they're somebody's sons," Charlie muttered as the wireless popped and crackled with the strains of "Be Careful, It's My Heart." "You can have your dance music now, Patsy."

"I think I'll just toddle off and get me beauty rest," she replied quietly, starting out of the room, then returning to place a quick kiss on Charlie's cheek. "Listen, old chap. I won't disgrace you with any Yanks. And you know you don't have to worry about Dawn."

He patted her hand absently and turned back to stare into the embers. Dawn put down the scone she'd been nibbling. She'd had to skimp on the recipe and it was flat and unappetizing. Making a mental note to get up early the next morning to queue up for the butter ration, she picked up the tea tray and trudged back to the kitchen. As she washed up the dishes she could hear Marge's voice start up in the same intimate, soothing tones she'd overheard from her parent's bedroom ever since she was a child.

THE FIRST TIME she saw U.S. Navy Chief Zac Mueller, she probably wouldn't have noticed him if the afternoon nurse hadn't pointed him out as being "a bit of all right." Propped up in bed, his right arm and hand swathed in bandages because his flesh had been peppered with shrapnel, Zac appeared rather sullen. He barely acknowledged her when she offered to give him a shave, but she recognized the gruffness as the defense of a man who was not comfortable with dependency. She kept up a gentle patter of small talk as she lathered his prominent jaw. By the time she'd finished shaving him, his bright blue eyes had softened. When she asked if he'd like to dictate any letters home, he passed his left hand through his dark hair and said "That sure would be fine," in that flat, broad accent that sounded strange to her ears. She cleared away the shaving gear and went to the volunteers' station to collect a pad and envelope.

"I hope you won't mind if this is written in pencil," she smiled, settling into the bedside chair.

"No problem. They'll be glad to hear from me."

"I expect so."

"Dear folks," he began self-consciously, "it shouldn't be long now before we can wind this thing up. Guess you've been reading in the papers that we've really been giving Hirohito's boys hell . . . no, make that giving them the works." He paused, staring into the mid-distance, the jaw tensing again. "I guess you must've got the money I sent by now. Homer can use it to build that new garage you've been wanting before the winter sets in. It sure is hard to think you've had snow already. The weather here is real warm so it sure doesn't feel like we're coming up to Thanksgiving. The people here are real fine too . . ." He turned his head to look at her. The sunlight from the window near the bed shone on her fine auburn hair, outlining the curve of her cheek, which had a rosy glow even without makeup. As she bent forward over the writing pad, the neckline of her dress fell away from her body just enough to show the edge of a hand-embroidered slip. As his gaze went down to her bare knees, she lifted her head. The gray eyes had an extraordinary compassion and openness. ". . . They've made us feel real welcome. I have to shove off now. And just sign it Zac."

"Is that all?"

"Yeah, well, I don't want to tell them I've been wounded," he said with a mixture of stoicism and guilt. "It'd just get them worried. Just put a P.S. saying I've mashed my thumb so a buddy is writing for me. And don't put anything showing that it's sent from a hospital, okay?"

"Whatever you like." She folded the letter and got to her feet. "I'll pop this in the post on my way home. Hope you're feeling a bit more chipper when I see you next."

"When will that be?"

"I'm in every Tuesday and Friday afternoon."

"I'll look forward to seeing you, er . . . ?"

"Mrs. Farrell. Dawn Farrell."

"Is your husband in the service?"

"He was in the RAAF. He was killed in action in the Middle East."

"Oh." He searched for some word of condolence but could find none. "Well, thanks again."

"Cheerio for now."

"So long, Aussie."

After her second week as barber and secretary, Zac confessed that he'd never been such a dutiful correspondent in his life. He told her he was to be released from hospital the next day and asked if he might take her out for an evening by way of expressing his gratitude. When she answered that she didn't like to be gone in the evenings because it meant she couldn't spend time with her little girl, he suggested that they could go on a picnic and take Faye along. Had he considered every possible strategy for winning her over, he couldn't have come up with a better suggestion. Since Ian's death, she had gone out with only one man, an old friend of the family who was home on leave. He had looked terribly burdened whenever she mentioned Faye's name, so she had rejected his offer for another date, feeling that any man who couldn't accept her child was of no interest to her.

She made sure that Charlie wouldn't be home when Zac came around on the following Saturday afternoon. He arrived punctually, looking very spiffy in his uniform and loaded down with packages. He presented Marge with several cans of peaches and pineapple juice, telling her that since he was regular Navy instead of a draftee, and a friend of the quartermaster to boot, he was entitled to some extras and wanted to share them with his friends. And he brought along a picture book of *Snow White* for Faye.

In the late afternoon when they came back from the picnic in King's Park, Dawn wanted him to leave them at the tram stop, but he insisted on escorting them to the house. As they turned the corner into her street, she saw Charlie watering the front lawn and braced herself for a chilly round of introductions. But Charlie had apparently been coaxed into politeness by Marge and shook Zac's hand warmly when she introduced them. When she came back outside after taking Faye in to her grandmother, Charlie announced that he was going to take Zac down to the local pub and shout him to a few beers.

It was after nine when they returned. Charlie was slightly tipsy and in an expansive mood. Steering Zac into the kitchen, he declared the Yank to be a bloody fine bloke who knew how to handle his liquor. Marge, mindful of the pattern of her husband's drinking days, had kept the supper warm and asked Zac to join them. Dawn set out the plates of mutton with mint sauce, roasted potatoes and turnips, apologizing for the meager fare.

Zac said that since he'd lived in an orphanage until he was five and had adapted to Navy chow since he was eighteen, the meal looked like a feast to him. His foster mother, Suds, was a plain cook, more interested in quantity than seasonings. His bright blue eyes, which rarely lost their tinge of suspicion, became gentle as Dawn heaped a second helping onto his plate. He couldn't take his eyes from her as she puttered around the kitchen. There was something about the careful, concentrated way in which she moved about, tending to her chores, brushing the fine auburn hair from her heat-flushed face, that soothed him. She looked so unaffectedly pretty in the print housedress; and the apron, tied tightly around her waist, accented the full, womanly lines of her body. She was so unlike the other women he'd known—the prostitutes and good-time gals that eyed him up and down, sat on his lap and quickened his blood with their sleazy, insincere propositions.

When they adjourned to the sitting room to listen to the wireless, the reports of battles and skirmishes seemed far away. He had often told his shipmates that he was in the war for his country and a paycheck; but now, warmed by the food and drink, witnessing the easy affection of this family, he began to understand what other guys meant when they spoke of fighting for their women and children or mentioned their longings for home. He left around midnight to go back to the base, pleased that he'd secured an invitation to come to dinner the following week.

The courtship was very proper, always with the background of the family. When taking Dawn out to a picture show or a dance, Zac might arrive early to help Charlie chop wood, or play in the sitting room with Faye. He was respectful toward Marge and treated Patsy with the good-natured teasing attitude of an older brother. Patsy always stayed up when her sister went out with "Super Yank." She would lurk in the passageway when she heard the door latch click, grab Dawn's hand, and pull her into her bedroom for a furious inquisition.

"Did you have a good time? Was the band wonderful? Did they play 'Besame Mucho'? I just love that song. It means kiss me in Spanish or something. Did he?"

"Did he what?"

"Cripes, you're dense sometimes! *Kiss you.* Did he kiss you?"

"No. He didn't kiss me."

"Why don't you tell me the truth?" Patsy said with disgust. "I won't tell anyone."

"I am telling you the truth."

"Well, I just don't believe you."

"Perhaps he's shy."

"Shy my eye! He only has to walk down the street and all the girls turn their heads around like their necks were made of India rubber. Even Mum says how handsome he is and you know she never talks about men that way. He's only thirty-four, isn't he? You're not past it at thirty-four, are you?"

"No, you're not past it at thirty-four," Dawn smiled. "I would have let him kiss me, but he didn't try. He *is* shy, at least about anything emotional. From the little he tells me, I don't think he's ever had any real attachment. Apparently his foster parents were very strict. Besides, he understands my position, I don't want to . . ."

"Oh, I'll bet you just acted all la-di-da and wouldn't let him near . . ." A muffled sound from the back of the house silenced her. "That'll be Charlie," she whispered after a beat. "You'd better get to your room before he comes down and gives me what for. But if you don't kiss Zac next time you go out with him just don't bother to come in here and talk to me."

"*You're* the one who pulled me in here," Dawn said with teasing indignation. "Mind your own bloody business and don't be such a pest."

"Oh, go bite your bum," Patsy laughed, kissing her.

Dawn crept down the hallway to the room she shared with Faye. She closed the door quietly, slipped off her high heels, and tiptoed to the child's bed. She stroked the leg that had kicked off the covers and put it back under the blanket. Undressing in the dark, she wondered why Zac had been so reticent. Of course he understood that she couldn't risk a trivial affair; but he'd been taking her out for over a month now and, though she could see in his eyes that he was attracted to her, the closest contact they'd had was on the dance floor. Just tonight, during a slow song, his rough cheek next to her own, she had felt a giddy expectation that made her legs go weak. She'd pressed into him, forgetting caution, aching for him to kiss her. But just as his arms tightened around her, when she was sure he was going to yield to the impulse, he'd spun her away from him saying he wished the band would pep it up because they were such good partners on the fast numbers. She sighed, crawled into bed, and shivered at the touch of the icy sheets. Ian had always kidded her about her cold feet. He would get into bed first, repeating his joke about being her human hot-water bottle, and watch her undress. "Don't put on the nightdress," he would say, "I'll keep you warm." And she would ease in beside him, constantly surprised at the heat of his body, which was warm even during the coldest weather.

She heard Faye whimper in her sleep, and got up and lay beside the child, crooning "It's all right, Mummy's here" until her own eyes fluttered shut.

When Zac finally proposed to her, he had only kissed her twice. He told her that he loved her. Said he was convinced that she would be an ideal wife. He even said that he might want to give up the military and move to Australia when the war was over because he shared her affection for her family.

On their wedding night, as she lay in the big double bed at the hotel and listened to him taking a shower, it occurred to her that she really knew very little about him. She longed to talk to him in an intimate way, with whispers, pet words, private bedroom jokes, to reveal all the passion she'd been forced to hide. She looked at the ridiculously expensive nightdress Patsy had urged her to buy, hoping the stretch marks on her breasts would not be visible in the moonlit room. As she heard him turn off the taps and flick the light switch, a tremor of expectation shuddered through her. Now she would see his body. Now she would break through all the reserve, show him how much she wanted him.

He came into the room wearing pajamas, strode to the windows, and pulled down the shades.

There was no question about his virility when he came to her; but his lovemaking was restrained, almost reverential, leaving her unsatisfied. She longed to tell him that he could let himself go, but couldn't find the words. Besides, she knew that the sort of freedom and trust she craved could not be asked for. It didn't come about instantly because they'd been pronounced man and wife. It would take time. As she rested her head on the matted hair of his chest and listened to the steady pumping of his heart, she was sure they would work it out. It would just take a little time.

He was transferred to the east coast a few weeks after the wedding.

She saw him briefly about five months later when he managed to get a three-day leave before returning to the States. Shortly after that, she discovered she was pregnant again.

> There'll be blue birds over
> The White Cliffs of Dover,
> Tomorrow, when this world is free . . .

She shook her right hand, almost numb from clutching the railing, shifted the baby's weight onto her other hip, and tucked the soggy ribbons of the bonnet under her chin. Nita stared up at her with Zac's bright blue eyes, reached for the ribbons, and stuffed them back into her rosebud mouth. Dawn dabbed her cheeks, took a breath of the chilly salt air, and put the nappie back into her purse.

"Oh, Mummy, are you crying again?" she heard Faye's voice pipe. "There's such a funny little lavatory downstairs. It's just like a cubby house." Her eldest daughter was at her side, still clutching the hand of the pretty young woman who'd volunteered to take her below.

"Thanks so much."

"Quite all right. We had a lovely time exploring the ship, didn't we, Faye?"

"Yes, and Mummy, Sheila promised to take me up the stairs all the way to where the flags are."

"Remember what I've told you about calling adults by their first names? I'm sorry, but I don't think I remember what your last name is."

"Rigby . . . oops, Hickock. I'm Sheila Hickock. I still forget to give my married name."

"Then it's Mrs. Hickock, Faye."

"But she's just like Patsy," Faye protested, struggling to understand the division between big ladies and girls.

Dawn looked at Sheila more closely. She was very young, probably not over nineteen. Despite her grooming, which suggested she must be a fan of the movie magazines, her manner was girlish. Perhaps it was the expression of defiance hardening the youthful features that had initially made Dawn think she was older. The wide brown eyes, framed with blond curls that had been swept up and clustered over the forehead in imitation of the Betty Grable style, were naive and expectant. Her teeth protruded ever so slightly and her real lip line, under the bright lipstick, had an almost childish pout. Her body was slender, with almost nonexistent breasts.

"I'll hold the baby for you if you'd like to take a rest," Sheila offered, teetering slightly on her high-heeled wedgies.

"I wouldn't want to trouble you. Babies have a way of mucking up your clothes," Dawn said quickly, noting Sheila's carefully pressed slacks and pale angora cardigan.

"Nonsense. I love babies. I'm going to have at least six myself," she answered enthusiastically, holding out her arms.

"Her name's Nita, and she wets on people sometimes," Faye cautioned, as Dawn handed the baby over. "And you have to be careful not to drop her . . . Mrs. Hickock."

"Don't worry, lovey, I won't."

"I don't think she needs to be changed," Dawn said as she thrust her hand under the baby's blanket for a quick check, "but she certainly needs to be fed. It's just that I can't leave the railing. My family's still down on the wharf. Was there any word about when we'll be getting underway?"

"One of the men told me any minute now."

"Are your parents still waiting?"

"No. They left ages ago."

Dawn noticed that the rebellious expression on Sheila's face changed momentarily to a look of doubt.

"My Mum and Da aren't too happy about my going."

"I don't suppose any of us can be really happy about it. I'm feeling homesick already. And of course we don't have any idea of what America will be like."

"It'll be wonderful," Sheila said rapturously, the eagerness returning to her wide brown eyes. "If my papers hadn't come through after all that red tape, I think I'd have dropped my knickers and started to swim across. They have everything in America! Besides, it's been over six months since my Billy was shipped back. He didn't even want to go home but he's got a combat decoration and lots of overseas service, so he scored high on the points system and they shipped him out."

"I haven't seen my new daddy since I was four," Faye put in.

"And that must've been ages ago."

"It is, because I'm five last week. My Nana made a cake with pink icing, but Nita couldn't have any cake because she just drinks mummy's milk . . ."

Dawn shot Faye the look that reminded her she was not supposed to intrude on adult conversation. "I wish my Nana was coming," Faye whispered, realizing that Marge was too far away to intercede for her. She tugged at the bow in her plaits, and peeked through the railings at the wharf.

"You see, Billy and I were only married for a few weeks before he left for the States," Sheila continued, "so you can imagine I feel like a race horse at the starting gate. Billy's home is in Virginia. I went to those orientation meetings the Red Cross gave for the brides and they showed photos of it. It's really lovely. Virginia, I mean. Just like *Gone With the Wind.* Beautiful old mansions and all. Of course they have modern cities as well. They probably have subways and nightclubs and. . ."

Sheila prattled on, interspersing her monologue with little laughs and exclamations. Dawn did her best to listen, but she thought she felt an increased vibration under her feet. A buxom nurse elbowed her way into position at her side, cradling a squalling infant. A garbled voice boomed over the P.A. and suddenly there was a burst of activity on deck. Passengers darted from the stairwells. The woman who had been conducting the chorus of singers herded her group over to the railing, raising her arm to start another song.

> Wish me luck as you wave me goodbye,
> Cheerio, here I go, on my way,
> Wish me luck, as you wave me goodbye,
> With a cheer, not a tear,
> Make it gay . . .

As the bleating of the tugboat was answered by the deep bellow of the ship's horn, a shout went up from the passengers. The crowd on the wharf echoed the cry and moved closer to the barricades. Dawn grabbed the baby back from Sheila and reached for Faye's hand. For a moment she lost sight of her family; then she saw Patsy's bright copper curls bobbing up and down. Patsy flung up both arms, wildly waving American and Australian flags. Charlie's right arm shot up and froze in mid-air. But it was the sight of Marge, standing calmly behind the rush of the others, that caused her the sharpest anguish. The rays of the setting sun hit the spectacles that Marge was now obliged to wear and her body looked very fragile in her dark patterned frock. "She's getting old," Dawn realized, the clarity of distance jarring her into a recognition that everyday contact had obscured.

She had a sudden presentiment that Marge would never have a protracted illness that would allow her to return and care for her, but would die quickly while performing one of the many gruelling household tasks that made up her everyday life. She longed to put her arms around her mother one last time, to embrace the birdlike body that had endured so much suffering without complaint. A great spasm of pain shuddered through her and she let out a wail that was not unlike the sounds she had heard from wounded men at the hospital. Faye looked up at her with frightened eyes, her small lips trembling.

"Why can't they come too, Mummy? I want Nana and Pop to come."

"Wave! Wave to them!" Dawn yelled hoarsely over the cacophony of shouts and singing and yoohooing. She pulled Faye's arm into the air and moved it up and down. "I'll be back," she cried as the ship maneuvered the channel and turned to face the brilliant sea. "I'll be back!"

The figures on the wharf became smaller and smaller, anonymous dots on a picture postcard of docks surrounded by green hills. As the chill breeze came upon them and rain clouds scudded across the horizon, most of the passengers scurried below deck. Dawn looked up at the tremendous, darkening sky and out onto the great expanse of ocean. She felt very small and unprotected. Her mind groped toward a vision of the future just as a woman finding herself in a long, dark corridor might grope her way along the walls, hoping to find an open door. She imagined Zac at her side, circling her in his strength, promising she would never again wake in the night gasping for his safety, assuring her that now, at last, she would have a home of her own: a place where she could love and nurture the children and express her devotion to Zac in ways that hadn't been possible thus far. Confusion, frustration and fear would all vanish. They would be supplanted by the joys of peace that only those who had suffered through a war could truly appreciate.

"Mummy? Mummy! Nita's crying and my legs are cold."

She started in a guilty way, realizing that she'd neglected the children. She was someone on whom others depended. Now was not the time to dwell on her own insecurities.

"Yes, angel, I'm sorry. We'll go down to the cabin now."

Sheila offered to come and help her with the children, but she said she needed a few minutes alone. After giving Sheila the number of her cabin, she cautioned Faye to be careful going down the steep stairs, and turned for one last look at the diminishing shoreline.

CHAPTER
II

SHEILA WAS SORRY when she saw Dawn and the children disappear. There was something sympathetic about Dawn, she decided, something pensive and caring in her gray eyes that inspired trust. It was too bad Dawn seemed to be so miserable about leaving Australia and so uncertain about what America would be like. But that sort of timidity always seemed to infect older people. She guessed that Dawn couldn't have been more than twenty-seven, but Sheila could already see the signs of cautiousness that always annoyed her. It was just like her parents. No sense of adventure. Whenever she tried anything new, from buying a pair of high heels to going off on holiday with her girlfriends, her mother would be seized with palpitations and her father would issue so many warnings that all the fun would go out of things. From the moment she'd introduced them to Billy they'd been muttering doom and gloom. They'd fought her every inch of the way about her wedding, and once they'd realized she was actually going to leave the country, their whining had become insufferable.

She heaved a sigh and gazed about, hungry for human contact. Two girls were strolling arm in arm, and over near the hatchway a couple of deckhands were chatting. Sauntering toward the prow, she saw a woman in a powder-blue suit sitting alone smoking a cigarette. She could have sworn she remembered seeing this same woman embracing a blowsy middle-aged creature with peroxide hair on the wharf, but now as she looked at her more closely it seemed unlikely that she would even know such a disreputable-looking person. Sheila inched her way over to the deck chairs and sat down, wondering how best to start a conversation.

"Thank goodness we're finally on our way," she said at last.

"Yes," the woman assented, sweeping the dark brown hair back from her cheek in a single studied gesture. She paused a moment, and then stretched out a pale hand tipped with long, carmine fingernails. "Gaynor Cunningham."

"Sheila Hickock. Pleased to meet you, I'm sure."

Resettling herself, Gaynor gazed out at the last vivid striations of the sunset and drew on her cigarette. Sheila looked into the oval face and tried to guess if Gaynor's dark, slanting eyes had been touched with mascara. She'd once tried to put some on herself, but her mother had said that it looked cheap and her father had warned her of eye infections. She'd been quite pleased when she'd looked at herself in the mirror this morning, but now, studying her companion, she suddenly felt frowsy. Gaynor had the aloof, implacable poise of those models in the fashion pages. The tailored lines of her suit were accented by a single strand of pearls and matching earrings. The froth of a lace slip peeked out over the long, sheer-stockinged legs. The glossy brown hair was parted in the middle and fell to shoulder length, framing the profile of a small, finely molded nose and a rather sharp chin. Sheila thought that Gaynor looked a lot like Gene Tierney and wondered what it would be like to have the blessing of real beauty. Sometimes, mostly when they were making love, Billy told her that she was the prettiest girl in the world. But as she looked at Gaynor Cunningham, she realized that no matter what efforts she made with her grooming, she would never be more than what the Yanks called "real cute."

"It's lovely up here on deck, isn't it," Sheila smiled. "I've never been on a really big ship before. My Da used to rent a little boat sometimes, and he and I would go sailing. We had some bonzer times, Da and I. It was just on the Swan River, of course. Nothing as impressive as this. My Da isn't a very athletic sort—he's a chemist, you see—but he did love to go on the little boat."

She felt her lower lip tremble. She never thanked Da for those outings, even though she was the one who'd talked him into them. But then, she never thanked Da for so many things. "I expect I'll take up sailing in America," she continued, feeling that if she could just keep talking she'd be able to control the quiver in her lip. "I don't know if there are many lakes in Virginia—that's where I'm going—but I expect there must be. Do you know anything about Virginia? I think they told me it's near New York."

The corners of Gaynor's mouth curled into an indulgent smile. "I'm not an expert on geography, but I don't think Virginia is anywhere near New York."

"Oh," Sheila replied dumbly. "I suppose it will take me a while to learn the map. I could draw a map of Australia and the British Isles when I was in the fourth standard. My mother always used to help me with my schoolwork. I won a prize for being able to name all the capitals of the world."

Why was she blathering on about her parents? This morning she'd been only too grateful to see the back of them, now she was dredging up silly memories and sounding positively juvenile. Perhaps she was feeling wistful because she hadn't shown them more consideration at her departure. But it wasn't her fault. She'd tried to overlook their disgustingly nagging behavior since she knew she wouldn't see them for a long time, but they had made it quite impossible.

Her mother had come into her bedroom last night, just after she'd finished packing. She had sat down on the bed, picked up a doll in a satin dress she'd given Sheila for some long-distant birthday and started into a boring reminiscence of what a delightful child Sheila had been. *She's been telling me that I* was *delightful, past tense, ever since I was four,* Sheila thought as she plunked herself down at her dressing table and started to wind her hair into pin curls. *I suppose I stopped being delightful once I gained the power of speech.* She concentrated on her reflection, not wanting to look at her mother's face once the lecture about marriage started. She knew it would be peppered with phrases like "woman's lot" and "wifely duties" and would wind up with a rehash of the anguish her mother had felt when she'd left her own parents and moved into town after Da had purchased his chemist's shop.

"But it's a wife's obligation to follow her husband, no matter what god-awful place he takes her to," her mother sighed as she automatically rearranged the things Sheila had packed.

Sheila examined a pimple forming on her chin and remained silent. She couldn't see that their home was so god-awful. Of course it was nothing much compared to the house she expected to share with Billy. But it was a good cut above what most of her friends had. There was the modern bathroom, a kitchen decked with most of the appliances that were advertised in the magazines but very hard to come by during the war, and Da's garden, which sent the perfume of roses through her bedroom window. And they had the luxury of a car that few of their neighbors could afford.

Even as a child, Sheila sensed that her mother's dissatisfactions with married life were not of a material nature. When mother nagged and pouted, Da always saw to it that she got the imported English china or the new lounge chair. But the acquisitions never seemed to please her for very long. No, her mother was soured on marriage for reasons that Sheila only dimly perceived until she started to be interested in boys. Then it struck her that the discontent that always floated about the home like a musty odor must have something to do with sex.

At fourteen Sheila tried to describe the delicious sensations she felt when the boy who lived down the street had kissed her, but her mother stiffened and told her to be careful. Such things were not to be talked about, not even between a mother and her growing daughter. Sheila thought that Da might understand, but she knew that she shouldn't discuss it with him. So she listened to the secretive talk of her girlfriends, watched love scenes flicker on the screen at the Regal Picture House, and tried to fill in the gaps in her information. When she fell in love with Billy, everything she'd only guessed about became brilliantly clear. Word had it that one could spot a girl who was no longer a virgin by the way she walked, but Sheila was sure that the giveaway was in the face. She was sure that the look of rapt involvement on her father's face when he pruned his roses, or the momentary satisfaction that crossed her mother's features when a new piece of furniture was set in place, were pale imitations of the dreamy, contented expression that stayed with her for hours after she'd been with Billy.

Now it was clear. The reason her home was so lacking in joy, despite its prosperity, was because her parents didn't like to sleep with each other. The knowledge turned a glaring light on all the constricting intricacies of their family relationships. Apart from embarrassing her, it also filled her with a secret sense of superiority.

She twisted a strand of hair around her finger and listened to her mother's voice drone on. ". . . because your head is so full of romantic nonsense. You'll be in for a rude awakening when you greet the real world. You've always been spoiled. Always been a daddy's girl . . ."

She opened her mouth to reply that it wasn't her fault, but then bit her lip and shoved the bobby pin into her hair, scratching her scalp.

"I know what it's like to be alone," the voice persisted. "You think it will be a piece of plum pudding when you get to America. But if you're unhappy, who are you going to turn to? If you have troubles, who will you call on? There'll be no one to reach out to, no one who'll care. You'll see the error of your ways, my girl. You'll forget your high and mighty ideas and wish you'd heeded my advice. Consider the fact that you barely know this boy. His mother hasn't even had the decency to write to us."

On and on she went, mixing all the slights and disappointments of her own life into a bitter brew that had nothing whatever to do with Sheila. *She's so bogged down in her furniture and her imaginary aches and pains that she can't even guess at what a great adventure I'm about to have,* Sheila thought, as she fastened the last curl and turned around.

"Mum, I'll be all right. You always say that I know how to get what I want, so I don't see why you're so worried. Now why don't you just toddle off to bed, and we'll all get a good night's sleep?"

"It's not too late, you know. You could wait and think about it for another couple of months and then, when you've had time to really reflect, there'll be plenty of opportunity to go over to the States. Why, I heard just yesterday from Mrs. Morgan that one of the girls who went over on the first transport got there and found out that the man she'd married had been deceiving her. He was already married to a woman over there and had two grown-up children. Can you imagine! Now that poor girl's going to have to come back home in disgrace."

She laughed as she tied the scarf around her pin curls. "Since Billy's only twenty-one, I don't think he's had time to become a bigamist, Mum."

"Yes. He's got more medals than hairs on his chest. And that's why I'm worried about what's going to happen to you," her mother cried with genuine anguish. "What sort of a position will Billy be able to get once he's out of the Marines? You told us yourself that he doesn't have any education. He may be a hero, but they don't give good positions to young men just because they're heroes. And you're still so young."

"Come on, Mum. Love conquers all; or hadn't you heard?" she said with the slightest touch of scorn. "I think I'll just go out and say goodnight to Da."

"I might have known that you wouldn't be persuaded. Oh, this war has just turned everything upside down. In my time . . ."

"Apart from getting you to a few more meetings of the Ladies' Auxiliary and forcing you to buy on the black market, the war hasn't touched you much," Sheila cut in. "Billy's brother died at Corregidor, think about that!"

"You're still wet behind the ears," her mother countered, breathing hard. "You've set out on this marriage knowing nothing. And why? Because you became infatuated with this American boy and you couldn't wait to . . ."

Her voice broke off abruptly. Sheila met her eyes, challenging her to complete the sentence, but she clenched her lips, tightened the sash on her dressing gown, and looked at the floor.

And wouldn't you just croak if you knew that we didn't wait, Sheila thought triumphantly as she continued to stare her down. Her mother moved to the dressing table, pretending to be busy with the toiletries.

"Shall I put this skin lotion in your case?"

"Don't bother. I'm traveling light as they say. I'm going to buy everything new once I get to America."

Comforted by the thought that this would be the very last time she would have to listen to these angry, convoluted sermons, she put her arm around her mother's shoulders, feeling magnanimous enough to squeeze her before she left the room.

She knew Da would be on the veranda. He always had a smoke out there before he went to bed because her mother complained that his cigarettes gave the parlor an unpleasant odor. She pushed open the door and stood quietly on the threshold, catching her breath.

"Da?" she whispered, as she made out his form at the far end of the shadowy veranda. "I've come to say goodnight."

"And goodbye," he muttered.

Her chest heaved with the agony of another unpleasant encounter.

"Oh, Da, please don't start up about all the awful things that are going to happen to me. I've just heard it all from Mum."

"Al'right, m' girl," he answered softly, rubbing his hand over his bald spot and staring out into the garden. "Al'right. You always did as you liked anyhow. Ever since you were knee high to a duck. You've always had your own will."

"That's the way you brought me up, isn't it?"

Neither of them said anything for several minutes. Sheila breathed the moist fragrance of the rose bushes and scratched the emerging pimple thinking that if they badgered her any more they were definately going to ruin her complexion.

"I've just pruned the 'Dainty Bess' bushes you like so much," Da said after a time. "If I don't have any unforeseen problems, I might be able to enter them in the garden show . . ."

His shoulders started to shake and he clutched at her arm. She took his hand and held it tight until he seemed to regain his composure. "I went through my papers today, Sheila. Found the application forms we'd sent to the university. You would have been the first woman in our family to go on in school, you know."

"I never really wanted to go, you know that, Da."

"But you're such a bright girl. Ever since you finished school and started to help out at the shop I've noticed how quickly you pick things up. You've a fine mind. You could be anything you set your heart to."

"Please don't. You promised you wouldn't."

"Did I promise? You've always had a way of thinking that if you wanted me to do a thing, it meant I'd already promised. Ah, you've been a trial one way and another, Sheila. But I don't know what life will be like with you gone from the house."

"A lot quieter, I expect," she tried to kid him.

"And no matter what I say, you'll be off tomorrow. Halfway 'round the world . . . I won't try to change your mind as your mother has. I just want you to know . . ." he reached into his vest pocket and took out an envelope ". . . this is for you. I wanted to give you a proper wedding, but you were in too much of a hurry for that. So I spoke to the clerk at the shipping lines and found out the price of the passage from the States back to Australia. It's all in here for you."

"I don't want it."

It was really too much that they had to inflict this sort of punishment during her last night at home. Even now that she was a married woman, they still nagged and babied her, tried to make her feel guilty and ungrateful. She supposed it had something to do with being an only child. She'd already told Billy that she wanted a large family because she wasn't about to make a single child the repository of all her hopes and expectations, the way her parents had done. Her mind drifted off to a pleasant domestic scene in a Jimmy Stewart movie. Donna Reed was the wife. Jimmy and Donna lived in a big house with a spiral staircase and lots of sunny bay windows. They had adorable children who played around a big Christmas tree. Jimmy had some big philosophical problems, but Donna was so lovely and understanding as the young matron that you just knew they'd be able to work them out. Of course you could tell by the way Jimmy kissed her when he came home from the office that they still liked to go to bed with each other. In the final scene . . .

She felt Da make another attempt to thrust the offending envelope into her hand. "Da, *please.* I don't need it and I don't want it. Billy's my husband now, and he's going to take care of me. Why don't you and Mum use the money to take that holiday to the eastern states that you're always talking about?"

He tightened his grip on her arm and made small choking noises. She felt very sorry for him, but if she broke down and told him how much she was going to miss him, he would probably lose all control. And then what would she do? Why couldn't he just rise to the occasion and be brave and funny like Spencer Tracy in *A Guy Named Joe*? Instead he had to give way, look small and defeated, and make her feel she was going to burst into tears. She turned abruptly and ran into the house.

The memory of her last private words with her father filled her with guilt and confusion. If only he'd been able to let her go with some grace, wished her luck or shared her hopes for her future, she was sure that she would have expressed her love. But of course that was out of the question. Nothing in their house could ever be simple or easy.

"Did your parents get all upset when you left?" she asked Gaynor.

Gaynor uncrossed her legs, lit another cigarette, murmured a non-committal "Mmmm," and stared out into the darkness.

It was obvious that Sheila was intruding on the woman's privacy. Recollections of her mother's instructions about good manners mingled with her sense of discomfort, but she stayed rooted to the deck chair, reflecting on the day's events.

Her mother, who had been crying ever since breakfast, continued to sob in the back seat of the car as Da drove them to the port. Sheila turned her head around several times and gave a comforting smile, but her mother kept on. Sniffling, dabbing her eyes with the limp handkerchief, she twisted her features into such an expression of self-pity that Sheila's compassion became muddied with impatience and anger. *Mum's playing the victim again. Woman's lot.*

"Oh buck up, old thing," she said when she could bear the blubbering no longer. "If you can't find the stiff upper lip we're supposed to have inherited from your posh English relatives, how's about a bit of the grit we got from Da's convict ancestors?"

A furtive grin creased the right corner of Da's mouth. Sheila felt proud that she'd been able to make him smile. Then he saw her mother's reflection in the rear-view mirror and promptly changed the grin to an insincere gruffness. "That's enough of your cheekiness, Sheila. Show some respect for your mother's feelings."

She flushed with frustration and anger. Here was the old pattern again: she'd say something, knowing full well that her father agreed with her, and then, at her mother's prompting, he would do an about face, and they'd both gang up on her. God, she was glad to be getting out from under it!

Staring straight ahead through the windshield, she watched the familiar streets and buildings go by. There was the Church of England Girls' School where, until last year, she'd marched every morning dressed in her gray uniform, turned-up hat and navy blazer. The tennis courts where she'd won second prize in the Women's Intermediate Competitions. Then onto the main street—Da's chemist shop with the new front windows displaying the big apothecary jars, the butcher shop, the library, Schnetzer's Dry Goods, the Town Hall and the greengrocer's. And further down the street, the haunts she liked the most: Tony's Fish and Chip Shop, the confectioner's and the beloved Regal Picture House. It already looked quite small and nondescript when she compared it to the skyscrapers, plantations and swimming pools that floated in her imagination.

Coming out of her daydream, she noticed that the speedometer on the dashboard was registering twenty miles per hour. Typical of Da to stifle any emotions by being overly cautious. Or perhaps he actually meant to make her miss the ship.

"You're going like a snail with rheumatism, Da. I've got to be on board by half past two, you know."

When they arrived at the docks, she was in such a sweat that she hurled herself from the automobile, leaving them to bring up the rear. An officer on the wharf told her the departure would be delayed. The thought of having to watch her mother carry on for another hour was more than she could bear. Da naturally wanted to stay when she told him about the postponement, but her mother was starting to have palpitations, and since she'd left her pills home in the rush, Sheila was able to persuade them to leave. She hugged them both, promised that she would write faithfully every week, and walked up the gangplank, dry-eyed and triumphant.

"WOULD YOU LIKE a cigarette?" Gaynor asked finally.

"No thanks." She'd almost blurted out that she wasn't allowed to smoke. Leaning back in the deck chair, she listened to the muffled clatter of dishes and the occasional laughter coming from below deck. They must be getting ready for the evening meal, but she wasn't the least bit hungry. Besides, being in a room full of strangers would only increase the loneliness that was beginning to gnaw at her. She stared out at the pale moon that had just become visible and turned to Gaynor with a tentative smile.

"Getting quite chilly up here, isn't it?"

"Is it? I hadn't noticed."

She could feel her mask of confidence slip a little further in the face of Gaynor's sophistication. What if she wasn't able to present herself favorably when she met Billy's mother? Mrs. Hickock hadn't answered her letter. Perhaps she was opposed to the match as much as her own parents were. Yet Billy had told her that his family were just "home folks"—whatever that meant. He'd said his dead father's chief occupations had been hunting and fishing, and that didn't sound very pretentious. He'd assured her that anyone who was "okay with me will be okay with them." Still, it wouldn't be the same as being around people you knew, your own family.

"Are you going to become a citizen?" she asked Gaynor suddenly.

"I expect so."

"I suppose a woman should adopt her husband's country. As in the Book of Ruth: 'Whither thou goest I shall go, Wherever thou lodgest I shall lodge, and thy people shall be my people.' That's really quite splendid, isn't it? Of course I may get a bit homesick . . . occasionally . . ." Her voice trailed off.

Gaynor snuffed out the remains of her cigarette, reached across to pat her hand, and then rose from the deck chair. Sheila felt that she had been granted an audience and was now being signaled that it was at an end. Perhaps she would go below and write Billy a letter. Better yet, she could look in at Dawn's cabin and offer to help with the children. That was the best idea. She knew she might end up in a puddle of tears if she didn't have someone to talk with now. "Well, cheerio, Mrs. Cunningham. Nice chatting with you."

Gaynor watched her wobble away toward the staircase. Alone at the railing, she planted her feet firmly on the deck, pulled back her hair, and faced into the wind. Her eyes pierced the darkness as a ripple of laughter bubbled in her throat, released itself and stopped abruptly just as it reached its crest.

"I don't give a good goddamn if I never see any of it again," she whispered. "I'm on my way now, and I'm never coming back."

CHAPTER

III

"SHE ROLLS as she pitches, honey," the sailor laughed as he passed the group of women sitting in deck chairs and noticed Dawn's pallid face. "Don't lose yer nerve. Tomorrow morning it's terra firma."

"These Americans!" Mavis Slocum muttered as soon as he was out of earshot. "They haven't any respect."

"Oh, they call everyone honey," Sheila explained. "It's just their way of being friendly." She stopped bouncing Nita on her knees and looked around the little circle for support of her statement, but Dawn lay perfectly still, too ill to get involved, and Patricia Guizquicz's freckled face was stuck in a map, tracing the route she would take from San Francisco to Detroit.

"Of course," Mavis went on, putting her knitting aside to tuck a strand of ginger hair beneath her turban, "no one can blame the Yanks for not having the proper respect for us—not after the way some of the women on this ship have behaved."

Sheila pulled the baby's dress up and down, playing peek-a-boo, pretending to be absorbed in its goos and gurgles while she studied Mavis. In many ways she reminded Sheila of her mother; she had a curiosity that extended itself just far enough to make a judgment, which she struggled to back up with bits of evidence that were often insightful but more often manufactured. She was not a homely woman, but her constantly agitated expression distorted any natural attractiveness. Shortly after meeting her, Sheila and Dawn had christened her Stickybeak because she was so nosey. Now, after countless afternoons on deck, her nose baked to a bright red, she actually resembled a hungry bird grubbing about for something to peck at.

"Why, just last night at the records requests," Mavis continued, eyes popping, "that Gaynor Cunningham asked them to play 'It's Been a Long, Long Time' and I thought 'Not for you it hasn't, dearie.' I've heard her pass my cabin on her way up to the officers' quarters long after everyone else has gone to sleep."

That woman's voice has all the appeal of a leaky tap, Dawn thought. Her eyes fluttered open. She looked across at Sheila, saw her open her mouth and then close it abruptly, deciding not to rise to Mavis's bait. She smiled weakly as Sheila swept her long blond hair back from her eye. After poring over a number of movie magazines, Sheila had decided to abandon her Betty Grable upsweep. Now she copied the flowing style of Veronica Lake, explaining to Dawn that she felt this would give her a more sophisticated look. But the glamorous hairdo and the makeup only served to make her look like an adolescent who'd gotten into her mother's cosmetics. Still, she was a dear girl. When seasickness had made Dawn so nauseous that she couldn't care for the children properly, Sheila had volunteered to move out of the dormitory and into her cabin. She was a real help—taking Faye to the nightly bingo games and picture shows when Dawn was too woozy to move from her bunk, and playing with Nita while Dawn lined up at the tubs to wash soiled nappies.

"It's just that her behavior puts us all in such a compromised position," Mavis droned on.

Lord, I hope I don't lose control and throttle her before we reach the shore, Dawn thought, squeezing her eyes shut and putting her arm across her forehead. She'd been seasick ever since they'd left Freemantle. Now they were only fourteen hours from San Francisco, and she could think of nothing more appealing than setting her feet on solid ground. She had marked off the days of the voyage as though she were a prisoner, thinking how much Zac would tease her when she confessed to being such a landlubber.

"I don't see what's so terrible about Gaynor going to have a drink with the captain," Sheila said finally.

"Where there's smoke there's fire. I knew that Gaynor was a ratbag the moment I set eyes on her. And it worries me because you know we're all going to have a rotten reputation with the Americans and women like her just confirm their worst suspicions."

"Why shouldn't the Yanks like us?"

"Because they'll think of us as foreigners with loose morals who got picked up in dance halls and stole their homesick boys."

"I met Carl at a dance," Patricia Guizquicz put in blandly, "but it certainly wasn't what you'd call racy. Dry sandwiches, a banjo, an out-of-tune piano and Father O'Herlity skulking around measuring the distance between the couples to make sure none of us girls were an 'occasion of sin' to the sex-hungry troops."

"Well, I don't think our national pride rests on any one woman's shoulders," Sheila reasoned, trying to sound mature.

"Personally, I don't care what anyone thinks of me," Dawn said tiredly. "Just as long as they find my passport in order and let me off this bloody ship."

"I only meant that *some* women . . . well, speak of the devil," Mavis whispered, inclining her head toward the staircase.

Gaynor was coming down the stairs, head erect, long limbs shown off to advantage in the brief halter top and white shorts. "Over here, Gaynor," Sheila yelled, damned if she were going to let Mavis dictate her choice of friends. Gaynor waved and started toward them. Mavis shoved on her sunglasses, grabbed Patricia's map, poked her nose into it, and turned her back. Gaynor paused for the briefest moment, and then moved past them without breaking her stride.

"No, thanks, Sheila," she called over her shoulder, holding up a book. "I'm just at a fascinating part of the story and I'm going to read for awhile." Strolling further along the deck, she found an isolated deck chair, settled down languidly, and opened the copy of *Forever Amber.* As the brisk sea breeze hit her naked legs, she thought it might be nice to be in that protective circle of other women. There was a certain calm in listening to the old wives' tales, the decorating tips, the gossip. Of course if you knew you were the object of the gossip the moment you left, it wasn't all that pleasant, and her sensibilities had been sharpened by experience to detect the most subtle social slight. She shifted her gaze back to them, saw Mavis nattering away *sotto voce.* For a moment, she felt like the outcast of a primitive tribe.

"Did you hear that posh English accent she puts on? 'Nooo, Sheila. I'm going to re-ad for a-while.' I can tell you, that accent's more from ambition than breeding. She doesn't even realize that it won't impress the Yanks because they can't hear the difference between a Pommy accent and ours. And I know she must've gotten that book from one of the men on board because it's banned in Australia."

"How do you know?" Sheila inquired mischievously. "Did you try to buy it?"

"She does have lovely legs," Patricia observed.

Mavis's eyebrows arched upward as her mouth turned down. "I'll bet she shaves them."

"Lots of American girls shave their legs," Sheila said.

"When a woman has responsibilities at home, she doesn't have time for all that Hollywood nonsense."

"I think American girls are beautiful," Sheila persisted. "They take much better care of themselves than we do."

"The only ones you've ever seen have been on the film screen. The rest are just ordinary like us."

"Well, I'm not going to be ordinary. I'm not going to let myself go to pot just because I'm married. I'm going to have my hair done every week and wear pretty negligees."

"You might have to change your tune once the first baby comes," Patricia Guizquicz warned.

"I don't think so. Look at Dawn. She has two kiddies and she still looks pretty."

"I feel like a wilted dandelion," Dawn laughed, struggling to her feet. "And I think I'll go below and try to freshen up for the last supper." She took the baby from Sheila's lap and called out for Faye, who was playing marbles a little distance from them.

"I won a green and a brown snake's eye," Faye panted triumphantly, holding up the marbles.

"That's very good, but we're going to get dressed for dinner now."

The child wrinkled her nose. "I hope they don't have that chicken with jam again."

"That's not chicken with jam, silly," Sheila said. "It's turkey with something called cranberry sauce and the cook told me that Americans eat it for all their holidays, so if you don't like it you can just bite your bum. If you hadn't been getting so many Hershey bars from the men who've fallen in love with you you'd probably have more of an appetite."

"I didn't eat the last one," Faye giggled, throwing her arms around Sheila's waist. "Mummy told me I have to share, so I put it under your pillow for a surprise."

"Then I'd best come down to the cabin to make sure I'm not going to be sleeping in a melted chocolate goo."

She nodded goodbye to Mavis and Patricia, called out a loud farewell to Gaynor, took Faye's hand, and followed Dawn's unsteady steps across the deck.

Gaynor waved back, crossed her legs and tried to become absorbed in her book. She was annoyed with herself for allowing that stupid Mavis to upset her. It wasn't as though she was unfamiliar with the type. She'd been dealing with Mavis and her ilk since she had been a teenager and was no longer intimidated by their slights and rejections. It had been a painful adolescent encounter with just such a "respectable" girl that had broken her heart and irreparably changed her view of human relationships.

Lela Waddington was the girl Gaynor most admired when she was fourteen. Besides having a physical maturity that made her classmates in the ninth standard look gangly and awkward by comparison, Lela was top of the class, and had a handsome older brother who was in his first year at the university and parents whose names appeared in the paper in connection with parties for the opening day of the races. When, through a remarkable stroke of good luck, Gaynor was shifted to the front of the class and given a desk next to hers, she almost expected Lela's golden aura to drift onto her like so much fairy dust. Recognizing Gaynor as the next brightest student in the ninth standard, Lela quickly gave up the struggle to maintain her competitive edge and formed an alliance with her. Lela referred to all the other girls in the school as "muggins" and said that she and Gaynor were the queen bees in a hive of drones. Gaynor studied very hard to keep her privileged position in Lela's eyes. It was only when the afternoon sun invaded the stuffy classroom and touched the edge of Lela's pale lashes that Gaynor found herself utterly unable to concentrate. Lela was so very beautiful.

When school was out for the day, they would ride their bikes down to the meadows near the train station and loll in the tall grass until they heard the whistle of the 5:10. They talked about history and hair styles, made up ghastly stories about the private lives of their teachers, debated about a woman becoming prime minister. Gaynor did Lela's algebra and Lela corrected Gaynor's French verbs. With the aid of some poems by Swinburne, a few Gothic novels and a biology text that Lela had swiped from her brother's room, they concocted a strange pastiche on the taboo subject of sex and swore a solemn oath that whoever married first would be honor-bound to discuss "it" with the other. Sometimes they would just lie together in the grass holding hands and looking up at the sky. The sweet intimacy of these afternoons almost made the secret horrors of Gaynor's life supportable.

Gaynor became a regular guest at the Waddingtons'. She was even allowed to accompany the family to their house by the seashore for one glorious weekend. She wanted to reciprocate Lela's invitations; but much as she adored her friend, she couldn't bring herself to divulge the truth about her own home life. Lela had riding lessons, pretty frocks, a father who inquired about her studies, a mother who wore afternoon dresses and instructed her on the proper etiquette of serving formal teas. What would she think if she knew that Gaynor lived in a smelly little house with broken windows and had a mother who cursed and threw things at her?

Instead of admitting that she had no memory of having a father, Gaynor said he had been killed in a car accident. She explained that Thelma, her mother, couldn't have visitors because she was often ill but didn't say that Thelma's poor health was due to the effects of too much gin. She glossed over Thelma's job as a barmaid and entirely suppressed any mention of the steady stream of "uncles" who bedded down at the house. Since Lela was too inexperienced to even guess that such ugliness existed in the world, she believed Gaynor's stories and thought it quite romantic to have a friend with such a tragic background.

But the weight of the double life was too much for a girl of her tender years. When the term started again after the Christmas holidays, Lela noticed that Gaynor was jittery and her eyes were often swollen and red. She begged Gaynor to confide in her, but Gaynor would only turn away and change the subject.

One afternoon when they were in the meadows, Lela made a wreath of wildflowers, placed it on Gaynor's head, and told her that she was the most beloved, truest friend of her life. Gaynor burst into tears. She made Lela promise never to tell what she was about to reveal and then poured out the whole sordid story. It had been bad enough before, she sobbed, but now her newest "uncle" had started coming into the bathroom when she was bathing. He had offered to give her ten shillings if she would let him watch her. When she had screamed at him to go away, he swore that he was going to tell Thelma that Gaynor had been showing herself to him.

Lela did her best to comfort her and said that she would manufacture some story so that Gaynor could come and stay at her house, but she was shocked and confused by Gaynor's confession. Her own mother had told her that girls were naturally deserving of respect, and if they found themselves in a compromised position, it was undoubtedly a reflection on their own conduct. She wondered if Gaynor hadn't somehow brought the scene on herself. She had noticed that Gaynor flirted with her brother sometimes. Mingled with her sympathy was a strange sense of betrayal and having been dirtied.

It was all Lela could do to hide her revulsion when she saw the miserable house that Gaynor shared with Thelma. The odor of the rotting wood floors, which were covered with cheap, cracked linoleum whose original color could only be guessed, was mixed with the smell of leaking gas. Gaynor had tried to improve the tiny room where she slept by tacking pictures of famous ladies in beautiful gowns to the walls. But the glamorous cutouts only accentuated the shabbiness of the chipped iron bedstead and the dingy curtains. Gaynor stuffed some clean underclothes into her school bag, scribbled a note to Thelma, and went into the back of the house to collect her toothbrush. When Lela heard a croaking male voice call out "Gaynor?" she bolted for the front door and stood panting on the patch of dirt where the lawn should have been. She felt as though she was about to vomit. As soon as Gaynor rushed from the house, they jumped on their bicycles and pedaled as fast as they could.

Two days later when Gaynor returned to the house to pick up some books, Thelma was waiting for her in a drunken rage. Seeing the bruise on her mother's left cheek, she knew there must have been a row with the latest "uncle." Thelma called her a nasty little bitch for having caused so much trouble and threatened to tell the police she had run away if she didn't come home that night. Gaynor was frantic at the idea of leaving the sanctuary of the Waddington house, but Lela had told her that she didn't think she could stay on without arousing Mrs. Waddington's suspicions.

As she sat in the meadow with Lela that afternoon, she talked about her plans for escape. Lela tore the petals from a wildflower and looked toward the train station, saying that it was silly of Gaynor to think about running away because she was only a girl. But Gaynor talked on wildly. She would get out, she vowed. Of course she was too young to know what to do now, but in a year or two she might be able to get a scholarship to go on in school, or perhaps a rich and handsome man would fall in love with her and ask her to marry him. Hadn't that happened to Jane Eyre and the Duchess of Windsor? They'd managed to make men fall in love and rescue them. Lela nodded but didn't say anything. Even before they heard the whistle of the 5:10, she checked the gold wristwatch her father had given her for doing well in her exams, brushed the grass from her school uniform, and said she must be getting home. As Gaynor put her arms around her and buried her face in her neck, she thought she felt her stiffen. Lela got on her bike, paused long enough to say that she wouldn't be able to go to the cinema on Saturday because her brother was bringing some of his university chums home for tea, and rode off.

On Monday afternoon, when the last bell rang, Gaynor gathered up her books and turned to Lela expectantly. Lela said her mother had asked her to come home early, so she wouldn't be able to take their usual ride to the meadows. When Gaynor offered to take her algebra homework, she sighed and said if she didn't start to master equations herself she was going to degenerate to the level of the "muggins and drones." Gaynor nodded and replied that she was going straight home to work on her French. She rode to the meadows alone and lay motionless in the tall grass until nightfall.

By the end of the week, Lela was saying "please excuse me" when she reached across the desks to dip her pen into the inkwell.

Ah yes, Gaynor mused, as she rested *Forever Amber* on her breasts and shut her eyes, she knew all about the respectable types. To *hell* with them! She was past the point where a scornful look from someone like Mavis, who didn't even have the class or the money to warrant pretentions, could injure her feelings. If women didn't trust her now it wasn't because she had a drunken mother, lived in a shack and lacked all the protections that allowed them to be "nice girls." It was because they intuited that she had the power to attract and manipulate men in ways that they thought unacceptable. They were jealous of her looks and her self-reliance. When the good women disdained her, it gave her a perverse satisfaction. She had something to be proud of: she had used her intelligence and polished her looks into something that passed for beauty. She had put her past behind her.

At sixteen, when she had passed her leaving exam, the scholarship she had hoped for did not materialize. At Thelma's insistence she took a job as a salesgirl at a local dress shop. She handed over the bulk of her meager salary for what Thelma called her "keep." The rest went for nice clothes, so that at least while she was away from home, she could look and feel attractive. But no wealthy savior appeared with a proposal of marriage. After six months at the shop her fantasies were equally divided between dreams of escape and thoughts of putting her head into the gas oven. Then "uncle" Joey appeared on the scene. He was a middle-aged bookie with a bulbous nose, a roller-coaster bank account and a roving eye. Gaynor waited until he'd hit a big win and said "yes" to his umpteenth proposition. Joey was amazed that such a delectable little virgin should fall into his lap. In order to ensure a repeat performance, he slipped Gaynor a five-pound note and said he thought it would be best if they didn't mention anything to Thelma. By the end of three months, Gaynor had enough cash saved to move out.

She rented a small flat on the other side of town and got a job at one of the best dress shops in the city. In no time at all her manner and grooming became indistinguishable from that of the customers, a transformation that only made her feel their condescension more acutely. She took a clerical training course and found a position with a firm of solicitors, but was forced to leave a year later when the senior partner's wife found out that she was having an affair with him.

Then, quite by chance, she ran into Lela Waddington's brother in the expensive little restaurant where she always went for lunch even though it meant she would have to scrimp on her supper at home. He courted her for several months. Even though he never invited her to the Waddington family home, he made increasingly passionate vows about his honorable intentions. Her mind told her that he would never propose, but she was so caught up in her dream that he *might* that she finally went to bed with him. Shortly after they'd consummated the affair he said he would have to go to England on business. A year later she saw his wedding photos in the society page of the newspaper.

The solicitor came into her life again, offering to set her up in a more attractive flat on the condition that he be her only visitor. She knew there was no future in it, but accepted, feeling that if she could enjoy pleasant surroundings and didn't have to spend her time working at some menial job, the bouts of insomnia and depression might lift. But her benefactor became obsessively jealous and after one of his destructive rages, the landlady had requested that she give up the flat. She moved again and took a job in a jewelry store. With the announcement of war, she volunteered to arrange dances and fundraisers. She started to go out with servicemen, making sure that she never gave more than verbal comfort to any man beneath the rank of lieutenant. Then the Yanks came to town. She saw the possibility of not only improving her life, but of changing it entirely.

"Oh, Gaynor." She heard Sheila's voice at her side. "It's almost dinner time. Aren't you hungry?"

"Not particularly."

"I'm not really hungry myself. 'Spose it's all the excitement of finally getting close to port. I've had butterflies all day. Do you mind if I sit down?"

"Not at all."

"I just looked in my address book," Sheila said, perching on the edge of the deck chair, "and I noticed that I don't have your address in the States. It might be fun to correspond with each other, don't you think? Compare our impressions."

"I'll be going to Ricky's parents' home in Kansas City first. Ricky is being detained in Washington until August, though he will have a few days' leave in another month or so. He thinks it might be more comfortable for me to stay with his parents until he's well and truly out of the service. After that, I'm not sure where we'll go."

"The papers say there's a terrible housing shortage in the States. I was afraid we were going to have to move in with Billy's mother, but there's a house that used to belong to his brother, so we can have that. I was so relieved when I heard that, because I don't want to see anyone but Billy for at least a month."

When Gaynor's eyes told her that she understood the implications of her remark, Sheila grinned and went on with a more intimate confession. "You know when we took our honeymoon at Cotesloe we didn't leave the hotel room for three whole days. It was the loveliest time I've ever had in my whole life."

"Yes, the war did have a way of intensifying things."

"I don't think it was just the war. I think it's being in love."

"I suppose that has something to do with it too."

Sheila twittered on about all the places she hoped to see on her train ride across the country, trying to make up for the rebuff she was sure Gaynor must have felt because of Mavis's unkind behavior. A deckhand came up to them and said that Captain Putney would like to invite Gaynor to his cabin for drinks.

"Captain Putney seems to be a very nice man," Sheila said, the slightest trace of a question wrinkling her forehead.

"He is, extremely nice," Gaynor replied as she rose and stretched, her breasts straining against the cloth of her halter.

"It's just rotten luck that your husband has to stay in Washington. I'll bet you're just crazy about him."

"Isn't everyone crazy about her husband?" Gaynor smiled, opening her dark eyes wide.

"I suppose so. I mean, I don't see how you can have a really happy family life unless you are."

"Then I guess you'll have a very happy family life, Sheila."

"I will. Believe me. Well, I'll just toddle off to dinner. Ta ta."

As she mounted the stairs to the captain's cabin, Gaynor had a rare sense of well-being. When Captain Putney had first started to be friendly toward her, she had assumed that he was interested in a shipboard romance and she had been cool toward him. In the course of one of their conversations over scotch in his cabin, she had been pleased to discover that sex wasn't the real focus of his interest. Of course his eyes would wander over her legs and breasts when he'd had a couple of drinks; but the main reason he was gracious to her was because her father-in-law, Richard Cunningham, seemed to be a man of much greater influence than her husband, Ricky, had ever led her to suspect.

She had known from the moment Ricky walked into the jewelry shop where she worked and purchased a precious opal pendant without even looking at the price tag that he must have an income above his Army pay. But he had never let her know, even when they married, that he was the scion of one of the most influential families in the midwestern United States. She had had to mask her surprise and pretend that she was already familiar with the senior Cunningham's reputation, while trying to solicit more information from Captain Putney. Ricky had told her a good deal about his schooling, his aspirations, and his mother, of whom he seemed very fond, but he had said precious little about his father. Apparently he wanted to protect himself from women who were only interested in his money.

Even though she wouldn't have given him a tumble had she not guessed that he was rich, she was fond of Ricky. Though not dynamic or mature enough to really be considered a knockout, he had the regular-featured, blond good looks of an Arrow shirt ad. When he talked about fighting to preserve democracy or held forth about the future of the world after the war, his gray eyes would become quite brilliant, and his gestures, which were usually restrained and somewhat clumsy, would become expansive, almost forceful. Of course his pronouncements were filled with an idealism that made her feel a gulf far greater than the two-year seniority she had on him, but he was undeniably sweet. He treated her to the sort of wooing that she and Lela had dreamed about so long ago. He brought her flowers and books of poetry, praised her intelligence, and asked her permission before he embraced her. She read his favorite novels and encouraged his plans to reenter Princeton after the war. Having had a year-long affair with a married Army major who was about to be shipped back to the U.S., she found Ricky's romanticism a pleasant contrast to the major's aggressive sexual demands and gifts of cash. It was touching to see Ricky struggling to repress his desires and treating her with exaggerated respect. She guessed that when she finally went to bed with him, a proposal would follow. The first time they made love, he stopped before he entered her, asked her to marry him, and promised to be gentle.

As she approached the captain's cabin, she heard the muffled sounds of a record player and an off-key baritone singing along to *Takin' a Chance On Love*. She smiled contentedly, whispering the lyrics, congratulating herself on the gamble that promised to be even more lucrative than she'd hoped for, and admiring her wedding ring. She tapped on the door. The voice broke off as abruptly as if she'd walked in on him singing in the shower. The needle scratched across the record and there was a brief, embarrassed silence. Apparently the captain, who'd told her the usual stories of making hootch out of hair tonic during the war, was already well into another victory celebration.

The door opened a crack and Putney's sturdy face appeared. The jaw, which had the shadow of a beard even when he'd just shaved, hung slack, and his eyes shone in greeting. "Good evening, Mrs. Cunningham." He flung back the door and motioned her into the cabin with an elaborate wave of his hand. He had already loosened his tie and was holding a glass of scotch. She settled into a leather chair as he returned to the improvised bar that took up part of his desk and poured her a drink.

"Ooops. Just fixed you a scotch and didn't even ask what you wanted. You'll have to excuse me tonight, Mrs. Cunningham. I'm in a mood of jubilation."

"The scotch is quite acceptable, and please call me Gaynor. We've known each other for a month and I've asked you many times before."

"All right then, Gaynor. And you might as well call me Tim. As I said before, you'll have to excuse me. Tomorrow I'm goin' to drop this cargo of snotty nosed kids and hysterical dames—'scuse me— and I'm goin' to be free. Gloriously free. Dammit! I'm going home! Do you know what that means to me? Last time I was stateside was when this ship was in San Francisco being altered to accommodate dependents. I was so busy I didn't even have time to buy a lobster or have a drink."

She laughed indulgently as she accepted her scotch. "To the U.S.

of A.!" he chuckled. He returned to the desk, sank into his chair, and propped his big head in his hands, his grin fading. "I sure hope it won't be changed too much."

"Well, I can't comment on that."

"Naw. I know that. Hey, what am I beefin' about? It's gonna be great. We bailed out the British and the French. We finished up the job a whole year ahead of time. Everybody's working. Everybody's got money."

"What will you do after you get back?"

"Y' see, my family's in the toolmaking business. Had a little plant in Indiana, but when the war came along the government invested a lot of money in equipment and they advanced us some working capital."

"Sounds very prosperous."

"Well, I don't know if we're gonna have enough money to renegotiate into the peacetime market. We sorta became a subcontractor to a much bigger firm and now it looks as though they want to consolidate and buy us out. You know the big guys really solidified their power during the war. That's understandable—they were the ones who could get the job done. But I have a feeling that now it's over, it's not gonna be so easy to make 'em come apart again. . . . Hey, I'm bending your ear and probably boring you to death."

"No," she answered frankly. "I don't know much about it, but I've always been interested in the wheelings and dealings of business."

"I guess if you're married to Richard Cunningham's son you'd have to be interested or else you wouldn't have much to say at the dinner table but 'pass the peas.' 'Course your husband won't be having any of the problems I've been talking about. Cunningham must have interests in every major company in the Midwest."

"I suppose he must," Gaynor said casually. "Ricky—my husband —hasn't really talked to me about it in detail."

"I guess it isn't exactly a romantic subject. I didn't really mean to bring it up. It's just that I'm a bit worried, underneath the excitement of getting back and all. I wish I'd been around so I had a better bead on things. My old man's pretty good at business and he's worked real hard, but he's getting on. And my brother—well, let's just put it this way: Four-F isn't just the Army's classification for him: he's only a partner because of the accident of birth. And it's all changed so fast that I think I'm gonna have a lot of catching up to do."

"I thought it was the American dream not just to catch up, but to surpass. I'm sure you'll be able to handle it."

"That's very reassuring, Mrs. Cunningham," he smiled, "but you know, being in the Navy has taught me a lot. I've seen guys who really had a lot on the ball—they could tear down an engine, make a decision on the spot—but that doesn't mean that they're going to be engineers or policy makers when they get back home. Did you ever hear the story about the lake where there were thousands of minnow and just a coupla big pike?" Gaynor shrugged, tossing her head from side to side and playing with the ice cubes in her glass. "Well," he continued, his eyes narrowing and rising to the ceiling of the cabin, "the pike were eating up all the little minnows, so the minnows finally got together and formed a committee and went to talk to the pike. The pike kicked the minnows' complaints around for awhile, and then they came up with a brilliant solution. They said, 'Stop complaining, fellows; from now on, we've decided that one minnow out of a thousand will be allowed to become a pike.'"

"And what did the minnows say?"

"Oh, they didn't want to cause any trouble, so they said okay and went away happy."

"I'm not sure what the moral is, Tim. But I certainly hope you get to become a pike."

"I'll drink to that," he laughed, his humor suddenly returning. "Or at least an angry minnow. But what am I telling you for? You're a pike already."

"Only by marriage, Tim."

"Really? Well you coulda fooled me. I would've guessed that your family had lots of loot."

She pulled back instantly from the intimacy of further disclosure and fixed the disinterested look of privilege on her face.

"We were . . . comfortable," she said softly. "Just . . . comfortable."

THE NEXT MORNING the women and children lined the decks of the ship clutching the American flags that had been handed out by the Red Cross, and peered into the dense fog.

"Cripes, if it's there I certainly can't see it," Patricia sighed, handing the binoculars back to Mavis.

"Of course it's there, silly," Mavis insisted as she retrieved the binoculars and put the straps around her neck. Turning to the women around her, she spoke in a high-pitched, commanding voice. "I hope all you girls remembered to put your addresses on that paper I had up on the bulletin board. Otherwise you won't be getting your copies of the newsletter. And remember that it's your obligation to keep in touch."

"Blimey, she's like a troop leader in the Girl Guides," Sheila said under her breath.

"Fair dinkum," Dawn whispered, "I expect she has sergeant's stripes sewn onto her nightie and makes her husband salute three times before approaching the bed."

They had been trading silly remarks back and forth all morning, trying to dissipate their nervousness. As relieved as they both were that the journey was at an end, there was still the reality of another round of goodbyes. Then each would set out on the last leg of the trip alone, without the comfort of a familiar face or helping hand, to struggle with passports, baggage, maps and train tickets. Another link with the past would be broken. The shared laughter over slang expressions or national jokes, not all that funny in themselves, but providing a recognition that fostered good will, would be gone.

"I know you all think I'm barmy," Mavis said in a no-nonsense voice, "but I know we'll all see the need to be in touch with each other and this newsletter idea of mine is a very practical way to accomplish that."

Patricia Guizquicz placed a freckled hand on her shoulder. "Sure, righto, Mavis. We all think it's a super idea."

A look of confused gratitude softened Mavis's face. She struggled to arrange her features into a firm expression that gave her some illusion of control. She knew that despite all of her efforts at socializing, she hadn't really made one close friend during the voyage. Nobody felt the sort of affection for her that she could see between Sheila and Dawn and she wasn't strong enough to eschew the company of other women as that snobbish, sexy Gaynor Cunningham seemed to do. She swallowed hard and tried not to think about the fact that Herbie had consented to marry her only when she got pregnant and her father threatened to go to Herbie's superior officer if he didn't "do the right thing." Had she presented him with a son, she might have been able to demonstrate her worth and secure his loyalty. But she had miscarried in her third month, when Herbie had already left for his home in New York. Now she feared that he would feel he had been railroaded, tricked into an unfortunate marriage, though she knew he would be far too honorable to tell her so. She had desperately needed to confide her anxieties to another woman, but pride and shame had always stopped her from taking the risk.

"The thing is we're so damned dependent," she went on in such an unnaturally quiet voice that she caught her companions' attention. "I mean any woman is dependent on her husband, but if he turns out to be a no-hoper, she can always run home to her family. We won't be able to do that. Most of us won't even have a friend to fall back on. So if your one-and-only turns out to be less than God's gift to woman, you'll be in a bit of a pigsty, won't you?"

"There, there," Dawn said quickly, touched by the only revelation of doubt she'd ever heard Mavis express but put off by its timing. It was a fear all of them shared to varying degrees, but to voice it now when they were finally approaching the shore, when there was an unspoken collective decision to put the best face on things, seemed insensitive.

"You've told us that Herbie is absolutely bonkers about you and I'm sure he is," Sheila muttered. The other women who were standing by joined in with "We're just a bit on edge today" or "It'll all turn out all right," and then fell silent, looking up into the murky morning sky, or becoming absorbed in the buttoning of a child's cardigan or the examination of cuticles—anything to escape the eye contact that might unleash anxiety.

"You can see it now!" Patricia yelped suddenly, her body straining forward. "Look! Straight ahead of us!"

She let out a shout that was taken up by the other women and children crowding the deck. Dawn hoisted Faye up so that she could see over the railing, while Sheila emitted squeals of excitement and hugged Nita so violently that the baby began to cry. Twisting her head around to the top deck, Sheila saw Gaynor, resplendent in a yellow linen frock with matching hat, puffing nervously on a cigarette. "We're finally here!" she yelled. Gaynor tossed the cigarette to the deck, ground it underfoot, and raced down the stairs, putting her arms around Sheila. With her free hand Sheila reached across and drew Dawn to her.

The three women stood together in an uneasy embrace, their eyes straining through the fog to catch the first glimpse of the great continent of America.

CHAPTER

IV

"THERE SHE BE. Kansas City!"

The young soldier with the thick glasses and the unfortunate hair-cut, who had given her his widow seat when they'd boarded the plane, leaned past Gaynor and smudged the window with his fingertips. She looked down. The vast flat planes of earth streaked with railroads and dotted with silos were giving way to a massive clot of buidings, the nexus of a great city. "This is the heart of America, lady. Can you see those cylindrical bins there along the river? They're the grain eleva-tors. And on over there are the stockyards. When the wind is comin' the wrong way you can smell 'em for miles. But the stronger the smell, the better the livestock business. Wow-wee! I sure am glad to be gettin' back home!"

Her stomach flip-flopped as she felt the plane dip closer to the earth. A stewardess sauntered up the aisle, checking safety belts and request-ing that the man behind them extinguish his cigar. The soldier was practically sitting on Gaynor's lap as he leaned closer to the window, racing on with his description of the city, so caught up in his enthusi-asm that he barely noticed she had taken out her gold compact and was powdering her forehead.

"I'll be gettin' back into school over to Hollister soon as I can," he went on. "I'm gonna finish up in animal husbandry and get me a farm and make a million dollars by the time I'm thirty. I've got so much catchin' up to do. If I hadn't had to go over there and wup those Germans, I'da been sittin' on my own stretch of land right now."

She snapped the compact shut and screwed her earrings tighter. She'd heard it all before: the frustration of the deferred dream, the need to make up for lost time: the serviceman's lament. Americans always seemed to be rushing into the future with the frenzy of a kid who's been handicapped in a foot race. Even the middle-aged ones, like her former paramour the Major, were possessed with a blind assurance and a frantic energy. She found the go-get-'em cockiness very appealing. She had gone out with Englishmen, Dutchmen, Australians and a lone Frenchman, and if, as her mother had once told her, "all men are boys," then the Yanks were clearly the most boyish of the lot. They strode the earth with the restlessness and virile energy of adolescent conquerors, too buoyed up by their newly felt power to be offensive even when they were rude.

As they touched down, the soldier welcomed her to the U.S. for the fifteenth time, gulped, and got tears in his eyes when he assured her that this was God's country so she'd have to love it. After snatching up his duffle bag, he remembered his manners and asked if he could help her with anything. She reminded him that her husband's parents would be picking her up, ducked out of his way as he reached over the seat to shake hands with the cigar smoker, and was on her feet, feeling more excited than she had ever been in her life.

Walking into the terminal, she felt a bit lost as she watched the other passengers being swept into tearful or boisterous embraces. The young soldier, surrounded by a slew of relatives, was tossing a small boy, who also had thick glasses and an unfortunate haircut, into the air and bellowing "It's great to be back" over and over again. Then an old Negro man in livery stepped up to her and doffed his cap. "Miz Cunningham?" he inquired politely.

She was still unaccustomed to seeing black skin and she gazed curiously into the deeply creased ebony face before she breathed, "Yes, I'm Mrs. Cunningham." He bobbed his face in front of her, a broad grin exposing a set of remarkably healthy teeth, and muttered, "Mister Ricky's wife." Replacing his cap, he started through the crowd, glancing back with a deferential smile to make sure she was following him. On the edge of the throng she spied a diminutive middle-aged woman dressed in a rose-colored suit, her blond and silver hair swept underneath a gray veiled hat. Ricky had shown her so many pictures of his mother that she recognized her immediately, but Etna was even smaller and more retiring than the photographs had shown. When she saw Gaynor, her gloved hands fluttered upward, faltered, and settled at her sides. Then she raised them again to frame Gaynor's face.

"Oh my. Ricky told me that you were beautiful, but he didn't do you justice. Even your photographs don't show you to advantage because they can't capture your beautiful coloring."

Through the veil, her eyes seemed either myopic or misty, having the same gray irises and softly wistful expression as Ricky's. Her face had the kind of delicate prettiness that blossoms briefly in youth but soon fades, as though the harshness of reality caused it to lose definition. She pressed the small pale lips to Gaynor's cheeks, whispered, "Welcome. Welcome dear daughter," and took her arm.

"WE CAN JUST go out to the car. Jackson will fetch your luggage. Jackson has been with us since I was about your age. I just don't know what I'd do without him." Etna guided her through the corridors and out into the central lobby of the airport, talking in such a quiet, genteel tone that Gaynor had to incline her head toward her to hear. "My dear, I am so sorry that I'm the only one to greet you, but Richard had some emergency meetings or something. I'm sure that you must be exhausted after your journey. Just the notion of getting on a plane would frighten me and of course you've had more to contend with than the plane trip—You've come halfway 'round the world. I spoke to Ricky long distance last evening and he said, 'Mother, do everything you can to make Gaynor comfortable.' Of course he didn't have to caution me. I'm more than happy, terribly happy to welcome you. I know Ricky is just heartbroken that he won't be able to get away from Washington for the next six weeks. He was so distressed to think that he wouldn't be here to greet you properly."

Gaynor was still feeling queasy and excited and barely took in Etna's chatter, which had the soft buzz of an insect. When they came out of the building and walked toward the large black Buick that was parked directly in front of the entrance, her attention was arrested. She took in the sleek polished lines of the automobile and was aware of bystanders looking at her. Etna opened the back door and she slid into the seat. Jackson emerged from the building in the company of another black man, huffing under the weight of her many suitcases. They deposited most of them in the trunk and Jackson brought the smaller bags into the front seat with him.

"Straight home, Miz Cunningham?"

"I do think that you might just drive by the old place, Jackson. That is, if Gaynor isn't too exhausted."

"Not the least bit fagged," Gaynor smiled as the car pulled away from the curb.

"It's just that we don't get into this part of town very often, and I thought that you might like to see the house where Ricky was born. It's not much to look at now, but oh, how I loved that house. I never really wanted to move but Richard insisted, and I must admit that he was right. This part of town isn't what it used to be. But the house holds so many memories that I still hate to think of leaving it." The car glided down the streets of fine turn-of-the-century dwellings that now had the dilapidated look of rooming houses. "There it is," she cried as they approached the largest house on the block. "Please slow down, Jackson."

"You don't have to tell me, ma'am. I pulled into this driveway 'bout more times than I can remember."

"We daren't go in," she said, almost to herself, as she stared at the hulk of the once impressive three-story house with its wide verandas and ornate gingerbread work. The lawn was parched to a dismal ochre, and shabby lace curtains flapped in the open windows. "Oh dear," she sighed. "The happiest years of my life were spent in that house. Ricky was born in the big bedroom upstairs—the second window on the right. The doctor was going to have me go to the hospital, but there were complications and the baby came faster than I'd anticipated. Ricky was premature, you know."

Gaynor nodded and craned her neck toward the upstairs windows of the old house. She wanted nothing more than a tall drink and a cool room, but knew she should indulge Etna's need to talk about her past and feign interest in the circumstances of Ricky's birth.

"We live in the Country Club district now," Etna explained after she had motioned Jackson to drive on. "Even though we've lived there for years and it's very nice, it will never be like living in that old house. I know I'm sentimental, but I don't have to explain that to you. It's something only another woman would understand. And that's the reason why I'm so glad you're here, because I've always wanted a daughter, and now I finally have one."

She reached over and touched Gaynor's arm again, smiling at her with soft, nearsighted eyes. They turned back and drove through the industrial section of town. Tall buildings, marble vaults, the railroad station, bridges, great vats and furnaces appeared and disappeared. The downtown section of the city was pointed out, but they skirted it to drive through rows of modest houses. There were corner stores, streetcar lines, bars and playgrounds. A cinema marquee announced *"The Best Years of Our Lives*—Coming Soon" and brightly colored billboards offered a startling array of goods and services, teasing the consumer appetites that had been suppressed during the war years and were now bursting to be unleashed. Gaynor's head pivoted around trying to take it all in. The vastness of it amazed and delighted her.

Etna chatted on, pointing out this or that landmark, usually in connection with some memory of what Ricky had said or done on that particular spot. Gaynor put in polite questions and made appropriate comments as her eyes flitted back to Jackson's dark hands on the wheel. She had always had a desire to drive a car and now the possibility of actually being able to made her heart race. She pictured herself at the wheel, turning the car this way and that, having the power to go anywhere her curiosity would take her.

At last they left the city limits and turned south, driving through miles of open pasture, meadows that had a Technicolor brilliance in the bright summer sunshine. Jackson passed two sparkling pillars that led into an enclave where trees met over broad, quiet streets and great expanses of clipped lawns fronted the entrances of partially hidden, magnificent homes.

"Here we are at last," Etna said as they turned into a winding driveway flanked by azalea bushes. She walked past the gently hissing sprinklers, inhaling the scent of roses and juniper, and followed Etna into a high-ceilinged entrance hall graced with a chandelier and ornate mirrors. "Would you care to join me in a glass of sherry, dear?" Etna removed the pin from her hat and placed it on a small cherrywood table.

"Righto," Gaynor said, trying to look casual as she followed her into the living room.

"I just love the way you talk: righto. That's an Australian expression, isn't it," she chirped as she crossed to the bar. "Did you ever see any of those darling little koala bears that you have over there?"

"They're rather hard to see, actually. You know the gum leaves that they chew on are apparently soporific, so most of the time they just hang about in the tops of the trees as though they were slightly drunk."

"But they're gentle, lovable creatures, aren't they?" Etna inquired in a concerned voice, handing her the glass of amber liquid.

"I think so. We lived in the city, you see, so I didn't have much opportunity to explore the bush except on holiday. My Uncle Joey had a station—a ranch I suppose you'd call it here—up in the country. I was sometimes taken there for holiday."

As she continued to talk about her trips to Uncle Joey's country place, she was only dimly aware that the story wasn't true. The imagination that had saved her from unpleasant realities in the past was as much a part of her as most of her real experience; and now that she was sitting in a cool, well-appointed room, sipping sherry from a tiny cut-crystal glass, surrounded by brocade furniture, paintings, a grand piano—by all the great and small things that bespoke wealth, she felt as though she were the fairy princess, released from an evil spell put upon her at birth. At last she was allowed to come into possession of all that was hers.

Etna poured herself another sherry and got to her feet, offering to show her through the house. She barely opened the door to the room adjoining the living room, explaining that it was "Richard's sanctuary," but Gaynor glimpsed a massive, bare desk and caught the pleasant smells of leather and tobacco. Crossing back through the entrance hall, they went through the dining room and out to the kitchen. A large-boned black woman, her crisp white hair drawn back into a chignon that accentuated her high cheekbones and slanting eyes, was kneading dough at the tiled sink. It was difficult to tell her age, since the back was ramrod straight and the coffee-colored skin was virtually unlined. Only the hair, a thickening about the waist and hips, and gnarled, wrinkled hands suggested she might be older than her mistress.

"This is Faustina," Etna said. "Faustina is Jackson's sister and she's taken care of me since I was just a bitty little thing back in St. Louis."

"I'm pleased to meet you," Faustina said in a low, melodious voice. "I sure hope that you'll be happy with us. Miz Cunningham, I think you'd better get out into the garden and be talking to James. I believe he's been putting too much fertilizer down."

Etna started out the back door and Gaynor followed her, aware that Faustina's benign gaze was still on her.

After a tour of the gardens and the tennis courts, her mother-in-law ushered Gaynor into Ricky's old room upstairs. It appeared to be preserved intact from his boyhood, with brown and yellow checkered spreads on the twin beds—"In case Ricky wanted to have a friend over"—a cowboy lamp and neat stacks of sporting equipment. Several pennants and a picture of Gene Autry adorned the walls. The only indications of the adult Ricky were the piles of books on the desk. Etna sat down on one of the beds and took a picture album from beneath it. She insisted on showing Gaynor countless photos: Ricky on a pony, Ricky graduating from Richland Manor Day School, Ricky going out on this first date with a plump, camera-shy girl in a ruffled dress, Ricky in his football uniform. Gaynor expressed a coy curiosity in the photographs, but it wasn't until Etna had closed the album and guided her along the hallway into the large, airy room that was to be hers that her interest revived. The windows, covered with white organdy curtains, opened onto the garden. A four poster bed that Etna said had belonged to her grandmother was in one corner; a desk and an elaborately mirrored dressing table, upon which a collection of silver brushes and combs already rested, was in the other.

"It's lovely," Gaynor breathed.

"The chests of drawers and the wardrobes are in this dressing room," Etna explained as she crossed the carpet. "I know it looks rather bare now. I was going to redecorate, but then I said to myself, 'Don't be interfering, Mother. You just wait and let Gaynor pick out what she wants.' There are some swatches of fabric for you to look at and if you don't like them, Jackson will drive you into town whenever you want to go. You don't drive, do you?"

"No."

"Neither do I. Richard tried to teach me when we were first married but he made me so nervous I just gave up."

"I'd like to learn."

"Then you shall, my dear," she smiled as she walked through the dressing room and flung back the next door, which led into a bathroom. Gaynor had been pleased with everything she had seen so far, but the bathroom absolutely took her breath away. The pale pink tile went from the floor to the height of her shoulders, giving back a shadowy reflection of her body. The porcelain tub was larger than any she had hitherto bathed in and could be shut off from the rest of the room by glass sliding doors. Next to the rack of fluffy towels, an opalescent dish contained bars of perfumed soap. And mirrored cabinets ranged above the sink, giving back the sharp image of her face.

"I think I'll leave you now and give you an opportunity to freshen up and nap." Etna kissed her again on the cheek and went out of the room.

Alone, Gaynor unpacked one of the suitcases, putting some of her dresses on the satin-covered hangers with little bags of sachet attached to them. Though she had selected her traveling wardrobe with great care, the clothes looked very nondescript as she placed them in the wardrobes.

While soaking herself in the tub, she envisioned all of the lovely things she'd now be able to buy. She patted herself dry with one of the monogrammed towels, walked back into the bedroom to survey her body in the full-length mirror, and collapsed onto the bed.

SOME HOURS LATER she awoke, checked the gold clock on the night table and saw that it was after six. She selected a red-and-white patterned dress that wasn't too creased, put on her makeup, and went downstairs. As she passed through the entrance hall on her way to the dining room, something stopped her. She paused and turned toward the living room, which was already gloomy with the shadows of nightfall, and caught the glint of a moving, shiny object. She peered into the dusky room to see Etna sitting on the couch, placing a glass on the coffee table.

"Yes, I'm in here, my dear."

"I'm sorry, I didn't really notice you."

"I suppose I forgot to turn on the lights. But sometimes I find it soothing to sit in the gathering darkness."

Gaynor paused on the threshold, waiting for her mother-in-law to turn on one of the lamps. Etna gave a nervous little laugh and rose from the couch, returning the glass and bottle to the bar.

"I do apologize for Richard being so late. He said he would try to make it home by six, but he's so busy that it's foolish to rely on him. I often take dinner alone, or sometimes I even sit in the kitchen and eat with Faustina just as I did when I was a little girl. It can be very comforting to sit in the kitchen, don't you find?"

There was a tremor in her voice and she seemed unsteady as she walked toward the hall and, without waiting for Gaynor, went into the dining room. Since she had most often witnessed the violent effects of alcohol, it took Gaynor a moment to realize that Etna was a little drunk. She unfolded her damask napkin and apologized for not coming down to dinner sooner. Etna lifted the silver bell next to her plate.

Faustina brought the steaks and salads to the table, her dark face appearing suddenly and then merging into the dimness of the candlelit room. Gaynor could feel the dark eyes playing on her with a curiosity that hinted at a more active intelligence than the pleasantly vacant look Faustina had worn at their first meeting. Etna seemed preoccupied, barely touching her plate and lapsing into long silences punctuated by flurries of conversation about the climate, the summer place on the lake, or Ricky's childhood.

Gaynor ate self-consciously, carefully muting the noise of the silverware and trying to understand how the mood of the house, so agreeably open and protected earlier in the day, had shifted into something morose and vaguely threatening. As Gaynor swirled her spoon into the puddle of baked Alaska, Etna drew her breath in sharply, unclenched the pale hand decorated with a single broad wedding band, and reached across the table as if to take Gaynor's hand. It was a foolish gesture, since the expanse of the table was far too great to allow them to touch.

"I belong to a book discussion group you might like to join," Etna said suddenly. "Ricky has told me that you love literature. I'm glad that he has chosen a wife who has the same interests as he. He's always loved to read—ever since he was a little boy. Richard always said that it would stunt his growth to be sitting about all day reading. But I tried to explain to Richard that there are many kinds of growth."

"Yes," Gaynor answered uncertainly, wondering what the imploring tone of Etna's voice was really asking for.

"So, you agree with us," she said happily. "Richard is . . ." she paused, her eyes fluttering around the dimly lit room and then settling on the candles, "a very determined man. His ideas are always very definite. I suppose that's why he's been so successful. I've never really understood all of his business dealings myself, but you see he's hardly ever wrong. And that's what makes it so difficult to . . . express the human element. He has very definite plans for Ricky's future even now. He's always had very definite plans for Ricky. Wanted him to play football when he was obviously better at tennis. Wanted him to get his degree in business or engineering even though Ricky knew after his first year at college that he wanted to be a professor of literature . . ."

Even though Faustina had appeared again, carrying a tray of coffee and cups, Etna kept on talking. Her voice had risen to a high, agitated pitch, her outstretched hand clenching and unclenching. Gaynor glanced up, wondering if the housekeeper was taking in the conversation, but Faustina averted her eyes, intent on pouring the coffee. It was impossible to tell if Etna was aware of her presence. Embarrassed, Gaynor cast her eyes down to the table. Faustina began to remove the dishes. As the dark hand moved to collect her mistress's dessert plate, it rested for the briefest moment on the pale, twitching one. Without acknowledging the touch, the hand stilled. Etna drew in her breath and dropped her voice.

"Not that Richard could possibly have anything against you—after all he hasn't even met you. I've tried to point out to him that there's nothing wrong with Ricky getting married so young. Age is only one factor in a marriage. It's spiritual compatibility, shared values, *caring* that makes a marriage work. And I trust Ricky's judgment. I know that I've brought my son up to be a good husband. He may be only twenty-four, but he already has a greater understanding of a woman's needs than many men who are much more mature."

"Yes, he's very sensitive."

"Of course it's a mother's prejudice, but I think so too. Once he gets back into school and the two of you have a chance to be on your own, I'm sure you'll have a happy marriage and raise a lovely family. Some of my friends have been distressed when they became grandmothers because they said it made them feel old. But I can't wait for the two of you to start a family."

Gaynor felt the corner of her mouth twitch involuntarily. Motherhood was certainly not a part of her immediate plans. She had never even allowed herself to think about pregnancy beyond taking precautions to prevent it. It was impossible to imagine the body that she was so proud of, whose beauty she was so dependent on, being disfigured and swollen with the presence of some alien growth. Taking her silence for shyness, Etna smiled across the table with an expression of contentment that almost made her look simpleminded.

"Oh Faustina," she called, her voice now lighthearted and girlish, "perhaps Gaynor would like to have tea instead of coffee. After all, tea is your national drink, isn't it?"

"To tell you the truth, I think that the Australian national drink is beer. You should have seen how the Yanks took to it. Apparently, it's much stronger than the variety you have here, so some of the boys weren't quite used to it when they first landed."

Etna bobbed her head to the side and let out a tinkling laugh, and Gaynor thought that she had put the conversation back on the track.

"Oh, let's call Ricky in Washington and tell him that you've arrived safely. He said that he'd call, but I know the General's number, so we can call him. He's always working late into the night. I know it's only his sense of honor that's made him consent to stay on for this extra time. I'm sure he'd much rather be with you. But it'll only be another month or so before he gets some leave and then we'll give you a really lovely party to celebrate and introduce you to everyone properly."

She blotted her thin lips with the napkin, rose from the table, still twittering, and crossed into the living room. Gaynor followed, pausing in the hallway to look at her reflection in the mirror. As she brushed back her hair and touched her little finger to the lipstick smudge at the corner of her mouth, the front door opened noiselessly behind her and a man appeared. Startled, she froze and without turning around, contemplated the face that was reflected next to her own image. For a split second she thought she knew the face. Then she realized that it was only the look she recognized: that cool, self-assured look of the truly powerful man—general, corporate boss, judge, statesman—that stared out from the pages of newspapers and magazines. His features were well defined and tanned, if slightly jowly. A crest of neatly combed silver hair accented the broad forehead and heavy-lidded eyes. His jaw was heavy and the mouth, which was held tight, relaxed to show a full lower lip as his gaze went down the length of her body with the smooth evaluation of a connoisseur. Under other circumstances, she might have asked if he would like to check her teeth.

"The long-distance lines are busy," Etna said, as she came back into the hallway. She stopped when she realized Richard was there, wavered for a moment, and then went over and stood on her tiptoes to put a dutiful kiss on his cheek. "Richard, this is Gaynor. We've been having such a lovely time getting to know each other." Her eyes flitted back to her daughter-in-law with a quick "don't give me away" pleading look.

"How do you do, Mr. Cunningham," Gaynor said as she advanced toward him, hand outstretched. His face broke into a well-practiced smile of conviviality, but he did not take the offered hand. "I think we should have a drink to celebrate your arrival." He disengaged himself from Etna, moved ahead of them into the living room, and called back over his shoulder, "You can tell Faustina to put the food away. I've already had something at the club." He fixed his own drink first, poured out the snifter of brandy that Gaynor had requested, and started away from the bar. Then, as if remembering that a certain amount of decorum was required, he asked if Etna would care for anything.

"Perhaps just a touch of brandy, dear."

He poured a small amount into another glass, unbuttoned his suit, and sat down in the large chair that seemed to be reserved for him. As Etna chattered about the bits of information that she had picked up from Gaynor during the afternoon, he sipped slowly, displaying an indulgent interest in her small talk. But his right leg jiggled occasionally with a nervous impatience, and his eyes kept moving back to Gaynor.

"Gaynor's a woman of commerce too. She was managing a jewelry shop when Ricky met her. I expect that she'll be much more intelligent in business conversations than I am."

"How did you come to be working there?"

"My Uncle Joey owns some opal mines," she said quickly. "He also has a number of sheep stations—ranches you'd call them—and he's in the export business. He knew the people who owned the shop and I thought it might be a lark to try my hand at it. Lots of girls were working during the war and I must say I found it rather interesting."

"Oh, my dear, your family," Etna exclaimed. "I've been so rude! Jabbering all day long about Ricky and never asking you anything. I know Ricky told me that you haven't any brothers and sisters and that your poor father died when you were very young. But you must have brought along photographs of your mother. Is she as beautiful as you are?"

"I don't have any photos with me."

"Putting the past behind you, eh?" Richard said with a sudden sharpness.

"Not at all. Just that in all the rushing about before I left I neglected to pack them. I must write to Mother and have her send some to me."

She resisted the impulse to take another mouthful of brandy and met his look with a steady, open-eyed innocence. He knocked back the rest of his drink without taking his eyes from her. "What the hell," he said, as he rose to replenish his glass. "Sometimes you're better off without families. I wouldn't give you a plug nickel for any of the bunch I came from."

"Richard! You don't mean that," Etna chided, though his remark had been uttered with complete conviction.

55

"Etna's very fond of her family. Or thinks she is. That's because they go back to the *Mayflower* or something."

"They don't go back to the *Mayflower*," Etna laughed. "But they did settle in St. Louis almost five generations ago. My great-great-grandfather built one of the oldest houses in the city. It's still preserved by the historical society. He was an explorer and a pioneer."

"He traded furs and killed a heap of Indians," Richard said bluntly.

"Dear me, Richard. What will Gaynor think of us if you say such awful things."

"I'm not put off by that," Gaynor said brightly. "I've always thought that one of the most attractive things about Americans was their ability to move on and not be bound by tradition."

"I'll drink to that," Richard said as he tipped back the glass. "Tradition holds you back. You've got to see a situation, size it up, and act on it in the best way for you, and that isn't always the old way. If we didn't know it before, the war taught us that. Tradition was that damned fool Chamberlain thinking that you could appease someone as powerful as Hitler by having tea with him. But we won the war because we knew how to make bigger and better equipment and deliver it faster than the enemy."

"We won the war because right was on our side," Etna cried. "The Nazis were evil men who had no fear of God or respect for other people."

"A rather simplistic view of power relationships. But have it your way, Etna."

"Perhaps we won because of both things," Gaynor said in a controlled voice, seeing that Richard's rebuff had caused Etna's lip to tremble. "We brought desire to win and the means to do it together."

"Isn't she an intelligent girl," Etna enthused, leaning over to touch Gaynor's hand. "I knew that Ricky would choose a wife who had brains as well as beauty. And you have to admit that she is a beauty."

"That she is. And now, if you ladies will excuse me."

"But we were going to call Ricky. Can't you wait just a few more minutes," Etna pleaded.

"I have some early meetings tomorrow. You wouldn't want the postwar economy to founder because I didn't get enough rest, would you? Tell Faustina to have breakfast ready at seven-thirty."

Though his face was slightly flushed from the two long drinks he'd just tossed off, Richard set the glass down on the bar with a hand as steady as a surgeon's, walked over to the couch, and patted Etna on the shoulder. Gaynor rose instinctively as he stepped toward her. She could feel the heat of his hands as he placed them on her shoulders. She dropped her head demurely. His lips touched the part in her hair. Moving quickly across the room, he turned in the doorway.

"I have some friends in the textile business who buy wool in your part of the world. I might ask one of them to look your Uncle Joey up."

"He's not in town very often," she blurted out, instantly aware that the words had come too quickly. She gave a little laugh and turned back to Etna. "It's funny that Uncle Joey should be in the wool business because he's always been referred to as the black sheep in the family. He went on walkabout with the Aborigines when he was just a young man, and I'm afraid that he still has a tendency to be a bit nomadic."

"Travel is always a broadening experience," Etna smiled.

"Yes. You never know what you'll find," Richard said blandly. He gave Gaynor an omniscient smile, faint but decided.

CHAPTER
V

DAWN SCRAPED the remains of mashed potatoes, peas and chicken bones into the bucket under the sink, and then thrust the plates into the steaming water. The screened window above the sink was open as far as it would go, but no breeze stirred the humid air. As she mopped the perspiration from her forehead with the back of her hand, she could hear Faye's piping voice rise above the indistinct conversation coming from the front porch. She hoped that the new environment would intimidate Faye into minding her manners. In the few brief hours since she had been at the house, it was already apparent that Suds, Zac's foster mother, ascribed to the philosophy that children should be seen and not heard, whereas Homer, Zac's foster father, seemed to have a more indulgent attitude toward the kids, looking at them with wonderment.

Suds had given Faye a stern look at the dinner table and told her there was no need to mash up her potatoes since it had already been done for her. She had also cautioned the child not to interrupt adults, though Faye was only asking for a second helping. And when Nita gurgled and smiled and spat out some food Dawn had been spooning into her mouth, Suds's bulky shoulders had stiffened with disgust. Dawn was so used to being alone with the children, or else in the company of Sheila, that she had not anticipated that their habits might offend. She tried to make allowance for the fact that Suds had not been with children for many years. Embarrassed, she had chided Faye softly and resolved to feed the children separately as long as they were staying with the Muellers.

She searched through the neatly ordered cabinets for some steel wool, and then scoured the pots vigorously. Suds had explained that though her baptized name was Harriet, her nickname was Suds because she liked everything in her house to be spic and span. Dawn held the frying pan up to the fluorescent light to make sure that it was scrupulously clean, dried it, and hung it on the hook above the stove. Wiping her hands on the apron and doing a last-minute check to make sure everything was inspection-proof, she picked up the bowl of wax fruit and placed it in the center of the table. Her eyes fixed on the framed cloth above the sideboard: "Jesus Is Always Welcome In My Home," in tiny embroidery stitches. She looked at it for a moment and then let her glance stray around the room. It was certainly larger than the kitchen at home. There were lots of conveniences: hot running water instead of having to heat the kettle, a big white refrigerator instead of the old ice chest with its rusty pan underneath to collect the drippings. Yet there was something almost institutional about the spotless white walls and the bare countertops. At home there was always the odd bottle of beer on the table, the portion of left-over cake, Patsy's books, a bowl of nasturtiums that Marge collected from the vacant lot down the street. She looked back at the framed cloth and smiled, wondering what her father would say about it. Probably something like: "Righto, Jesus is welcome in our house—as long as he doesn't eat too bloody much." Then Patsy would giggle and Marge would shake her head and cluck her tongue to hide her smile. She missed them all so terribly. She had devoured the air letters from Marge that had been waiting for her when she arrived in Ohio, but the moment she had finished reading them the comfort they gave melted away and she found herself more bereft than ever.

The screen door slammed and Faye raced through the living room into the kitchen.

"Mummy, you'll never guess! There are little flies all around the yard that glow in the dark. They're called lighting bugs, and Daddy says I can catch them and put them in a jar. Where do they keep the jars?"

"I'm not sure, lovey . . ."

Zac came in behind her, his bright blue eyes smiling, his khaki shirt opened at the neck. He winked at Dawn as he strode past her and reached into one of the cabinets. "Suds says that extra jars are kept up here. Hey, here's one. Now run along, and watch where you're going 'cause it's dark outside." He patted her behind and she ran out of the room. As soon as he heard the screen door slam, he put his arm around Dawn's waist. "How you doin', Aussie? You didn't have to volunteer to do the dishes all by yourself, you know. You must be real tired after that train ride."

"It wasn't just the train ride. Oh, it was horrible for me on the ship, Zac. First of all, there were no washing machines and we had to line up to do the nappies. Then there was an epidemic of measles on board —well, you can just imagine that. Over fifty spotty, scratching kiddies and everyone afraid that the women who were pregnant had to be kept away from them, which was pretty difficult to do . . ."

Her voice cracked as she felt all of the accumulated fatigue of the journey. She put her head on his shoulder, feeling that if she just allowed her eyes to close she would fade away into oblivion. He touched her hair gingerly, clearing his throat. He had been overwhelmed with emotion when he'd met them at the station, feeling a rush of unexpected pride when Dawn had placed Nita in his arms. But it had been hard for him to connect the squirming baby, with eyes exactly the same blue as his own, with that last brief weekend he'd spent with Dawn. When the child had started to whimper and reached up to pull his hair, he was embarrassed at his clumsiness and the tightness in his throat, so he'd handed her back to Dawn.

"The baby's beautiful, Dawn. She's just beautiful."

"I think so too. You know, whenever I'd get really truly fed up— just get the pip about everything—I'd look at those eyes of hers and I'd think, 'I've got a part of Zac here with me.' " She wanted him to ask about all the details of the birth. Of course she had written some of it to him, but she hadn't been able to express the anxiety and joy she'd experienced or to confess to the irrational anger of feeling deserted by him. "I've missed you awfully."

"I've missed you too. Couldn't believe it when I first saw you today. You looked so skinny."

"I know. I was so seasick I just couldn't eat. I think I must've lost over two stone on the boat."

"Not stone, pounds. And it's not a boat, it's a ship."

"Righto, ship. I kept saying to myself, 'Zac's going to be very upset when he gets a look at this bag of bones.' Even with the nursing, my breasts have shrunk down to nothing."

"You know the old saying: 'More than a handful's a waste.' "

"I don't think I've ever heard that one," she laughed, turning his hand over in hers, then placing it on her breast. "I think you must've picked that one up in one of those places you haven't told me about yet."

He touched her tentatively, and then drew away and held her at arm's length. There were dark circles under her gray eyes. The cheek-bones were more pronounced, giving her face a worn and fragile look. During the separation, he had often taken out the photo he carried in his wallet, but now he had difficulty reconciling the real face with the smiling black-and-white image. The fact that she was standing in Suds's kitchen and wearing Suds's apron increased his disorientation. He had not really imagined what she might have gone through in his absence, but as he looked into the questioning, caring eyes, the strangeness began to evaporate and he felt a protective tenderness toward her. He started to draw her into his arms.

"Now, now. You lovebirds will just have to knock it off," Suds said as she bustled into the kitchen. Zac's face flushed. He pulled away and dropped his arms. Suds strode past them toward the refrigerator, letting out a laugh that seemed to be routed through her nose and sounded like a horse's whinny. Opening the refrigerator door, she folded her arms beneath her pendulous bosom and surveyed the contents with narrowed, ferreting eyes. "Guess we don't have many leftovers," she sighed, shaking the little sausage curls that surrounded her heavy-featured face. "I was gonna get myself another piece of that lemon meringue pie. Guess I'm just not used to having so many people to feed."

"I'll give you some money to go grocery shopping tomorrow," Zac said quickly.

"Now, Zachariah, how can we go shopping on a Sunday?" she whined. "We'll get by. Dawn honey, I think it was real sweet of you to offer to help me like this by doing the dishes."

She shifted the wax fruit slightly, re-folded the dish towel and placed it over the faucet. "Now I want you two to quit smoochin'. Come on out to the porch, Dawn, and tell us all about yourself and your country. Say, did I tell you, Zac, that the Fletcher boy brought home a girl from overseas too? She's Eyetalian and don't speak much English, so they're having a heck of a time figuring her out. But you know I said to Homer when Zac first joined the Navy—oh, ages ago —I said, 'I'll just bet Zac is going to come home with a foreign girl. I just bet he will.'"

There was something about the intonation she gave to the word "foreign" that made Dawn feel not only alien, but somehow not quite clean. Suds motioned for them to follow her and started into the living room, which was crowded with heavy furniture and tables covered with doilies and ceramic figurines.

"Guess I'll have to pack up all my pretty little what-nots now that there's a baby around," she said, pausing to touch a miniature duck.

"I suppose it wouldn't be a bad idea," Dawn said. "Now that she's at the crawling stage, Nita does love to get into everything."

"Well, I taught Zachariah right from the first when we brought him to live with us that he wasn't allowed to touch. Might as well start teaching them respect for other people's property from the very beginning, otherwise they don't learn."

She stood at the screen door and waited for Zac to open it. Dawn pulled the cotton housedress away from her sweating back and stepped down onto the porch. Homer was sitting on the glider, cradling the baby in his arms and whispering a soothing gibberish, though the child had already fallen asleep. Dawn sat down next to Homer under the single yellow lightbulb and looked out onto the street. The rows of two-story wooden houses were separated by concrete driveways. Almost all had screened-in porches and here and there a special decoration appeared on the square of front lawn—a bird bath, a plaster statue of a Negro wearing a jockey's outfit. Taking a deep breath of the still, humid air, she watched Zac move away and sit on the front stoop. Faye darted about in the bushes trying to capture lightning bugs. Suds moved out of the dim circle of light, picked up a palmetto fan and a glass of iced tea, settled her bulk into a rocking chair, and fixed her eyes on Dawn.

"You mustn't let the children stay up too late. They're tired from that train ride and we'll have to get up early for services."

"I'm not sure if it would be a good idea to take the baby," Dawn answered uncertainly, taken aback that Suds had decided that they should all attend church without bothering to inquire if they wanted to. "Nita doesn't seem to have much of a religious persuasion. When I took her to be christened she howled throughout the ceremony, and wet right through her nappy and dress onto the priest's robes."

"Zac didn't tell me you were Catholic," Suds said.

"I'm afraid I'm not a very good one. I don't even go to Mass every Sunday. My mum's very regular about it. Especially since my brother was killed. But most of the time she ends up going alone."

"What about your sister and your father?"

"Patsy likes to stay in bed and read on Sunday because it's her only day off from work. And Charlie doesn't have much time for religion —unless, of course, you consider socialism a religion."

"That's not a religion," Suds said in alarm.

"No. I only meant that as a joke. Dad helped to organize his union during the Depression and even though he's too sick to go to work anymore, he still gets all dressed up and goes to the union meetings."

"He's a good-hearted guy," Zac mumbled as he stood up, stretched, and walked across the lawn to Faye. As she watched him pick Faye up and hurl her into the air in an effortless movement, Dawn wished that he might have stayed on the porch, taken a more active part in the conversation, helped her bridge the gap between Suds's questions and her own misunderstood attempts at humor.

"And what church do you go to?" Dawn asked.

"We're baptized in the Pentecostal," Suds declared solemnly. "I guess you must have been baptized. What all religions do they have in Australia?"

Dawn responded to the interrogation as best she could. She had never heard of the Pentecostals, but thought it better not to ask too much about them. Sitting under the yellow light, answering Suds's rapid-fire questions, she felt rather like a suspect at a police lineup. She longed for the evening to come to a close, so that she could go upstairs and be alone with Zac. Finally he came up onto the porch carrying Faye, who had adorned her fingers with squashed lightning bugs. He tickled her until she squirmed in delight, and then dumped her into Dawn's lap.

"Oh Mummy," she squeaked, displaying her jar of captives, "I'm glad we came to America. I love these creepy crawlies."

"You'd best make sure that child isn't feverish," Suds cautioned. "We've had a lot of polio cases this summer. The Pritchards' eight-year-old has come down with a real bad case. His little legs are all twisted and it seems like he might never walk again. One day a child might be runnin' around and the next . . ."

Faye's eyes went saucerlike as she listened to the details of the Pritchard boy's misfortunes. As Dawn stroked the sweet-smelling perspiration from her daughter's forehead, she let her hands cup over the child's ears.

"Is it always so muggy here in the summer?" she interrupted when she could bear the grisly description no longer. "I could do with a few swallows of cold beer."

"We don't favor liquor in this house," Suds said curtly. "If you're just thirsty I'll get you an iced tea."

"Don't you have beers?" Faye wanted to know, wiggling around in Dawn's lap. "My Pop always has beers. Sometimes he lets me have the foams."

"I was talking to your mother," Suds said firmly.

Faye shrank back into Dawn's body, putting one sticky hand around her mother's neck and inserting the thumb of the other into her mouth. It was a habit that she had given up years ago, but she looked so glum that Dawn decided not to chide her for it. But Suds's sharp eyes glinted through the darkness and fixed on the offending thumb.

"I thought you knew how to be a nice little girl," Suds said immediately. "You're way too old to have your hands stuck in your mouth. If you suck your thumb your teeth will grow all bucked out and then your daddy will have to pay lots of money to have a man put tin wires in your mouth."

Faye looked up at Dawn to see if this horrible prognostication might be true, then slowly drew the thumb out of her mouth and started to kick the glider. Dawn stilled her foot and stroked her hair with a steady, soothing hand.

"I can remember all those years when Zachariah was growing up. There's never any end to the aggravation you have with a child. Landsakes, I never had a moment's peace. If he wasn't sick he was gettin' into trouble at school. And disobedient! There were times when my hand was red raw from trying to smack some sense into him."

"He was a wild one sometimes," Homer chuckled, "but he was a good kid too."

"Homer. I do wish you wouldn't keep interrupting me when I'm tryin' to tell something," Suds said impatiently.

Homer went back to whispering nonsense to the unconscious baby.

"Still, God didn't bless me with a child of my own, so when I saw Zachariah—'course that wasn't his name then—when I saw Zachariah that day at the foundling home I knew that the Lord wanted me to take him in and give him a good home. He was one sad-looking little tyke. Abandoned, you know. We didn't have much money back then and I knew that it would be a struggle. Homer was all against it . . ."

"I liked the kid from the first," Homer muttered under his breath. Suds went on with her recollections of hardship and sacrifice until Faye's half-closed eyes drooped shut, her body relaxing heavily on Dawn's breast. Zac had taken up his position on the stoop again, his back turned to the porch, his hands slowly tearing at a clump of grass. Dawn looked at his knotted neck muscles, thinking that he had been about Faye's age when he'd been brought (at divine directive, according to Suds) to live with them. Dawn had never met anybody who thought they had a direct line to God before; nor had she encountered any woman who had such a martyred attitude about being a parent. Her heart went out to Zac with a new understanding as she imagined all the trials and hurts that he must have suffered at a time when he should have been encouraged and nurtured.

"I think I'd better take Faye upstairs and put her to bed," she said, when Suds paused in her litany long enough to draw a breath.

"The bed's all made up in that little back room next to yours. It used to be for storage, but I had Homer carry all the stuff down into the basement; and I borrowed a crib for that little one."

"Thanks. That was good of you," Dawn said as she handed Faye's limp body to Zac. "I can take the baby now, Homer."

"Oh, I'll carry her up," he replied, never taking his eyes from Nita's face.

"You heard her say she wanted to take the baby, Homer. Why are you so cantankerous?"

Homer lifted the baby to Dawn with a resigned smile. "See you in the morning," Suds called after them, as though annoyed that sleep would remove them from her grasp. Dawn undressed the children and put them into their beds. It was all she could do to wash her face and slip into her nightie before her own eyes started to droop. She had imagined being in bed with Zac so often, but now that he was finally putting on his pajamas and moving in beside her, she felt only confusion and fatigue.

"I know it's rough," he whispered. "I've been looking for a place ever since I got transferred back here, but there's no place available that'll take kids. I requested to be here at the recruiting station, so we're stuck for another six months."

"Then your hitch will be up, right?"

"Yeah. Then I'll have to decide whether to sign up again."

"I thought you were going to get out for good."

"Let's talk about it some other time. Right now I just want to hold you."

"Please do," she sighed. "Please do."

He rolled toward her and took her in his arms. Her ears strained for the slightest noise in the house. Except for one brief moment of abandon, he too seemed apprehensive and constrained. Afterwards she got up and opened the bedroom door a crack, so that she might hear the children if they stirred in the night.

SHE WOKE UP as the sun was rising, its pale light filtering through the window and giving the bare room with its hooked rug, single dresser and old wooden bedstead a dappled, pleasant glow. The house was hushed. Propping herself up on her elbow, she looked at Zac's face. Though he appeared to be deep in sleep, his mouth slightly open and his jaw slack, his forehead was creased in a frown and his eyes were squeezed shut as though he were forcing himself to remain unconscious. She stroked his head and touched his shoulders. He turned toward her, already in a state of arousal. With his eyes still closed, he pulled her to him roughly, stirring the desire that had deserted her the night before. Her own eyes began to flicker shut as she relaxed, yielded to the long-awaited pleasure. Then she noticed that the door was still open. "The door," she whispered, moving out of his arms, "let me shut the door." He blinked and released her. She tiptoed across the room, carefully shut the door, turned back to him, and slipped the straps of the nightdress from her shoulders. His eyes opened wide with dazed surprise. He tossed back the sheet to welcome her as she walked slowly toward him, feeling proud and beautiful. She knelt down beside the bed. He traced the lines of her neck, reached for her breasts, and then drew her to him. They lay, full length, bodies pressing into each other with growing urgency.

There was a sharp rap at the door.

"Rise and shine," Suds's voice boomed. "I'll have the coffee ready in ten minutes." She thudded down the stairs. They lay staring at each other—Dawn in stupified disappointment that brought her close to tears, Zac with a look of murderous rage that immediately iced over with sullen compliance. They could hear the pots and pans being slammed about in the kitchen with such force that the din echoed all the way up the stairs and through the closed door. Dawn reached out to touch him, but he sat up abruptly, swung his feet onto the hardwood floor, and stood up.

"I suppose we have to go to church," she said, hoping he would offer some resistance.

"I guess so," he muttered sourly, starting toward the closet. "Suds will have a heart attack if we don't. I'll try to borrow the car from Homer and take you and the kids out for a drive this afternoon."

She dressed quickly and woke the children, who were still cranky, and hurried them downstairs. Zac sat at the table as Suds piled heaps of bacon and eggs onto his plate. His eyes seemed glazed. Dawn ironed the girls' best dresses, so she had no time for breakfast. Then Homer backed the '39 Plymouth out of the garage and they all piled in: Homer at the wheel with Zac beside him; Suds, Dawn and the children squeezed into the back seat. "Read in the paper that General Motors said we'd get those assembly lines from guns to auto parts in six months, but with all this union trouble we still don't have no parts in the stores," Homer said as he gunned the motor, swerved around the corner, and missed the stop sign. Dawn was amazed that Suds said nothing about the maniacal abandon with which Homer drove, but Suds was already absorbed in a description of the virtues of the new preacher.

The service was even more bleak than Dawn had imagined it might be. A gaunt young man with a florid, acne-scarred face shouted about the impending apocalypse and exhorted the congregation to prepare themselves because they were the chosen few who recognized the wrath of the Lord. Whenever he yelled "Je-*sus*" it was spat out of his mouth with such force that it seemed to be more of a curse than a holy name. Dawn watched Faye anxiously. The child's face was pale and chastened; she twirled her hair nervously with one hand and stuffed the fingers of the other into her mouth. Dawn made up her mind that she would work out some way to keep the children away from church services as well as the dinner table even if she, to preserve harmony, would be obliged to go through the ordeals herself. Shutting out the grim preacher's calls to the Christian life, she found her lips moving in a silent prayer of her own. It was addressed to no one in particular, but expressed the same desperate need for help that she had felt when her husband and brother were killed, and when Zac was still away on maneuvers: "Please help us. Help us to find a place of our own. Help Zac to stand up to her. Help him to love me as I love him."

AFTER SIX WEEKS in the house, Dawn found that she was still losing weight and in a state of nervous near-collapse. Suds advised her to eat —"If there's one thing a man don't like it's a skinny woman" and "I don't know how long you're gonna be having that child at the breast. Bottles are more sanitary, but if they do it that way where you come from, you should at least know that you have to eat good to keep your milk." Dawn did her best to force food down, but even when she thought she had an appetite, her stomach would rebel as soon as she brought the fork to her lips. She was constantly on guard lest the children do anything to upset the rigid order of the household. She chased after them, mopping up spills, cautioning them not to touch, scolding in a voice that was alien to her ears and turned Faye's usually bright and curious expression into a resentful scowl. Trying to make herself useful in any way that might make up for their intrusion into Suds's territory, she cooked, washed, ironed, cleaned, and weeded the garden. But after thanking her for her help, Suds always managed to find fault: "Dawn honey, it's real sweet of you to water the garden, but I do think you're giving those tomato plants a mite too much," or "Landsakes, all those dishes done! 'Course *I* always put the rinse water into the big pan 'stead of running it over them."

When she wasn't instructing her on the right way to do things, Suds turned the conversation to her favorite topics: blighted marriages (usually the woman's fault), incurable protracted diseases, and the impending end of the world. At first Dawn tried to turn the talk around to less calamitous subjects but this only seemed to annoy Suds, who would stare at her disgustedly, as though she had unmasked a coward who was unable to face the darker, and therefore more real, side of life. Then she would continue about the neighbor's son who was in an iron lung, a stillborn baby, or a veteran who had run amuck and murdered three people.

Suds's grisly tales didn't seem to faze Zac. Whenever she started up, his eyes would film over as though he were driving down a road he had traveled a million times before, so nothing more than reflexive attention was required of him. Even Homer seemed to have mastered the skill of retreating to some private place in his mind while remaining physically present. On the quiet he would play with Nita, or sneak Faye the occasional candy bar, but when he was around Suds, his demeanor was as dull-eyed and cowed as an indentured servant. He was gone from the house from dawn until supper time. When he returned from the factory, he would perform the tasks Suds had set for him, lap up his food, and go to sleep.

Zac assured her that he was making every effort to find them a place to live, so Dawn crossed her fingers and tried to take whatever small pleasures she could from her daily life. When Suds wasn't around to lecture her, she felt a quiet satisfaction in smelling a stack of freshly laundered clothes or preparing a new recipe. The children were also a source of comfort and joy; Faye showed real aptitude when Dawn started to teach her to read, Nita made the transition to solid foods without much fuss. Once, when she and Zac managed to sneak out to the local bar for a hamburger and a couple of beers, she was light-hearted for the entire next day. She kept a stack of magazine pictures of pretty, brightly decorated homes in the drawer next to her under-wear. She remembered her mother's words about patience being one of the finest of womanly virtues.

Once Zac got the use of a station wagon from headquarters, he began to stay out later, explaining that he had a lot of work to do. She would bathe the children and put them to bed, always taking time for the nightly story and whispered conversations with Faye. Afterwards she would drag herself downstairs, push aside the lunch pail that Suds always prepared in advance for Homer's six o'clock departure to the tire factory, take out her airletters, and begin to write home. She censored any mention of her unhappiness, saying only that the Muell-ers had a washing machine, that she had mastered the art of making pies, that Faye was delighted to find the local drug store sold many flavors of ice cream, that the housing shortage was still acute but they were hopeful of finding something soon. Sometimes she would imagine Charlie, Marge and Patsy sitting around the table with her, arguing and laughing. Then she would creep up to bed and collapse.

When Zac was late, she would invariably wake up after a few hours, check the clock, and then lie motionless staring at the shadows on the ceiling until she heard the station wagon pull into the drive. Assured that he was safely home, she would often feign sleep when she heard him sneaking up the stairs. It wasn't that she didn't want him to make love to her, but the act was usually so constrained and furtive that it had little possibility of joy. And the notion of becoming pregnant under the present living conditions filled her with terror. Besides that very real fear, there was something about the smell of the Sen-Sen on

Zac's breath that stifled her desire. It wasn't that she minded his going out with the boys after work—that was a masculine habit she'd grown accustomed to early in life. But it made her lose respect for him to know that though he was worldly and courageous in many ways, he was afraid to face down the woman who might be lurking in the hallway waiting to sniff his breath. In her own family there were knock-down drag-outs about differences of opinion and habit, but none of them would have thought to be hypocritical. The hope that Zac would assert himself lingered long after it was obvious that he had neither the desire nor the will to do so, and mingled with her own resentments at the thousand daily compromises she forced on herself in order not to ruffle Suds's feathers.

She might never have risked a showdown with Suds on her own account, but one day, when Suds took off after Faye, the bottled-up frustration and anger could no longer be contained.

It had been an extremely trying day. Zac had come home late the previous evening and though he wouldn't admit to it, had awakened with a hangover. He had barely spoken to her as she prepared his breakfast. She had burned her arm while doing the ironing. When the mailman came, she was excited to see that she had a letter from Virginia, but after reading it, she became more depressed.

Dear Dawn:

It's me, Sheila. I've been wanting to write to you for such a long time. Billy and I have a little house up in the hills near Blacksburg. It's rather like living in the bush, though I'm having to learn the names of the new flora and fauna. Billy's mother is very sweet and understanding. I've called her Ma from the very beginning. Still, there's no one else that I can really talk to. I have to admit that I've been homesick, though I haven't dared to write to Da and Mother about it (you know what they'd have to say). I still love Billy very much, though many things aren't what I expected them to be (no skyscrapers or subways; in fact, they don't even have a tram line here). I know you must be terribly busy with the kiddies, but I'd love to hear from you as soon as you have the time. Tell me all about how things are going with you. Has Nita started teething yet? Give Faye a big hug from her Auntie Sheila.

Your true friend, Sheila

P.S. I think I might be pregnant.

Dawn worried about Sheila most of the day, wishing she'd been more specific about her life in Virginia and wondering why she'd mentioned the pregnancy in such a casual way. By the time supper rolled around, she was so tired that she wanted to soak in the tub and block out all of her insoluble problems, and go to bed.

Suds had put the ham-and-potato casserole on the table and was already badgering Homer for starting on the Jell-O and celery salad without pausing to say this prayer of thanks. Faye had gone off to play with some children who lived four houses down. Though Dawn had cautioned her that she must return when the little hand was on six and the big hand was on twelve, she had not come home. Dawn went to the back door and called for her several times, and then excused herself to walk up to the O'Connors'.

Mrs. O'Connor welcomed her at the back door, saying that Faye was playing with her boys in the rumpus room and inviting Dawn to come in for an iced tea. She apologized for not having reminded Faye of the time. The child had asked her to tell her when it was close to six, but she'd been on the telephone and had neglected to do so. Why didn't they both stay for dinner, even though it was only beans and franks? Dawn thanked her for the invitation but said that it would be impossible for them to stay, since Mrs. Mueller already had the dinner on the table. She took Faye's hand, said goodbye, and started across the backyards.

"Look how pretty the sunset is tonight," Dawn said as they strolled across the freshly watered lawns. She paused, sniffing the honeysuckle and grass. The sounds of clattering dishes, laughter and radio music coming from the houses filled her with an aching nostalgia. "This is my favorite time of the day, you know. Do you remember last summer when we took the tram to Rockingham beach at night? Pop built a fire and we caught prawns and roasted potatoes and sang songs."

"It's still light. Can I go out before my bath, Mummy?" Faye asked, looking around for lightning bugs.

"Do you remember?"

"You had a fat tummy. You wouldn't go in the water with me."

"That's right."

"Patsy went with me and we played fishes."

"So you do remember."

"Mrs. O'Connor lets Paul and Jimmy go out after they eat. They get to play near the street light."

"We'll see what time it is when you've finished dinner. Don't forget, you have to finish everything on your plate. And you have to try harder to remember what I've told you about the time. In the summer, the days seem longer but . . ."

". . . But the clock hand still goes around."

"That's right." They reached the back door, from which no sounds issued. "So you have to be especially careful when I ask you to watch the time."

They stepped into the kitchen. Homer was already spooning into the upside-down cake. Suds sat in front of an untouched plate of congealing casserole, her hands gripping the edge of the table as though to prevent herself from hurling herself across the room. Another plate of food was set in front of the chair where Dawn sat, but there was nothing in Faye's place.

"Sorry about the mix-up. The time got away from us, didn't it, pet?"

"Where's my plate? Mrs. O'Connor was having weenies and beans and I like them better . . ."

"Please tell Suds that your're sorry you're late for tea," Dawn said as she moved toward the cupboard to get another dish.

"I've already put the food away," Suds said in a quivering voice. "If children don't mind and come to supper on time, then I figure they just don't need any supper. I make food to be served hot and on time."

Dawn decided not to mention that it was she who had fixed the meal. She paused, her hand in midair, wondering what would be the most diplomatic manner in which to handle the situation. Faye's eyes shot over to her, begging for an explanation of the tension she intuited but did not understand. When her mother said nothing, she mumbled that she was sorry, and cast her eyes down at the linoleum.

"Sorry doesn't count," Suds snapped.

"Mrs. O'Connor forgot to tell her the time," Dawn said tiredly, not daring to encounter the accusation of betrayal she saw in Faye's eyes.

"Mrs. O'Connor shouldn't be relied upon to do anything. I don't think that it's fitting for a little girl to be running around with those wild O'Connor boys. Everyone knows that the O'Connors are just trash."

"She has to have someone to play with. The O'Connors seem like a nice family to me."

She could feel the blood rising in her cheeks. Homer scraped the last drops of sugar syrup from his bowl, patted Faye's head when Suds wasn't looking, placed the bowl in the sink, and shuffled out. His skulking departure made Dawn feel as though she were swimming against the tide, being pulled into a strong undertow.

"Look," she said, articulating each syllable in a desperate attempt to put the trivial disagreement into perspective, "I'm sorry and Faye is sorry. It's not as though we'd invited the bloody Queen of England for high tea. I'll heat up the food and I'll wash up afterwards."

" 'By their deeds ye shall know them.' I know a disobedient child when I see one."

"This isn't a religious debate, Suds," Dawn said hotly.

Suds's large shoulders started to quiver, and her eyes became fierce and inflamed. Dawn told Faye to go to her room and wait until she brought her dinner up to her; then, feeling that she had gone too far, she turned back to her mother-in-law, ready to proffer another apology.

"Look, Suds . . ."

"The O'Connors were having weenies and she likes weenies! I never heard such sass. If she was my child I'd be cutting a switch this minute."

"But she's *not* your child," Dawn shouted, bringing the plate down hard on the table.

She heard a sharp crack.

"You broke my plate! I've had that plate for over twenty years and you broke it!"

Dawn stared stupidly at the half of the plate she was still holding in her right hand. An instant and painful contrition seized her, making her mouth open and close in mute apology. With a clumsy movement of her other hand, she started to scoop up the shards.

"Dear Je-sus, save us from the sin of anger . . ." the voice, once again cool and triumphant, began.

Before she knew what she was doing, Dawn had hurled the remaining half of the plate against the wall and ran out of the room, sobbing.

When Zac finally came home, she heard Suds meet him at the door. At first she strained to hear the conversation that hissed from downstairs, but then she decided that whatever was being said made no difference to her.

As Zac mounted the stairs to their bedroom, he was filled with a sullen frustration. All during his service in the Navy—in Nicaragua and China, but especially during the war years—he had been assured and decisive, capable of seeing a situation and acting on it in a quick, effectual manner. He had commanded men, seen half the world, been offered a commission and turned it down. He had even managed to save a few lives. He had been, though he would not have known how to express it, caught up in the great drama of history, playing a minor but not insignificant part. Now he was reduced to settling domestic squabbles between hysterical women. The situation made him confused and impatient. More than that, he couldn't think of a solution, which only increased his sense of impotence.

When he saw Dawn, tense and upright, sitting on the edge of their bed, he slumped against the doorjamb. She did not even ask him to close the door, as she usually did when she had something to say. Instead she turned her red-rimmed eyes directly to him.

"I don't care if I live in a tent, Zac. I have to get out of this house."

CHAPTER
VI

IT WAS THE strangest waiting room Sheila had ever been in. There was an old sofa covered with hastily sewn blue canvas, a rickety playpen filled with grubby, chewed toys, and a single large table littered with books on prenatal care and a few torn magazines. The walls were whitewashed, but had smudges of children's fingerprints near the baseboards. An abstract painting of a mother and child, several medical charts of the female reproductive system, and a photograph of the late President, F.D.R., and his wife hung on the walls. A stick of wood propped up the single window.

Peculiar as the room was, Sheila's attention was focused on the woman sitting across from her on the blue sofa. It was impossible to tell the woman's age. Her hair was lusterless, parted on the side, drawn back and tied with a piece of cotton cloth. The taut skin of her cheeks and neck suggested youth, but the eyes were listless and vacant, the forehead marked with deep furrows, the mouth sunken as with an old woman who had removed her dentures. The woman stared straight ahead of her, unmindful of Sheila's gaze. From time to time she would take a limp handkerchief from the pocket of her checkered housedress and, in an automatic, dazed fashion, wipe the runny eyes and nose of the infant hunched next to her. The child could not have been more than a year and a half old, but the woman's ill-fitting dress was strained over another burgeoning belly. As she looked at her, the queasy feeling that Sheila had been having for the last couple of weeks threatened to erupt into a violent fit of the heaves. She fished in the leather purse a girlfriend had given her as a going-away present, taking out the soda crackers Billy's mother had given to her. Ma said that soda crackers were good for morning sickness. It was now five o'clock in the afternoon and the nausea had persisted ever since she had gotten up in the morning. As she stared at the tattered, defeated woman, Sheila almost hoped that she might have some serious illness, such as an ulcer. Anything would be better than being pregnant.

The door marked "Do Not Enter" was opened. Another woman, back swerved, her great belly leading her tiny body, started across the room. Sheila's eyes followed her as she fumbled for the door knob and exited. Then a deep scratchy voice with an accent she didn't recognize called out, "Next, please." The woman on the sofa lumbered to her feet.

The door to the inner room was swung back impatiently. A short stocky woman, her hands thrust into a white coat, stalked in. The nose was so prominent that it was the first feature to command attention. Above it, two bright eyes the color of metal gleamed with authority and restlessness. Two wings of iron-gray hair flew out from the strong face. The eyes surveyed the room with lightning speed, acknowledging but immediately passing over Sheila, stopping on the woman and child.

"Does Chester have a cold again?" she demanded, moving swiftly toward the child and taking its face in her hand.

"No'm. I don't rightly know what he has. He's been waterin' like that 'bout five days now . . ."

"All right, bring him in; I'll take a look at him first," she said shortly, turning on her heel and motioning them forward.

Sheila's heart sank. For the umpteenth time that day she felt close to weeping. Billy's mother had said she didn't see the need for Sheila to be going to a doctor. All she had to do was wait for another couple of weeks and then Nature would let her know for sure. Ma was so happy about the prospect of being a grandmother for the eleventh time that Sheila didn't have the nerve to tell her that she was terrified. She explained to Ma that she'd never had a proper physical examination before she had married Billy; that she wanted to know *now*. Ma had suggested that she go to Dr. Helen, whom she described as being "from up North, kinda perculiar, but good hearted." Sheila found her formidable and unsympathetic, not at all the friendly outsider she had been hoping for. It crossed her mind that Ma had recommended Dr. Helen because she was not particular about pressing for payment for her services.

She stuffed the soda crackers back into her pocketbook and stared at the diagrams of the female reproductive system. She had never seen such drawings before. It was very difficult to imagine that anything like the two weed-shaped "ovaries," the brilliantly colored "Fallopian tubes," the vaselike "uterus" containing the tiny pea "ovum," existed in her body. It certainly didn't seem to have much relationship to being in bed with Billy. But then, nothing that had happened to her lately bore any relationship to her notions of how things would be. From the moment she'd stepped off the train six weeks before, feeling jubilant, totally in command of her destiny, she had been plunged into a world of shocks and surprises.

The train had pulled in to Blacksburg at midnight. She had had her forehead pressed to the window for an hour, but was unable to see anything except an impenetrable darkness. Finally, as the train slowed down, she saw a cupola-shaped station house with a single light shining from a window. The platform was deserted except for a potbellied man with his thumbs around his suspenders, a ragamuffin child bundling newspapers, and a lanky young man wearing overalls and a collarless shirt. Had the young man not let out a yell, bounced on the balls of his feet, and lurched toward the train, she would not have recognized him. His light brown hair, which had been neatly slicked back during his service in the Marines was now longer, falling over his high forehead and into his deep-set, greenish eyes. His mouth, with its long upper lip and loosely held fleshy lower one, was framed with the beginnings of a moustache. As the train pulled alongside the platform and she steadied herself, getting ready to disembark as soon as it halted, he ran alongside, his face cracked into a broad smile.

"Honey, I thought you'd never get here," he cried as he lifted her from the step and held her, not letting her feet touch the ground. "I been 'bout to bust open every day waitin' fer y'."

The Negro porter stepped down behind her, waited a moment, grinning at them, and then tapped Billy on the shoulder. "I sure hate to interrupt y'all, but we don't stop here but for a minute, so's we gotta unload the young lady's luggage."

Billy released her and helped to heave the suitcases onto the platform. The porter tipped his hat, wagging his head slowly from side to side. "'Bye, young lady. Sure do hope you like the U.S.A. And best of luck," he yelled, jumping back onto the train.

The potbellied man snapped his suspenders, yelled something unintelligible to the raggedy boy, and shuffled into the station house. Billy's mouth came down on hers. The whistle hooted three times. When he finally let her go, she stood, slightly off balance, and watched the train disappearing into the darkness. The light had been turned off in the station house; the fat man slammed the door to the ticket booth and disappeared.

"Truck's over here," Billy said as he reached down for the bags. "Don't y' bother trying to lift that one, honey. I'll come back for it." She followed him as he scrunched up the gravel walk toward a pickup truck. Throwing open the door, he helped her climb up, let out another whoop, and raced back to the platform for the other bags. She peered through the windshield at the full watery moon and the brilliant stars that hung in the midnight sky, and then looked around at the ghostly forms of unlit buildings near the tiny station. He slid in beside her, squeezed her knee, and fiddled with the key in the ignition before the motor wheezed, choked and rumbled into action. "I sure was worried 'bout y' comin' all that way cross-country by yerself, but Ma said 'If'n she's got the gumption y' tell she has, she's gonna be all right.' Ma's jest about as excited as I am that y're finally here. Since Tom was killed and Paralee took the kids and moved back to Prathers Creek and Lonnie and Ivy went on up to Cincinnati, she's been real mournful. She wanted to come along to the station, but I said no. Then she wanted us to come back to the house, but I told her she was jest gonna have to possess her soul in patience and wait to see y' tomorra. Tonight I want y' all to m'self."

Her cheeks dimpled as she listened to Billy talk. He was what her girlfriends called the "strong, silent type." Usually he spoke so little that she would have to remind herself to stop chattering so that he could get a word in edgewise. She was so intent on looking at his wildly excited face in the glow of the one functioning dial on the dashboard that she barely noticed they had left the town in less than five minutes. Billy ground the gears as he shifted down and they began an ascent into black, thickly wooded hills.

"I must say I can't see a thing," she said as she rolled down the window and sniffed the night air, "but it does smell lovely."

" 'Lovely'—oh I've missed hearing that funny li'l way y' have of talkin'. Tomorra when we get up I'm gonna take y' fer a real long walk and tell y' all the trees and flowers and all. They're real different from what y' have back home. We don't have no jacaranda or Kangaroo

Paws, but we've got pine and dogwood, honeysuckle . . . gee, I'm talkin' mor'n I have in m' whole life. Tell me, how was yer trip?"

"I don't know where to begin. I was at sea so long that I thought they'd never let me off the boat. I met this very nice woman and helped her with her kiddies. I suppose she's the first real friend I've ever had—I mean now that I'm grown up. I really hated to leave her. Oh, when I got off the train in St. Louis, I got lost. The first person I asked directions from was very posh and snooty. She asked if they didn't have information booths where I came from. Then I met a man on the train who asked me where I'd learned to speak English so well. I must say, I think some Americans are frightfully ignorant about Australia . . . I'd started to be a bit homesick, but now that we're together, everything's grand. I must say, we are going into the bush, aren't we?" she exclaimed as the old pickup jolted and bounced away from the paved road and wheezed onto a dirt track. "It's so dark I can't see my hand in front of me."

"That's Ma's house over there," he said, cocking his head toward an indistinct blur of white. "Y' know m' grandpappy on Daddy's side got this here land for tradin' a mule or somethin'. We been livin' on it since, 'cept for when Daddy worked at the mines over to McDowell County. I swear I could walk it blindfold."

They bumped across a wooden bridge. The headlights shone briefly on the trunk of an old tree. Several dogs ran alongside the truck barking furiously. Billy switched off the headlights and the ignition. He took her hand, yelling out to the dogs, who quieted immediately. Her hearing, more acute because she was sightless, picked up the croaking of frogs and the insistent clicking of insects. He guided her up some steps, and then swung open a creaking door. She pulled back and put her arms out to him.

"I think you're supposed to carry the bride over the threshold. But it's so dark I can't even see where the threshold is."

He swooped her up into his arms and carried her into the house. She clung to him, kicking off her high heels, burying her face in his neck. He lowered her onto a bed.

"What about the bags?" she whispered as he undid the buttons on her dress.

"They can wait till mornin'. Everythin' can wait, 'cept this."

They undressed each other hurriedly; but when they were nearly naked he drew back from her, kneeling upright on the bed. The moonlight through the window limned the contours of his flat hairless chest and long arms, which were powerful but still lacked the heavy musculature of a fully grown man. He put a bony hand forward; his gold wedding ring glittered as he traced the areolas of her breasts. His hands went up into her hair and removed the pins one by one with gentle solemnity. Pressing her back onto the mattress, his lips and hands moved slowly down the length of her body. Her legs moved apart as he kneaded the flesh of her thighs and buried his head in her stomach. When he lifted his head again to look into her face she realized that he was crying.

"Great God, I never had anything as wonderful as you in m' whole life, girl. I'll never treat you mean. You're m' one and only beautiful bride."

She pressed his face to hers, kissing the warm salty mouth, clasping his buttocks and guiding him into her—the penetration tearing cries from both throats. Coming home. Recognition and surprise melding together in a moment that shaped all time and longing into a tumultuous joy, violent but absolutely still at its center.

They lay apart, her leg thrown limply over his, her hands moving in slow aimless circles, caressing the smooth, tight flesh, pausing to feel the blood coursing through the pulse points, pressing deeper to discover the very bones. Then, the fingers relaxing again, soothing, light, trusting the intimacy, lolling in it, waiting for the next surge to begin. Her hands went down to the coiled moist weight between his legs. He squirmed and laughed, rolling her over on top of him.

"Guess we shouldn'ta sold that ol' stallion, girl. Y'all didn't tell me you were a horsewoman," he teased as he arched and twisted beneath her. Tenderness gave way to playfulness as they pinched and bit each other, tore at the sheets and finally came to another riotous lurching finale, entirely different but as intimate as their first coupling.

"Do y' give yet?" he panted, turning her over onto her stomach and licking the perspiration from the back of her neck.

"Not me," she laughed. "I'm a pioneer woman."

Afterwards they lay, drained and silent, his hand resting on her angular hipbone, looking into each other's eyes. Another great harvesting of love had united them again. The secrets of the flesh making them initiates into all the mysteries of the world.

The memory of that reunion still made her tingle. She looked blankly at the reproductive charts on the wall: "Sperm Penetrating Ovum" and "Multiplication of Embryonic Cells." Could that drawing of a tiny lump, no bigger than her fingernail, resemble something inside her at this very minute? Could the multiplying cells, already another human being, be lodged in her belly, causing her stomach to turn, her breasts to swell, her bladder to demand countless trips to the bathroom? It just couldn't be true.

She had always imagined that when she conceived she would announce it to Billy sitting in their comfortable living room, looking angelic and slightly mischievous, knitting a tiny garment in pastel wool. When Billy asked her what she was doing, she would lower her eyes, smile shyly and remain silent. Then his questioning expression would change from confusion to an illuminated grin and he would say something like "Gee whiz honey! I'm going to be a father! Why didn't you say so?" She had seen that in a movie the name of which she couldn't remember. The film seemed so much more pleasant than the secretive mutterings she'd heard from her mother about so-and-so "having another bun in the oven." Now she forced herself to concentrate on the diagrams, mouthing the unfamiliar words, hoping they might provide a clue to the mystery.

"Now don't forget what I've told you, Mrs. Dalton: give Chester lots of liquids. I noticed that the store down the road has oranges for sale. If you can afford it, he should have some juice. And put him to bed for a couple of days—that should help you to stay off your feet. Remember, you must take the white pills I gave you and if there's any breakthrough bleeding, you must come back to see me immediately."

The woman nodded glumly, hoisted the runny-nosed child onto her hip, and moved clumsily toward the door.

"No, no, Mrs. Dalton," Dr. Helen said emphatically, "put Chester down and let him try to walk. Just take your time." She drew in an agitated breath, straightened her stocky shoulders, waited until Mrs. Dalton was out the door, and then turned to Sheila. "I'm sorry you've had to wait so long. Please come in."

Sheila followed her into the inner room. Dr. Helen motioned her to sit down next to the cluttered desk, whisked a pen out of the pocket of the white coat, and drew a fresh piece of paper from the drawer.

"All right, dear, what's your name," she said quickly.

"Sheila Hickock."

"Age?"

"I'll be twenty in two months."

"And what seems to be the trouble?"

81

"I . . . I'm not sure. I think I might be pregnant."

"Do you remember when you had your last period?"

"About nine weeks ago. I haven't been very regular lately. I've been traveling a lot and I thought perhaps . . ."

"Yes. That can sometimes disrupt the cycle," the doctor cut in. "Well, I'll listen to your history while I'm examining you and write it down later. Go into the bathroom and give me a urine sample. Then take off your clothes, and put on one of the robes that are hanging behind that curtain."

She tossed the pen back onto the desk and looked at Sheila with an expression that might have been either fatigue or boredom. Sheila got up uncertainly and went into the bathroom. When she reentered the room Dr. Helen was scribbling notes and didn't look up. She walked over to the corner, where a curtain had been strung on a pipe that protruded from the ceiling. As she took off her dress and panties, she read the framed diploma on the wall; most of it was in Latin, a language Sheila had been forced to take at the Church of England Girls' School. She pictured herself sitting in the classroom wearing the crisp gray school uniform, her long plaits tied with navy-blue taffeta ribbons, reciting "Hic, haec, hoc, huis, huis, huis" in unison with her mostly serious, sometimes smirking schoolmates. But she could no longer remember what any of the Latin words meant. She did manage to make out that the doctor's name was Helen Abromovitz and that she had graduated from the Columbia University School of Medicine in New York City.

When she came out from behind the curtain, clutching the baggy robe around her, Dr. Helen indicated that she was to get up on the table.

"Have you ever had a pelvic examination before?"

"No. I've never been sick in my life. Except for measles and those childhood things."

"Just lie back, put your feet up here in these things—they're called stirrups. It might be a bit uncomfortable, but it won't hurt. The more relaxed you are, the easier it will be," she said as she drew on a rubber glove.

Sheila obeyed, settling on the table, breathing slowly through her mouth and trying to conceal her embarrassment. She stared up at the ceiling. The image of the brown water spot that bled through the ceiling right above the bed she shared with Billy superimposed itself on the clean whitewash. She shut her eyes. Her mother had cautioned her that when she came to her new home in the United States she would be in for a rude awakening; it seemed cruelly ironic that the warning, which Sheila had dismissed at the time, should have turned out to be literally true. Because the morning after the jubilant love-making that had marked her arrival, she had opened her eyes to an unexpected and shocking reality.

SHE HAD BEEN asleep for only a few hours when the sharp, insistent caw of a crow nudged her into wakefulness. She rolled over onto her back, dimly aware that her bladder was full but trying to find a more comfortable position that would allow her to ignore it and drift back to sleep. Blinking at the misty green woods that appeared through the unadorned window, her gaze moved upward to an ugly brown water mark on the ceiling above the bed. Her eyes went wide in disbelief as she took in the rest of the room. The walls were roughhewn unpainted wood adorned with a paper calendar and a photograph of herself and her parents that Billy had taken on their wedding day. The only furniture, except for the iron bedstead, was a small table with washbasin and pitcher and a crudely made chest of drawers on which a rifle had been placed. As she sat up and swung her feet down onto the bare floor, the springs of the mattress creaked and she felt an uncomfortable twitch in her lower back. She had been vaguely aware the night before that the mattress was not firm, but now she felt the lumps and sags acutely. Barely taking in Billy's body, which lay sprawled in an oblivious heap in the sagging middle of the bed, she got up slowly, moving to the doorway. The adjoining room had the same raw wood walls, another iron bed, a table covered with chipped linoleum, several rickety chairs, and a sideboard on which tin dishes and pots were stacked. She looked for another door which might lead to a bathroom, then peered through the screen door, past the dogs sleeping on the porch, across the dirt yard toward a smaller shack. She rubbed her hands over her eyes, hoping to banish the unbearably shabby rooms. She had never seen anything like it in her life. Was it possible that she had made love for hours, sheltered in a velvet black-ness, relishing the silvery outlines of Billy's body and her own, only to wake up in this hideous shack? It knocked her backwards in aston-ishment, and she felt for the seat of one of the chairs and lowered her body into it without looking.

"Hey, honey, where are y'," Billy's voice drawled.

She couldn't answer because she didn't know. He appeared in the doorway, groggy and contented, a sheet draped around his loins. "If you're goin' to the outhouse y' better let me fetch y' yer shoes. Don't have to worry 'bout puttin' anythin' else on—nobody around for miles. What's the matter, girl? Don't y' feel good?"

"I . . . it's . . ."

He bent down next to her, his eyes alert and concerned, trying to discover why she sat, naked, still as a statue. She stared past him, her eyes rolling about in stupefied incredulity.

"I know the place ain't much," he said finally. "I tol' y' Tom and Paralee and their young'uns lived here 'fore he was killed. I've saved most of m' G.I. money, but I didn't want to go out and buy nothin' till I saw what y' wanted. I'll take y' down into town tomorra and y' can get yerself some things."

"There isn't any running water?" she asked numbly, eyeing the pump near the sink.

"Nope, but there's a tub out on the porch and we can fill it up real easy. Besides, I had a bathroom built for Ma with my musterin'-out pay. I hope y' don't mind, but she's gettin' a little old to be going outside when the weather gets bad. I know it's kinda sad-lookin' after what y' come from, but things are improvin' up here. We got the electricity while I was away in the war. 'Fore that we used to have them kerosene lanterns. Ma use to cook in a ol' wood stove, but now we jest be usin' the wood stove for heat. We're hooked up to bottled gas . . ."

He chafed her hands to try to banish the dazed expression on her face, and talked on about how things had changed since his childhood, hoping that the improvements, which seemed momentous to him, would bring her to a more optimistic view of the place. He had expected that she would want to spiffy it up here and there, bring a womanly eye to it; but he had had no idea that she would be so bitterly disappointed. When, after he'd first started taking her out, he'd commented on the opulence of her parents' home, she'd told him that she didn't consider their luxuries worth a damn because they were only a substitute for loving feelings.

"It's so . . ." she gulped, unable to find words to express her disappointment.

"It ain't so bad," he said defensively. "I'll fix it up—do whatever y' want. After the war it sure looked like heaven to me, 'cept for the fact that you weren't here yet."

He sat down on the floor, bewilderment and apprehension twisting his face. When she didn't speak, he rose and went back into the bedroom, appearing a moment later with another sheet and her pair of red high heels with the bows on the front. Handing her the sheet, which she wrapped around herself in a slow, protective motion, he bent down and slipped the shoes onto her feet. She got up without looking at him and walked out into the morning sunlight. The dogs yelped around her. She crossed the dirt yard unsteadily in the red high heels.

He had already pulled on his overalls and was kneeling, barefooted, stuffing wood into the potbellied stove when she returned.

"I done told y' it wasn't much, Sheila," he said without looking up. "I done told y' all about it."

"I know you said it was in the country, but when you said it wasn't fancy I thought you were being modest. You're always so bashful about everything—even your medals from the war. And when you said you went hunting and fishing, I thought you meant, I don't know —hunting with horses and red caps on your head and fishing on boats and . . . well, I thought . . ."

Her face contorted into a silly smile, then twisted into a grimace of self-accusation as she struggled to control her tears. He guided her back to the chair, stroking her with numb, consoling hands. "Go on, honey, tell me."

She tried to think of words that wouldn't injure his feelings; but just when she thought she'd mastered herself and could speak again, a deep sob tore out of her. He had seen her cry only once before, after a fight with her mother, and it had been nothing like these uncontrollable gasps. He helped her back into the bedroom. She pushed his hands away, falling on the bed and burying her face in the pillow. He stood helpless, and then unwrapped the sheet, covered her with it, and lay down next to her, afraid to touch her.

When at last she seemed to have spent herself with weeping, she rolled over, exhausted, hiccoughing sobs still coming out of her swollen mouth. He took her hand and held it hard until the sounds subsided and she nuzzled into the crook of his neck. As she fell asleep, he stared up at the water-stained ceiling, miserable. *I knew she was too good for me,* he thought, *but I tolt her so when I asked her to marry me. I never tried to lie or lead her on. I guess I shouda taken pictures of the place or somethin'. But I didn't have a camera.*

Creeping out into the kitchen later in the morning, she saw him sitting on the porch whittling a piece of wood, the dogs at his side. He did not acknowledge her presence. She went to the sink and began to pump water into the basin. She washed her hands and face, pressing the cloth to her puffy eyes, determined not to look at him again until she had regained her composure. Walking back to the bed, she opened the suitcases he had placed there while she was asleep and took out a crisp summer dress. "You can do anything you set your mind to, Sheila," her father had said. She resolved to learn about things, discover what sort of houses were available in town, find out what Billy's job prospects were and encourage him to pursue them. It wasn't as though Billy wasn't strong or willing. And they loved each other. It was out of the question to turn her back on the promises she had made only eight months ago. Equally impossible that she should admit that her parents were right. All right, it was a pigsty, but she had the will to get out of it. And they loved each other.

"Oh, Billy?" she called as she took the mirror from her pocketbook and applied a bright smear of lipstick. He came to the door apprehensively. "You sure do look pretty," he said, amazed that she could pick herself up from the anguished heap she had been a few hours before and transform herself into the spunky girl he was crazy about.

"I suppose the first thing we'll have to get is a mirror. You know how vain I am. Now I think I'm ready to go meet your mother. And I certainly hope she takes a liking to me right away because I want to make use of her bathtub."

As they jolted down the hill to Ma's, she recalled all of the terrible trials that Luise Rainer had suffered as the peasant wife in *The Good Earth*. Luise had struggled and prospered and she would too. She was already leaning out of the window questioning him about the plants and trees. When he flicked the cowlick from his forehead, she thought how handsome he looked and wondered how many hours of visiting they would have to go through before they could get back to the privacy of the battered iron bedstead. "We'll be all right, matey," she whispered as she bit his ear. "The two of us will be all right." She did not even consider the possibility that there might be three of them soon.

"YOU CAN RELAX now, Mrs. Hickock," Dr. Helen said as she snapped off the rubber glove and tossed it into the sink. "Tell me, do you use any method of birth control?"

"No. I didn't know anything about it except . . ."

"Withdrawal? Yes. Well, if you've been having intercourse regularly there is a strong possibility that you might be pregnant. However, you seem to be in good physical condition. You can come back and get the results of the pregnancy test in another week."

"I didn't know it would take that long," Sheila said softly.

"I'm afraid so. If you are pregnant the hormones in your body will change almost immediately. The change will show up in your urine. We send your urine to the laboratory. It's injected into an animal. The laboratory technicians will look at the change in the animal and determine if you are pregnant."

Dr. Helen realized that in giving the explanation she had all the animation of a fourth-grader reciting the multiplication table one hundred times, but she was too tired to articulate the information with more verve. Nevertheless, she saw that the girl's brown eyes were attentive and that she seemed to absorb what was being said. When she'd first seen Sheila in the waiting room, she'd observed the pretty dress, the carefully groomed hair and the touch of makeup that separated her from the usual run of downtrodden hill women, but she'd been too harried to give her much attention.

As Sheila disappeared behind the curtains, she slumped into her chair and lit a cigarette, coughed, and stubbed it out. It had been one of those days. Called to the hospital before dawn on a complicated premature delivery, she had driven straight to her office at ten o'clock to find six women and ten children standing on the lawn, their faces as forbearing and patient as mistreated farm animals. That look of stolid endurance usually touched her heart; but this morning she felt an uncontrollable fury at their passivity, mentally cursed their complicity in their own victimization. She had ushered them into the waiting room, pulled on her white smock, and called for the first one, cautioning herself to put in a word of cheer. It was so difficult for her not to lose her patience when she had to remind one of them for the umpteenth time about the need for proper diet or the necessity of taking medication. She took them in turn, apologizing for keeping them waiting, though she knew that none of them would complain. Rummaging through her desk, she dispensed pills and salves to those who were absolutely too poor to go to a druggist.

By early afternoon she had finished the coffee in her Thermos and gone through a pack of cigarettes. She had to call her housekeeper to ask if she would be kind enough to deliver more Camels and a couple of sandwiches. She wolfed down the sandwiches, one ear tuned to the steady wailing of a child beyond the door. When she went to the bathroom to swallow some digestive medicine, she noticed that her hand was shaking. The warnings of colleagues she had left behind in New York rang in her ears. Ob/Gyn in the hills of Virginia? That was for crusaders, neurotics or Reds. She'd get little cash and less thanks. Days like today made her think they might be right.

"Sit down and tell me a little bit about yourself, Mrs. Hickock," she said when Sheila crept out from behind the curtain. "I noticed that you have an accent. Are you English?"

"No. Australian."

"And how long have you been in the United States?"

"I've only been here about seven weeks. I married my husband over home. He came back here and I followed him."

"I see," she said, noting the apprehension in the brown eyes. "And does your husband have a job or is he going to school?"

"Neither," Sheila answered, lowering her eyes. "We've been living on the G.I. benefits but they're going to run out soon. He has tried to find something, but you see he doesn't have an education and they're laying people off at that munitions factory, and the other factory where they make overalls says they don't need any help . . ."

Her lip began to tremble. She fished in her purse for a handkerchief. When she couldn't find one, the tears began to roll down her cheeks. "I'm terribly sorry. It's really not like me to give way like this, but lately, I just don't seem to have any control over anything. I . . . I . . ."

Dr. Helen's face softened. She pulled a slightly soiled handkerchief from her breast pocket and handed it to Sheila.

"So you're upset about the possibility of being pregnant, is that it?"

"Yes. No. I don't know. It's not that I don't want to have a baby. I love my husband very much and I always thought that we'd have lots of children; but you see I had no idea what living conditions were like here. I suppose it was awfully naive of me, but I thought all Americans had money. I just supposed that Billy would find work."

"There now. First of all you may not be pregnant. I know that you're very anxious about it so I'll call the laboratory and ask if they will rush the results. Are you living in a decent place? Do you have healthy things to eat? What about his family?"

"The place is—I don't know how to describe it—I'd never seen anything like it in my life. We do have plenty of food. Most evenings we drive down the road and take dinner with Billy's mother. She's really a remarkable woman. I don't mean that she's educated or anything like that, but she's terribly kind. She had six children herself, though only three of them are alive now. After all she's seen and gone through, I really don't think that anything fazes her, so I couldn't very well tell her how I was feeling. Billy is . . ."

The words tumbled out. Not only was she able to talk about the shack, her relationship to Billy, and all of their financial problems, she even started to tell Dr. Helen about her home in Australia.

"Yes, that's the next thing I was going to ask you: could you write to your parents and ask them for financial assistance?"

"In the first place Billy would be ever so hurt if I did that. He knows that they didn't approve of him, and it would be such a blow to his pride. In the second place, I know it sounds pig-headed but I just can't bear to admit that they were right and I was an impractical dreamer. Can you understand what I mean? It's probably wrong of me, but I have to stick by things I start."

"Yes, I do know what you mean," the doctor said, stubbing out another cigarette. "In any event we can talk further about what you're going to do when we get the results of the test. In the meantime, perhaps we can have a little chat about birth control. I hate to ask you to undress again, but if you're willing, I think it would be a good idea if I fitted you for a diaphragm. You'll want to use it until we find out the results. I know it will be difficult since you don't have any running water in the house—that's the problem for most of the women here, but I know you'll make the effort until you and your husband get on your feet."

She picked up the telephone, calling her housekeeper to put the pot roast in the oven and tell Mr. Abromovitz that she would be late for dinner. Feeling that she was getting her second wind, she pulled pamphlets and boxes out of her desk, pleased that she had such an intelligent patient to talk to. "I know this looks like a strange object," she said as Sheila got up on the table again, "but it's really quite an advance. The Egyptians were the first people who left us any record of their birth control methods. They used to pack the vagina with a combination of herbs, honey and leaves to prevent conception . . ." The voice became vibrant again as she warmed to her subject and noticed that Sheila was listening with rapt attention. It was the first time in ages that Sheila's mind had been engaged with anything other than her own troubles and fantasies. Her quick intelligence clicked into gear, temporarily releasing her from her own concerns.

When she finally left the office, armed with several booklets and a tiny box, she walked out into the twilight to where Billy was waiting in the truck.

"What did they tell you?" he asked anxiously.

"We won't know until next week."

"Y' sure seem to be in a better mood than y' were when y' went in. I was gettin' real worried about y'."

"I found out all sorts of things. Things nobody would ever talk to me about before. The whole thing—getting pregnant I mean—it's just marvelous. There's all sorts of unbelievable things I'll have to tell you about and show you."

"Y' want to do that now? I thought that since we were in town, I'd like to treat y' to the movies."

"The movies! That would be even better," she cried as she hugged him and he turned the key to start the sputtering motor.

CHAPTER
VII

"SCOTCH?" RICHARD asked without looking up from the bar.

"No thanks," Ricky answered.

"Thought that hitch in the Army might have taught you how to drink."

Ricky loosened his tie and decided not to rise to the bait. Leaning against the archway that separated the entrance hall from the living room, he looked up the stairs where Gaynor had disappeared. When she had met him at the airport she'd looked even more beautiful than he had remembered. He wanted nothing more than to follow her upstairs, take her in his arms, and make love to her. Failing that, he might have gone out to inspect the garden with his mother, sat in the kitchen and chatted with Faustina, or had a smoke with Jackson. There would have been some pleasure in being with any one of them. But he knew that as soon as the bags had been carried into the house he would have to go into the living room for a father/son interrogation.

Nothing really changes, he thought as he sauntered across the room with self-conscious casualness; *Maybe in the world, but not in family relationships.* He threw himself into one of his mother's overstuffed chairs, registering the same inability to control his body that he always felt in Richard's presence. At least when he'd gone into the Army, and because of Richard's connections had found himself an aide to the General, he'd had the consolation of knowing when he was supposed to snap to and when he was allowed to be at ease. He had almost been comfortable, while hating himself for it, with the military protocol that outlined his behavior to those who were above and those who were below him. And for a few liberating months, when he first met Gaynor, he had actually believed himself released from the crushing authority and ridiculous values of men like his father. The knowledge that he could gain the love of such a woman was proof of his worth. It helped to heal the division between rebelliousness and deeply felt inadequacy; fostered the hope that he was strong enough to set his own course and follow through with it. But it took only an hour back in Kansas City before his confidence started to wither.

His eyes roved around the room. If memory served, the lamps near the couch used to have cream-colored rather than beige silk shades, but apart from that, everything, right down to the placement of the silver-framed baby pictures on the piano, was the same. He didn't have to look at his watch to know that it must be just after five on a midsummer's afternoon. The shadow of the elm tree that fell through the bay window had just reached the second swirling border of the carpet. If he looked to the left he would see the cluster of pink tea roses in the pewter vase that had belonged to his mother's mother. If he looked straight ahead, he would see his father's implacable, never satisfied gaze fixed on him. He shut his eyes, wanting to save at least one of his senses from the oppressive recognitions, but there was no escape. The clink of the ice cubes being dropped into the glass and the sound of the scotch being poured seemed louder.

"Now that I think about it, I guess I will take that drink."

"Good for you, son."

Don't call me 'son.' I'm not your son anymore.

"Why are you smirking like that, Ricky? And why the hell do you have your eyes closed? You're not shellshocked, are you? You didn't see any real combat."

"No, Dad. I didn't get into combat." *I wanted to go in as a regular dogface, but you made sure I wouldn't be exposed to the front lines.*

"You did get malaria though, didn't you?" Richard asked coldly, as though contracting the disease was another example of weakness.

"Yeah, there's always a chance of a recurrence, but if I stay in good shape I figure I'll be okay."

Richard handed him the drink, drew his own chair up, and looked at him closely.

"You did see some action though, didn't you? I remember you wrote to your mother about being shelled in, where was it, Leyte? Luzon?"

"Yeah, one of those." *I was scared shitless. When I heard them coming overhead I started to pray. And you remember that I voiced my first doubts about the existence of God when I was eighteen. I made Mom cry.*

"It must have been rough. Jimmy Richardson has told us a few gory stories down at the club. He brought back a whole album of pictures and quite a few Jap souvenirs."

He would. "I'd just as soon not talk about it, Dad. It's over with now."

"I have no intention of getting bogged down in the past, Ricky. In fact the reason I wanted to talk to you before your mother takes over with all the social engagements is because I want to know what you plan to do with your future."

I've told you a hundred times. "I'm going back to Princeton. I've contacted one of my old professors and it looks as though I can do an accelerated program and get my Ph.D. in about a year and a half."

"But where will that get you?"

Impossible question! Away from here at any rate.

"Look, Ricky," Richard continued in the controlled, reasonable tone that Ricky had overheard for years in business conversations, "I know we've had our differences in the past. When I say I'm looking toward the future I mean it. You were the kid who had his head stuck in the history books, so you'll appreciate what I'm saying: the country is in a unique historical position. Of course it's been a bit rocky with all the munitions and military support plants shutting down. But that's only temporary. We've been getting hell from the unions, but anyone with a brain knew that would happen once the wartime no-srike pledges came to an end. We'll retrench. Unemployment is less than two percent and there's about a hundred and forty billion dollars in liquid savings floating around—that's three times what it was about fifteen years ago. Not only do people want things, but they're going to have the money to buy them, inflation or not. There's going to be a boom. A big one."

Statistics again! Christ, he's a robot. "Yeah, Dad. I've had time enough to read the papers."

"The greatest consolidation of business in recent history is going to happen now. I want you to come down to the office. I'll show you the whole setup. You want to get into manufacturing? Real estate? Hell, they did the first Washington-New York television transmission a couple of months ago. That might be more in your line. I've got some connections with NBC, own a bit of stock there. Get in on the ground floor."

"I guess you haven't been listening to me. I'm going back to school. I'm going to write my thesis. I'm going to become a professor."

Richard's eyes narrowed and he jiggled his left leg impatiently. "Ricky, I'm giving it to you straight," he said, the sententious bonhomie leaving his voice. He almost seemed to be pleading. "I'm not trying to order you around, but if you turn down what I'm offering, you do it out of a perversity that you'll live to regret."

"Gee, Dad . . ." *You poor bastard. You've got hold of the cookie jar and now you want to dole them out because it might increase your pleasure. On top of the wheeling and dealing you want the added power of magnanimity. Not with me, buddy. I've said thank you for the last time.*

"Look, you've never had a real honeymoon, from what Gaynor tells me. Take her, go away. Go anywhere you want. Consider it my gift. Then, when you come back, you'll take over some of the business. Have something concrete to give your own son."

What I want to give to my son is something you'd never be able to understand. Because it's not material and you can't understand anything about intangibles. I want to make my son feel confident, full of self-respect, capable of love.

"I'm sorry, Dad. I'm really sorry to disappoint you, but my mind is made up. I'm going back to Princeton."

"And how will Gaynor take your decision? You think she'll want to keep house in a dingy little kitchenette while you sit around reading Walt Whitman and F. Scott Fitzgerald?"

"I don't think she'll mind. You see, she loves me."

She loves me in a way Mother could never love you because you never gave her a chance. With your almighty business deals and your women—don't think I don't know—you've helped to make her into a pathetic cipher. I'll never, ever forgive you for that.

"Have you talked to Gaynor about your plans?"

"Sure. Not recently of course, but before we were married."

"How long did you know her before you asked her to marry you?"

"Long enough . . . What is this, Twenty Questions?"

Richard fell silent, leaning forward with his elbows on his knees, twirling the ice cubes in his glass. The late-afternoon sun hit the top of his silver hair. For the briefest moment he seemed bowed down, uncommonly vulnerable.

Christ, the old stoneface is really depressed. Maybe this is the time to open up, tell him what I really think of him. Give him back a dose of his own medicine. . . . No. That would mean I was following his lead again. 'Identifi-

cation with the aggressor' I think the psychology professor called it. Not me. I'm not like him.

"Hey, Dad, I have to go back to Washington on Sunday, but I'll go out on the golf course with you tomorrow if you like. I know you'll lick the pants off me, but what the hell . . ."

Richard pulled his head up abruptly, the features set in a familiar expression. The lips were curled in a tight smile, but the eyes said what the mouth did not: You know nothing. You are an object of contempt to me.

"I hope I'm not disturbing you boys," Etna called from the hallway. She stopped at the arch, hands clasped demurely together, eyes misty.

Oh, she's dottier than she ever was. Look at that expression: same sentimental look she has when she puts the statue of the baby Jesus under the Christmas tree or takes out that old Norman Rockwell calendar of the father and son fishing together. Poor, dear Mother. I'll never forget the time when I was twelve and she caught me with both hands under the bedcovers and said she'd fetch the calamine lotion if I had an itch!

"Etna, Ricky and I are . . ."

"I think we've finished talking," Ricky said, rising to his feet.

"Oh, good. I don't want to rush you, but you know the Richardsons are coming for dinner. I hope you aren't annoyed with me for inviting them tonight, but Mabel and Fred were so anxious to see you again. Jimmy's coming too, but you needn't worry because Betty can't make it. I had to include her on the guest list for the big party tomorrow, but there's nothing to be upset about. Mabel tells me that Betty has found a very acceptable young man, and it's probably serious."

Betty. Years of hide-and-seek and croquet while the parents sat on the lawn drinking and snotty Jimmy teased the dog. I took her to the prom two years in a row, tried to French kiss her and made her cry. Wonder if she still splashes herself with White Shoulders and worries that her thighs are too big to look good in tennis shorts. Should've written to her. But she's such a deb type. No courage. Not like Gaynor. Gaynor didn't care about her virginity once she knew I really loved her. She was willing to give it all to me.

"I guess I'll go upstairs now, Mother."

"Yes, dear, do that. But don't take too long to unpack because the Richardsons are due here in about a half hour and Faustina is fixing a special dinner with all your old favorites."

THE FAINT clackety-clack of the lawnmower became the machine-gun fire of Ricky's dream. He jerked the sheets around him and buried his head in the pillow, frantically trying to camouflage his prone body. Turning in what he thought was a pup tent, he came up against soft flesh. The noise stopped. Filled with gratitude and relief, he tried to merge himself with the body. Gaynor. Half conscious, he fumbled beneath the sheets, found the hem of the satin nightdress that had wiggled up around her thighs, and slithered it up to her stomach. She stirred, pushed his hand away with groggy irritation, and rolled away from him. He fondled the shoulders and back, moaned into the mass of sweet-smelling hair. The clackety-clack started up again. He came full awake, and realized that he was in his parents' house.

The previous evening came back to him in a rapid montage: The afternoon contest with Richard had been bad enough, but he hadn't even had time to talk with Gaynor, let alone make love to her. He had come down to dinner in a welter of frustration. The favorite dishes of his past—sweet potatoes with marshmallows, roast beef, peas and hot biscuits—were being brought to the table. Faustina smiled expectantly, waiting for him to show his affection by scarfing them all up. But in the present company his appetite withered so completely that he was barely able to finish the first helping. Jimmy Richardson bragged about the war like a slightly sadistic coach giving a Monday-morning chalk talk after the big game. Mabel Richardson looked Gaynor over with obvious suspicion, which she tried to cover by being effusively polite and asking moronic questions—"What *do* you eat in Australia, my dear? Not kangaroo, I hope!" His mother made repeated trips to the kitchen—"to make sure everything is all right"— though everyone knew she was taking a few belts from the bottle she kept under the sink. Fred and Jimmy—and even, he had thought for a brief, paranoid moment, his father—eyed Gaynor's V-plunge neckline. Gaynor had told him it was the "New Look," but he thought it rather too revealing.

Once or twice, after dinner, when he feared he might lash out at all of them, he'd refilled his glass and gulped it down. A mistake. He couldn't even handle the beer at the old fraternity parties or the more recent officers' bashes; the hard stuff put him under completely, making him seem disinterested when he only wanted to be quietly attentive, ascerbic when he wished to appear humorous. When the Richardsons finally left and he followed Gaynor to the bedroom, he was half drunk and totally exhausted. His accumulated eagerness for lovemaking had turned him impatient and clumsy.

He blinked to remove the unpleasant pictures of the previous evening from his inner eye and stared around the room. He had noticed yesterday that the room was very different. Now he took in all the changes. A rose satin bedspread, which had replaced the old white candlewick, had slipped from the bed and fallen onto the carpet. There was a chaise longue where the desk used to be. Fine wallpaper with clusters of silver flowers and little beige stripes matched the cloth draped around the vanity table. Several full-length mirrors adorned the walls. It was all so sumptuously feminine that he felt he might be an overnight guest in the chambers of a courtesan out of a Zola novel. He caught a glimpse of his confused face in one of the mirrors and slid back down into the bed. Of course it was only natural that his mother and Gaynor would redecorate. Only natural that he and Gaynor should sleep here. It would have been impossible for them to go to bed in his old room. Just walking in there, seeing the school pennants, framed diplomas and photos of the football team on which he had played, an indifferent quarterback, made him wince. Somehow Gaynor had found a niche, settled in so completely that he felt as though she—and not he—had grown up in the house. He turned to her more insistently, kissing her full on the mouth.

"Good morning, darling," she yawned.

He started to undo his pajamas, but she pecked him on the cheek, threw back the sheet, and stepped onto the carpet.

"Hey, come back here," he demanded, reaching for her. She glided away from him, peeked out of the window, and then looked at the little gold clock on the night table.

"Oh, Ricky—it's after nine. We should get dressed."

"To hell with that. You think last night was enough to quench my burning passion? Come over here, m' wench."

"But we can't. Faustina must have breakfast on the table already. You know how early Richard gets up, even on the weekends. What will they think?"

"The truth I expect."

"But Jackson's taking me for a driving lesson at ten."

She was already pulling the brush through her hair and examining her complexion in the mirror. He lay back, still fingering the buttons on his pajamas, his eyes staring at the ceiling.

"Darling, you know I'd like to stay in bed, but I just feel . . . I don't know . . . uncomfortable."

"I know what you mean," he said. Last night when they'd finally gotten into bed he'd noticed that she seemed more reticent than he'd remembered. It hadn't occurred to him that she too might be sensitive to the strain of being in his father's domain. As she hurried into the bathroom, he looked at her with tenderness, trying to formulate plans that would assure them of privacy.

"I only have a few more months with the General. If you're really unhappy here you could come to Washington with me. I should have given you that option before, but I hated to think of you living in a hotel with no one to talk to. I'm so damned busy that I wouldn't be able to spend much time with you. Still, it might be best if you came back with me."

"No. I can stick it out here. I think it's just hunky dory," she called out.

"You're being real brave about it, but I know it's hell being away from each other. I knew I was being a sucker when I said I'd stay on for the extra time; but the General has treated me decently, and I just didn't think it would be honorable to walk out on him now. He's a queer duck, y' know. In the field he was totally confident, but now he's back at the War Department he's like Julius Caesar waiting for the Ides of March. Thinks he has enemies everywhere. Thinks the demobilization is going too fast and that we're going to be caught with our pants down again. Did I tell you that the day after the Japanese signed the surrender he turned to me and said, 'Now we're going to have to turn around and fight the Russians.' I've tried to explain to him several times that there's a difference between the civilian and the military mentality. It isn't that people don't care about our commitments, it's just that the guys who've been overseas are so anxious to get back to their regular lives. 'Course the way things are shaping up . . ."

He heard the shower go on. Slipping his feet into slippers, he started to go to shower with her, but paused to fling open the window. A moist morning breeze fluttered the curtains, and an odor of fertilizer mixed with the fragrance of the flowerbeds penetrated his nostrils. He stood still, his imagination superimposing huge spirals of smoke and flame on the lush green lawns. The gardener, who was running up the knoll toward the tennis courts, became a soldier frantically scurrying for cover. Transfixed, he clutched the sill until he heard the shower being turned off.

"So," he said, turning quickly from the window, "if you can stick it out here for another couple of months, we'll get a place near the college by September. Professor Lucas is already looking around for us. I don't care if it's two rooms with a privy down the hall, so long as we're together."

"*I* care if it's two rooms and a privy down the hall," she yelled back.

"Well, we'll do the best we can. We'll be living on the G.I. Bill, so even if I get a teaching assistantship, we won't be able to play the ponies this year."

He padded over to the bathroom and leaned against the door, watching her slip the sheer print dress over her head.

"I'd so much like to have a real house of our own, darling," she said as she turned her back to him and offered him the zipper. "I'm sure Richard would give us a loan."

"Sure he would. He'd love to. That would be just another hook into me so that he could ask about what I'm doing and then tell me what I *should* be doing instead. The interest is too high. I don't mean the money, I mean the emotional interest. You've seen my father enough to know: he doesn't give gifts, he makes investments."

"I don't think he's like that at all. He seems to be uncommonly generous."

"Honey, I've known him for twenty-four years. Believe me."

She moved past him into the bedroom, hiking the dress up above her knees and snapping the hook of her garter belt onto the top of her nylons.

"You do look like a Petty Girl," he grinned as he shuffled after her and put his arms around her. "Suppose we sneak up here after your driving lesson? You could tell them you have to wash your hair for a couple of hours."

"I'll try to, but there is this huge bash of a party planned for tonight. It's so important to Mother that it be a success, and I've promised to help Faustina with the hors d'oeuvres."

"Gee, you're sweet. I'm so glad you like Faustina."

She smoothed the dress over her hips and reached for her lipstick, not wanting to discuss her relationship to the housekeeper. There was a strange tension between them that she couldn't quite put her finger on. At first she'd put it down to resentment on Faustina's part because she was obliged to do a good deal more ironing and cleaning. But Faustina never seemed ruffled by any increase in her work load; in fact, she always volunteered to perform the extra tasks that added to Gaynor's comfort. Still, there was something about the woman that made Gaynor uneasy. She was never able to penetrate past the watchful eyes to discover what Faustina might be thinking. Whenever she tried to look at her directly, Faustina would drop her gaze and call her "ma'am" in that mellow, compliant voice. So she abandoned her effort to understand the housekeeper, feeling that as a mistress she need only be concerned with the performance of servants and not their personal attitudes.

"Maybe I should book us a room at a hotel, like the old days," Ricky persisted, coming up behind her and putting his hands on her hips. "This time I wouldn't even have to lie when I put Mr. and Mrs. on the register."

"Do you think that would take the thrill out of it?" she teased.

"Nothing can take the thrill out of it. I'm crazy about you, Mrs. Cunningham," he said as he pulled her to him. "Now run on down and tell Faustina to keep the flapjacks hot. I'll be there as soon as I take a shower. A *cold* shower."

He ate his flapjacks and gulped the Prairie Oyster Faustina had set near his plate, while Gaynor waited impatiently for Jackson to finish supervising the men who were setting up the tables and umbrellas on the back lawn. Fortunately Richard had already left the house; when Gaynor left, honking the horn and waving happily as she backed out of the driveway, Ricky had a chance to go into the kitchen and talk with Faustina. She was attending to preparations for the party with the same concentrated energy the General put into a battle plan, but managed to tell him in the subtle code language they'd developed over the years that his mother's drinking was no worse and that Etna seemed happier now that she had a daughter-in-law to fuss over and go shopping with. When the skinny, nervous black girl who had been hired to assist with the party came into the kitchen, he went out into the garden. Etna, wearing her battered straw hat and garden gloves, was crooning contentedly to herself as she selected blossoms for her flower arrangements. They talked about his health, his future plans and the George Orwell book he had sent to her, which, she confessed, she found too grim to finish. He helped the workmen to set up the tables, and by lunchtime the frustrations and weird imaginings of his waking hours had been banished.

In the late afternoon, when all the preparations seemed to be near completion and Gaynor had finished helping Faustina with the hors d'oeuvres, he signaled her that they should try to sneak upstairs. There was a furious honking and Jackson appeared at the back door, his eyes wide and his face split into an outrageous grin. "Don't know how he did it, but Mister Cunningham's gone and got himself a fine new chariot!" There was a general hubbub as they all ran out to the driveway to see a sleek, silver Cadillac convertible with Richard sitting at the wheel.

"Why didn't you tell us you were going to guy a new car?" Etna gasped. "I didn't even think you could get anything like this these days."

"You can get anything you want if you know how to go about it," Richard said quietly, looking at Ricky.

"It's a beauty, Dad." *Pathetic! He feels angry because he can't get me to do what he wants, so he runs out and buys himself a new toy. Or maybe he's just trying to impress me with the fruits of capital.*

"Mighty fine," Faustina grunted. "Mighty fine."

"You must be feeling a good deal younger than I," Etna laughed, "if you intend to go racing about in such a wild-looking thing."

"What do you think of it, Gaynor?" Richard wanted to know.

Gaynor was standing as though transfixed by a divine vision, her hands moving reverently over the upholstery, her nostrils flaring slightly. "I think," she whispered, "that the smell of anything brand new is absolutely the best smell in the world. How fast will it go?"

"Miz Gaynor is sure a natural behind a wheel," Jackson laughed, "long as she remember she's not in a racing competition."

Gaynor shot him a look and he excused himself and walked back to the house.

"It goes as fast as they make them to go," Richard smiled. "Do you want to take her out, Ricky?"

"Maybe later." *And have you sitting there waiting for me to either fall in love with it or have an accident? Not on your life.*

"It sure is fine, Mr. Cunningham," Faustina said again. "I could jest stand here and look at it 'til my eyes pop outta my head, but we got about fifty people comin' here in a hour or so."

"Yes, we do," Etna agreed. "I do wish you'd decided to buy it when we all had the time to go for a spin."

"Yeah, we'd better get upstairs and start to get ready," Ricky said, taking Gaynor's arm. She gave the car a last longing look and followed him into the house.

"Fair dinkum, that car's about the most incredible thing I've ever seen," she cried as he closed the bedroom door.

"I've got a DeSoto jalopy I left with my friend, Evan, in Princeton. When we go back there you can scoot around in that."

"Ricky, do you really want to go back there? I mean, even if you want to finish school, isn't there somewhere around here you could go?"

"That's out of the question for a hundred different reasons," he said as he unbuttoned his shirt.

"Do you think I could persuade you to reconsider?" she asked coquettishly, flopping on the bed and starting to unroll her nylon.

He was so overjoyed to be looking at her in the privacy of the bedroom that he didn't even hear the question. As she flung the stocking onto the carpet and started to unroll the other one, he felt an enormous sense of gratitude, and congratulated himself for having such a beautiful, uninhibited wife. He had taken a lot of razzing from the other guys when he'd turned down their offers to visit whorehouses. They'd said he was either a nut or a coward to forgo the pleasures of the flesh when they might all be blown away tomorrow. But he knew that he'd rather live with a dream than a disappointing reality. It would have offended his sense of aesthetics to go off like a Cro-Magnon hunter indiscriminately stalking his prey. And now his vision had been rewarded: he was blessed with a desirable and willing wife. An endless series of matings—intimate and varied—stretched before his imagination, intensifying his immediate physical need. He had trouble taking off his pants, and instead of undressing her he pulled up her skirt. He wanted to channel himself into a lengthy and sensual coupling. As he entered her he tried to concentrate on mathematical formulas (a trick an old college roommate had guaranteed would prolong performance), but his desire was now so excruciating that he was out of control. "I love you," he muttered over and over again. Then he collapsed in a spasm.

His perspiration had not even begun to dry in the twilight breeze coming in through the open windows before she wriggled out from under him.

"Damn this party. I wish we could just spend the rest of the night in bed."

"You'd better hurry up," she said as she pulled off the crumpled dress.

"I think I did that already," he sighed. "I'm sorry."

"I meant hurry up and dress. I'll shower first if you don't mind," she said casually, shutting the bathroom door.

He reached for one of her cigarettes on the night table, and sat staring down at his naked feet, which looked large and ugly upon the swirls of the beige-and-rose carpet. He switched on the bedside radio.

The plaintive voice of the crooner struggled against the back-up of the brassy orchestra:

> Long ago and far away,
> I dreamed a dream one day
> And now, that dream is
> here beside me . . .

"Ricky, what's the matter with you?" she said as she emerged from the bathroom holding a towel around her dewy skin. "Get a move on."

He stayed in the shower for a long time, concentrating on the steaming water that was hitting his back, trying to clear the tangle of thoughts from his brain. When he came out, she was already sitting at the vanity wearing a black strapless gown, touching her lashes with mascara. For a moment he just looked at the dress and wondered how they engineered it to stay up by itself.

"The brassiere is boned on the sides," she said, catching his look in the mirror.

"It still looks pretty dangerous to me," he answered as he pulled on his pants.

"Do you have to wear that uniform?" she asked, never taking her eyes from her meticulous grooming. "Everyone else will be in black tie."

"Thought you women loved the uniform. At least that's what the recruiting officer told me. Said it was an absolute guarantee of female adoration . . . I feel a bit bored with it myself, but since I'm still officially in, I think I'd better wear it."

"I hope you're not going to be one of those chaps who can't adjust to peacetime."

"Not me. I've been praying for it."

"You don't have to pray for it, love. It's already here."

"That dress is new, isn't it?"

"Yes. Bought it for the party. Etna took me on a shopping trip to Petticoat Lane. We went to all the shops. The minute I saw this I absolutely fell in love with it."

"How can you fall in love with a dress?"

"Manner of speaking, Ricky. You educated types take everything so literally."

"It looks expensive."

"I think it was."

"You *think* it was," he said impatiently, searching under the bed for a missing shoe. "Honey, I don't want to be cheap, but I'd hoped that you might be able to save a little of the money I've been sending to you."

"But Etna said we have an account at the shop," she said defensively.

"We? No, Gaynor. *We* don't have an account at the store. My father does."

"Oh Ricky, all my life I've wanted to just walk into a place and say 'that's what I want' without asking the price. I don't suppose you can understand that because you've been able to do it all your life."

"Do you think most people in the world feel that way when they go out and buy something?"

"I'm not most people," she snapped. "I'm me."

He tugged on his shoelace and cursed when it broke. Throwing the remaining part of it onto the floor, he continued to curse under his breath. "Dammit to hell. I hope Faustina has an extra pair of laces somewhere."

"See what I mean? You've always been taken care of. Always had people around to do things for you." She remembered that when he had walked into the jewelry shop where she'd worked, she had first noticed him because he had bought the opal pendant without asking the price. "I don't see why you're so angry with me. After all, I just want to make a good impression."

"I'm not angry with you," he shouted. "And this good impression stuff—where does that crap come from? Last night at dinner when Richard started in about your rich uncle who has ranches in Australia I almost fell off my chair. Why would you want to tell him that baloney? I can see where you wouldn't want to talk about your mother, but that's no reason to start inventing things."

The face that had been so serenely lovely a few minutes ago stared back at her, contorting into hard, ugly lines as she struggled to control her anger. She took the top from the perfume bottle, but her hand started to shake, so she put it down. No. There was no point in trying to explain herself. That might be construed as nagging. If she wanted to exercise any leverage with him she would have to play the role of the compliant wife. He couldn't understand her. *How* could he understand any woman when he only thought of them in terms of poetry and pinups? It was all very well that he'd put her on a pedestal—at first the change from the pawing, demanding men she'd had to deal with was refreshing—but she couldn't expect him to really know her or, for that matter, really make love to her. He was only capable, albeit with the illusion of unselfish devotion, of being utterly and completely self-involved. Another quiver of rage went through her. Reaching for a cigarette, she knocked over the bottle of perfume. She watched it leak onto the vanity table, knowing that if she moved to pick it up she might explode with violent fury.

He reached for the overturned bottle and wiped up the spill with his fingertips. It filled him with panic to see her, pale and unmoving, squeezing that damned cigarette and looking at her reflection as though she had just seen some hideous vision. He had no desire to dominate her. Couldn't she see that he would do everything to avoid the domestic bullying he'd witnessed and despised all his life? But he couldn't confront her. The rigid, angry mask in the mirror was too threatening. He touched his wet fingertips behind her ears. As the sounds of the band that Etna had hired for the party started up, he felt incredible relief.

"It sounds as though the party is starting, dear."

"I suppose so," she said numbly.

"I'm sorry. I didn't mean to upset you. I need your help. I guess I should have told you more about the setup here before you came. It's much more complicated than you think."

"I just don't want . . . I don't want anyone to think that you've married beneath you . . . that you've made a mistake in choosing me."

"How could anyone ever think that? I'm proud of you. Please. Forget everything I said. Now let's go downstairs."

"If you don't mind, I'd like to stay up here for a minute—I haven't quite finished with my makeup."

He nodded, gave her shoulder the sort of squeeze of affirmation he might give to a buddy on a football team, and walked out.

As soon as she heard his footsteps running down the stairs, she picked up the silver hairbrush and hurled it across the room. *Goddamn him to hell!* It was so bloody unfair. How dare he castigate her for wanting acceptance and comfort and pleasure? Those were the things that any sensible person desired. But he had never had to face deprivation or make harsh decisions. He was a rich momma's boy with idealistic pretensions. Much as he railed against his privilege, and wanted to get away from it in order to assert himself and do things the hard way, he had been protected from reality all his life. And what was the point of having a rich and powerful father if you didn't use his help? He had no idea what he was turning down by rejecting Richard's offers. He thought it would be more noble to sit with his face in a book for the rest of his life.

She paced the room until her rage was spent and the sounds of voices from downstairs intruded on her thoughts. Looking at herself in the mirror, she arranged her features into an expression of aloof composure and walked out onto the landing, peering over the bannister.

The first guests had arrived and were milling about the entrance hall. The young Negro girl in the oversized maid's uniform stood rigidly by the door. Richard, scotch already in hand, directed a corpulent man into the living room while Etna, a corsage pinned to the shoulder of her blue lace dress, fluttered among the guests like a spinster music teacher on the night of the annual recital.

"Gladys, do you know Mr. and Mrs. Phelps? I think you were introduced last year at the lake . . . George, this is Kay and Donald Manchester. You'll probably recognize Mr. Manchester from the firm of Potter, Manchester and Little . . . my, isn't it muggy . . . not that you look it, Iris. Iris is president of the garden club—yes, isn't the name appropriate! Why don't we all go out onto the terrace? The band has already started up and some of the young people will want to dance . . . no, Sue Ann! I wasn't excluding you when I said young people . . ."

She ushered them through the double doors onto the terrace. The Negro girl let her spine relax and pulled at her stockings in preparation for the next onslaught of guests, then straightened to attention again. No one really seemed to notice her, but if there was any criticism of her deportment she might not be hired again.

Gaynor took a deep breath and started down the stairs. She hesitated as she saw the fat man exit the living room and bounce toward the terrace. A second later, Richard came out of the living room. When he saw her in the classic but revealing strapless dress, her long brown hair sweeping her exposed shoulders, her head held high with just the trace of uncertainty about her vivid mouth, he stopped and stared. *Goddamn it,* he thought, *she may be a climber, but she sure knows how to put it together.*

She caught the glimmer of admiration in his eyes before he reverted to his usual look of appraisal. He held out his hand. When their fingers touched, neither of them moved.

"Girl, why you standin' there like God took away the use of your limbs?" Faustina hissed as she bustled into the hallway toward the young girl. The slanted eyes cut over to Richard and Gaynor, then immediately arced back toward the front door as though she hadn't noticed them. "Don't just cement yourself like a garden statue," she continued to upbraid the young woman. "Come on back to the kitchen and make yourself useful 'til you hear the bell chime again." The girl hitched up her white organdy apron and trailed after her.

"The dress is perfect," Richard said. "Come on. I'll introduce you to these clowns and fix you a drink."

She tossed her hair back, straightened her back so that her breasts looked high and invulnerable, and prepared to make her entrance.

CHAPTER
VIII

BY ELEVEN O'CLOCK even those guests who wished to appear fashionably late had arrived, and were bouncing to the music, soaking up the liquor, flirting or talking business. Gaynor had taken just the right amount of champagne to loosen her tongue without dulling her responses. She'd given her speech about how much she loved America so many times that it had the glib but seemingly spontaneous tone of a celebrity's response to a stock question. The women were polite and the men drooled from a respectful distance as she told each of them what he wanted to hear. It was just as well that she was in a mood to sparkle, because Ricky was making a terrible showing. Even when he stood with his arm around her, the perfect picture of uxorious devotion, he made no attempt to hide his boredom with small talk and became downright rude when any of the men tried to discuss business with him.

He knows what's required at these things, Gaynor thought bitterly, listening to one of his cynical, intellectual remarks to Donald Manchester. *If he isn't willing to go along with it, why the hell didn't he have the guts to tell Etna to call the whole evening off?* When she saw Kay Manchester shoot a disapproving glance at Donald, then fix a tolerant smile on her aseptic mouth, Gaynor complained that Ricky hadn't danced with her all evening and guided him onto the area of the terrace that had been cleared for dancing. He held her very close and murmured endearments into her ear until he saw a young woman in a polka-dot voile formal walk out onto the terrace.

"Betty Richardson," he exclaimed, releasing Gaynor and pulling her after him. "Gaynor, this is Betty. Betty was my childhood sweet-heart. Betty, this is Gaynor, my wife."

"I'm very pleased to meet you," Betty said, smiling out of a broad freckled face with earnest blue eyes. "This is Roger Elmsly."

They chatted awkwardly for a few minutes until Roger, full of eager, oily charm, asked Gaynor to dance. Gaynor decided that the dumpy girl with her bob of light brown hair and out-of-fashion dress was no competition, and allowed herself to take Roger's perspiring hand and be led away.

"I suppose I should say something original like 'long time no see,'" Betty said quickly.

"How long has it been? When I came home on leave two years ago?" *Light years. But yesterday. When I look at that open, intelligent face . . . What a good kid she is. Not a breath of recrimination even though I didn't answer her letters.*

"If you keep staring at me like that I'll think you've noticed that I've gained another ten pounds but you're too polite to mention it. Seems unfair that brother Jimmy got the slim body and the long eyelashes, doesn't it?

"You got the brains *and* the looks."

"The kids in my third grade class tell me that, but you've known me too long to stoop to flattery."

"Speaking of brother Jimmy, he was over here last night with your parents. I though the war would be enough to make all of us grown-up, but I couldn't see that the experience had any noticeable affect on Jimmy."

"You're telling me," she whispered. "I came down to breakfast yesterday morning and found him teasing the dog. It reminded me of that time on the lake when we were about eleven years old. Remember? We caught a frog—you wanted to write a story about it, I wanted to keep it as a pet, and Jimmy wanted to cut it up 'for scientific purposes.'"

As they laughed together her eyes filled with the same old tender-ness.

Please don't look at me that way. I can already see your mother over there watching us and she still has the look of a predatory matchmaker.

"Would you like to dance?"

"Oh, dear. Jimmy's still a braggart and a sadist and you still ask me to dance when you don't know what to say to me. Nothing ever changes."

Nothing ever changes. That's what I was thinking yesterday. You know it too. You just have a sweeter nature than I do so you're not so bitter about it. "If you don't want to dance, how's about sneaking up to the tennis courts for a talk? I'll get you a drink. Want to wait for me or should I meet you up there?"

"Oh, I think we can walk off together. In the first place almost everyone's too pie-eyed to notice; and in the second place, with a wife like Gaynor, you're probably the only married man here who isn't angling for an affair."

"Don't tell me the moral tone in the charmed circle has degenerated in my absence," he grinned as he motioned for the waiter.

"No, it's about the same. Still more petting and gossiping than real cuckoldry. Not that I'm in a position to know. There does seem to be an increase in the divorce rate, but they say that has something to do with the war."

He handed her the drink and shouldered his way through the throng. As they set out across the lawn, she filled him in on the lives and loves of former friends and schoolmates. When they reached the first clump of shrubbery, he held her drink while she balanced herself against a tree trunk and took off her shoes.

"And what about you?" he asked when they'd settled on one of the benches near the courts and the din of the party had faded into the background. "Think you'll get hitched to that Roger fellow?"

"Good heavens no! I guess it must have been Mother who planted that seed in your brain. She's been trying to plant it in mine too. Ever since I started getting birth announcements from my old sorority sisters, she's really upped the ante. And now that Jimmy's back, he puts his two cents in as well—talks to me about the wasted lives of old maids and other such subtle stuff. Of course I know that Roger would slip the gold band on my finger if I wanted it. He's a manager at one of Dad's plants and now that Jimmy's back in town I think he feels he may be in a precarious position. I let him squire me around to these parties so that I won't look like too much of a misfit, but the thought of waking up next to him makes me want to giggle." She wiggled her toes in the grass, threw her head back, and looked up into the starry sky. "I used to think that the worst thing about growing up was that I wouldn't be able to go barefoot. Now I know it's the pressure to get married. Honestly, I feel as though I'm a stock they've invested in that keeps dropping in value and they don't know how to unload it. But

I 'spose that most of the marriages in our set are like that—more financial transactions than love affairs. You're one of the lucky ones. I always though you'd make a wonderful husband . . . not for me of course," she added quickly.

"Yes, I'm lucky. If you got to know Gaynor, you'd know how lucky I am. I don't just mean that she's beautiful. She's exceptionally bright, too. When we were first going out she made me feel so much at home. She'd read all of my favorite books . . ."

"Well, I have yet to meet a man who asked me for *my* list of favorite books," she said, running her hand over the bench. Even in the moonlight he could see that the averted face had a wry smile. "I don't mean to be sarcastic," she apologized. "I just mean that the qualities one looks for in a mate still seem to be very different for men and for women. I can't imagine myself wanting to spend the rest of my life with someone because he was attractive, compliant and thought that I was the focus of his entire life, but that does seem to be what most men want in women. And most of my female friends profess to want an equally superficial though entirely different list of qualities. . . . At any rate, you're happy and I'm glad for that."

"Yes, I am happy." *Have a little spunk, Ricky. She's not after you anymore. She's really trying to talk to you, and she'd probably understand if you tried to talk to her. Besides, you've never really had a close woman friend. It might be nice. Women are easier to talk to than men.*

"I haven't been all that happy this weekend. The separation from Gaynor has been hell, and I have to go back to Washington tomorrow. There are so many things about her I just don't understand yet. And there are so many things about the family that I haven't had time to talk to her about. Richard's been breathing down my neck and it's still more than I can cope with, but Gaynor doesn't really see what he's like."

"Yes, I can imagine," she said after a pause.

I'll bet you can. Nothing like an old friend. You don't have to struggle to give them the background. Close, wordless comfort. I'd like to hold you, hug you, let you know that I really do care about you in ways that I can't express. But open as you are, you might misinterpret it.

They were silent, breathing the damp night air that almost obliterated the memory of the muggy day, comfortable in being away from the blare of the music and the pretenses of the social scene.

"Does Gaynor understand about your going back to Princeton? You are going back, aren't you?"

I'm not sure if she understands. Yes. She must understand. After all, she loves me. "Yes, I'm going back."

"I think it's brave of you. I don't mean you should get the Purple Heart or anything; but it does take some guts to get up and leave. I think Jimmy wanted to get out on his own when he first came back from Europe. But it's so easy to slip back in when you have it all there for you on the plate. 'Course being one of the fairer sex I don't even have the option of becoming a junior partner, so I'm in no position to talk about what I'd do . . . but, Lord, I do wish Jimmy could have gotten out and tried to grow up alone. I can just see him, fifteen years from now, chasing the employees instead of the dog."

"I don't think that I should get credit for courage—there's really no alternative for me. Of course Richard doesn't understand. He thinks I'm being perverse—don't have the proper respect for money. But it's not that I scorn all the power and possessions—I'm still grateful in some mixed-up way that I was born with the silver spoon. It's just that the *process* irks me. You see, I couldn't get any satisfaction out of closing a deal, or beating out the competition and making a killing. Even when you're on top like Dad is, you still have to enjoy the process because it takes such a phenomenal amount of energy. I thought I wanted to get away even before the war, but now I absolutely have to. When I actually saw guys dying and I was afraid that I might get it myself—well, I knew I could never do something I hadn't chosen, or something I didn't respect and care about. I actually *felt* my own mortality, and it was a helluva lot different than reading about death in some philosophy book."

"I think I know what you mean. That recognition of mortality can drive some people into hedonism—they want to get what they can to make it comfortable while they're still around. But it can also turn a person in the other direction—make them want to do something worthwhile. You know I've been taking some graduate classes over at K.U. and I've noticed that the mood of the campus has really changed because of the vets. They're so serious. A lot of the students don't like it. They know the buzz boys are ruining the curves on the exams, because they're actually coming back to study. And I guess some of the girls are a bit surprised by the direct propositions they've been getting. Seems that the vets feel they lost so much time that they don't want to take a girl to four dances, three swim parties and meet her folks before they try to kiss her. Some of the girls think that the women overseas made them lose their manners. But I know it's something more than that. The mood is changing. And even if there's some horrible backsliding—all that most of the girls ever talk about now is having a home, and being good wives and mothers—ultimately, we'll all have to deal with the changes . . . and on the taboo subject of the battle of the sexes," she laughed, "I thought I'd tell you that I finally lost it."

My god, Blushing Betty telling me that she's "lost it"—things really have changed . . . I wonder what she's like in bed? Somehow I never even thought about it. Even when I made those fumbling passes at her I never really fantasized about her. I only did it because she was there and female. Still, I have heard guys say that the homely ones can really surprise you.

"I don't know why I'm making this confession to you," she continued, when he didn't say anything. "I guess it's because you're my only social contact outside of Mom, Dad, Roger and fifteen third-graders."

"Should I ask why, how or with whom?" he smiled.

"Why?: because it was about time. How?: the usual way I think, though I'm still pretty inexperienced in these matters. Who?: a vet I met last year."

"So where is this young Lochinvar?"

"He's left. Gone back East to Columbia University. As a matter of fact I'm going back there myself. Not because I want him to reward my virginal sacrifice with marriage. To be perfectly honest I think he only went to bed with me because he knew I wouldn't insist on all of the preliminaries. But I've applied to Columbia grad school in sociology. I find that I'm losing patience with my nine-year-olds. It isn't their fault; I just don't feature myself reading *Fun With Dick and Jane* and waiting for menopause."

"Sociology, huh," he said blankly, still taken aback by her candor.

"Yes. When I explained to Mother that it was about society, I expect she thought I'd study the family tree and how to give parties. Anyhow, I have to try my wings or lose respect for myself."

"You know, I really admire you, Betty," he said as he put his arm around her. "When we were kids I always thought you were different, but when you hit fourteen you just seemed to slide right into the mold."

"God knows I tried. Put lemon juice on my face to bleach the freckles, improved my tennis game—not to the point of being competitive you understand, but just enough so my backhand would get more attention than my legs—I even learned to dance. But the whole kit and kaboodle just wouldn't take. So . . . if I'm back in New York in September, you and Gaynor will be out in New Jersey and we'll be able to visit. And speaking of Gaynor, I think we've abandoned her long enough. We'd better get back."

"Yeah, you're right. I've been having such a good time talking with you that I wasn't paying attention," he said with surprise as he watched her put her shoes back on. "You've been the best part of the whole trip."

"Likewise I'm sure, Lieutenant. Likewise."

They walked hand in hand across the lawn. The crowd had thinned out and the band had slowed to a plaintive rendition of "All or Nothing at All." Five or six couples, either in a state of preparatory amorousness or advanced drunkenness, clutched each other and stumbled to the music. Jimmy Richardson, exhausted from recounting past battles and working out the tactics of future ones on the fields of commerce, had passed out cold, the upper half of his body sprawled across the buffet table. The men had taken over the garden chairs, clustering in small groups, talking about the state of the economy or swapping off-color yarns. The women had gathered near the buffet table, seemingly oblivious to Jimmy's inert body. The Manchesters, in another of their public domestic disputes, squared off near the bar and hissed audible insults to each other. Ricky delivered Betty back into the company of her mother, who immediately pulled her aside and suggested that they go to the little girls' room.

"How's it going?" Ricky asked, putting his arm around Etna and interrupting her conversation about the fundraiser for the historical society.

"Just grand, dear. Charming party, don't you think?" she cooed, ignoring the fact that Donald Manchester had just shouted "For Christsake, Kay, get off my back! If you don't like the new governess, *you* fire her!"

Oh God, let it end. Let me lie down in peace with my wife and escape this madness. "I don't see Gaynor, Mother. Any idea where she is?"

"My dear, I just don't know. I believe Faustina said she and your father and some other people left about a half hour ago to have a fling in the new car."

WHEN RICHARD saw Ricky and Betty leave the party, he downed the remains of his third scotch and excused himself from Donald Manchester, who seemed to take advantage of every gathering to unburden himself of his marital dissatisfactions. Moving to the edge of the crowd, he sat down at one of the lawn tables and focused his attention toward the terrace. His daughter-in-law was dancing with Jimmy Richardson, following his clumsy lead with grace, ignoring the fact that Jimmy was having trouble keeping his eyes away from her cleavage. When Jimmy's hand moved from her waist to the exposed flesh of her back, she twisted in time to the music, forcing the hand to return to its proper place, her eyes flashing a cool warning. *I wonder how many passes she's blocked,* Richard thought. *Probably about equal to the amount that she's accepted. Goddamn son of mine's still wet behind the ears. He wouldn't have a clue what she's about. He'd have been better off with that little dumpling Betty. Probably would have married her if he hadn't thought it would please me.*

As the band started into "Blues in the Night," Gaynor whirled away from Jimmy, her long legs flashing through the slit in the dress, her breasts, which had that slight droop Richard found most desirable, bouncing slightly as she swayed to the music. Richard uncrossed his legs, realizing that his palms were sweating just as they had the first time he'd sneaked into a burlesque show at sixteen. Hearing Etna's girlish laugh, he turned to see her chattering to one of her cronies from the garden club, and nervously rearranging the parsley on one of the huge platters Faustina had set on the table. Two bright circles of pink stood out on her cheeks, making her look more pathetically doll-like than usual. *Christ! Has she ever felt even a twitch of pleasure that didn't come from looking up her genealogical charts or playing with her baby boy?* He crossed his legs again, motioning the waiter for another drink.

"There you are, Richard," Lonnie Diamond boomed. He pulled up a chair, yanking part of the lawn with it, and put his moon-shaped face close to Richard's. "I've been trying to get your ear all night. Been talking to some of the fellows down at the Legion and we're gonna have to move fast on this G.I. housing provision. You know we were successful in blocking the original bill where the government was gonna spring for housing loans at an outright three percent and finance it through the FHA. So now that we've convinced them to work through the banks with conventional and higher financing, we've gotta take advantage of it. I know you couldn't come to the meeting of the National Association of Real Estate Boards, but we decided that . . ."

Behind the expression of attentiveness he always displayed to underlings, Richard felt a wave of indignation mixed with a very rare sense of self-pity. He had amassed a fortune. He had connections that reached from Washington to San Francisco. For what? For a silly, tippling wife he hadn't slept with in years? For a weakling son who masked his ineffectual rebellion as idealism? They didn't care about him. They didn't even care about the money he'd fought for. Why, he'd seen more gratitude and excitement glittering in that Gaynor's eyes this afternoon when he'd brought the new car home than he'd elicited from either his wife or son in years.

"So we know we've got some congressmen on our side already, but not enough. If you could talk to Walker," Lonnie rushed on. "Hell, a word from you could swing him around and then we'd be sure of the votes. He knows he can't win the next election without your support. Besides, his son-in-law is in the construction business and he's already started to soften him up . . ."

Why the hell had she married someone like Ricky? She couldn't be in love with him. It must've been that she smelled the money; wanted a passport to respectability. He didn't even have to check out the stories she'd told about her dead father, her invalid mother and the moneyed uncle she supposedly had in Australia. He'd identified the flash of fear in her eyes when he'd hinted that he was on to her game. In the six weeks she'd been at the house, she hadn't received a single letter from home (a fact that seemed to have escaped Etna's attention); and her obvious delight in luxuries did not bespeak a girl who had grown up with them. It all added up. Of course Gaynor was pretty smooth. It took an old hand like himself to see through her. But he'd played some games himself—years back when he'd had to be less than honest about the extent of his capital to swing a deal. That took guts. Even though she must be a tramp, he had to admire her for creating another self, and putting it over on most of the yahoos. But she still didn't have it down to a fine art. She didn't realize that if she was powerful enough she'd never have to make up stories. If you carried yourself with the proper authority, people didn't seek explanations. She'd figure that out in another couple of years.

". . . and since Ricky's going back to Washington tomorrow and he's got the General's ear, I thought perhaps . . ."

"No, Lonnie. Ricky's out," Richard said, momentarily alert to the conversation. "He's not interested in business. He's going back to Princeton. Wants to become a college professor."

"Yeah, I think I heard that," Lonnie commiserated. "What can y' say? Maybe it's just this veteran's adjustment problem or whatever they call it. He'll probably pull out of it."

Richard could feel the anger welling up, out of control now because of the booze. He had been so enraptured with the first sight of his son, so hopeful of what Ricky might accomplish, so proud of his own ability to provide him with a leg up. His own old man had never given him more than the back of his hand and he knew that because of his disadvantage of birth he could never be more than a behind-the-scenes dealer of power. But he had dreamed. He had imagined a brood of educated, privileged sons who could reach for the top with clean hands. He had wanted to see gracious, beautiful daughters upon whom he could lavish gifts, and promote into successful marriages. But Etna had been too frail. She had almost lost her life giving birth to Ricky. During the infrequent times when they "honored the marriage bed" as Etna termed it, she had taken precautions not to conceive, though she never discussed these precautions with him. So Ricky had been her great love from the moment he came out of her womb. And Etna, despite her apparent frailty, had succeeded where Richard had failed. She'd molded their only son after her design into a lily-livered sob sister.

"Did you hear what the nurse said to the guy with the prostate trouble?" Lonnie asked, realizing that he'd made a mistake in bringing up the subject of Ricky, and quickly riffling through his file of dirty jokes. He wheezed with premature laughter, recovered himself, and started the story again. "So there he is, incapacitated, and this luscious nurse comes into the room and says . . ."

Richard's eyes flitted back to Gaynor. The band had concluded a number and she was heaving with mock exhaustion, placing her hand on her breast and begging off from her next partner. Tossing her hair back from her face in that studied but totally winning gesture, she turned a demure smile toward one of the older ladies and started to give another interview about her reactions to the United States. The expression of implicit understanding iced with cool innocence that she displayed toward the men now changed into an unctuous politeness that would have done credit to a diplomat's wife. *What a waste of talent that she should have become Ricky's. Why, Ricky would be down for the count after a single round in the sack with a woman like that,* he thought as he felt the blood rush to his head.

He finished off his fourth scotch and forced himself to look into Lonnie's bloodshot eyes and give a grudging laugh, even though he'd heard the joke twice before. Encouraged by even a halfhearted response, Lonnie started up again: "You see this guy was out on the golf course and the caddie had lost his balls, ha ha, so the guy says 'How many holes do we have to go?' and the caddie says . . ."

It wasn't until last night when he'd watched Ricky follow Gaynor up the stairs that he'd realized the full extent of his lust for her. He'd let Etna totter up to their bedroom alone, saying that he wanted to stay downstairs to go over some papers. Sitting at his desk, capping and uncapping his fountain pen, his ears strained to hear any sound that came from the bedroom above his study. The hostility he'd felt toward Gaynor began to shift to Ricky as he imagined his son fawning over her, fumbling and sighing instead of taking hold, mastering her, and seizing the obvious pleasures she had to offer. The picture of them in bed together filled him with bitterness. Ricky could scorn his money and power but still enjoy the reward that was his only because of them. He'd paced the study, gripped by a sexual need that he had not felt so acutely in years. Of course he'd taken his satisfaction with expensive, faceless women, but that was just another business transaction. He knew in advance what the moves and the final payment would be. There was no challenge in it. No engagement of his real force. And therefore, no sense of victory. Just looking at his beautiful daughter-in-law made his throat dry up. There was something about her that suggested that though she'd probably had many lovers, there was a part of her that had never really been touched. She was wrapped in a cocoon of narcissism, desirable but never desiring. That protective veneer could never be removed layer by layer, but perhaps it could be ripped away. He felt the mixture of untested power and tenderness of a hard-bodied youngster stalking his first piece.

"Well, listen, Richard, I guess this isn't the time to be talking business," Lonnie apologized as Richard stood up. "I'll give you a call at your office on Monday."

"You do that, Lonnie," Richard said as he moved toward the terrace.

He stopped her just as she was excusing herself from a circle of admirers and saying that she had to go and powder her nose. "Would you like to go for a ride in the new car?" he asked casually.

Her lips parted and she looked around quickly to see if anyone was listening.

"Wouldn't it be rude? I mean, do you think we could?"

He didn't bother to answer, but headed through the french doors into the house. After checking to see that all of the guests were either dancing, eating, or talking, she paused for the briefest moment, and then followed him.

Richard stood on the front steps until she came up behind him, and then, without looking back at her, crossed the lawn. She tried to keep up with his pace, but her high heels sank into the wet lawn and the long skirt hindered her stride. Slowing down only made her feel affected. It was maddening; no matter how much her confidence increased with other people, she was never at ease with Richard. She did not see him frequently—there were days when he left the house before she got up and returned after she went to bed; but whenever he was around, she felt that same conscious desire to please, the same lack of poise that had marked their first meeting. No matter how hard she tried to impress him with her gentility, her manners, her knowledge of events, those cold, evaluating eyes would stare her down. She knew she had been judged and found lacking, but her anger at his hostile appraisal was quickly replaced by the desire to win him. Perhaps this evening the antagonism had at last been overcome. He must have noticed what a favorable impression she'd made on all of the guests, and she knew his eyes had never left her when she was dancing with Jimmy Richardson.

She had felt a return of some of her power as she pretended to be unaware of his attention. *No matter what he thinks of me, he finds me desirable,* she thought. *That's the root of the hostility.* She would manipulate his attraction, flirt with him a little in a sweet ingenue way that would please his ego, lubricate the friction between them. He had probably suggested the drive so that he could speak to her privately. It was important to both of them to bring Ricky around, and when she told him that she would do everything in her power to make Ricky take a more sensible attitude toward his future, they would become allies.

"Jackson says I'm really coming along with my driving," she said in a high-pitched voice. He swung the door of the convertible open on the driver's side. She gathered up her skirt and got in, thinking that he was going to let her try the car.

"Maybe you can take it out later. Right now, I think I'll drive."

There was something in his voice—a hint of threat or promise, a challenge—that sent an odd tingle through her. She slid obediently across the seat. As he got in and turned the key the powerful motor purred instantly. Her stomach turned. Perhaps she'd had too much champagne after all, perhaps she shouldn't have left the party. He guided the car out of the driveway, driving it slowly through the broad avenues of the enclave. The great trees clasped their branches protectively overhead; the still humid air wafted the scents of the cultivated gardens; the grand houses, luminous in the moonlight, bespoke a cherished, civilized domesticity.

As he reached the fields that surrounded the estates, he paused for a moment. His eyes became glistening pinpoints as he focused on the road leading into the open fields.

"Now let's open her up," he said, almost to himself as he pressed down on the accelerator.

The night air raced by them, lashing her hair into her face, sending the smell of new upholstery into her nostrils. He negotiated a turn at giddying speed, righted the wheel, and plunged onto another country road. She gripped the seat with the near-hysterical pleasure of a child on its first roller-coaster ride. They were going too fast for her to make out anything on the side of the road. She let her head fall back and turned her face to the blackness of the sky. Her mouth fell open, lips drawn back over the bright teeth in an expression of extreme emotion that might have been pain or pleasure. A low growling sound came from her throat. On and on they went, the well-sprung car eating up the uneven surface of the road, oblivious to everything but the sensations of driving, catapulting through time and space, moving with incredible power and speed.

With an abrupt movement that almost sent her hurtling through the windshield, he spun the car into a clump of trees. It trembled to a stop. She stared straight ahead, gasping, the sudden cessation of the motor and the lashing wind creating a stillness that sealed off the world. He turned to her slowly, his eyes penetrating the darkness.

"I know who you are," he breathed heavily as he took hold of her. "I know who you are because you're like me."

CHAPTER
IX

HELLO CHUMS:

It's your old friend Mavis Slocum, the Kangaroo Courier! Guess we're all licking our wounds to see that the Aussies were defeated in the Davis Cup, but there's lots of happy news from our fellow war brides!

Hope you all had your radios tuned to "Queen for a Day" when Ruby Keller was on. They thought her accent a bit of a lark (guess we've all grown weary of those "You talk funny, where are you from?" questions), but Ruby didn't mind the razzing because she won: a washing machine, a ten-piece mahogany bedroom set, a stove, a pressure cooker, a year's supply of bed linen, one of those wonderful new home freezers and a trip to Manhattan!!! I look forward to seeing her during her trip to New York.

Wish I could show you all the photo that Gaynor Cunningham sent to me of her home in K.C. It's a veritable mansion!

Winnifred Thomas tells us that she's expecting. (Oh, oh, Winnie! You didn't waste any time, did you!)

Janet White relates an amusing but slightly off-colour anecdote: seems she was having dinner with some people and mentioned that someone was a "pimp." She said the faces around the table went scarlet. She checked with her husband and found out that the American expression for that word is "tattle tail." When the Yanks say "pimp" they mean a procurer. So watch your language, girls! They say "napkin" instead of "serviette," "trunk" instead of "boot," and you don't get a ladder in your stockings, you get a run in your nylons.

Moina Miheil is living outside of Washington, D.C., with hubby Kent, who is doing research on one of those great new medicines that end in "myacin." She tells us that on a trip to the capital, she actually caught sight of President Truman!

Have to close now, as my one and only is taking me on the town to see that great new musical *Annie Get Your Gun.*

Keep those cards and letters coming, girls, and don't get too homesick.

Cheerio for now,

Mavis

Dawn folded up the letter, put the pacifier back into Nita's mouth, and stared out the window of the station wagon. They had passed the prosperous, downtown section of Portsmouth and were driving through a shabby commercial neighborhood of seemingly deserted shops. As they approached a railroad crossing, Zac shifted the car into neutral and waited for the train to shunt by. Faye bounced impatiently in the back seat.

"Are we almost there, Daddy? I want to see our new house."

"Just a few more minutes, honey. And I've already told you, it's not really a house. It used to be a grocery store, but it's the best we can do just now. I'm sure your mother will make it livable."

"Of course I will," Dawn said simply.

Ever since the blow-up with Suds, the atmosphere at the Mueller household had become, if possible, even more intolerable. Dawn had offered her apologies and redoubled her efforts to get along with her mother-in-law. Suds grudgingly accepted her offer of peace, but now added the sins of pride and anger to her endless list of Dawn's wrongdoings. Even though Suds continued to complain about the disruption that the children caused, she told Zac that she was deeply hurt to think that they might want to move. But if Dawn was eighty percent compliance, she was twenty percent determination and grit. She continued to voice her need to get out into a place of their own and when Zac told her that he had discovered a store front that could be rented as an apartment, she urged him to take it, sight unseen.

As the car pulled up to the curb on the grimy, uninhabited street, she imagined the comfort and ease in which Gaynor Cunningham must be living. Still, it was not luxury that she craved. Any place where she could be surrounded by familiar objects, know that her children were safe and that her husband was beside her, would be enough for her. She gathered Nita up and stepped out onto the pavement.

"This is it," Zac said as he opened the door to the store. "Gioffre's Groceries and Luncheonette" was marked on the plate window and a bell tinkled over the door as they went in. The room was large, divided by a counter. There were rings on the linoleum where chairs and tables had been. The floor was littered with cardboard boxes and a hand-lettered menu was tacked to the wall.

"We're going to live here?" Faye squeaked. "It's all funny and dirty."

"Just button your lip for a minute," Dawn said as she looked out the fly-specked front window. The bakery across the street was partially boarded up. The photographer's studio next to it had a faded "Closed" sign on the door and hand-tinted photographs of bygone weddings and graduations gathered dust in the window. Beside the studio was a shoe repair shop. She could make out a dim light in its recesses, but whether or not it was still open for business or used as a dwelling was a mystery.

"They're supposed to raze the whole neighborhood in another six months and start a new housing development, but I guess we won't be here by then," Zac said, standing in the middle of the room with his hands on his hips.

"Well, at least they won't be creating any displaced persons," Dawn replied as she made a mental note of the yardage it would take to shield the front window from the depressing sight of the street. "Right now it looks as deserted as a pub on a Sunday morning."

"I know it's a real mess," he apologized. "But you said you'd move anywhere, and the only other place that was available wouldn't take children."

"Why not?" Faye asked.

"Don't sit down on that floor in your good dress. And don't be asking so many questions," Dawn said as she walked into the adjoining room. It had apparently been intended for storage, but the heavy bedstead and chest of drawers showed that someone had lived there. Dawn drew her breath in sharply, put the pacifier back into Nita's mouth, and walked on into the kitchen.

"Good job it's summertime," she sighed as she eyed the mammoth commercial refrigerator and double sinks; "we can crawl into these fridges on hot days."

Zac looked around helplessly.

"Oh don't worry, love," she said as she came close to him. "I said anyplace, and I meant it. A bit of elbow grease—correction, a *lot* of elbow grease—and I'll have it shipshape in no time. I think I can curtain off that counter top and put a bed behind it for us and use the rest of the front room for a living room. The girls can have what, I suspect, was the storage room."

"You're being a good sport about it, Dawn. It won't always be like this, you know."

"Too bloody right. It'll be a lot cleaner day after tomorrow."

"Sorry I won't be here to help you fix it up," he said guiltily. "I just can't do anything about those orders for the statewide tour of the recruiting stations, but I should be able to give you a hand before I leave."

The tour had come at an inopportune time, but Zac's guilt was outweighed by a sense of relief. He was comfortable with guns and radar screens, not household improvements. He had a kind of scorn for men like his foster father who were goaded into being handymen for their wives. The place was lousy and he wished that he might have done better by Dawn and the girls. But he had searched long and hard and now at least part of his obligation was fulfilled. As Dawn talked on, asking his choice of colors for paint and curtains, soliciting his preference on the arrangement of nonexistent furniture, he listened with half an ear, already mapping out the route he would take when he hit the road.

When they returned to the Muellers' and announced that they would be moving the following day, Suds implied that they were being spendthrift and said that it was too bad they were moving on the Sabbath; otherwise, she and Homer would have helped them.

She sat on the porch the following morning, rocking back and forth and reading her Bible while they loaded the car with their suitcases. As they got into the car, she put her arms about Zac stiffly, and intoned: "Hear, my son, the instruction of thy father, And forsake not the teaching of thy mother; For they shall be a chaplet of grace unto thy head, And chains about thy neck."

The part about the chains is certainly true, Dawn thought as she thanked Suds and hugged Homer. She laughed out loud as they pulled away from the driveway, but when Zac asked her why she was acting so giddy, she said it was because it was a beautiful day and the weather made her lighthearted.

"Lighthearted. Lighthearted. Lighthearted," Faye chanted as she reached forward into the front seat and put her arms around her mother's neck. "Mummy's lighthearted!" The two of them giggled together with a deep and jubilant understanding.

The morning after Zac had left on his trip, Dawn dressed and fed the girls, put Nita into the buggy, told Faye to hold on to her skirt, and set off up the street in the direction of the still flourishing shops. Looking at the purse that was nestled in the buggy next to Nita's chubby legs, she felt a pleasant sense of well-being. It was good to have some money again. Not that Zac wasn't generous. Whenever she told him that she needed money, he would reach into his wallet and peel off some bills. But it was so demeaning to have to ask for it, especially since it was always for minor things—toilet articles, stamps, treats for the children. During their stay at the Muellers' the living expenses had been handed over directly to Suds, and this distribution of monies had made Dawn feel that she was somehow unworthy of responsibility. Now that she had a large chunk of cash with which to change the blighted storefront into a livable apartment, she felt challenged and energetic. She was determined to present Zac with a bright, comfortable home when he returned, and to show him how thrifty and enterprising she could be.

For days she waged war on the grime and rust that coated every surface and was embedded in every cranny of the old store. Putting Nita in the playpen and talking to her as she worked, Dawn scoured and scrubbed, stripped and spackled, varnished and painted from early morning until late afternoon. Then she would break from the tedious labors and march the children four blocks to a municipal playground. The place was called Lakeside Park, though there was no lake to be seen. The dried grass and creaking swings and seesaws mirrored the neglect of the grubby and mostly unattended children who played on them. She kept a close eye on Faye, encouraging her to expend the energy pent up during the morning when she was confined to the apartment, hoping that she would exhaust herself enough to go to bed without whining. After feeding and bathing the children, she would sit at the sewing machine and fashion slipcovers, pillows and curtains. Then, when the distant whistle of the train reminded her that it was time to go to bed, she would shower, write her letters home or to Sheila, and collapse.

In the mornings—her hearing tuned to the baby's slightest sound—she would stagger, half-conscious, into the back room, pick Nita up, and bring her back into the double bed. As Dawn tried to drift back into the warm world of dreams, Nita would clutch at her neck, poke fingers into her mouth and ears, and wiggle about, gurgling and squealing. Soon Faye would appear at her side, touching her cheek and whispering, "Time to get up, Mummy. Why's Nita in bed with you? What about me?" Dawn would fling back the covers and Faye would climb in. Then the blissful half hour—bouncing, caressing amid the tossed sheets, marveling at the baby's tiny features, answering the amazing questions that Faye came up with (Who was the first person to plant a carrot? If cows have milk, why don't fishes have milk? Where do people go when they die?). At such times she felt an overwhelming love for her children. A feeling that had no beginning and no end. It obliterated the irritation she had felt the previous day, when Faye had tipped over an entire can of paint and Nita had clutched the bars of the playpen, opened her mouth so that the pink tonsils showed, and bellowed for thirty minutes straight, though Dawn had checked to see that she was fed and dry. She would be awash in the pleasure of their presence, awed that they should have come from her body, fearful and protective lest any harm come to them. After they had played for a while, Faye would ask for breakfast and Dawn would drag herself up from the bed and begin another round of daily chores. It was only after a week and a half of constant labor, when the store started to shape up into something resembling a home, that she became acutely conscious of her loneliness.

She had put the girls to bed and padded into the living room, surveying the curtains she had made out of yards of parachute silk purchased from the war-surplus store and dyed a sky blue. She complimented herself that the draperies camouflaged the gaping window and blocked off the sight of the street so well. Sitting down on the slightly dilapidated but now acceptably covered maroon couch, she took up her sewing. When she was sure that the girls were asleep, she tiptoed over to the radio. It was a purchase that she hadn't intended to make, but Faye told her that all the kids at the park talked about the serials, so she had relented. Kneeling on the floor, she turned the knob and watched the orange light suffuse the dial. The familiar voice of Danny Kaye came forth:

"My sister married an Irishman."
"Oh, really?"
"No, O'Reilly."

Hoots of laughter came from the brocade cloth and lyre-shaped wood that covered the speaker. She slumped back, resting on her heels, remembering her family's habit of gathering around the wireless before they went to bed, the affectionate banter, the tea and scones, the smell of resin drifting from the logs in the fireplace. In the afternoons when she did the ironing or the laundry, it seemed less lonely to listen to "Stella Dallas" or "Our Gal Sunday," but sometimes in the evenings, the sound of distant voices coming over the airwaves increased her sense of isolation.

She switched the dial to off and started back toward the couch. There was a knock at the front door. Her heart leaped. Perhaps Zac had come home unexpectedly. But it wasn't likely that he would cut his trip short. Approaching the door cautiously, she pulled aside the curtain to see a wizened, gnomish face under a brown felt hat. The man's small body was dressed in a three-piece suit and he was carrying a basket of tomatoes and a bottle of wine. She opened the door a crack.

"Please allow me to presenta myself. I'm your neighbor from across the street. My name is Vittorio DeLongini."

"Yes," she replied uncertainly. "You're the gentleman who has the boot repair shop?"

"That'sa right. I think you been seeing me when you walk with the little girl and the baby."

"Please come in."

"I see you got up these nice curtains now, 'steada the blankets. You maka everything so nice in here," he said, his watery brown eyes taking in the room. "I see you every day. Always working. I think you do a first-rate job."

"Why, thank you so much," she said softly. "Please sit down . . . I'm talking quietly because I just put the children to bed."

"I'ma so sorry if I disturb. I like to talk to the children too. Now I'ma old man I never sleep much anymore so I forget that you have to put the bambini in their beds so soon."

"May I offer you a cup of tea?"

"If you like to have some please, but also I brought a gift to warm your house. Wine, and tomatoes from that patch of garden I have at the back of my store."

"That's very kind of you. You know, I was beginning to think that I was the only person living on this block."

"That's the way the man who owns alla this property want it to be," Mr. DeLongini said as he settled himself on the couch. "I was friends with the Gioffre family who rented this store. They gotta move maybe eight, nine months ago. Everything die in this part of town—alla the people go away. Now they gonna tear down all the buildings and make up new houses. New houses that all looka the same. You're going to a lot of trouble to make everything nice, but in six months maybe, in come the bulldozers."

"I don't expect that we'll be here longer than six months. My husband is in the service and his tour of duty will be up in December. Now let me see if we have a corkscrew."

"I bring with me," he said proudly, waving the bottle of wine in one hand and rummaging in his pocket with the other. "Shall we sit in the kitchen?"

"Why yes," she smiled, "that would be lovely."

When she'd set two jelly glasses on the table, he uncorked the wine, sniffed it with obvious relish, and poured it. His rheumy eyes, set in a face that resembled the wrinkled leather of an old pair of shoes he might have worked on, took in the green-and-white checked curtains, pale green paint and bunch of daisies sitting in the window.

"Yes, you maka all nice. Very pretty, like the lady of the house."

"I thank you for the compliment. Sometimes it seems like such dumb work—housework I mean. You just get everything clean and then it's time to clean it again, so that it seems like a negative action instead of a positive one. But if someone notices it, that does make the difference."

"To a most beautiful lady," he said gallantly, raising his glass. "I'm thinking by the way you talk that you are also not born in this land."

"No, I'm not," she laughed, amused at the flourish of his toast. "I'm from Australia. I've only been in the States for a few months and I have to confess that I'm still very homesick."

"To your homeland then," he said, clinking his glass to hers, "and to mine."

She sipped her wine and looked at him intently, wanting to ask him how it had been for him as an Italian in the United States during the war. In the town where she was born there were very few foreigners, and they stayed mostly to themselves, plying the trades that were associated with their nationalities. Her mother might say "Go down to the Italians" when she meant to send her to the greengrocers, or "Pop in at the Jews" when they needed fabrics or dry goods. But there was little socializing beyond business. Though not as feared or hated as the Germans or Japanese had been during the war, the Italians had been the butt of many jokes.

"When did you come to this country?" she asked.

"I'm here from when I'm eighteen in 1894. I am living in New York, New Jersey, Cleveland—oh, I sure do get around! Now, I'm surprised to find myself to end up here . . . ah, youth is a mistake, manhood a struggle, old age a regret," he said pensively.

"And your family?"

"Sure. Sure. I have them from New York to Napoli. But no one with me now. My wife, *Dio la benediccie,* has been dead for almost fifteen years. God did not bless us with children, and alla our relatives here are moved to California. I am glad my wife did not live to see the war. Always I promised her that I would take her back to the village where we were born. I don't think such a village is beautiful to most people. I was happy to leave it to come and find my fortune here when I was young. But once I am here, I would remember . . . I remember how the tomato plants grow so big. I remember how the women go down to wash the clothes on the big rocks in the river. My nephew Angelo was in the American army. He sent to me a picture of my village. Even the rocks in the stream are bombed away. It was a terrible thing. A terrible thing for all of us."

He wagged his head slowly and touched the corners of his eyes with his hand. "But I don't come to your home to tell you sad stories that you already know. Tell me about your family. Tell me about the little ones."

The openness of his conversation caused her to throw aside her reserve. She'd had no opportunity to speak to anyone about her loved ones since leaving the ship in San Francisco. Now she found the family album, always one of the first things unpacked, and talked animatedly about her mother, father and sister, recounted the idiosyncrasies of this or that aunt or cousin. He poured himself another glass of wine, listening intently, telling various anecdotes about members of his own clan. When the whistle of the train hooted, he rose a bit unsteadily and put out his hand.

"It has been most pleasurable for me to share this evening with you," he said formally.

"For me as well, Mr. DeLongini. I would like you to come and share dinner with us tomorrow. It would be a treat for Faye to meet you. She misses her grandfather so. The children are some company to me, but lately I've thought I might go a bit dotty if I didn't have an adult to talk to."

"I would be honored to come. Also, I will tell you that I will sit the babies when you have shopping to do."

During the next week Mr. DeLongini became a regular guest in the house. He would drop by in the evening to bring Dawn a newspaper or the children some sweets. In the afternoons, Faye would run over to his shop, sit on a high stool near the workbench, and watch as he painstakingly repaired the shoes of one of his few remaining customers. On the Fourth of July they took the bus downtown to the park to see the fireworks display. Mr. DeLongini regaled Faye with a passionate if not altogether accurate history of the American Revolution as the rockets burst in the sky. The night before Zac was due to return, Dawn invited him to dinner again, but he refused, eyes twinkling, saying that he was not so old that he couldn't remember that a husband and wife would want to be alone after a separation.

Dawn scurried about, making sure that the finishing touches were put on all the repairs, stocking the refrigerator with the beer, ham and pies that Zac liked. She planted Faye in front of the radio with a coloring book and told her to knock on the bathroom door if Nita woke up, and then disappeared into the bathroom to the shout of "Hi yo, Silver." As she soaped up her body, she made plans for the evening. She would let the children stay up for supper because they were so eager to see their father, but she would put them to bed immediately afterwards and break out the bottle of wine Mr. DeLongini had given her. Then she and Zac would turn on the radio, dance and perhaps neck a bit before they went to bed. At last they would be alone in their own place. She had felt bitter and neglected when Zac had refused to stand up to Suds and didn't seem to perceive her own unhappiness, but the weeks of separation had softened the angry feelings. Now she felt a resurgence of hope about their future.

By Christmas time Zac's hitch in the Navy would be over. No more shifting about. No more evenings spent alone. He might revive his idea of returning to Australia. Then they would have a permanent home, perhaps even be able to afford another child.

Toweling herself dry, she scrutinized her body and was pleased to see that it was taking on some flesh again. She'd run herself ragged fixing up the apartment, but at least she'd been relaxed enough to start eating properly. She was beginning to look more like she did when they'd first met. She pushed fingerwaves into her damp hair, put her housedress into the laundry hamper, and put on her best underwear. Pulling on an embroidered blouse and a pair of slacks that she'd been obliged to leave in the closet during her stay at the Muellers'—Suds had quoted something from Deuteronomy about it being an abomination that a woman should wear that which pertaineth to a man, though Dawn couldn't imagine that the Israelites had been too awfully concerned with slacks—she stood up on the toilet seat to survey herself in the mirror above the sink, and felt almost pretty.

By ten o'clock, when Zac still hadn't appeared, she soothed Faye's disappointment and ordered her to bed. She finished ironing the baby clothes that she was going to send to Sheila, then wandered into the living room and took up a magazine. Too full of anticipation and anxiety to concentrate on reading, she flipped through the pages, looking at pictures of fashion and furniture. When she saw an article titled "Are You the Wife He Wants to Come Home To?" she tossed the magazine aside with annoyance and stretched out on the couch. Why was it that she spent so much of her life waiting? She had waited to grow up, waited to be married, waited for the girls to be born, waited for the war to be over, waited to have a place of her own. She waited for her period to come. Waited for sales so that she could buy what she wanted at the right price. And she waited for Zac. It seemed as though most of her existence was a round of mindless tasks punctuated by expectation. The only indications of change were the stretch marks on her breasts and stomach, the faint lines that were being etched around her eyes and mouth. But of course there were the children. She could see change in them. Nita was beginning to form words, could stand up by herself and crawl about quite independently. Faye could read now and help with household chores without causing too much damage. And her curiosity and intelligence were amazing. Yes. The children showed growth and change, and she had fostered and guided it. When they grew up, she would make sure that they had enough education to choose something more than a life of drudgery.

She had dropped off to sleep when she heard the tinkling of the little bell above the front door. Zac, his tie loose, his hat tilted at a rakish angle, crept in carrying several packages. She propped herself up on her elbow and blinked at him.

"Hi. Sorry I'm so late. When we get a bit more cash we'll have a phone put in so I can call you."

"Darling, I'm so glad you're here," she said, stretching out her arms toward him. "Did you have car trouble? I did start to worry about you. Isn't it silly? When someone you don't much care about is late all you feel is annoyance, but when it's someone you love, you can't stop your imagination from turning grisly. I was starting to get worried. Kept imagining accidents—all that sort of thing. Do you want some food?"

"Naw. I'm fine," he said as he dumped the packages on the table and bent down to her. "How're the kids, Mom?"

"They're fine. Faye was awfully disappointed when I wouldn't let her wait up. I expect she'll be bouncing on your chest first thing in the morning."

"She'd better not be. I'm bushed. Hey," he said, looking around for the first time, "you've done a terrific job on this place. It really looks great."

"Do you like it? I'm so glad if you do. I had a helluva time getting these curtains up by myself. And I was afraid I'd strained my back moving the furniture. But it does look a bit of an improvement, doesn't it?"

"It's swell. You can be a deckhand on my ship anytime."

"Thank you very much," she laughed, "but I'd rather be the gal waiting in port."

"Sure."

Taking off his hat and putting it on her head, she stretched full length on the couch, pulling him to her. He kissed her, but when she started to unbuckle his belt, he sat up abruptly, muttering something about being embarrassed to pet on the couch like a couple of kids.

"Right behind those curtains is a little nook we can call our very own bedroom," she whispered.

"Yeah . . . well, I'm feeling kinda dirty from the road. Think I'd like to wash up." He disengaged himself and got up from the couch. "While I'm in the shower, maybe you'd like to open that big package. That's for you. The smaller ones are for the kids."

"Zac," she cried, touched by his thoughtfulness. "It's not even my birthday."

"Tell you the truth, I can't remember when your birthday is. Can't even remember when our anniversary is."

"Our anniversary is in two months, but since you're sweet enough to bring me a present now, I won't even send you a note to remind you."

"Okay, Mom," he said, as he started toward the back of the apartment.

Putting the latch on the bathroom door, he undressed, started the shower, and stood watching the steaming water bounce onto the tiles, afraid to turn and catch a glimpse of his face in the mirror. When he was a child, Suds had always told him that his sins showed on his face. For years he had believed this was true. Suds seemed to be omniscient about even his minor infractions and her wrath came down on him with terrible force. It wasn't until he was eleven years old that he realized that it was his own guilty looks, not the mark of Cain or any outward sign, that gave him away. From then on, he had cultivated a distant and cocky expression, though the fear of an awful female intuition that could sear through the mask and go straight to the heart still haunted him. But Dawn had greeted him as though everything was all right. She hadn't even complained that he was hours late. He took a deep breath and stepped into the shower, scrubbing himself brutally.

The episode the night before hadn't really been his fault. It hadn't even been in his mind to pick the woman up. He had only stopped into the bar for a quick one before going up to his hotel room. He'd noticed the woman's platinum hair, luminous in the dim light, but even as he was drawn to it, he knew that it would be brittle to the touch. She'd asked him to buy her a drink. The way she'd looked into his eyes and said "Thanks, Chief" as she touched her glass to his let him know that he could take her back to the hotel without too many more questions asked. He excused himself and went to the men's room. As he washed his hands, it crossed his mind that he might take off his wedding ring. But that seemed deceitful. Besides, he loved his wife. He would have one more drink and leave.

It had been a rough trip. Eagerness to enlist, at a fever pitch just a few years ago, had given way to a deep desire to forget about defense and return to normal life. It had been hard to meet the recruitment quota. He knew he was supposed to be as happy about the end of the war as everyone else said they were, but he had had no idea what it would really mean to him. By chance, he had run into an old buddy. He remembered him as being particularly courageous, but now the guy was pumping gas and worrying about house payments. It seemed a sorry comedown from the sense of purpose and adventure they'd once shared. And it depressed him even more when he tried to think where he himself might fit into the peacetime economy. He knew about artillery, radar, the operation of submarines. Where would such know-how provide him with money or respect now? How could he possibly hope to provide for Dawn and the girls? He was going to be thirty-six soon. That was too old to make a major change. Besides, he loved the Navy. It had given him escape, a salary, prestige, a place in the scheme of things. Even the thought of being in civilian clothes upset him. And he knew he would miss the company of other men.

When he'd finished the second round, the woman placed her hand high up on his thigh and proposed a toast to peacetime. He said he didn't know if he could drink to that, but drained the glass anyway. She lolled her bright head on his shoulder, oblivious to the fact that he was staring straight ahead into the murky mirror behind the bottles.

"So how's about it, handsome, wanna tell me about the battles you've been in?" He could have slapped the silly smile off her drunken face right then.

"Not particularly. Want to tell me about yours?"

Instead of being insulted, she tossed her head back and laughed uproariously. He threw some bills on the bar and started to get up. "Hey," she said, surprised, "I didn't mean to insult you or nothin'. Thought we could have some fun." He paused. Her fingernails dug through the cloth of his uniform as she clung to his arm. The thought of returning to the hotel room alone was too much for him. He was sick of feeling his head go round and round with the same problems. And there was something about this kind of woman that enticed him more than any other type. With a woman like this he didn't have to pretend to be steady or reliable or good. He could clutch, demand, expose himself without running the risk of shocking her. And in the morning . . . why, he would never have to see her again, never have to deal with her suspicions or her needs.

He rubbed his flesh vigorously with the towel and reached for the pajamas that Dawn had put on the hook near the mirror.

DAWN HAD SLIPPED into her nightdress and was sitting on the edge of the bed brushing her hair. The package he had brought for her lay unopened in the middle of the bed. It had irked her slightly that he had called her "Mom" and broken off the embrace. Still, she thought as she drew the brush methodically through her hair, she couldn't expect him to call her sweetie or darling forever, like a couple of school kids. Perhaps he had taken to calling her that because of his attachment to the children, or because he wanted to show that he was glad to be home. And, though he'd commented superficially on the apartment, she wished he'd taken more time to observe all the work she'd done. But this wasn't an appropriate time to tell him about her grievances. Not when he'd just returned.

"I wanted to wait until you came to bed before I opened my gift," she smiled, when he appeared in the alcove dressed in his pajamas.

She reached forward and pulled the package to her, carefully slipping the ties from the box and rolling them up.

"You needn't bother to save the wrapping," he said.

"Don't 'spose I'll ever get out of the habit of saving things. Growing up in the Depression and then the war made me feel guilty about being wasteful. I know it's had the opposite effect on some people, but it's made me cautious . . . oh, what the hell," she laughed, tossing the wrapping on the floor. She hoped that the gift would be something pretty and intimate, though the box was too large and heavy for perfume or lingerie. As she tore at the tissue paper, she looked up at him flirtatiously. She opened it, swallowed, tried to hide her disappointment. "Thank you, dear," she said in a throaty voice.

"It's a pressure cooker," he said blankly.

"Yes, I know."

"That's why I was late tonight. I stopped off at a store to get things for you and the kids. There's a little booklet there inside of it. The saleslady told me that it cuts cooking time in half. You can make all sorts of things. Stews . . . you know, all those things you make."

"Yes. Thanks, Zac."

She set the box down by the side of the bed and slipped in between the sheets.

"Do you think we should set the alarm?" he asked as he sat down beside her and reached to turn out the bedlamp.

"Whatever for?"

"Well, I told Suds that we'd bring the kids over early tomorrow morning."

"Zac! Not tomorrow. Not on your first day home. I'd just like us to be together. Besides, I've met this really charming old man from across the street and I've asked him to come over so you could meet him. He's been so good to us while you've been gone."

"Stepping out on me, huh?" he said with a broad smile.

"Hardly. In the first place he's about eighty years old. And in the second place, having two kiddies to take care of doesn't allow much time for gallivanting. But he's very sweet. Can't we just put off seeing Suds and Homer 'til later?"

"Hell, honey, what are you talking about? First you say you want to be alone and then you tell me you've invited some old coot over! Be reasonable, for God's sake."

"How was I being unreasonable?" she asked, sensing that he was trying for some reason to pick a fight with her.

"Forget it. If I have to explain it, you probably wouldn't understand anyway."

He switched off the light, kicked at the bedspread and yanked the sheet about him. Why was he so angry, she wondered. She had indulged in so many fantasies of what tonight's reunion would be like; she had done everything to prepare for a pleasant homecoming. What had gone wrong? As he turned his back to her, their legs touched. She reached out tentatively to stroke his back, desperately wanting to make it up with him.

"Darling, let's not fight. Not tonight. It's the first time we're in bed together in a place of our own. I know it still doesn't look like much, but once you're out of the Navy and we get a real home, you'll see how beautiful I'll be able to make it."

"What do you mean, once I'm out of the Navy?" he barked. "What the hell do you suppose I'm going to do once I'm out of the Navy? Be a janitor or a short-order cook?"

"I don't know what you're planning to do," she whispered, afraid their voices would wake the children. "Whenever I've tried to talk to you about it, you've always said it wasn't the right time. I just assumed that . . ."

"Don't assume anything. I'm telling you right now, I don't think I could get any sort of decent job."

"But you haven't tried yet, have you? If you started making inquiries, something would turn up. You're bright and hard-working and you know a lot about machinery . . ."

"I know a lot about ships and artillery."

"Still, if you started looking around . . ."

"Christ! I come home after two weeks on the road and all I get is a cross-examination."

"I'm sorry," she said sarcastically, moving to her own side of the bed. It was so unfair that he should treat her like this. She hadn't complained about the work or the waiting, yet he was acting as though she was as demanding as Suds. Her sense of injustice revived the hostility she'd felt about living at the Muellers', sharpened her disappointment at the gift of the pressure cooker. She lay awake, listening as his agitated breath quieted to a soft, snoring sound, her rage subsiding into a fatigued and despairing hurt. She had just about dropped off to sleep when he reached over, putting his hand on her hip.

"Sorry, Dawn. I guess I'm just tired."

Her body was rigid beneath his touch. Much as she wanted to respond, she felt that if she yielded now, without pressing for a further explanation of his feelings, she would be opening the door to further disregard. "I'm tired too," she muttered in a barely audible voice.

"Well, I guess we'd both better get a little shuteye," he yawned, drawing his legs up to his chest and wrapping his arms around himself.

CHAPTER
X

RICKY TURNED the page of *Themes of Social Class in the American Novel,* rubbed his eyelids, and then flipped it back again. He had read the same paragraph at least three times and knew damned well that he hadn't absorbed a word of it. Squinting up at the clock on the library wall, he noted it was 4:45. He sighed and shut the book. He had to pick Betty up at the train station at 5:10. He reached for his overcoat, careful not to disturb the snoozing student sprawled across the table from him. Leaving the library, he pulled his muffler closer to his chin and looked up through the bare trees lining the quad. The icy air tingled with a hint of the first snow, which had been predicted for that night. He imagined the soft flakes coming down, covering the bleak scenery with the muffling beauty of real winter. Gaynor had never seen snow before. Perhaps she might respond to its magic as he did, feeling that winter, in its own demanding way, had a special loveliness. But it wasn't realistic to think that she would delight in a snowstorm. She took little interest in nature. The change of seasons, which meant so much to him, was only an occasion for her to examine her wardrobe and find it lacking. And she had been so despondent lately that he wasn't sure anything could make an impression on her.

At first he had assumed that she was going through some sort of hormonal change connected with early pregnancy. His friend Evan, who was a brilliant young psychiatric intern, had told him that he shouldn't be surprised at mood shifts or erratic behavior. The pregnancy had not been planned; and, in addition to coping with that surprise, Gaynor was undoubtedly going through adjustment problems with her new environment. But there weren't any changes or shifts in her moods. She had only shown a steady decline into an almost catatonic state of depression.

He wrenched open the door of the old DeSoto, tossed his books into the back seat, and turned the key in the ignition. The motor groaned, refusing to turn over in the cold. Cursing its sluggishness, he banged his hand on the dashboard, then tried again. "Goddamn it, start, you lazy son-of-a-bitch," he cursed until it finally grunted and turned over with a steady, wheezing sound. If he took off before it had reached a reluctant purr, it might stall in traffic. He threw back his head and stared at the sagging fabric covering the ceiling while he waited for the motor to warm up. He and Evan had joked about the car, Evan saying that you had to treat a motor the way you treated a woman—know its idiosyncrasies, baby it along. Ricky smiled, remembering the conversation. "You're such a grouchy bastard lately," he muttered to himself. Between researching his thesis, working as an assistant teacher, worrying about Gaynor, it seemed that he was always fatigued and short-tempered, ready to fly off the handle at the least provocation. When he'd heard through the grapevine that his students had christened him "the Dancing Bear" because of his gruffness and nervous movements, he'd pretended to laugh it off, but he'd been hurt by the nickname. He had always imagined that he would be a self-possessed and sympathetic teacher, but apparently his manner didn't live up to his self-image. Just this morning, when a student had turned a paper in late, he had been so severe that the kid had been close to tears. He reminded himself that he should have a firmer grip on his temper, whether alone or with others. He always did his best to control his impatience with Gaynor, but the irritations were deflected onto those around him.

He opened the glove compartment and inspected the small gift-wrapped package of perfume. He had wanted to buy Gaynor something nicer for her birthday, but she said that she didn't want maternity clothes and the jaunty little fur hat she'd admired in a shop window was beyond his budget, so he'd had to settle for the Chanel instead. Pulling away from the curb, he checked his watch, gunned the motor and headed down Nassau Street. He began to chew his lip and have second thoughts about the wisdom of the surprise party. He knew that she loved social occasions and when the notion of the party had first occurred to him and then Betty had agreed to help out, it had seemed like a great idea. But Gaynor had been so withdrawn of late that Ricky was afraid she might look upon the guests as an intrusion. And she'd probably be annoyed that he hadn't alerted her so that she could fix herself up in advance.

The truth was, he thought sadly, he could no longer predict her reactions to anything. He had anticipated that she would be disappointed with the garage apartment. Even though it was quite a find by current standards of student housing, an efficiency apartment behind someone else's house was quite a comedown after the luxury of the Country Club Estates in Kansas City. But he had had no idea that she would react so violently to being pregnant. The news, which she had announced only a few weeks after her arrival in Princeton, had filled him with joyful expectations. Since she had never expressed any desire to be a mother and had told him that she was taking precautions not to conceive, he suspected that she might not be as delighted as he. But he had hoped that she would warm to the idea. It had taken him several months to realize that the preoccupied expression on her face was not a madonnalike contemplation, but the symptom of a deep withdrawal.

Once he had realized the depth of her unhappiness, his enthusiasm about the baby had been replaced by a bleak determination. He *would* make her feel better, he vowed with the same dogged determination that had earned him A's in those classes for which he had no natural liking.

He cast about for things that might interest her, and take her away from her sullen preoccupation with herself. Putting aside his studies, he took her to films and lectures. He introduced her to Evan's wife, Caroline, who was also pregnant, thinking that the two women would share common interests. But Gaynor said that she found Caroline an insufferable simp and preferred to spend her days alone rather than in the company of any of those dreary veterans' wives. He bought her flowers, took her out to dinner as often as he could afford, brought home articles and books. But often, when he returned from the university, he would find the books unopened, the dishes in the sink, the tiny apartment in disarray, and Gaynor, glass of scotch in hand, sitting near the window. Sometimes she wouldn't even acknowledge his presence when he came in. If she had neglected to go to the grocery store, he would race out to the corner market and then fix the dinner. Immediately afterwards, she would go to bed. He would sit up at the kitchen table, a scarf over the lamp so that the light would not shine into the other room, and read until well after midnight. When he joined her in bed, she reacted to his touch with annoyance and some-times outright distaste. Finally, he had appealed to Evan for advice. Evan suggested that Gaynor might need some professional counsel-ing, but when he'd mentioned that possibility to her, she had screamed that she wasn't insane and wouldn't think of such a thing.

HE PULLED the car into the parking lot and rested his head on the back of the seat for a cat-nap. Hearing the train chug into the station, he dragged himself out of the car and stood on the platform, watching the commuter passengers get off.

"Hey, handsome, help me with these shopping bags, will you?"

He turned to see Betty, her cheeks rosy with the chilly air, lugging a couple of shopping bags. The sight of her, a brightly colored knit hat pulled down on her head, her face broad and smiling like a kid out of the Our Gang comedies, changed his worried expression into a sardonic grin.

"Sorry, I didn't see you. What the hell have you got in this bag?" he asked as he took one.

"I didn't know if you'd have time to shop, so I stopped at every deli on 114th Street and cleaned 'em out. I also went to a classy Viennese bakery and got a chocolate cake and some candles. You did tell me that Gaynor likes chocolate, didn't you?"

"Hell, I don't know what she likes," he confessed as they walked toward the car.

"I think ladies' magazines and movies suggest ice cream washed down with pickle juice for pregnant women. But never having been pregnant, I had to take a chance with the chocolate cake. How're you doing?"

"To tell you the truth it's been pretty rough," he said as he yanked on the car door. "Don't know what's been the matter with me lately —I've just felt frustrated about everything."

"That's not abnormal for a guy with an old car who's also in grad school. Everybody I know who's getting a Ph.D. goes from exhaus-tion to cynicism and back again in hourly cycles. I'm up to my eyeballs in unfinished papers myself."

"Where's your boyfriend? I thought you were going to ask him to come along," he said as he started the car.

"He's busy. I only get to see him every couple of days. When he's not studying he goes to veterans' meetings. Sometimes, when I'm real lucky, he sneaks down the hallway and spends the night, but I don't know how much longer that can last. The landlady seems to be on to our immoral relationship and I have a feeling she may ask me to move. I would have to find the only Puritan property owner in the entire city of New York."

"Why don't you just get married and make life easier for yourselves?"

"Does being married make it easier?" she laughed, taking off her mittens and blowing on her hands.

"I used to think so. At least if you were married to him you could bump into each other while you were cleaning your teeth."

"I hope I don't have to change my notion of romantic love to include dental hygiene. Hey, doesn't this heater work? I'm frozen . . . fact is, he hasn't seen fit to ask me."

"He's a fool. No one could hope to get a better wife than you'd be."

"Stop sounding like you're an irate relative who wants to make him do the right thing by me. If it's not in the cards for me to marry, I'll just go on with my work. Tell you the truth, I'd go on with my work anyway. Moving away from home and going to Columbia has been really good for me. I'm not unhappy."

"You're a brick, Betty. You really are."

"Ever heard of anyone getting the hots for a brick?" she grinned. "Let's get going and stop by a liquor store. I've been smart enough not to cut off relations with the old man until I'm solvent and I'd like to treat us all to a bottle of classy scotch."

She rearranged the packages at her feet, looking at him out of the corner of her eye. In just the last few months his face had lost much of its boyish looks. The hollows under the eyes gave him a maturely handsome aspect, but as he ground the gears and pulled out of the parking lot, she noticed the tension in his neck and the slight twitch that moved the corner of his mouth. It couldn't just be the work. He was fond of studying, always a tiger about proving himself academically. The strain must come from more intimate pressures.

"Boy, I hope I've done the right thing in planning this surprise party," he said.

"'Course you have. Gaynor will be delighted that you thought of it."

"I don't know, Betty. I just don't know what her reactions will be. You know when I first met her, I thought she was so self-possessed, so independent. But lately . . . I guess she's taken the pregnancy pretty hard. I feel guilty about uprooting her. She was happy in Kansas City. But you know how things were. Even apart from getting the degree, I absolutely couldn't think of living there. I know she looks like the Golden Girl, but actually she's had it pretty rough. Her father was killed when she was just a kid, and her mother was apparently pretty selfish. Gaynor just left home and tried to make it on her own rather than live with her. I mean, their relationship was so bad, she never even wanted me to meet the old girl. And now I've uprooted her again."

"If her relationship with her own mother was so dreadful, that might account for her having so many negative feelings about being a mother herself," she said cautiously.

"Yeah. I don't know. Sometimes . . . well, she'll get this almost waxen expression on her face, doesn't want me to touch her. It really frightens me. I know she needs someone to talk to—I've even suggested analysis. I've encouraged her to get into a group or maybe even take a class, but she doesn't make friends easily."

"Perhaps I could ask her to come into the city for a day. I wouldn't mind showing her around. But if she's as depressed as you say, it might be a good idea if she'd seek some psychiatric help."

"You know, during the war I used to have all these grandiose notions about how I was going to change the world. Now I don't even know how to make the person I love most feel happy. I just feel helpless."

"You mustn't take all of it on yourself, Ricky. Perhaps it's just not in Gaynor's character to take enjoyment in the things you care about . . . brrr. It is cold, isn't it? Did I tell you about this class I'm taking with Professor Conrado? He is the wackiest . . ."

What kind of a friend could she count herself if she avoided his intimate confessions and blathered on about trivia, she asked herself. But how could she talk to Ricky about Gaynor? Despite his 140-plus I.Q. he was an emotional moron when it came to his wife. The first time she had seen them together she'd guessed that the relationship was one-sided, and subsequent meetings had confirmed her initial impression. Gaynor had a materialistic streak that would always be in opposition to Ricky's idealistic nature. It was obvious that Gaynor took no interest in Ricky's studies or his future plans. But how to say any of this to him? Especially when she was still attracted to him and wasn't wholly sure that her observations weren't prompted by jealousy. And what would it benefit if she did say it? Being in love wasn't a rational decision taken with one's best interests in mind. You could fall in love because of a touch, a look, a gesture, the length of the beloved's eyelashes. And Ricky was obviously in love with Gaynor.

"Oh, Ricky, look," she cried, turning her face upward as they got out of the car and walked to the liquor store. "It's starting to snow."

GAYNOR HAD OFTEN imagined herself, resplendent in protective furs, driving through a snowstorm. Now she stood by the single window of the apartment, clutched the cardigan to her chest, and stared out at the first flurries of white drifting through the sky. The second-hand space heater that Ricky had bought just last month popped and crackled. Yanking the extension cord from the wall, she shivered and wandered into the kitchen. She held the ignited match until it started to burn her fingers. One corner of her mouth twisted upward as she envisioned her body lying gassed on the floor. Would Richard come to the funeral? She lit the stove, and reached for another pack of cigarettes. Moving slowly past the bookcases, the unmade Murphy bed, and the cheap reproduction of Chagall's "Lovers in Springtime," she pressed her forehead to the window.

"No two snowflakes are alike," Ricky had told her last night when they'd heard the storm warning on the radio. He'd recounted his own enchantment with the changing seasons, told her stories of sledding and snowmen. Sometimes when she'd notice his struggle to interest her in everything from the novels of Theodore Dreiser to the price of oleomargarine, she would feel sorry for him. Then, looking at his pleading, lovesick, uncomprehending eyes, the pity would shift to contempt. But who was she to be contemptuous of Ricky? Dreamer though he was, he had withstood all pressures to give up his silly academic career. He was doing what he wanted to do. While she, considering herself wiser, was stuck like a figure in a glass paperweight, the forces of life swirling around her like snowflurries.

She touched the windowpane, saw the flakes fly onto it, melt and disappear. It seemed as though they vanished into nothingness, leaving no impression at all. Yet, staring into the yard, she saw that they were accumulating, covering everything with a powdery whiteness. She thought of the men in her life. They had floated by and vanished, leaving no individual mark, yet an accumulation. There were the "uncles" her mother had brought home, remembered not by faces but by a strong sense memory of stale liquor and tobacco smells. Stupid that other women said things like "you never forget the first one." She hadn't consciously thought of Uncle Joey in years. But that wasn't so strange, for even as he was having her on her mother's grubby bed, she'd tried to put her mind elsewhere. What she recalled now was not his persistence or her own curiosity and disgust, but the crisp five-pound note he had pressed into her hand afterwards. Then there was the old solicitor. He had stood behind her and watched her type so that she was bound to make mistakes out of nervousness. The relief she'd felt when he'd called her into his office and she'd realized that he had not been passing judgment on her work, but had been peeking at her shiny hair and youthful neck, sniffing her out. What a pathetic creature he'd turned out to be. Yet, at the time, he had personified what little she knew of power in the world. After him, Lela Waddington's brother. Why couldn't she remember his name? And the Frenchman who talked philosophy and wanted her to wear her stockings in bed. The American major with his cache of black-market loot. And . . . and . . . the faces melted again. She saw the reason, or what she had thought at the time to be the reason, for going with each of them. But now she felt the weight of it all, was appalled at her misjudgments, frozen in disgust at her complicities. Yet how, she wondered, could she have done otherwise? For each of them had promised some possibility of escape, if not enjoyment.

She stubbed out the cigarette and reached for another. Turning back to the window, Richard's compelling eyes and mouth imposed themselves on her own reflection. It was still impossible to understand why she had given way to him so easily. She had known even as she yielded to the first embrace that it was dangerous, threatening to her survival, but she hadn't been able to resist. For the first time in her life, she was in love. It wasn't the sort of love she had imagined when she had lain in the meadow with Lela whispering about flowers, kisses and promises of undying devotion. It was something mysterious, obsessive, eclipsing and hopeless. How could it not have been so? Richard was father, teacher, boss, seducer—the embodiment of all male power. How naive of her to think that by becoming his lover, she might be able to exercise control over him. It should have been obvious from the beginning that his lust was interwoven with his desire to humiliate his son and his wife. She had known it but blinded herself to it, thinking that somehow she could ally herself with his power. But instead of becoming his conspirator in the fight to bend

Ricky to his will and hers, she had only been his means of unmanning Ricky in the most destructive way he could devise. But her need for his approval had been greater than her understanding of his motives, or her own.

From that first night in the convertible, she had been seized by the obsession that takes place when hidden desire, so deeply buried in the psyche that its force can only be felt but never assessed, merged with hungers of the flesh. She had barely been able to look at Ricky the next day when she drove him to the airport. Kissing him on both cheeks, she had begged him to reconsider his plans to go back to school, and had forgotten him as soon as the plane lifted into the air. Then she had driven downtown to meet Richard at a hotel. It was the beginning of a series of afternoons of prolonged and violent lovemaking that gave her the gratification she had only experimented with in private and long since ceased to dream about. There was no possibility for coyness or inhibition. Richard had said that he knew who she was because she was like him. Here was the raw, blinding act of mutual use. Afterwards she would lie panting, the ceiling above her tilting, the sounds of all the world banished. But the release was never more than momentary. She would get up like an exhausted fighter, clean up, wait for the announcement of the next round. Until one afternoon, as she lay sprawled on the sheets, watching Richard check his gold watch and prepare to leave for a meeting, she realized that, more than anything in the world, she wanted him to say that he loved her.

Even had he been willing to make such an admission, which of course he was not, it would not have meant anything to her life outside of that room. He had not risen in the world without an understanding, and at least an outward respect, for conformity. He might, as she did, despise society in his heart, but he would never jeopardize his position in it. He was married to a woman of position, who even in her twenties must have shown signs of what she would become. She might not have been dependent on the bottle or sad in that vague, defenseless way—Richard's indifference and flashes of outright cruelty had fostered much of the downhill slide—but still she had always been a proper, socially advantageous mate. Richard would not leave her. Certainly not for his son's wife. There were limits to acceptable behavior, even among the most powerful.

Before the affair, his manner toward Gaynor at the house had been suspicious and hostile. Once she had become his mistress, he became politely aloof. They might have tasted each other's sweat just hours before, but when she sat across from him at the dinner table, he could look straight through her as if she were invisible. She waited for the next round they would play out in secrecy, yearned for the combative excitement of being in bed with him. But the inequity of their positions and her constant desire for him began to fill her with a sense of humiliation, captivity and hopelessness. After a time, she stopped writing the long letters begging Ricky to change his mind. She wanted to leave and seek the peace of her young husband's devotion.

Much as she knew that she and Richard were alike—that their similarities were the foundation of their house-of-mirrors sexuality—they were different. She needed the approval of society, though she was bound to mistrust it once it was given. Richard, her senior in years and authority, considered it his due and gave it little mind. She longed for beautiful things. The satisfaction of Richard's whims were never more than a phone call away. She sought wealth. He already had it. But the most important difference was that she was a woman. Two weeks before she was due to depart and join Ricky in Princeton, she found out she was pregnant.

She had visited a gynecologist whose name she found in the phone book. His office was in a sufficiently off-beat part of town that he would never have recognized her name even if she had given it. After he told her that her tests were positive—a fact that astounded her, since she had never been pregnant before and always took precautions —she had driven for several hours, finally parking the convertible at the spot where Richard had first taken hold of her. She sat there for hours, until the autumn sky had darkened into a vivid dark blue. She considered getting rid of the child, though she had no way to do so without some help. And there was no one she could turn to. When she drove back to the house, Etna was in a predictable state of nerves about her absence. Richard barely looked up from his papers. She strode past him to the telephone, called Ricky, and told him that she wanted to come to Princeton a week earlier than planned.

THE SNOW had become heavy, no longer gusting against the window in flurries but coming straight down from the dark sky with the persistence of rain. She bowed her head and drew in her breath sharply. It was hopeless. Whatever plans she'd had of living in style or being with the man she thought she loved were dashed. She had to get back to him somehow. But how? Hearing voices on the stairs, she started, blinked at the glowing coal of the cigarette. She must have forgotten the time. Ricky was already home.

"Surprise!" she heard a high-pitched female voice call out as the front door was flung open. "Hey, it's dark in here."

Ricky reached toward the kitchen ceiling and pulled the string of the lightbulb. Caroline and Evan Eckleberg, Betty and Ricky, their caps and heavy coats covered with snow, their arms laden with packages, stood and stared at her.

"Whatever are you doing standing there in the dark, Gaynor?" Caroline said, her pretty eyes going wide in disbelief. "Don't you know that everything you do while you're pregnant affects the unborn child? If you mope around in the dark, he'll probably grow up morbid and unfriendly."

"Maybe she's just saving electricity," Evan laughed, crossing toward her. "How you doin', kid? Your old man brought us all over to celebrate your birthday."

"I see," she muttered, pushing her hair back from her forehead.

"Well, let's not stand around. Let's get these coats off and open a bottle," he laughed again, seeing how distressed she looked.

"Happy birthday, darling." Ricky took her hands. She forced a sociable smile to her lips, but her eyes were furious. When he reached out to touch her hair, she turned away. Betty was sitting on the unmade bed removing her galoshes. She took in Gaynor's reaction to Ricky and moved toward her quickly.

"Hello, Gaynor. Happy birthday," she smiled, extending her hand. "Hope you don't mind us all barging in on you like this. Ricky was afraid that you'd be feeling homesick and I thought a surprise party might be a good idea. I must say experience should have taught me to be more careful. The only other time I gave a surprise party for anyone, it was a bon voyage for a sorority sister. She had a terrible argument with her parents the day of the party, they cancelled her trip, and she arrived in tears."

"No, I'm all right, Betty. I took a late-afternoon nap. I'm afraid I must look a fright." She brushed her hair back in the old studied, graceful gesture.

"The first nine months are the hardest," Caroline chortled, struggling out of her coat and smoothing the navy maternity smock with the demure lace collar. "I only have two more to go, but I was just drug out for the first five. I've been feeling a lot better since I've been taking the prenatal exercise class, and those activities at the Veterans' Wives Club have made me feel as though I'm back in the swing again. Now why don't you come to our Thursday kaffeeklatsch, Gaynor? It'd be so good for you."

"If you'll all excuse me, I'll just go into the bathroom and pull the brush through my hair," Gaynor replied stiffly.

"Just consider yourself lucky to even have a bathroom," Caroline went on. "We only have one down the hall. I'm always afraid that this wild-eyed chemistry student who has hair growing out of his ears and looks like Frankenstein is going to burst in on me. Honestly, Evan, if my daddy could see what you've brought me to, he'd never have consented to give you my maiden hand in marriage."

Gaynor felt her stomach turn as she hurried into the bathroom. It was just like Ricky to make some "loving" gesture that was totally out of touch with her needs. *Goddamn him!* Her hands shook as she fumbled in the cabinet for her lipstick and power. Her face was flushed with anger. Pulling off the cardigan, she saw the front buttons of her dress pulling against her breasts. No matter how hard she tried to suck in her stomach, which had always looked so attractively taut in midriffs, it was already beginning to protrude. She gripped the edge of the sink and swore at herself. She wouldn't let someone like that syrupy, holier-than-thou Caroline see her out of control. She would rise to the occasion, though the thought of the occasion made another wave of rage and nausea sweep through her. She had never dreamed that she would be spending her twenty-seventh birthday sitting around a kitchen table watching a bunch of students and their wives swill beer and babble about books and baby formulas. *How could Ricky be so stupid!* she thought with a blind, hot hatred.

"I'd like a whiskey," she said, walking back into the room.

"Do you think you should?" Caroline asked. "I don't think you're supposed to drink when you're pregnant."

Gaynor sucked in her breath and looked at Evan, who was busy with the drinks.

"Will you pour me a drink, or should I do it for my bloody self?"

"No. I'll pour you one," he answered cautiously. "Straight up?"

Betty looked up from the sink, where she was hurriedly washing the dishes. "One drink shouldn't hurt—after all, it's her birthday. I hope you have an appetite too. I've brought a truckload of food from the city."

"Ginger ale for me," Caroline said sweetly.

There was an embarrassed silence as Ricky finished straightening the bed and Evan poured the drinks.

"You know what I read in the paper today?" Caroline chirped enthusiastically. "We're in something called the baby boom. Yes, that's what they're calling it. Seems as though all the couples who have been waiting all through the war to start their families are all doing it at the same time! I have a friend who's living in veterans' housing at the University of Wisconsin—well, it's only five acres of trailers really, but they call it the state's most fertile five acres. Isn't that a howl? And they've organized the trailer park so well: they have a nursery, a cooperative grocery store, their own police, even a softball team—just about everything you'd ever need."

"Except for the softball team it sounds a bit like what the Nazis were trying to do at Lebensborn," Gaynor said acidly, taking a sip of her drink. "All that fearfully earnest breeding. Like little rabbits."

"You know the joke about what the corporal said when the reporter asked him what was the first thing he was going to do after the war?" Evan asked, waving his pipe in the air.

"I'll bite," Ricky replied.

"He said, 'First thing I want to do is hump my wife, and the second thing I want to do is take off these damned army boots.'"

"Evan, what a way to talk," Caroline tittered, pleased that her marital status now made it possible for her to hear off-color jokes.

Gaynor knocked back the rest of the whiskey and pushed the glass across the table for a refill. Her eyes met Evan's; he smiled uncomfortably and poured another shot into her glass. He had never seen a woman who had her combination of beauty and self-possession before. Even though her cynical remarks about pregnancy were quite a change from Caroline's obsessive chatter on that subject, he felt that it would betray his lack of sophistication if he showed that he was shocked. He was sure there must have been some deep and tragic trauma in her life to have made her appear so brittle. The delicacy of her features, the grace of her movements, the throaty voice with the accent that sounded more English than Australian, were so intriguing. Gaynor noticed the appreciative curiosity in his eyes and held his gaze over the rim of her glass. The liquor scalded her throat and warmed her. Having a man look at her in that old, fascinated way restored some of her confidence. She would find a way out. There was a knock on the door.

"Must be Andy and Cynthia," Ricky said, hoping that the party was finally getting underway. Andy, a rather rotund, pompous Economics major, and Cynthia, who was so shy that Gaynor had at first thought she might be a little retarded, bustled in. After another piling up of coats and discussion of the snowstorm, they all sat down to the table where Betty had heaped piles of roast beef, pastrami, cole slaw and piroshki.

"What are these little pastries?" Caroline wanted to know as she helped herself to a second one.

"Piroshki. It's the Russian version of a meat pie."

"Wherever did you get them?"

"Oh, there are lots of different restaurants and delis up near Columbia."

"I'm not sure I should trust eating anything Russian," Caroline sniffed.

"I think these go back to the czars—not these particular ones, they're supposed to be fresh. But the recipe is pretty old."

"But Russian," Andy said. "Since I read the transcript of Churchill's Iron Curtain speech, I don't want to touch anything Russian."

"Don't forget what the Russians went through in the war," Ricky said between bites. "During the siege of Leningrad they were lucky to be eating the neighbor's cat."

"Please, my stomach," Caroline squealed.

"Does that give Joe Stalin the right to be a son-of-a-bitch?" Andy inquired.

"I wasn't talking about Stalin. Christ, Andy, you think eating a meat pie is an endorsement of foreign policy?"

"That's the way all of you guys in the literature department are," Andy grinned. "Always soft on the Commies."

"Yeah," Betty said, casting an affectionate glance in Ricky's direction. "Tolstoy seduced him and Dostoyevsky done him in for good. Listen, I didn't mean to start a political argument by bringing piroshki. It's just that the old guy who makes them is kinda sad-looking—has hairs growing out of his ears like your neighbor the chemistry student," she winked at Caroline, "so I felt sorry for him and bought two dozen."

"Hairs growing out of his ears!" Caroline yelped. "That does it for me. Ever since I've been PG I've had the weakest stomach. I don't have any political bias—gee, I leave that stuff to the boys—but hairy ears? I draw the line at that."

"Now, Caroline," Evan said, taking Gaynor in because he thought perhaps she was interested in worldly concerns, "it's up to everyone, regardless of sex, to think about politics. Especially now. We didn't fight the war for nothing."

"Nope," Andy concurred, "we fought for our lousy sixty-five dollars a month in G.I. benefits. And do you realize that because a college graduate will earn more during his lifetime, the federal tax on his added income will more than pay for education and training assistance from the VA?"

"But that's all up the road," Caroline put in. "I want Evan to be out of school *now*. We'd already been pinned for six months when they drafted him, and if he hadn't gone away he could already be practicing by now and we wouldn't be living in a boarding house with the bathroom down the hall."

"Don't complain, sweetheart. Princeton broke a two-hundred-year-old rule just to allow students to have wives on campus."

"That was bloody big of them," Gaynor smirked. "Though I guess if someone is still a student, they usually haven't taken on the responsibilities of marriage."

"Women should be allowed to live anywhere, and study anywhere," Betty put in as she gathered up the plates.

"Women don't want to study," Caroline insisted. "What's the point? They don't do anything with their education anyhow. Most women just want to have a comfortable home and raise a family. I mean unless they're the sort who can't get anyone to marry them."

Betty's mouth opened and closed abruptly. Gaynor looked at her and the two of them, unlike in almost every way, stared at each other for a moment of inchoate, confused acknowledgment.

"Hey, any woman can get a guy to marry her if she pets with him long enough in the back seat of a car," Andy said quickly. "Besides, I don't want to talk about women . . ."

"But they're one of the most fascinating subjects in the world," Evan protested.

". . . I want to talk to Ricky about why he wrote that letter to the Daily Princetonian. I don't see why he's being so hardnosed about not supporting Veterans of Foreign Wars. At least they're for the vets. And Ricky's been screaming that we should get behind this American Veterans' Committee. I just think they're a bunch of pie-in-the-sky visionaries."

Ricky took another sip of his drink, pushed back his chair and gave Andy a quizzical look. "Am I supposed to take 'visionaries' as a slur?

One of the strengths of American Veterans' Committee is that we're not just out for a personal grab. We're concerned with the needs of all citizens. Did you know that the American Legion just teamed up with the real-estate lobby to make sure that we couldn't get a three precent government loan on housing? Now we'll have to go through the VA with regular lending institutions—the banks and financing companies. I happen to know about that because my father is a big wheel in real estate, among other things, and I know there was a lot of dealing behind the scenes to push that so-called 'compromise' through. If we don't get a handle on big business and the lobbyists now, they'll be running the show for the rest of our lives. For the rest of our childrens' lives."

"Hey, you really are an orator when you get going," Andy said sarcastically, seeing the change that came over Ricky once he got hold of a subject. "If you feel this hot about everything I think you should go into politics yourself. You're good-looking and vets are making it big this year. Look at that guy Kennedy up in Massachusetts. Did a helluva campaign. If your old man's got the loot, why don't you get him to stake you to a real career?"

"I'm not interest in running for office. I'm just a concerned citizen."

"Besides, he can't stand his father," Gaynor drawled, turning to give him a challenging glance.

Evan tapped out his pipe and pointed it toward Ricky. "So what are we seeing here, buddy? The righteousness of a good college liberal, or a guy who's still battling an Oedipus complex?"

"Trust you to turn everything back to Freud," Caroline sighed. "I blame the Army for that."

"You blame the Army for Freud?" Betty inquired archly.

"I just meant that Evan was perfectly content to be a regular doctor before the war. But since he worked in those Army hospitals he got all interested in traumas, so now we have to sit around for another couple of years while he sees all those nut cases."

"The health of the mind is as important as the health of the body," Evan said earnestly. "Your life has been so uncomplicated that you don't even know what a trauma might mean."

"I do too know what a trauma means: it means having to hurry to take a bath so old hairy ears doesn't break in on me."

"Aw, that'll be over soon," Andy comforted her, amid hoots of laughter. "Another couple of years you'll be livin' on Park Avenue and Evan'll be holding the hands of a bunch of rich ladies who can't decide whether or not to get their fifth divorce. And when he tells 'em to go ahead, I hope he'll recommend me as their lawyer."

"You are a cynic," Ricky shook his head. "And I bet if I scratched you I wouldn't even find a disappointed idealist."

"If you scratch me in another three years all you'll get is some of the wool from my Brooks Brothers suit," Andy laughed. "Look at things straight for a change, Cunningham. Society's changing. There are bound to be a lot more divorces and I can make money on them."

"What do you think, Betty?" Ricky asked, wanting to include her in the conversation. "You're going to be a sociologist and your field is family life."

"I think Andy's prognostication is probably correct, but I don't think I can say anything definitive about why."

"But why should people want to get divorces?" Caroline begged, as she sidled over to the sink and grabbed a leftover piroshki.

"Shifting economic and demographic patterns, changing notions of roles within the family—all that stuff I'm learning about. But more to the point, I think it's because people find out that the person they *think* they've married isn't the person they've married. If that happened to grandma and grandpa, they'd just grin and bear it. And if it happened in Pago Pago, it probably wouldn't make a helluva lot of difference because the only time they'd have to see each other would be at the yam harvest or something. But we—our society—we have the expectation of romantic love. That means you have to have a specific, one and only person to satisfy your heart. And given our attitudes about sex and courtship, you don't really get much of a chance to know the other person. It's all highs and lows, moonlight and illusions. Daily life is something else. I believe most people fall in love with an image. Unrequited passion blinds them to any knowledge of character. And it takes a long time to really know what makes someone tick. You're certainly not in the best position to be an intelligent observer if you have hearthrobs every time the object of your affection comes into the room."

"But that's the *fun* of being in love," Cynthia put in, looking fondly at Andy.

"And that's why there's such a difference between loving and just being in love. When you really love you've got some idea of what you've got, what you want, who the other person is. Being in love . . ."

"I don't see the difference at all—loving versus being in love—I really don't know what you're talking about," Caroline said with a hint of hostility. "I bet you just say all this because you haven't really been in love with anyone yet."

"I've been in love," Betty said quietly. "But let's not turn this into a true confessions. . . . I guess I can't really back up anything I've been saying. I was talking about my impressions of things."

"Not very scientific," Evan joked, wagging his pipe at her. "Not that the social sciences can ever hope to be truly exacting in their analysis, but you really must seek to have a more objective attitude."

"Since I'm talking about people, I don't suppose I'll ever be really scientific," Betty conceded, and then, with a wink she added, "that would be most unloving."

"You see," Andy laughed, "let women into the discussion and it just slips and slides away from any concrete issue."

"You're a lousy misogynist," Ricky said. "And that's not appropriate to the celebration of my wife's birthday. What say we bring on the cake, 'cause I'll have to take Betty to the station pretty soon."

He got up to turn off the light.

They sat in the darkened room while Betty lit the candles. As they all sang "Happy Birthday" Ricky looked across the table, his eyes begging forgiveness for having made a mistake by planning the party. Gaynor, warmed by the liquor and Evan's furtive and admiring glances, gave him a relaxed smile. He beamed at her as she opened the gifts—a pair of mittens from Andy and Cynthia, a Shetland scarf from Betty, a pattern book for baby clothes and several skeins of pastel wool from Caroline.

"Dammit, I left your present in the glove compartment," Ricky said.

"Then I guess it can't be a mink coat."

"On a professor's salary it'll never be a mink coat," Andy reminded her. "God knows I've tried to wise this guy up, but he's just not interested in money. The only way you'll ever get a mink coat is when his old man croaks and leaves you his fortune."

"And I expect that he'll have gone through with his threats to disinherit me by that time," Ricky said. "Now, any of you want to walk down to the car with me? The snow's stopped and the streets will be beautiful in the moonlight. Besides, Gaynor's never seen snow before."

"Sure, let's get a taste of that sobering, icy air," Evan said gamely, helping Caroline on with her coat.

"Then it's a snowball fight and a ride to the station." Ricky was in good spirits now. Gaynor had smiled at him. The party had turned out better than the first half hour had promised. Perhaps when they came back home, Gaynor would be willing to go to bed with him. She had been so loving during the courtship that he just couldn't believe that her withdrawal was permanent.

After Andy, Ricky and Betty tossed a few snowballs at each other, a neighbor called out from an upstairs window to keep the noise down. Gaynor, who had already crawled into the front seat of the DeSoto, leaned out of the window to bid Cynthia and Andy goodnight. Ricky offered to drive Evan and Caroline home after he'd taken Betty to the station. When he got out to wait on the platform with Betty, Caroline had already fallen asleep in the back seat. Evan shifted her head from his shoulder, and leaned toward the front seat. Gaynor had opened Ricky's gift and was slowly dabbing the perfume on her neck. Breathing in its fragrance, he watched her profile as she tossed her head and touched it behind her ears. When she took out a cigarette he held the lighter for her. "I hope you had a good time tonight." She drew on the cigarette, her eyes holding his, then let her lashes droop and turned abruptly toward the window.

"It was very good of you to come," she said distractedly. She rolled down the window, pulled the frosty air into her lungs, and coughed. Feeling his eyes still on her, she shifted her position so that her face and hair were illuminated by the street lamp.

"I don't mean to pry," he went on softly, glancing at Caroline's inert form, "but Ricky has told me that you've been having some problems adjusting to being away from home. I guess it must be very lonely for you—strange country, never being able to talk to your family."

"If you only knew," she smiled wistfully. "No, Evan. I want to be honest with you. It isn't really that I miss Australia. I didn't have much of a home life to speak of. I know you'll find it hard to believe because I've been so despondent ever since you've known me, but it's really not like me to mope about. I just . . . sometimes, I just . . ."

Her lips trembled. She dropped her head for a moment. Then, shaking her hair and giving him a bright smile, she seemed to be on the brink of breaking off the conversation.

"Perhaps you should seek some professional advice."

"With our money situation the way it is, I don't see how I can. And

I have to admit I'm a bit afraid of it. I've always thought of myself as a very private person."

"Look, I do see a few regular patients in addition to my work load at the clinic. It wouldn't be ideal of course, because it's preferable that the psychiatrist not know his patients personally. But if you really feel the need to speak to someone, I could arrange some time for you, at least for a preliminary interview. Then I might be able to steer you on to someone else."

"That's terribly kind of you, Evan," she murmured as she reached over the seat and took his hand. "Terribly kind."

SHE VISITED his tiny office three times a week for almost a month. With the intuition that had guided her through every relationship save that with Richard, she revealed what she chose to reveal and watched the effect of her confessions on him, though he tried to remain blandly professional throughout. She told him about her mother, carefully shifting the facts of her maternal neglect to a different social context. Thelma was presented as being uncaring because she took long vacations in Europe with cruel, aristocratic lovers, rather than because she picked up any rummy who happened to be in the bar at closing time and stayed out for all-night binges. She spoke of the isolation and struggle of the years when she lived alone, mentioning the various men who had persistently but unsuccessfully sought her favors, and of how, not from passion but from a desire for security and peace, she had accepted Ricky's proposal of marriage, without really knowing much about him.

Sometimes, caught up in the retelling of an event, the essential truth of which could never have been manufactured, Gaynor would be tempted to confide in him. But she always stopped herself before the really upsetting revelations; for Evan, though understanding, would surely have been shocked, and he was only a means toward her escape. She was, on these occasions, impressed with her own artfulness in transforming reality while being faithful to its emotional core, and thought perhaps she should have pursued a career as an actress. For when the tears welled in her large, beautiful eyes, they were not forced. She was genuinely at her wit's end to change the misery of her life. But the tears were never so uncontrolled that she was not aware of their effect on Evan. When he fumbled in the breast pocket of his tweed suit to find a handkerchief, or nervously packed his pipe, she could see the studious, eminently rational expression drain from his face and couldn't fail to notice his own inferior role-playing. Besides, it was a point of honor with her that her real breakdowns should always occur in private. Without that one defense, she sensed that she might truly become emotionally unbalanced.

Then one afternoon, as she drew her handkerchief from her purse and dabbed it to her eyes, he was overwhelmed, as she knew he would be, not by the sight of a patient in distress, but by the helpless near-hysteria of a woman to whom he was sexually attracted. He lurched from the neatly organized desk and sat beside her. It was only a matter of minutes before the pseudo-paternal, comforting hand had slipped from her shoulder and moved toward the opening of her dress. She returned the hot embrace, but as he was forcing her backward on the couch, she pulled away, contrite and confused. He got up and returned to his desk, blushing violently as he rearranged his notes. She waited until he was sufficiently composed, stuffed the handkerchief back into her purse, and straightened her clothes. Rising, she said haltingly that perhaps she'd better not come to the office again. He mumbled a few inaudible words of apology, then became predictably businesslike. Without mentioning his own lapse of professionalism, he said sternly that he felt she must keep coming to their sessions for her own good. He definitely expected to see her the following week.

It took two more sessions of watching him struggle with his conscience and assume a fatherly and somewhat condescending attitude before he moved to the couch again, covered her neck and face with kisses, and told her that he had been thinking of her constantly and was probably in love with her. Again she responded, then pulled back, reminding him of the betrayal that their consummation would involve. He was her husband's friend. She knew his wife. No matter what the strength of her personal feelings for him—and she implied that they were as deep as his own—she could not live with herself if she gave way to him. Yet the temptation of seeing him, even being in the same town with him, was so great that she might not be able to resist much longer. Might it not be best if she could get away? Go back to Kansas City and stay with Ricky's parents for the rest of her pregnancy? She had already told him how fond she was of Etna, and having no real mother of her own, she felt the need to have another woman around. She wasn't in love with Ricky—she had already confessed that—yet Ricky was really so good to her. If she announced a separation now it would be so destructive to his work. And what about poor Caroline?

Perhaps, she said distractedly, stroking the hair back from his forehead, perhaps, if he could persuade Ricky that she would be better off, owing to her shaky psychological state, in Kansas City, that would facilitate a less hurtful break. It would allow both of them to really examine their feelings before they made a commitment for which they might both feel enormous guilt. Of course she wasn't sure that was the way out. All she could think of now was how very much she wanted to make love to him. . . .

Afterwards, full of remorse, he told her that he would talk to Ricky and suggest that for the sake of her mental health, she should return to his parents' home.

CHAPTER
XI

THE ICY January wind howled around the shack. Sheila woke up with a start, thinking that the baby had given her a strong kick. Then she realized that the accumulated snow on the tree overhanging the house had been dislodged by the wind and was falling on the roof with a dull, thudding sound. Blinking, she took the book that was propped up on her belly, set it on the bedspread, and then crossed her hands over her abdomen and lay waiting to feel the baby move. The last few days it had been as active as an acrobat. She pushed her swollen feet into the pink satin slippers that her parents had sent in the Christmas package, pulled the blanket around her shoulders, and walked slowly into the kitchen. Opening the door of the potbellied stove, she threw in some more wood. In a moment she would have to tug on the heavy coat and struggle to get her feet into her rubber shoes for a trip to the outhouse, but for now she sat at the kitchen table and stared out the window at the heavy frost that covered the woods.

It hadn't been so bad during the summer and autumn. Still in the early stages of her pregnancy, after the initial period of morning sickness she'd felt remarkably healthy. She had gone for daily walks to pick flowers and berries, while Billy, his rifle slung over his arm, described the countryside and took shots at the occasional squirrel or rabbit. She was still too squeamish to eat the furry creatures, but Ma seemed grateful enough for the catch and would cook them up in stews. Even when the first snows came she was still able to get about without too much effort. She did her best to try to fix up the house, but since there was so little money available and she had no special talents in domestic arts, it was only slightly more comfortable than it had been when she'd arrived.

Every Wednesday, after her regular checkup, she would stay in Dr. Helen's office, filing, tidying up, and caring for the kids who came in with their mothers. Her duties helped pay off the bill, but more than that, the Wednesday afternoons gave her an opportunity to be with Dr. Helen.

When all the patients had been seen, the two of them would sit in the office sharing cups of the strong black coffee from Dr. Helen's Thermos and talking. Dr. Helen was a human encyclopedia. She talked over a wide range of subjects, often expressing points of view totally new to Sheila. She gave her books, made up reading lists for her to take to the local library, encouraged her to think about what she might do with herself once the child was born. Billy was surprised and a little uncomfortable to discover that Sheila could be a book-worm, but she told him that before she'd hit adolescence and become captivated by the movies, she'd always had her nose in a book. Prior to the galvanizing discovery of the opposite sex, she had been thought by her teachers and her father to have quite a good brain. Now, as the child grew in her body, the seed of a notion about what she might do with herself afterwards began to grow in her mind. Seeing Billy's insecurity about being a good provider, she had kept these thoughts to herself, discussing them only with Dr. Helen and casually mention-ing to Ma that she might like to find a job once the baby had been delivered. Thus the last months had been spent in a dreamy but thoughtful state of anticipation.

But lately the weather had been so inclement. She had grown too large to move about freely, and since Billy had taken a job at the overall factory and needed the truck to go to work, she had become a virtual prisoner in the house. She spent the mornings doing what-ever chores were necessary and in the afternoons she crawled back into bed and read until Ma came by to keep her company and help her with the evening meal. The days were long and lonely, but know-ing how miserable Billy had been when she'd finally persuaded him to take the factory job, she tried not to complain.

It was a crushing blow to his manhood and sense of freedom to be confined indoors and forced to punch a time clock. But she had made it clear that even if she were willing to accept a life of deprivation for herself, she would absolutely not allow her child to grow up in need. Mute and unhappy, Billy had given way to her demands.

It wasn't that Billy was lazy. He had boundless physical energy and would eagerly set about any task that she asked him to perform around the house. But he was not a self-starter. The war had opened up new horizons for him, but once back in the hill country, there was no outlet for his energy and courage except in hunting and occasional drinking bouts with his cronies who owned a still. When Sheila had suggested that he go to college on the G.I. Bill, he had shamefacedly confessed that he'd never finished high school. He was too embarrassed by his deficiencies and his age to try for any further education and moped about the house in moods of inarticulate frustration that not even their most intimate moments of pleasure could alleviate.

The realization that Billy was not the sort of man who would ever get out and make his way in the world on his own frightened her. Her whole notion of what their married life would be like was based on an expectation of Billy as leader and provider, she the faithful follower. But now it was clear that if they were ever to improve their lot, it would be her responsibility to direct them both. Yet she had no clear idea of what she might do to guide them into greater happiness or success. She was, as her mother had predicted, inexperienced and foolish, weighed down by responsibilities she had eagerly but heedlessly taken on.

Sometimes she would wake in the night, shivering under the pile of Army blankets and the patchwork quilt Ma had made for their wedding present, afraid to wake Billy because he had to get up at six to start for the factory. She would lie motionless, eyes clenched shut, feeling the baby inside her and wondering about their future. To calm herself, she would visualize her old room at home: the little girl's room with its ruffled bedspread, collection of dolls and wardrobe full of party dresses. There she had only to step out of the door to be in Da's rose garden, only to walk down the street to meet schoolmates confectioner's who would stroll with her to confectioner's, tennis courts or movie houses. She knew somehow that her nostalgia was out of proportion to her feelings when she'd actually lived there, but the memories made her feel warm and safe.

Once, right after Billy had started to work at the factory, heavy rains had caused the water stain in the bedroom to leak. She had moved the bed so it wouldn't get wet, put a pail underneath the leak and then climbed up on a chair to inspect the damage. When the chair tipped over and the bucket spilled, she sprawled on the floor, knee skinned, heart beating wildly, torn between tearful despair and a raging tantrum. Dragging herself up, she rushed to the chest of drawers, found her pen and paper, and began her first truthful letter to her father.

Da,
    I'm homesick and utterly miserable. You were right about everything. I was too silly to realize what I was getting into. I remember so well that last night at home when you offered me the money to come back. I was too full of pride and dreams to accept it. I miss you so much. I am so unhappy now that I think I'll have to come back . . .

But that afternoon she got a letter from her mother that was so full of caution and complaint that she was immediately reminded of the real situation in her parents' home. She could not hope to return, especially not with a baby. She tore up her letter to Da.

Besides, Billy was so loving and excited about their child. She had heard stories that men were often embarrassed by their wives' pregnancies or likely to stray to other women, but Billy was even more devoted than before. He was his taciturn, controlled self on the rare occasions when he took her to a local dance or movie; but when they were alone he was affectionate and solicitous. He listened carefully while she read the manuals on child development, kidded her that for the first time in her life she had noticeable breasts, and stroked her changing body with something approaching religious awe. Even if they'd had a spat during the day, he seemed to find her wholly desirable when they went to bed. And when she fell asleep he would turn her back to his chest and rest one hand protectively on her belly.

She lumbered up from the table, stoked the fire and put the kettle on. There was a knock at the door. Without waiting for an answer, Ma came in, slamming it quickly behind her.

"Whew, that wind outside has jest about froze m' bones. Looks like you got some more mail today, daughter," she said, holding up a letter.

"I've just put the kettle on. Will you have a cup of tea?"

Ma took off the heavy man's coat and removed the old felt hat. "Don't be troublin' yerself. I'll fix it. Guess by now I learned how to do it right."

Sheila was always amazed at Ma's rugged vitality. It was easy to see, from the crevices that marked her weather-beaten skin and from the deep-set, weary eyes, that she had had a harsh, demanding life. Yet she still walked with the determination of a woman who has a destination or an important task before her. Sometimes her stoicism was almost annoying. Sheila couldn't imagine that she could survive six pregnancies, the death of a husband and three children, and years of poverty and still move with such vigor. Mostly she was awestruck by such endurance.

"Aren't y' gonna open that there letter?"

"Oh, it's just another one of those stupid Kangaroo Courier things from Mavis," Sheila sighed, looking at the postmark.

"I din' notice. Thought it might be from yer friend Dawn," Ma said as she rinsed the teapot with scalding water.

"Just listen to this drivel: 'Belated Happy New Year from the Kangaroo Courier! It's Mavis again, offering apologies for not getting around to sending this sooner. Here's hoping that Father Christmas (whoops! make that Santa Claus) brought each and every one of you whatever your little hearts desired. Herbie and I have been busy moving into our very own, brand new, split-level house in a place called Levittown. Seems a fellow named Levitt, full of Yankee ingenuity, bought some potato fields in Long Island and has set up a one-thousand-home new town. A thousand dollars down, seventy-nine dollars a month for Mr. Kilroy to move into a three-bedroom house complete with venetian blinds and landscaping. Boy am I happy! Can't wait to meet the neighbors. They're all young couples on their way up—like us.

" 'Aileen Ferry says that hubby Paul has a new job . . .' "

She broke off abruptly as her eyes flew to the hand-scrawled message at the bottom of the page:

Sheila: just to let you know that Patricia Guizquicz has gone back home to Perth. Seems her husband took her to some dreadful little town near Detroit and most of the people there, including his relatives, didn't even speak English! When he started knocking her about, she decided she couldn't take it anymore. Naturally I wasn't going to print any such unhappy news in the Courier, but since you were friendly with her on the ship, I thought I'd let you know. Isn't your baby due soon? Do keep in touch . . . Cheerio, Mavis.

"You don't look so good, Sheila. Is that grandchild of mine kicking the daylights out of you again?"

"No. I just heard some bad news. One of the girls I came over with has left her husband and gone back home. I didn't know her really well, but we were friends on the ship."

"I'm sorry y' had to get bad news, especially since it's so close to yer time."

"It's just that she was such a chipper girl. She seemed to have so much pluck. I'm sure she would never have left if it weren't intolerable. Apparently her husband started beating her up."

"Then it was time to leave and go back to her folks. Hard times is one thing. Beatin' is somethin' else. Least ways you know that Billy won't ever raise his hand to you."

"No," Sheila smiled wanly. "I don't expect he would."

"I tried to raise him gentle. Didn't have to try too hard though. He's natural-born kind."

"I think that environment has a great deal to do with how a child develops," she said, quoting one of the books she'd just read.

"A good home can help to straighten out the crooked ones some, but any mother'll tell y', you can tell their nature right from the beginnin'. Now Tommy, he was diff'rent. Gave me lots of trouble in the birthin' and never stopped hollerin' from the first day he drew breath. I knowed when he went off to the war I might never see him again. He could get into a heap o' trouble even in peacetime so I figured when the Marines tolt me he was a hero and all, that somehow he was lookin' to get himself killed. I've never said that to no one before, but I've knowed it in my heart."

The fatalism of Ma's remarks stirred the hopelessness that Sheila was constantly battling. She sat, silently staring out the window, until Ma reached across the table for her hand.

"There's something I've been wantin' to say to y', Sheila. I've been pesterin' myself jest how to put it. I haven't been out in the world much myself—why, I was borned in Prathers Creek and went right up to the mines in McDowell County when Big Lonnie and I got married and I was young'r 'n you then . . . Billy tolt me right after y' come that you wasn't used to livin' this way. 'Course I suspected that y' come from rich folks. Then, when I saw that Christmas package they sent y' with them fancy slippers and nightdresses and all, I knowed my suspicions was right. But you never let on to me about it. I see you've stuck here by him even when he was outta work. I know y' love Billy 'bout as much as he loves you. I seen you sufferin' through, but you stuck with him. What I mean is . . . I feel like you're one of m' own now. I'd be real sorry to see y' leave."

"I've never thought of leaving, Ma," she lied, squeezing the wrinkled hand. " 'Whither thou goest I shall go.' "

"I don't know 'bout that," Ma smiled. "My grandma tolt me: 'When you get married, you gotta take the fleas with the dog.' Now I know that Billy needs a little push to get him going. I know he's not happy with this here factory job, and he won't want you to go to work either. But after the baby's come, if you want to go to work and you can find somethin', y' won't have to worry, Sheila. I'll take care of the house and the baby."

"I'm going to think about it, Ma. Not right after the baby's born, of course, but maybe later. Dr. Helen has been talking to me about going back to school. She thinks I would be a good grade-school teacher, or possibly I could have a nursing career. It's been at the back of my mind for some time, but I haven't wanted to talk about it to Billy until I really knew what I wanted. And I do want to move. I've hesitated to tell you that, because I know how attached both you and Billy are to the country up here, but if I was going to do anything at all, I think I'd have to be closer into town."

"But that would mean that I'd have to move in with you, and that could cause a heap of problems."

"I don't think so. Believe me, you'd be more of a help than a burden. Besides, I wouldn't like the idea of your living up here alone. I don't know, Ma. To tell you the truth, I can't think clearly about anything just now. I know the baby isn't due for another month, but it's been moving about so much that I have a feeling it may come sooner. All I can think about is that I want it to be healthy. I've had such morbid imaginings lately . . ."

"All right, daughter. It's gonna be all right. I jest wanted you to know that I see what's goin' on and that I care for you and I'll help y' any way I can."

"I appreciate that, Ma. I really do. You don't know how much it means to me that you've said this."

JUST BEFORE MIDNIGHT, lying on her back listening to the hoot of a screech owl echoing through the lonely woods, she felt a pop like a minor volcanic eruption in her belly. She lay perfectly still, all of her senses tuned acutely to her own body. It couldn't be. She had more than a month to go and everyone said that the first was usually later than expected. She had probably just had too many of Ma's biscuits at supper. She listened to Billy's steady snores, and then struggled to a sitting position and groped for her robe. Standing up unsteadily, she felt her way along the wall until she was almost to the kitchen, then clutched at the doorjamb with both hands and sucked in a deep breath as another contraction shuddered through her.

"Billy," she whispered, trying to find her voice.

"Where are you?" he croaked, turning over and fondling the pillow. As she turned on the light, he sat bolt upright, open-mouthed and startled. Stumbling to his feet, he moved across the room, half conscious.

"Is this it? Are y' sure?" he asked, blinking into her face and weaving on his feet.

"No, I'm not sure, I . . ." She felt another upheaval, warm liquid running down her legs. "Yes . . . Yes. I'm sure."

"VJ Day," he yelled, dancing around her.

He helped her back to the bed and ran to the wardrobe, pulling on his pants over his long underwear and muttering to himself as he searched for her overcoat. In his confusion he scattered most of the clothes on the floor, then rushed back to her. He helped her on with the coat and tried to ease her up.

"I can't go barefoot. Even around here they don't go barefoot in winter," she said impatiently.

He crawled under the bed, looking for her rubber boots.

"They're out near the front door," she cried, tugging at the sheets, her eyes going wide. "Oh, Billy, we look like Laurel and Hardy."

He pushed her feet into the boots.

"How do y' feel?" he asked, as he helped her toward the door. "Are the pains comin' fast?"

"I don't know. I feel like I did before the intermediate tennis competition—sweaty and nervous; afraid that I'm going to make a mistake."

"You won't make any mistakes, honey. Now jest holt on tight and I'll get y' down to the hospital fast as I can," he breathed as he kicked one of the yelping dogs aside and helped her into the cab of the pickup. He dropped the keys on the floor and hunted for them as she settled into the seat. He scrounged about her feet and she sat, biting her lips and trying to count the minutes between contractions. After what seemed like an eternity, he found the keys, turned on the motor, and pushed the gears into reverse.

"Stop," she cried, as he'd almost righted the truck and was turning onto the road. "I forgot my robe and my pretty nightdress."

"Hell, girl, you can't worry 'bout that now."

"Yes, I can. I want them. My slippers too. I'm not going to be sitting in hospital looking like a wreck. Please go back and get my things."

"It ain't gonna be my fault if'n you drop that baby right on the road," he said as he lurched the truck back into the yard. He leaped out and raced toward the house, the dogs milling around him. While she sat shivering, he kicked open the door, and soon ran back out, the bundled-up frilly nightdress and satin slippers in his arms. He dropped one of the slippers, retrieved it, and jumped back in beside her.

He gulped, paused to hug her and smooth the hair back from her perspiring forehead. "I got 'em. Now what?"

"Get me to the hospital and call Dr. Helen."

"Sure. Sure," he said, shaking his head and grinding the gears. "Now you jest holt on tight. I'm goin' down that there hill like greased lightnin'."

She groaned as another contraction started, clutching the seat with one hand, holding the other over her belly.

"We're gonna have a baby! We're gonna have a baby right to-night!" he whooped as the truck careened over the wooden bridge, bounced onto the road, and hurtled down the hill.

"I never thought it would be like this," she breathed, her eyes glued to the violently moving headlights. "Oh, dear God, I never thought . . ."

"Holt on, girl. I'll get you there. Holt on," he cried, slamming the accelerator to the floor.

"I never thought . . ."

A tremor of laughter rippled through her already shaking body. Billy, wildly staring at the highway that was lurching in front of them, took his hand off the wheel long enough to find her hand and squeeze it hard. "I . . . never . . . thought . . ." she gasped again, convulsed in wracking, hysterial laughter. He jerked his head around for a split second to look at her, and then a hoot of uproarious joy came from his throat. They laughed together, tears stinging their eyes until the next spasm ripped through her body.

After fifteen hours of labor, when she cried out for a mother she didn't love and a husband she adored but couldn't rely on, she followed Dr. Helen's instructions and pushed William (after Billy) Spencer (after Spencer Tracy) Hickock into the world.

———

CHAPTER
XII

"IF THAT KID belonged to me I'd take the hide off his little behind," the man sitting next to her said between clenched teeth.

"He does seem to be rather a handful," Gaynor answered, staring across the aisle at the brat in the red beanie. The boy was only about six years old, but his features were those of a malicious old man. He had thrown a tantrum as soon as the plane took off, kicked the seat in front of him until the passenger had asked to be moved, and then whined until his mother had given him candy bars. Now, feet sprawled in the aisle, his wizened chin smeared with chocolate, he gaped at Gaynor with a mischievous, challenging look as though he sensed her dislike for children and was plotting to punish her for it.

"I've got a couple of kids myself," the man went on, grateful for some reason to engage her in conversation. "'Course the wife takes care of them most of the time. I travel a lot. I only have to put up with them once in a blue moon. But boy, kids can really cramp your style, know what I mean?"

Gaynor nodded, folded her hands over her stomach, and looked ahead of her. She'd undone the zipper of her suit part way but could feel the fabric taut against her belly. Nothing made her more miserable than feeling that she wasn't attractively outfitted. She'd told Ricky that she needed a new traveling suit, but of course he'd said that they couldn't afford it. She had put on a bulky sweater and draped her coat about her. She could feel the man's eyes giving her the once over the minute she'd taken her seat next to him, so apparently she didn't look pregnant.

"This your first time going to Kansas City?" the man asked after a pause.

"No. I've been there before. I have relatives there," she said coolly.

"Must be your husband's relatives, huh?"

"Yes."

"I figured that out because I saw your wedding ring and I also noticed that you had an accent. English, isn't it?" he beamed, as though his observations were a sign of superior intelligence.

She nodded again and folded the coat closer around her. Why wouldn't this damned bozo leave her alone? She was in no mood to put up with fumbling flirtations from a middle-aged man on a business trip, and she knew that the sight of a woman traveling alone was enough to excite the erotic imaginations of men of his type. He probably hoped for a quick weekend fling in another town and his next move would be either an inane question about her homeland or, if he were a fast mover, a suggestion that they explore the city together.

"Visiting relatives can't be much fun for an attractive young woman like yourself. Relatives never take you out on the town. I'm from New York myself, but, like I said, I travel a lot on business. I'd sure love to show you around while I'm here."

"Thank you, but I don't think I'll be going into the city."

"You should. No reason why you couldn't break away for an evening out. Nothing serious—just some pleasant company. You don't have any kids, do you?"

"No . . . If you'll excuse me for a moment."

As she got up the coat fell from her shoulders and she saw his eyes travel down the length of her body. His face went red as he half rose from his seat.

"Oh . . . gee . . . excuse me," he said, flustered. "I didn't mean to offend you. You see I didn't notice . . ."

She started up the aisle toward the bathroom, feeling a biting anger toward him. Not that she was interested in his clumsy propositions. It was just that her pregnancy seemed to mark her as an untouchable, beyond the pale of admiration or desire. To most men her condition was a source of embarrassment. She yanked back the door to the washroom, turned the lock, and leaned against the wall, easing the zipper of the skirt down another few inches. God, how she hated being like this. When she tried to think about the baby—and most of the time she tried not to—she couldn't imagine anything more than a featureless lump. It was a parasitic growth that had invaded her body and disrupted her life. It made her feel that whatever tenuous control she had once had over her life had been lost.

Just this morning, when she was rushing around packing her suitcase, she had felt a sharp kick, and then noticed a few spots of blood on her underwear. She had immediately emptied the last of the scotch, taken a hot bath, and gone out in the snow to jog about, hoping against hope that she would miscarry. But there had been no more signs of trouble. The child who was destroying her present and shaping her future clung to her womb with the same tenacity as all the miseries of her past. And what would it mean to Richard even if she told him?

"I won't think about it now," she whispered as she brushed her hair and repaired her makeup. "I just won't think about it." No matter what was happening in her body, at least her face was still beautiful. She touched her fingertips gently to her cheeks, stared at her reflection until she felt a glimmer of her old self-confidence, and then walked back to her seat, head held high. The man had opened his briefcase and seemed to be absorbed in his papers. The brat across the aisle grinned at her. As she sat down, she felt something on the seat. Reaching beneath her, she came up with a handful of sticky popcorn.

"Alexander," the boy's mother bleated, "look what you've done! I told you that you couldn't have any more Cracker Jacks if you kept taking them out of your mouth. Now you've scattered them all around and spoiled that pretty lady's suit."

Alexander put both hands on his beanie, staring across at Gaynor with wide innocent eyes, his mouth twisted in a triumphal smirk.

"I am *so* sorry," the woman gushed on. "I know Alexander seems to be a naughty boy, but children do get so bored when they're traveling. Once you've had your own you'll understand just what I'm talking about. How long is it until you're due?"

"Is that lady going to have a baby?" the child shrieked at the top of his voice. "Is it inside her right now?"

Gaynor clenched her hands and resisted the urge to throttle the little monster. The pilot's voice announced that they had begun their descent.

Etna, wrapped in a mink coat that seemed to diminish her body, was standing in front of the group of people waiting to greet the passengers. As soon as she saw Gaynor, she inched forward, her gloved hands fluttering up, her pale eyes anxious.

"Oh, we're so glad to have you back. How are you, dear? How was the flight?"

Gaynor turned her cheek to receive the kiss, looking around for Richard. She hadn't really expected that he would come to meet her, but her heart still sank when she realized he wasn't there. She wondered bitterly why Etna, who was one of the most solitary women she'd ever known, persisted in saying "we." Perhaps it was a royal form of address she'd learned in one of the fancy schools she'd attended in her girlhood, or maybe it was just a pathetic need to pretend that she and Richard were a couple.

"Thank you, Mother," she said softly, consciously using the word for the first time and watching its effect on Etna.

"But you mustn't say thank you, Daughter. You're part of the family, after all. And now I'm not just a mother. I'm going to be a grandmother as well. I'm so happy about it. I just longed for you and Ricky to join us during the Christmas holidays. But now you're here, we're going to take the very best care of you. Jackson is waiting to get your bags, so we might as well start toward the car," she smiled, linking her arm through Gaynor's.

As they neared the main doors of the terminal, Alexander and his mother walked past them. The boy spotted her, stuck out his tongue, and then yelled "hubba hubba" before his mother managed to jerk him through the doorway.

"That little beast," Gaynor said vehemently. "God, how I hate children like that."

Etna raised her hand to signal to Jackson, casting a nervous sidelong glance at her daughter-in-law. The force and bitterness of her outburst toward the child in the beanie amazed her. Of course Ricky had telephoned her privately, explaining that Gaynor was emotionally overwrought, but he hadn't given her any details. He had mentioned a psychiatrist, and that was enough to alarm her. Being of the old school, she viewed psychiatry with mistrust and embarrassment, and thought it somehow unmannerly to discuss personal problems outside of the immediate family. She hoped that Gaynor would confide in her, though she had no idea of how to raise the subject of Gaynor's "depression."

"Welcome home, Miz Cunningham," Jackson smiled as he held open the door of the Buick. "Sure is fine to see you again. I don't suppose you'll be wanting to drive, will you?"

"Not just now, thank you, Jackson."

Sinking into the upholstery, Gaynor was silent for most of the ride, answering Etna's apprehensive questions in monosyllables. But when they drove into the estates she sat up, glad to see the vast lawns blanketed in snow and the luxurious cars parked beside them. When Jackson eased up the long driveway leading to the Cunningham mansion, the lights from the many windows seemed to promise comfort and protection. Faustina opened the front door, her dark face placid, her almond-shaped eyes full of that veiled curiosity that always made Gaynor uneasy. But the sparkling chandelier, the vase of carefully arranged hothouse flowers reflected in the mirror, the pungent logs burning in the living-room fireplace were enough welcome for her. "It's good to be home," she said in such a cheerful voice that Etna felt reassured. They took off their coats and gloves and settled into one of the sofas. Faustina appeared again, carrying a silver tray.

"Egg nog," Etna called brightly. "Faustina always knows just what will hit the spot. You know she nursed me all during my time with Ricky. I know you're almost ready to serve dinner, Faustina, but I don't suppose a little nip could hurt our appetites. Would you put the brandy decanter on the table?"

Faustina walked noiselessly to the bar and found the decanter.

Etna paused before she poured a liberal jigger into her own glass. "Shall I pour some for you, my dear?"

"Please. I've really been fine regarding food and drink," Gaynor answered. Her eyes darted up to the housekeeper, wanting her to leave.

"I think that will be all," Etna said formally. Faustina nodded and left. Even in a distraught state, Gaynor was still conscious of Etna's behavior toward the servants. It was one of the few areas in which she had something to learn from her mother-in-law, and it still amazed her. Faustina not only knew all of Etna's life, she had nursed her through illness, put her to bed when she was sloshed, calmed her when she was raving. Yet Etna could dismiss her in that ladylike but imperious tone of voice and never think it unkind. That was the way people born to wealth behaved: they were awash in a dependency they never had to acknowledge, they could be affectionate one minute and treat those who served them as though they were invisible the next. She watched Etna nervously rearranging things on the coffee table and thought how stupid the woman was not to realize her power. If only she had this money, this house, she would know how to use it.

"Now tell me, dear, how are you?" Etna began after another agonizing pause. "Ricky tells me you've been . . ."

"Depressed. That's the word the psychiatrist used to describe it, anyway. I don't know what to say. I just found that I was terribly lonely. I didn't want to lean on Ricky too much—you know how much work he has to do—but he was away most of the time and I was left in that little apartment. Perhaps I just needed . . ."

"The company of another woman. I understand. Naturally, I wouldn't want you to be alone. Especially at a time like this. You're so far from your own mother. I suppose she's the one you really want to have near."

"I wish I could say that was true, but it's not," Gaynor started softly. She went into another story of her relationship with Thelma, even more sanitized than the version she had told Evan, watching Etna's face change from concern to shock and finally melt into an expression of sentimental compassion.

"I had no idea your mother was so uncaring about you. I'd wondered why she didn't write to you, but still, I'd never imagined . . ."

"I don't really brood over that anymore. Or at least I didn't. Now that I'm pregnant, it does seem to bother me more."

"You just have to put it out of your mind. That's what I do whenever something unpleasant comes up. I concentrate on something pleasant, like my garden, and I just put any nastiness out of my mind."

"But it was so difficult to do that when I was left alone all the time back in Princeton. And I was afraid that you would think I was deserting Ricky by coming back here."

"Nonsense. Ricky told me that you'd both made the decision for you to come back home until the baby was born. Much as he'll miss you, he knows that we all have to do what's best for the baby, don't we?"

"I knew you'd understand," Gaynor whispered, putting on a brave smile.

"Now let's go in to dinner. I don't want to keep Faustina waiting. I'm sure Richard won't be home until late—even though he's very pleased that you've come back to stay with us."

SHE TOOK HER place at the candlelit dining table as Etna, now in the voluble mood that came over her after the first few drinks, talked of doctors, diets and possible names for the baby. Even as she enjoyed the well-appointed table, the carefully seasoned food and the soft shadows of the room, Gaynor kept looking toward the door in anticipation of Richard's arrival. Etna had obviously been glossing over his reaction to her return. She picked at the shrimp and tried to imagine what sort of reception she would get from him.

"So we couldn't name the baby that, could we?"

"I'm sorry, I wasn't listening," Gaynor said, pushing her plate aside.

"I was saying we couldn't call the baby Richard. Oh, I remember when Ricky came home one day—just a little thing he was—and he said, 'Mother, I don't want to be called Richard. That's Father's name. I just want to be Ricky.' So from that time on, I always called him Ricky. I suppose it hurt Richard's feelings. He was so set on having a son who was like him in every way. Men are strange about those things, don't you think? If they're interested in children at all, it seems to have something to do with their pride. They just want the child to emulate them. With a woman it's different. Mother love is special."

"Would you mind very much if I didn't have dessert? I'm afraid I have a bit of a headache and I'd like to go to bed early."

"You just run on upstairs and soak in a hot tub," Etna soothed, getting up and putting a protective arm about her shoulders. "I'll see you first thing in the morning. I am sorry Richard didn't come home for dinner. But then . . . you know Richard."

"Yes. Yes, I do."

Around midnight, when the house had been still for over an hour, Gaynor drew on her robe and crept downstairs. She had tried to sleep, but her ears were strained to hear when he might come in. The light was still on in the entrance hall. She walked into the living room without bothering to turn on another light, poured herself a brandy, and curled up on the couch. Lying in the semidarkness chain smoking, she heard the clock strike twelve. She poured another drink and stretched out again, starting to feel groggy. The front door opened. She lay stock still as he took off his coat, walked past her toward the bar, and fixed himself a scotch. Turning slowly, his eyes glinting in the darkness, he looked at her coolly. "So you're back."

"I didn't think you'd noticed me."

"I don't have to see you, Gaynor: I can smell you."

"I take it you mean that as a compliment to our intimacy," she whispered, making her voice as light as possible. She wanted to rush to him, tell him how she'd longed for him, beg him to help her. He snorted and settled into his leather chair.

"So what's the problem? Weren't the libraries at Princeton enough to engage your agile mind? Or was it just a case of poverty coming in the door and love flying out the window?"

"I never said I loved him."

"And if you had, I'd have known you were lying."

"I married him because I thought he had money," she said flatly. "Is that what you want me to admit? All right. I admit it. You wouldn't be such a hypocrite as to criticize me for that, would you? Not when it's the thing you care for most in the world."

"Is that what you think," he answered tonelessly, swirling his drink.

"Yes. That's what I think. Perhaps sometime when we have a brief hour together you might care to correct my misunderstanding."

"We don't have to talk. We understand each other well enough as it is."

"Would you mind fixing me another drink?" she asked, her voice lethal with controlled rage.

"Drunkenness isn't becoming to expectant mothers, my dear. I did hear that piece of news, didn't I? I never thought you'd be the type to get trapped into maternity, but you are carrying his child, aren't you? I am going to be a grandfather."

She drew herself up and stared at him, articulating every syllable. "Not exactly . . . and now, how about that drink?"

He had risen from the chair before the meaning of the words hit him. He stopped, his back to her, and then turned in slow motion, his eyes boring into her.

"Surely that must have occurred to you, Richard."

"Are you positive?"

"Yes. I knew it before I left. You're rather good at mathematical calculations, aren't you? You can figure it out when the little bastard is born."

"Why didn't you . . ."

"What? Tell you?" she cut in. "I'm not even sure why I'm telling you now. Of course I thought of trying to get rid of it, but I didn't have anyone to turn to and I'm afraid I wasn't thinking very clearly."

"Get rid of it?" he said hoarsely, appalled. The ice in his glass began to tinkle as his hand shook.

"Yes, I . . ."

He raised his hand to stop her from talking and moved back to his chair. When he'd first heard that she was pregnant he'd despised her, felt that she had taken some sort of revenge, outwitted him in some dark, female connivance that he couldn't unravel. He had never connected their afternoons of lust with her conception. But she must be telling the truth. She might lie to others, but she wouldn't lie to him, if only because he had convinced her that he could see through everything she did. Besides, she had nothing to gain by this confession.

"Well, it's too late to talk about that now. I'm already six months along."

His heart contracted. There was a clutching in his guts that was entirely separate from the frantic calculations of his brain. He knew intuitively that she was telling the truth. This child, his child. The long-abandoned dream of a son to follow after him. And this time he would mold the child successfully, without interference. He would correct all the mistakes he had made with Ricky. He would be young again.

"It won't affect you very much," she continued bitterly. "I'm the one that's pregnant, after all. There's nothing you can do about that."

"I will provide for it," he said, almost to himself.

"As a doting grandfather?"

"I will have to think about this . . ."

"But I thought you knew everything, Richard," she hissed.

"I said I will provide for the child."

"It may turn out to be the most expensive piece of ass you've ever had."

He came toward her swiftly, grabbing her by the arms, lifting her off the couch. "Shut up," he ordered. "Just shut up!" Part of her triumphed in seeing him lose control and show some emotion. She stared him down until his grip loosened, but when his hands went up to her neck, caressing it with hot, trembling fingers, she pulled in to him, burying her face in his chest.

"I tried to make it work with Ricky, but I couldn't. I know it sounds melodramatic, but I was so miserable I wanted to kill myself. Do you think I want to be here?" she cried in anguish. "I haven't anywhere else to go."

There was a noise from the back of the house. He dropped his hands, moving away from her and picking up his drink. Faustina, wrapped in a white candlewick robe, stepped into the light of the entrance hall.

"Miz Cunningham?" she said softly, pausing in the doorway. "Is that you?"

"It's me," Gaynor said stiffly. "I'd just come down for a glass of milk when Dad came in."

"Would you like me to fix you some cocoa? Or can I get you anything, Mr. Cunningham?"

"No, thank you, Faustina," Richard said brusquely. "I've had my nightcap."

"Sorry to disturb you," she murmured, still lingering.

"Not at all. I think it's time to turn in anyway."

He tossed off the rest of his drink, kissed Gaynor paternally on the top of the head, and walked quickly into the hallway. "I'll talk to you tomorrow, Gaynor. I think you should try to get some rest." He mounted the stairs and Faustina drifted back into the shadows of the dining room. Gaynor lit another cigarette and stared into the darkness.

THE NEXT three months were the most miserable of her life. She was coddled by Etna and the servants, Ricky wrote to her almost daily, but Richard made a point of not being around. And despite her longing, it was a relief not to have to see him. The projected date of her delivery came and passed. She had been like a prisoner, counting off the days until her release, but now she was like an insane person, trapped and tortured with no hope of freedom. Then, one afternoon in early April, as she sat in a garden chair with Etna's mink coat draped around her shoulders and watched her mother-in-law potting iris bulbs, she felt the first spasm.

Etna fluttered around like a bird in a dust bath, ordering Faustina to fetch the overnight bag and call the hospital. Jackson, speechlessly efficient, assisted her to the Buick. He chauffeured her to the hospital, careening through stop lights, frantically honking the horn when they were stuck in traffic, while Etna, her battered garden hat still on her head, squeezed her hands and prayed.

Her most vivid memory of the birth was the exit sign over the door of the delivery room. The blurred figures in white ordered her to push, to breathe, to relax, to push again. She tried to follow their commands, but the pain was so great she couldn't concentrate. A doctor she had never seen before was summoned because she wasn't "progressing." He snapped on his rubber gloves and ordered a spinal block. Behind his masked face she could see the exit sign. When he asked for the forceps, she lunged forward, straining to get off the table. A fiercely impatient expression came into his eyes. He moved over her, blotting out the sign. Hands forced her backwards. No exit.

"POOR LITTLE TYKE, had a rough time getting out," the figure that was stroking her head said.

"Am I still alive?"

"Used up all of his glucose. They've put him in the incubator. He's only six pounds twelve ounces—that's small for full term, but he's going to be okay."

"Am I still alive?"

The nurse removed her hand and looked at the chalky face. Its eyes searched the room, then drooped shut. She'd been told this one had been a real lulu—caused a lot of trouble in delivery. That was always the way with these rich bitches. They never helped with the labor. They were always more concerned with themselves than with the baby.

"If you can hear me, then I guess you're alive, aren't you, Mrs. Cunningham?"

"Yes," Gaynor whispered, trying to grasp the logic of what had just been said. "But is he here?"

"Your husband's flight arrived hours ago. You were in labor for a long time, you know. He's in the waiting room."

"No . . . I mean . . . is he here?"

The nurse turned on her heel and left the room.

IT WAS ANOTHER three days before she was allowed to leave the hospital. The baby was put in her arms. Ricky steadied her elbow and helped her to the car. She got in gingerly, her whole body feeling like one big bruise. Now that the baby was out of her body, it wasn't much different from the way she had imagined it while it was inside. It was a sallow little lump. Its eyes were shut and the scars of the forceps were livid on its forehead, ugly as the mark of Cain.

"Did oo have a tewwible time, sweet thing?" Etna cooed, tucking the blanket around the hairless skull.

Gaynor handed the baby to her and slumped back. Ricky put his arm around her and kissed her cheek as Jackson turned around and beamed. "Sure is goin' to be strange, havin' a baby 'round the house. There he be: Richard the Third."

"Not Richard the Third, Jackson. That's a monster character out of Shakespeare," Ricky laughed. "He's to be called Joseph, after Etna's father."

"Joseph. That's from the Bible," Jackson nodded sagely, as he pulled away from the curb. "Joseph means 'the Lord shall add to me another son.' Ol' Jacob said that. See, he'd just about given up, but when he saw that li'l baby, he said 'and the Lord shall add to me another son' and that li'l boy got to be his very favorite child."

Gaynor retreated to her bedroom as soon as they got back to the house. Faustina gave Joey his formula, carried him into the bedroom, placed him in the antique bassinette, and closed the door. Gaynor looked at the ugly little face, and then squeezed her hands on her still puffy belly. At last it was over. She flung herself onto the chaise longue and opened a pack of cigarettes, glad to be away from Etna's baby talk and Ricky's solicitude. When she heard him come in, she pretended to be sleeping.

"Darling," he whispered with the lingering soft tones that real affection gives to the word, "why don't you let me help you to bed."

"Did Richard come home yet?"

"No. Mother talked to him right after dinner. He's still in Los Angeles. He sends his love to you. Hey, you shouldn't be smoking when you're about to fall asleep."

As he tried to take her hand, she grunted, her eyes flickering open, and reached out for the smoldering cigarette. He was always hovering over her like some benign vampire. The very fact that she had to move her legs aside to make room for him irritated her.

"Don't feel bad, honey," he soothed, mistaking her annoyance for disappointment. "Richard will be back late tonight. You know he never pays much attention to anything but himself and his deals. Hey, I forgot to tell you Betty called. She says to congratulate you and tell you that she's going to throw a big christening party once we get back home."

"The baby should be christened here. Think how disappointed Etna would be."

"I absolutely have to get back tomorrow. Spring finals aren't too far away and I had a helluva time getting off as it is. I guess you won't be well enough to go back with me. You can follow along next week."

"I can't go back there, Ricky. I was just miserable there."

"But we have the baby now."

"That would only make it worse. You don't seem to understand: being in that crummy little apartment makes me physically ill. Besides, the doctors say Joey needs special attention."

"My God, Princeton isn't the outback. There are fine doctors there too."

"But I don't know how to handle a baby. Faustina can take care of him here."

"You'll learn how to take care of him. Caroline's doing just fine. She'll help you and . . ."

"Christ! Don't wish that on me."

". . . and there are plenty of books on child care."

"Do you think everything comes out of a book?" she snapped, stubbing out the cigarette.

"But I've missed you so. It's been hell going to bed alone, worrying about you and the baby. I want what's best for Joey too, but don't you see how unnatural it would be for us to be apart at a time like this?"

"So now my feelings are unnatural?"

"I didn't mean that." He shifted around, ran his hand over his face, and tried to think of a more reasonable approach. "Apart from the expense of traveling, you know how I feel about being in this house. I have obligations at school. I can't keep coming back here to visit you. And we've been apart for most of our married life. You've just got to come back to Princeton with me."

"Are you ordering me about?"

"Why are you twisting things like that? Goddamn it, you're my wife. I want you with me."

"I'd hoped my first night at home would be peaceful," she cried with agonized patience. "I don't feel well enough to argue. I'd think that after all I've been through, you wouldn't want to push me into any decisions."

She pulled away from him and flounced over to the bed. As he watched her he felt no anger, just the despairing acceptance of the great gulf between them. No matter how much he denied, rationalized or excused her behavior, he had to admit that he didn't understand her. He had wanted to believe that making love to her, going through the marriage ceremony, had joined them inexorably. He had trusted that the workings of her mind would become as accessible to him as the tiny black mole near her right hipbone. But he had been hopelessly naive. He didn't know her at all. He couldn't know her because she wouldn't open up to him. And she wouldn't open up to him because—and now his consciousness reeled away from the painful truth—she didn't really love him.

He turned out the light and undressed, looking down at the tiny, lost figure in the bassinette for a long time before he crawled in beside her. He listened to her breathing, his hand poised, yet afraid to touch her.

Please turn to me. Or let me reach out to you. I know you've been unhappy, but we can ease each other's hurts. This should be a happy time for us. I know I'm always thinking "should," but we should be happy now. We should. Bend to me, darling. Please.

RICHARD WAS ALREADY sitting at the table sipping his morning coffee and reading the newspaper when Ricky came down to breakfast.

"Well, where's the boy?" Richard asked, without greeting him.

"Gaynor will bring him down in a minute."

"Heard she had a pretty rough time of it."

"Yes." *You actually had a ring of concern in your voice. Is it possible that you're human enough to be concerned? Could you mellow into an indulgent grandfather? Get down on the floor and play with trains? Not likely.*

"So what are your plans? Are you staying, or do you have to get back to school?"

"Even in academia, we do have a schedule. I'm leaving this afternoon."

"And Gaynor and the baby?"

"She's still feeling a bit rocky and the doctors want to see Joey again. So I guess they'll stay on for awhile."

"Of course," Richard said offhandedly.

CHAPTER

XIII

DEAR SHEILA:

Sorry I've been so long answering your letter. With all the packing
I've been running around like a chicken with its head cut off. The
children and I are finally on our way to California. After last winter
in Ohio, I expect that it will be a change for the better. The girls
loved the snow, but I was nearly round the bend having to keep
them inside so much of the time—as far as I'm concerned, snow
belongs on Christmas cards . . .

Dawn steadied the notebook on her lap, glanced across the compartment at the sleeping children, and then looked out the window
at the flat Arizona landscape. Her eyes felt gritty as she watched the
first bright rays of pink and gold illuminate the barren plains. She had
slept very little the night before—Nita had been cranky and Faye was
so excited about the adventure of sleeping on a train that she had
jabbered and asked questions long after Dawn had turned out the
light. Now, as the train clacked along, she felt too anxious and tired
to really enjoy the spectacle of a desert sunrise.

I'm not altogether happy about the move. I've been shunted
about so much that I'd just like to have someone stamp me and send
me through the post. As you know, I'd been hoping Zac would get
out of the Navy . . .

He had come home the week after Christmas, thrown his coat and hat on the sofa, and walked straight to the refrigerator for a bottle of beer without saying hello to her. Even before she'd looked at his face, she could tell something was bothering him. But she had learned that if she asked how he was feeling or what was wrong, he would probably accuse her of interrogating him. She hoisted Nita up from the kitchen floor and carried her to the playpen in the living room. Then she gave Faye a plastic bag of white oleomargarine and told her to sit by the radio and knead the button of dye that would make the margarine turn yellow. She turned down the flame under the pots, pulled a chair up to the kitchen table, and poured some of Zac's beer into a glass.

"I still miss Aussie beer."

"This is just as good," he replied.

"You've said yourself that it isn't."

Off on the wrong foot: she shouldn't correct him. "Did you see the snowman out on the street? Mr. DeLongini helped Faye to make it. Poor old chap looks so frail I'd think a strong wind could knock him down, but he insisted on staying out there and playing with her. I don't know how he puts up with these winters at his age. He told me he'd always thought he'd go back to Italy when he got old, but since the war that's impossible."

"Then I guess his pal Mussolini shouldn't have started the war."

"Oh, for Pete's sake, Zac, Mussolini wasn't his pal. Vittorio hasn't been in Italy in sixty years. How long do you have to live in this country before people stop thinking of you as a foreigner?"

"Long enough to stop criticizing it."

"I wasn't criticizing it. But it's a democracy, isn't it? People are allowed to criticize."

"A person's country is like their family; it's okay to criticize it if you're part of it, but it's a different thing with outsiders. Hey, I didn't mean anything about him personally," he said, vaguely aware that he was manufacturing antagonism because he had unpleasant news to tell her. He got up from the table, hitched up his pants, and started to pace back and forth. "I know he's a nice old guy."

"There was a sale on pot roast, so I'm fixing that tonight. With lima beans. I know you like lima beans." She felt a bit simpleminded reading off the dinner menu, but the storm warnings were up, and it seemed the most harmless thing to say.

"Fine." Pot roasts, sales, neighbors, snowmen—all the trappings of domesticity. Everything seemed to get buried under that avalanche of trivia. But that was married life. Some guys even seemed to like it. It suffocated him. Made him itchy and tense. No matter how fondly he thought of her and the kids when he was away, as soon as he hit the door and saw the litter of toys, he felt as trapped as he'd been in his boyhood when Suds had kept him indoors reading religious tracts when he'd wanted to be chasing down the alleys with the other boys. He knew now that he shouldn't have asked her to marry him. But being wounded had given him a vulnerability that he was afraid to express to anyone. And she had been so kind and pretty and decent, making him wish for a life of order and peace. He just hadn't thought ahead to the years of dentist's bills, crying kids, daily responsibility. Hadn't realized that she would always be there asking for his attention in that quiet, expectant way that was worse than any outright demand.

He looks like a bloody caged lion, pacing back and forth like that, she thought as she straightened the silverware and waited for him to speak. Back and forth, back and forth, from the sink to the refrigerator. He'd wear a path in the linoleum if he didn't settle down soon.

He stopped and cleared his throat. "I might as well tell you," he said in that brusque, forced lower register that men used to one another when they wanted to sound businesslike.

"Tell me what?" Why couldn't he just talk to her instead of using that phony, tone of voice?

"I re-enlisted last month. My orders came through today. We'll be going to San Diego."

"San Diego?" she said blankly, trying to picture a map. "Isn't that in California?"

"That's where it used to be so I guess that's where it still is."

"But Zac . . . !"

"I'm leaving next week. You and the kids can follow soon as I find a place. It might take me a couple of months."

"Why didn't you tell me? You'd agreed to discuss it before you made a decision."

"I did discuss it. With my superior officer."

"You don't live with your bloody superior officer, do you? Why didn't you talk to me about it?"

"I've shipped over. That's that. I don't want any backtalk about it."

"For how long?"

185

"Five years."

"How could you do that? You'll be over forty by then. It'll be even harder for you to find anything. And there must be so many things you . . ."

"You don't know what's out there. I do."

"Why are you talking to me as though I were a first-class seaman? I'm your *wife*! Don't you think I have any right to be part of these decisions? They affect my life. They affect the children's lives."

"You're not bringing home the bacon, are you? Listen," he went on after a pause, feeling guilty that he'd been so sharp with her but afraid that if he apologized or voiced his own confusion about the decision, he would loose all authority, "I don't want to fight about it. I have looked around, Dawn. There's nothing I can do. Where the hell am I going to fit into a peacetime economy? All I know about is weapons and how to deal with men. And there's nothing for you to worry about. They're gonna be putting the fleet into mothballs, and I'll only be going out on maneuvers once in a while . . ."

She sat perfectly still, vaguely aware that he was still talking. His words had no more meaning than the hiss of the pressure cooker. He had made his decision. She would be moved again as though she were a piece of furniture and someone had walked in and stamped a new address on her back. She wouldn't see the tomato plants come up in the back of the shop next summer. Wouldn't have Mr. DeLongini to talk to. Wouldn't be able to enroll Faye in the school she had already visited. She would be moved to another place where she wouldn't know a single soul.

A rush of steam burst from the pressure cooker. Nita was screaming. As Dawn jumped up, reaching toward the stove to shut off the gas, the top of the cooker flew off, sending a geyser of boiling steam onto her arm. She yelped in pain, threw a dishcloth on her scalded flesh, pushed Zac aside and ran into the living room. Nita was sprawled on the floor beside the playpen, a cut on her head, bawling hysterically. Faye was backing off, whimpering, "I didn't mean to hurt her, Mummy. I tried to help her out and she just dropped."

"I've told you time and time again not to lift her, haven't I? Haven't I?" she shrieked. "Why don't you listen to me! Why doesn't anyone listen to me? Am I invisible or something?"

Faye wiped her nose on her sleeve and burst into tears. Dawn picked the baby up and rocked her back and forth, trying to calm her so that she could get a better look at the cut. Faye's weeping reached a new crescendo, her eyes fixed on her mother accusingly. Dawn was instantly contrite. It was horribly unfair that she should take out her frustrations with Zac on the child. She reached over and tried to pull Faye to her, but she wrenched away and ran into the bedroom.

"Hey, Dawn . . . Dawn . . ." Zac knelt beside her imploringly. As he took her by the arm and tried to turn her to him, his fingers dug into her scalded flesh. She jerked away, her lips pulling back over her teeth in a painful grimace. "I'm sorry, Aussie, I didn't mean . . ." The tears welled in her eyes and a harsh, gasping sound came from her throat. He stood up, staring helplessly, then pushed past her and grabbed his coat.

"Goddamn it. I can't stand all this crying! All this goddamn noise! I'm going out."

"Good. Go out. Leave!" she screamed after him. "Find another bloody war to fight. That's all you men are good for anyway."

. . . I suppose the worst thing about Zac's being in the military, apart from the fact that he's gone so much of the time, is our being uprooted from family and friends. I can't express myself well in a letter, Sheila, but how I'd love to sit down, share a cuppa and have a real talk with you . . .

The suitcases and bundles were stacked by the door. Faye, dressed in her spring coat, a white hat with daisies and her new pair of white gloves, watched out the unadorned front window for Suds and Homer to arrive. Dawn stood near the big commercial refrigerator in the bare kitchen and looked at Mr. DeLongini, who sat on the last rickety chair holding Nita and wiping his eyes with his stained pocket, handkerchief.

"Don't feela so sad, Dawn. I been telling you they gonna tear down alla the buildings here anyway. My sister in California, she write me come live with her. My nephew's in the garbage transport business there and he's making a lotta money. Who knows? Maybe I go. Maybe I even see you in California. It'sa warm there. Sun alla the time. You gonna like it better. You'll see."

"I'm going to miss you. The children will miss you too. You're a grandfather to them. Oh, Mr. DeLongini, I miss my family so much."

"Calla me Vittorio. How many times I tell you? You maka me feel like I'm a headstone in a cemetery already."

"I've thought of trying to go back home. You know that. But how can I go back? In the first place I haven't any money. I'm not equipped for any sort of work."

"Whatta you mean? You work alla the time like a little donkey. You're a mamma. Whatta you talkin' about?"

"But I'm not even a good mother lately. I've been so nervous. I yell at Faye all the time, and I can't really explain to her why I'm so upset. I know she resents me. She thinks somehow Zac went away because he couldn't get along with me."

"Don't you worry. She's a strong little girl, like her mamma. Maybe she have to grow up to understand, but she will understand. You be pappa and mamma both. It'sa hard for you. But you remember, you don't do her no harm. It's all right. The song a mother sings in the cradle is heard ina the coffin. How you think I keep goin' so long? 'Cause I remember whata my mamma tell me: Life is sweet. I'ma never gonna give up. You won't either."

"I know our mothers influence our lives. That's why I feel so responsible. But it isn't always for the good. Look at Zac. Sometimes, when I just ask him a question, he gets so angry. I think he sees his mother standing in front of him instead of me."

"You don't have to say. I'ma nosy neighbor, you know. But I ask you now: do you wanna leave him? Do you love him?"

"Sometimes no," she said after thinking for a long time. "Then other times—oh, I look at him and see how lonely he really must be. But it's a loneliness I can't hope to comfort. I know that now. I used to think I could make the difference. Now I know I can't. It's very hard to love someone when you realize that you can't really make any difference."

"Mummy, they're here. Can we go to California now?" Faye cried from the other room.

The bell over the front door jingled. Mr. DeLongini got up, handed Nita to Dawn, and brushed off his suit. "Don't let her make you nervous," he whispered.

Suds marched through to the kitchen with Homer in tow. She stopped and stared at Dawn and Mr. DeLongini with as much shock as if she'd found them in bed together.

"I hope you're all ready to leave, Dawn. We have a long drive and my back has been bothering me today."

"We're all ready, Suds. Mr. and Mrs. Mueller, this is our friend Mr. DeLongini."

Vittorio blew his nose, stuffed his handkerchief into his suit pocket, and bowed. Suds looked at him as though he were a specimen of some colorful but possibly poisonous insect, then turned her attention to Faye.

"I don't see why you've got that child dressed up like a doll. Those white gloves will just get filthy on the train."

"She's looking like a little daisy," Mr. Delongini said, putting his arm around her.

"We'd better get organized," Suds cut in, " 'the way of the sluggard is as though hedged by thorns.' "

"If you wouldn't mind, I'd just like a minute to say goodbye to Mr. DeLongini."

"But we've got to get going. I read in this morning's paper that there was a terrible accident right near the train station—a whole family just had their earthly bodies mangled beyond repair and . . ."

"In private, please. I'll be right with you."

"Well!" Suds whined with martyred dignity, backing into the living room, "I guess Homer will just start loading the car. I don't see how you've managed to accumulate all this stuff in the time you've been here, Dawn. Why, I've lived in my house for over twenty years and . . ."

Dawn swung the kitchen door closed, blocking off the stream of complaints, and turned to Vittorio. He put his arm around her, reached into his breast pocket, and took out a little gold necklace.

"Non piangeri, cara. Non piangeri," he cautioned, fastening the locket around her neck. "This is remembrance of me. Stop now, otherwise you maka old man lose dignity and cry too."

"Thank you. Thank you for everything. You know I'll miss you."

"Don't have to say what I know, Dawn," he said softly, taking her chin in his hands. "Such pleasure I have from you and the babies. Such pleasure. And good for you too—I teach you how to make the ravioli, remember?"

"Are you coming or not?" Suds yelled through the door.

Dawn sucked in her breath.

"Lika the song says, every cloud has a silver lining," Vittorio winked. "At least you won't have to put up with the *biggota* anymore." She shook with silent laughter as they hugged each other.

. . . So Zac has found us a place to live. It isn't exactly a dream house. In fact, it's a Quonset hut on the Navy base, so I don't know what to expect. Still, a little elbow grease ought to make it livable.

CHAPTER

XIV

"SHEILA, HONEY, you'd better put that letter away. It's ten after three and that gang is gonna be landin' on us any minute," Della Mae shouted from behind the grill.

Sheila read the last line of the letter: "Hope the baby clothes I sent for Spencer fit. I'll write to you as soon as I know my address and phone number. Love, Dawn." She stuffed it into her apron pocket, tucked a strand of hair underneath her hairnet, and started to shovel ice into the row of Coke glasses. The half-hour respite between the lunch crowd and the gang of teenagers who came in after school was over. She didn't know which group she thought was worse. The lunchtime customers were mostly working men, transients and truckers. They said little, even to each other, and usually left tips. But sometimes the sight of them, munching their hamburgers, picking their teeth, sopping up the thick flour gravy Della Mae smeared on the daily special (be it fried chicken, pork chops or ham), made Sheila feel queasy. The afternoon crowd of bobbysoxers was rowdy. They blew the paper off their straws, danced around the tables, and yelled to each other over the constant blare of the jukebox. And they rarely left tips. When she'd first started working at Della Mae's the teenage boys had tried to flirt with her until Della Mae told them that Sheila was a married woman with a baby. Now they called her Mrs. Hickock and made her feel as old as God. Still, she liked Della Mae and could usually get through the day without too much trouble. But today had been an exception.

In the first place she hadn't had enough sleep. Spencer was now sleeping through the night, but this morning he had started crying before the alarm went off. She'd dragged herself out of bed and picked him up, afraid that his whimpering would wake Ma. Ma slept down the hall, but her ears, trained over a lifetime of maternity, could detect the slightest sound from Spencer's crib. Sheila lugged him back to the big bed, but he squirmed and gurgled so much that Billy woke up. Billy played with the baby while she went into the kitchen to start breakfast. Just as she was about to put the eggs and grits on the table, Spencer dozed off, and Billy, checking the clock, said that they could probably go back to bed for twenty minutes. She didn't really like to make love when there was a time limit, but when Billy looked at her with those sleepy green eyes and traced the outline of her mouth with his fingertips, she hurried into the little bathroom and put on her diaphragm. At least she had an indoor toilet and a bath now, even if it did mean going to work to help pay the bills. And Billy had never complained about moving down from the hills, though she knew that he missed them terribly.

As she looked at her reflection, puffy-eyed and straggly-haired, she wondered why Billy should want to make love to her. She'd planned to wash and set her hair this morning, but there wouldn't be enough time. Anything she did, even down to a five-minute respite to shave her legs, had to be worked out on a basis of priorities. Now the priority was twenty minutes in bed, though she scarcely had the energy or inclination for sex. It wasn't that she didn't want him as much as she always had. It was just that there was so little romance or sense of freedom in it anymore.

After they'd made love—and by some magic it had been enjoyable —she'd knocked on Ma's door to tell her that they were leaving. Then she had taken Billy to the factory, stopped off to do the grocery shopping, and helped Ma straighten up the house. She had ironed her apron and driven to work at Della Mae's "Honest Home Cooking." She'd sliced pies, mashed potatoes, and set tables until the regulars started to arrive. In the midst of the lunchtime pandemonium, a heavy-set stranger, his hair slicked back with Brylcreem, had taken a booth and pounded on the table for service. She'd rushed over and stood, pencil poised, to take his order. As he leered at her and fanned himself with the menu, she noticed the grime underneath his fingernails. He looked her up and down, and then drawled, "Ah'd like a breast and a couple of thighs. Now, come to think of it, ah'd like the whole young chicken." A few of the men who'd overheard the remark snickered. Several turned away in embarrassment. She blushed to the roots of her hair, hurried to the kitchen, picked up someone else's order of fried chicken, and plopped it down in front of him without looking at him. When he'd gone she stood staring at the dirty plate and the fifteen-cent tip beside it. If her father could see her now! Suffering the indignity of such a crass proposition . . . "Hey, Sheila, how's about another tad o' cream on this here pie?" another customer called out. She pocketed the coins.

After lunch, as she sat in the washroom that reeked of ammonia and hamburger grease, transferring her tips to her purse, she looked at the handful of coins and tried to figure out which ones the man had left. She selected a nickle and dime and flushed them down the toilet. Even as she did it, she knew that it was a ridiculous gesture. But, she thought as she washed her hands, most of the things people went through to protect their dignity were equally ridiculous.

She slipped her swollen feet back into her loafers as the first group of high-school kids came through the doors. It was hard not to feel self-pity as she saw the girls waltzing in wearing new springtime dresses, laughing about dates and dances. She was only a couple of years and a lifetime of experience away from them. They tossed their books onto the tables and eyed the door until the boys came in. Then they made a beeline for the jukebox. She didn't have to guess what button they were going to push—the same crazy lyrics of the hit songs went round and round in her brain as though she were a hamster in a wheel.

> Open the door, Richard,
> Open the door and let me in,
> Open the door, Richard,
> Richard why don't you open that door?

"Two cheeseburgers, an order of fries with lotsa ketchup, two lemon and one cherry Coke with losta ice," the skinny, effeminate boy who was the resident comedian called out as he grabbed one of the girls and twirled her around.

"Ah tolt you kids this place ain't licensed fer dancin'," Della Mae yelled through the opening that separated the grill from the fountain. "If'n y'all can't find somethin' else to play 'cept that damned silly song ah'm gonna yank the plug on that there machine."

"Oh, Della Mae, how come yer so mean 'bout everythin'?" one of the more attractive boys who was already testing his charm with the ladies called back. "You know the only reason I come in here is 'cause you remind me of Jane Russell, and I got a terrible crush on you."

Della Mae looked every bit of her fifty years. Her only resemblance to Jane Russell was a very large and now pendulous bosom that, she'd confided to Sheila, made it difficult for her to sleep on her stomach. She yelled back good-naturedly that she didn't want any more of his sass, and threw the burgers on the grill, whistling along with the jukebox.

"I jest think it's disgusting the way you boys carry on 'bout Jane Russell," one of the girls said as Sheila put the Cokes down on the table. "My mamma says that it jest goes to show that the country is goin' downhill when there's no respect for ladies anymore."

"I respect her. Believe me, I respect her," the boy said, rolling his eyes. "Not your mamma—Jane Russell. You know I spent 'bout all my allowance seeing that movie. I've seen it four times now."

"You oughta be 'shamed of yerself. The pastor at our church says that movie oughta be banned. I sure know that I won't be seen goin' to the Paradise while that's still on."

"Whatcha gonna do? Sneak in?"

"Well, what's it all about anyway?"

The boys poked each other and guffawed while the girl's friend put her arm around her and whispered into her ear.

"You think that's a hot one? Wait'll next week. I seen previews fer it the other night. It's called *Duel in the Sun*."

"You know what this cousin of mine who lives in California wrote me? They got a new thing there called the drive-in movies. You jest drive inta this field or somethin', and they have a big ol' screen up front with li'l boxes that you put on yer car so's you can hear the sound. Don't even have to get out of yer car. I sure wisht they had somethin' like that 'round here."

"Are you kiddin'? They never have anythin' good 'round here. That's why I'm trying to talk my daddy into sendin' me to college up to Washington."

"I'm goin' to Richmond myself. Soon's I graduate you watch my dust."

"Sez who? Your mamma won't let you stay out later'n eleven o'clock."

"Sez me. Mrs. Hickock, did they have movies and all where you come from?"

"Certainly. I used to go to the movies all the time. Except we called them the pictures or the cinema . . ."

"The cinema? That's what my granddaddy calls 'em."

". . . and in the summertime, we even had open-air pictures. No cars, of course. You took a blanket in case it got chilly and there were canvas chairs set out on the lawn. The boy who took you would usually buy you a box of chocolates and . . ."

"Sheila, pick up on those burgers," Della Mae bellowed.

She rushed back to the counter as another group of kids pushed through the door.

"Hey, about this movie I was tellin' you about—*Duel in the Sun*," the comedian went on, "they won't even let anyone underage in 'cause there's this scene were Jennifer Jones goes fer a swim and this guy takes her clothes."

"Yer pullin' m' leg."

"No. Honest. There's pictures of it in *Silver Screen*. Wait up a minute and I'll show y'."

He dashed over to the magazine rack and came back, riffling through the pages of the movie magazine. Della Mae was out from behind the grill in a shot, wiping her hands on the spattered apron and reaching for the magazine.

"This ain't buying the baby a new dress or payin' fer the one she's got on," she said sharply. "I'm runnin' a business here, not a library. Folks don't wanna be buyin' magazines when y'all have mussed up the pages."

The table quieted down as she marched over to the rack, narrowed her eyes, and looked at the picture. "Oughta be called *Drool in the Sun* from what all I can see." Howls of laughter broke out. The kids started to shout out their orders again. Sheila fixed two banana splits and carried them over to a table where two girls were sitting with their heads together, whispering.

"So he pulls out this big ol' orchid corsage see, but then he asks me if he can pin it on me. I almost died! 'Cause I'd let you talk me into wearin' those falsies and I jest knew that he knew and he knew that I knew . . . oops, thank you, Mrs. Hickock."

She hurried to the back booth where the lovebirds always sat, holding hands and looking into each other's eyes, oblivious to the racket around them. Waiting to take the order, she watched the boy turn the girl's hand over, touching her fingertips as though they were fragile and might break.

The girl that I marry will have to be
As soft and as pink as a nursery

"That's our song," the girl smiled up at her.

"Two Cokes, please."

What if she gets in trouble? Sheila thought as she scooped the ice into the glasses. Then, in amazement, *Oh God, I'm starting to think like my mother.*

At five-fifteen Della Mae ordered the stragglers to go home to their parents. Sheila closed the door after them, slipped her shoes off her sweaty feet, and checked her orders against the money she had put in the cash register: seven sundaes, two banana splits, four sodas, six hamburgers, eight orders of fries, one coffee (that must be the sophisticate who was heading for Washington), and twenty-one Cokes. As she counted out her two dollars and eleven cents worth of tips she sang absentmindedly:

> A doll I can carry,
> The girl that I marry,
> Must be.

"That song's even sillier than the other one," Della Mae laughed as she dipped the glasses into the rinse water. "Only time my husband carried me was the first time he took me to the hayloft. Then ah carried him on m' back fer the next thirty years. Oh, fergot to tell ya, Billy called and said you should pick him up an hour late 'cause that son-of-a-bitch foreman is makin' him work overtime."

"Did he say that? I mean, did he call him a . . . you know?"

"Sure. He's a plain-talkin' man."

"I wish he didn't have so much trouble with people at work."

"Hell, honey, least ways he's willin' to work. If ah'd married a man like that ah'd think ah'd died and gone to heaven. Y'all through with them receipts?"

"Yes, I'm finished," she said wearily.

"Okay, sugarpuss, see y' tomorra."

Sheila rolled her apron up in a ball and stuffed it into her purse, then pushed the screen door open and walked out onto the lot behind the restaurant. She climbed into the pickup and revved the motor. She and Billy had had a fine old time careening around town when he was teaching her to drive. She was so proud of herself when she got her license that she'd borrowed Della Mae's camera and had Billy take a picture of her sitting at the wheel, but the truck had looked so sorry that she'd decided against sending the picture to her parents.

She pulled out onto the main street wondering what to do with her hour of free time. The library was still open. She hadn't had any time to read since the last months of her pregnancy. She missed the romances that helped her leave her own troubles behind and enter into a world of hunting parties and balls, where beautifully dressed heroines contained throbbing passion in heaving bosoms and protected their virtue until rich and brooding heroes asked for their hand and whisked them off to mansions where, presumably, they lived happily ever after. She even missed the textbooks that Dr. Helen recommended. But the last time she'd checked out books from the library they'd sat unopened on the bureau until they were past due. If she went to the library, she'd see those stacks and stacks of books she'd never have time to read and just feel frustrated and ignorant.

The pickup seemed to move of its own accord into the older residential section of town. If she saw Dr. Helen's car parked in the driveway, she would pay her a call. Even if Helen wasn't home, it would be pleasant to drive along the graceful, tree-lined street. The house she had talked Billy and Ma into renting was an improvement over the shack in the hills, but it was still crowded and jerrybuilt, with doors and windows that wouldn't shut properly and a smell of rot in the wood that no amount of cleaning seemed to alleviate. Where the lawn should have been there was only hard-packed reddish clay that wouldn't support the growth of anything but a few tenacious weeds. Some of the neighbors used their yards as automobile graveyards. On Saturday nights the men would congregate around the hulks of dismembered Fords and Chevies, drink their beer and moonshine, and relive the adventures they'd had before the transmission dropped or the crank shaft gave up the ghost. During the day, slews of grimy-faced children played house amid the wreckage.

But on this street the lawns and the cars were well cared for. The spring breeze rustled through overhanging trees, making a protective shushing sound broken only by the whir of a lawn mower and the notes of a simplified Chopin waltz. Her imagination took her behind the walls of the comfortable houses to see china plates on lace tablecloths, pastel-colored nurseries, vanities lined with jars and bottles of perfume. She had scaled down her expectations a great deal during the past year, yet even this modest version of domestic bliss seemed impossibly remote. But some women had this, and more. According to Mavis's reports in the Kangaroo Courier, Gaynor Cunningham was just like those heroines in the novels: she'd married a man who had given her a mansion. Strange to think that they'd once been in the same circumstances—women who'd taken a chance on love and had left their past behind them—yet the results of their gamble had turned out so differently. And Dawn Mueller. She hadn't wanted much at all, just a home where she could be safe and loved. Even that seemed to be denied her. It didn't seem to matter much whether one had grandiose or modest dreams, because a woman's destiny was so bound up with that of the man she married.

She was so engrossed in her thoughts that she passed Dr. Helen's house and had to back up. The blue sedan was in the driveway. She pulled up behind it, walked to the open back door, and called out to announce herself.

"Come on in. I'm in my study," the deep voice called out.

Sheila walked through the kitchen. The neat countertops, frilly yellow curtains and decals of fruit plastered on the cabinets marked this as the territory of Dr. Helen's housekeeper. Her own study was very different: piles of books spilled over from the shelves that lined the walls, the furniture invited you to put up your feet, and the desk was littered with ashtrays, specimens of rock and lichen, a Thermos of black coffee, snapshots of children and grandchildren, and a gold-framed wedding photo.

"Did she seem to be resting comfortably?" Dr. Helen asked into the phone as she welcomed Sheila with her eyes, swept a heap of medical journals and newspapers from the chair near the desk, and motioned her to sit down. "I'm talking to the hospital, be with you in a minute," she whispered, crooking the mouthpiece between her ear and shoulder and reaching for a cigarette. "Uh-huh," she returned to the caller, "then I think we might cut back on her medication . . ."

Sheila studied the wedding photo. She had seen it before, but it always captivated her. Here was Helen, thirty years younger and almost as many pounds lighter, dressed in white satin, seated in the traditional pose that had gone out of vogue long before the picture was taken. She looked almost tiny beside the tall young man with bushy eyebrows and receding hairline who was standing behind her holding the back of her chair. Her eyes had that questioning, almost fierce expression that brought a premature wrinkle to the middle of the brow. Her chin was thrust forward as though balancing an invisible object on its tip. Her thick, dark brown hair was cut in a stylish bob. Sheila looked from the image of the handsome young woman to the stocky nervous figure standing next to her. The wrinkle in the forehead was a permanent crease now, surrounded by countless smaller lines. The assertive chin had a few folds of flesh beneath it. The hair was still thick, but gray. It must be very strange to feel yourself getting old. Were you the same inside, but totally different outside?

"That's right. Now what about the five-year-old I admitted this afternoon?" Helen demanded, ignoring the cigarette smoldering in the ashtray and reaching for another. "Uh-huh. All right . . ."

Since she and Dr. Helen had expanded their relationship from doctor/patient, Sheila had learned a good deal about Helen's early married life. Helen had met Morris Abromovitz at a political rally when they were both students at the university. They had become "comrades"—Sheila supposed that meant lovers—and when Helen had discovered, during her first year of medical school, that she was pregnant, Morris had insisted on marrying her. With the help of her grandmother, who was a suffragette, they had managed to continue their separate studies through the birth of three children. Morris had finished his Ph.D. in botany and apparently knew as much about plant reproduction as Helen knew about the human variety. Helen had set up a limited practice in their New York apartment. Morris had become a professor. During the war he had worked for the government. But with the children grown and the war coming to an end, they had seized the opportunity to put their youthful radicalism into practice. Over the objections of their children, Morris had accepted a professorship at Virginia Polytechnic Institute so that Helen could set up her birth control and child care clinic. "I know my children thought we were crazy, but that's the thing about children," Helen had explained. "To them you're always the one with the toothbrush and the checkbook. They don't understand your dreams."

"So I'll drop by the hospital around seven," she was saying now. "Thanks. Goodbye." She dropped the receiver back into the cradle, settled herself into her chair and puffed on her cigarette.

"What a day! Sheila, my dear, you can't imagine. I had to have a five-year-old girl hospitalized. The kid's on the verge of pneumonia. When I asked the mother why she hadn't brought her in sooner, she told me she'd been rubbing the child's chest with skunk liniment.

Skunk liniment! I thought I was gong to burst a blood vessel. Then I had a fourteen-year-old girl who's already six months along and looks like a child herself. The father's only sixteen, she tells me. Not that it makes much difference, apparently he disappeared two months ago. Oh, if I had my way, every adolescent would have to take one class in sex education and another in economics."

"If you say that too loudly, the city fathers will want to tar and feather you."

"They'd have to hear me before they got their hackles up, and since they aren't about to listen . . ." She ran her hand through her hair, pulling it to its full length, then letting it go. "And the worst of it is that I gave absolutely no comfort to the mother with the skunk oil or to the pregnant girl. I get so impatient with people that I just bark and make them feel worse."

"That's nonsense. You help lots of people."

"But my bedside manner hasn't improved one iota. I'm as much of a klutz as I was during my internship. I remember the first time I had to examine a man. When I asked him to drop his pants he backed up as though I was going to rape him. Then I said something very smooth like 'Do you think I care, I've seen it before' . . . Coffee?"

"No, thanks," Sheila smiled, picturing a young Dr. Helen stalking a terrified patient protecting his crotch.

"Ah, I didn't mean to complain so much. So how are you?"

"Just . . ."

"Don't tell me, I can see. Chronically fatigued. Well, it's the young mother's disease. No known cure but cash and willing female relatives. So how's Ma?"

"She's well. I . . ."

"Didn't I tell you to get some surgical stockings while you're working at Della Mae's?"

"Yes, you did. But they're so ugly."

"Wait'll you see a varicose vein, then you'll know from ugly."

"Haven't seen any veins yet, but my feet are killing me. It's not really my feet, though. You wouldn't believe this chap who came in today. Big burly fellow who made the crudest remarks to me. Oh, I didn't know whether to throw a plate at his head or burst into tears."

"What did you do?"

"Neither," she answered miserably, twisting a strand of hair. "I flushed his fifteen-cent tip down the toilet."

"You're so impractical, Sheila. You should have thrown the plate at him and kept the tip." She laughed as she poured herself a cup of coffee, and then, noticing Sheila's wounded expression, reached across the desk and patted her hand.

"I didn't mean to be unsympathetic. I'm sorry that masher insulted you. I guess the only way to keep your spirit up is to keep telling yourself that this waitress job is only temporary. You have filled out your application for nursing school, haven't you?"

"No. It's still sitting on the bureau in the bedroom. That's where I file all my unfinished business. Every day I tell myself that I'll fill it out, but the days just seem to go by. I don't know how to catch up with them. I just sleep and eat and work. Sometimes I don't even have time to play with Spencer. I don't even wash my hair. How could I possibly have the energy to go to nursing school?"

"But you could handle it, I know you could. You'd make a first-class nurse. I watched you when you helped out at the clinic. You're intelligent, efficient and compassionate. And you have lots of that bedside manner I was talking about. That's a real talent, you know."

"But I hate to think about leaving Spencer. No decent mother would leave her baby."

"But you're away from home most of the day as it is. You trust Ma with him, don't you? The difference would be that you'd be studying for a career that would give you a better income and some self-respect."

"I just don't know where I'd get the money to go back to school," Sheila went on, knowing that she was voicing the same old objections, equally aware that Dr. Helen would have an answer for every one of them.

"You've told me that your father wanted you to go on in school. If you'd only write and ask, I'm sure he'd be willing to help you with some money."

"He felt that way before I was married. Even if I could persuade him to send me something—and I just don't know what that would do to Billy's pride—my mother would think it most peculiar. She thinks that when a girl gets married she should stay at home and take care of the house and the children. It's just not normal for a married woman to be starting out on a career that's going to take years of training."

"Your mother doesn't realize the circumstances of your life, does she?" Helen asked between sips of coffee. "Oh, I know all the reasons why you feel you can't tell her the truth, but isn't it foolish to let her judgment stand in your way?"

Not when she's been so right about so many things, Sheila thought. Why had she even brought all of this up? Helen was like a dog with a bone, especially when it came to urging people to take charge of their lives. She just didn't acknowledge the fact that the gap between desire and action was greater for most people than it was for her. She was encouraging, but she was also tiring.

"It's your life, isn't it? You cut the umbilical cord when you married Billy and left Australia," she persisted. "And you have started to take control of it. Why, I remember what a frightened little rabbit you were that first day I met you. Since then you've had a baby, moved, learned to drive, started to work."

"Yes. And I feel . . . tired. It would be three whole years before I'd become a nurse. I'd be the only girl in training who was married and had a baby. You see, Helen"—she bit her cuticle and wondered how best to explain herself—"you're exceptional. It isn't hard for you to be an outsider. You just barrel on through with all this amazing courage. But I'm ordinary. In my dreams I'm not ordinary, of course, and sometimes I do get little flashes of ideas that make me want to have courage. But I'm not Joan of Arc. I just don't have the strength for any of it. And three whole years . . ."

She felt she was on the verge of tears and groped in her purse for the wadded-up apron. Helen leaned back in her chair and looked out the window. Perhaps she was pushing the girl too hard. It was one of life's ironies that young people, who had so much real time before them, were cursed with an impatience that made them think three years was close to an eternity. She had been like that herself, though any references to her own struggles would probably just make Sheila feel worse.

Her eyes caught a plant growing in the windowbox and she recalled an evening early in her love affair with Morris. He had wanted to take her out for a walk, but she had sat, hunched over her desk, frantic that she would not be able to place well in the next day's exam. He'd kissed the back of her neck and tried to kid her along, but she'd exploded at him and he'd left the apartment. Later, after she'd sobbed her frustration into her notebook and blurred all of her notes, he'd reappeared, placed a budding azalea in front of her, and yelled, "Hurry! Hurry up and grow. Helen won't put up with you unless you grow overnight." Yes, she had felt all that youthful impatience. Even thirty years and the balance of Morris's more easy-going philosophy of life hadn't been able to mellow her much.

"I know three years seems like a long time, Sheila," she continued slowly. "I know you're feeling tired and overburdened. But you've told me yourself that Billy can't earn much money. You love him and you wouldn't think of leaving him. And then there's Spencer. So, like it or not, it's up to you. You don't picture yourself slinging hash at Della Mae's in another three years, do you?"

"I don't know," Sheila answered defiantly.

"On top of the financial problems, that would be a real waste of your talents. God gives us burdens. God also gives us shoulders. You fill out your application and write to your father. I'll drop a letter to the Radford School of Nursing and ask them to make an exception and admit you even though you're married. Because you *are* an exception, Sheila. You're not ordinary. None of God's creatures are ordinary."

"I didn't know you were so religious."

"Not so it shows, I hope."

Sheila shoved the apron back into her purse, squared her shoulders, and got up. "I'll have to think about it some more."

"Don't think about it too long," Helen warned, rising to her feet and putting an arm around her shoulders. "Knowing you, I probably shouldn't have tried to appeal to your reason. I should have reminded you of Rosalind Russell playing Sister Kenny."

"You're absolutely right. I do give myself the pip sometimes with all my woolgathering."

"Imagination is a beginning, isn't it?"

Driving through the twilight toward the factory, Sheila pictured herself, starched white cap perched on her head, walking briskly down a shiny hospital corridor on a mission of mercy. If she saw pain, she would know how to ease it. If a patient was frightened or cranky, she would have the power to soothe and comfort. Instead of letting her days slip by in a dreary round of eating, sleeping and counting tips, she would live intimately with the mysteries of life and death.

But three whole years of study? Why, she'd be twenty-five—a quarter of a century old—before she was ready to graduate. It was such a long time. Not only for her, but for Billy and Ma as well. It would mean more scrimping, less time with Spencer, continuing sacrifices. . . .

Billy was leaning next to the door marked "Employees Only" when she pulled up to the high wire fence that surrounded the factory. He reached down for his lunch pail, loping toward her with a slow, graceful gait. His shoulders were hunched. As he reached the pickup, she saw his eyes were troubled. "Sorry if I've kept you waiting, lovey. I popped in to see Helen and . . ." She slid across to the passenger side; but instead of climbing up into the cab, he stared into the sky.

"Christ, I might as well be in the slammer, much as I ever get to look at the sky anymore. See there, the first star's comin' out."

"Star light, star bright, first star I see tonight . . ."

"C'mon, girl. Save the baby talk fer Spencer."

"I can see you're in a chipper mood." She tried to jolly him as he crawled in beside her, draping his arms on the wheel and resting his head on his hands. "Bad day?"

"I swear to God, Sheila, that foreman's got it in fer me. It ain't that I don't do the work, either. Y' know I jest bust m' ass. I reckon he jest cain't stand to see another man that he cain't push around, an' the fact that the other guys like me jest makes it worse. He rides me all the time. Called me back on the line 'fore m' break was over, then tells me I'm gonna have to work overtime. Only reason he's over the resta us is 'cause he sat out the war. Reminds me of this sergeant use 't ride me all through basic. Christ, I hate it."

"I understand." She moved closer, rubbing the taut muscles of his neck. "It isn't the work one minds, it's the lack of respect."

"Y' said a mouthful there," he muttered, turning on the ignition and tearing out onto the road. "You have a rotten day too?"

"Mmm." Best not give him another reason to feel angry by mentioning the man with the dirty fingernails who'd insulted her.

After she'd helped Ma with the dishes and put Spencer to bed, she ran a comb through her hair, put on some lipstick, and asked Billy to drive her into town to buy an ice cream. "I'd think that'd be the last thing y'd hanker for after lookin' at it all day long," he grinned, hoisting up his pants. "But c'mon if y' want to." It always improved his mood when he was able to give her something she wanted.

They drove along in silence. Billy hummed one of the plaintive mountain tunes she often heard Ma sing around the house. She had no recollection of ever having heard her own mother sing. At first the relative lack of conversation among her, Billy and Ma at mealtimes had bothered her; now she enjoyed it, counted it as part of their intimacy. But this evening, she wasn't content to mull her own thoughts while enjoying Billy's physical presence. She was trying to think about the best way to approach the subject of nursing school.

"You know, I was talking to Helen today," she began slowly.

"Hey, did you see that car?" Billy jerked his neck forward, stared out of the windshield, and followed the shiny new Oldsmobile with his eyes. "Hell, I wonder who y'd have to know to get a car like that. Never seen anythin' like it 'round here before."

"Yes. It's a beaut," she nodded. "So we got to talking and Helen mentioned that she'd write a letter of recommendation for me if I decided to go to nursing school."

"Nursing school?"

"Yes. I've mentioned it before," she continued casually. "Remember when I was helping out at the clinic, I mentioned how much I thought I'd like to be a nurse."

"Sure, but . . ."

"I can't go on at Della Mae's forever, Billy."

"I never thought y' would. Soon's I get some more money . . ."

"It isn't just the money, Billy," she cut in, already having decided she would soft-pedal the financial aspect. "Helen thinks I'd be good at it, and I'd really like to give it a go."

"But how could you? I mean, that's fer girls who aren't married an' all. I don't think they'd want no married girl startin' in school."

"During the war lots of women who were married did all sorts of things."

"That was different. They prob'ly wouldn't let y' in now."

"I had very good marks in school. If we hadn't gotten married I probably would have gone to the university."

"But y' are married now. Y' have Spencer now."

"I know that," she said patiently. "But it's not as though I'm not already working."

"That's only in the afternoons, and it's only temporary." He said it with so much conviction that she knew he was getting defensive.

"But I'd like to do it, Billy. I *know* I'd like it. And I'd be good at it too. It would be something I could be proud of."

"I'm not sayin' y' wouldn't be able to handle it, but hell, they don't let y' go fer free. We'd never have the kinda cash it would take fer y' to go."

"I've already thought of that," she countered quickly. "I could write to Da and ask him. I'm sure he wouldn't mind. He would've blown a year's tuition money giving us a posh wedding if we'd let him.''

"But we didn't want to," he replied with increasing strength. "Y' do remember that, don't y'? They didn't want y' to marry me, and we said to each other that when we got married we were gonna make it on our own.''

"I know—I know we said that. But this is different. It's not for anything frivolous. It would be a loan.''

He pulled the truck up to the curb, but made no move to get out. He turned toward her. "I cain't let you do that, Sheila. Goin' to yer daddy like that. It's jest not right.''

She braced her feet against the floorboard and pushed her spine into the seat. She knew she'd be able to get over all of his objections save this one, for this was a point of pride, not of reason. She would have to move very delicately now, being careful not to wound. Only then could she make him understand that by advancing herself she did not mean to move away from him.

"Billy, don't think about how we feel as somebody's children; because I agree with you: we aren't children anymore. Think about how we'd feel as parents. If Spencer came to you and he needed money to go to school, you'd try to help him, wouldn't you?''

"Nope.''

"No?''

"Well, sure I'd try to help him. But I'm gonna make it clear to Spencer when he's growin' up that onct he's married that means he's taken on responsibilities. I'm not gonna have him be like these no-count guys I've seen 'round here, jest havin' kids and don't worry 'bout nothin' but hooch and cars. If'n he don't understand that, I won't let him get married.''

"You didn't ask anyone's permission, did you?'' she asked slyly. "And besides, Ma helps us, doesn't she? Not with money, but in a thousand other ways.''

"Ma's not judging us wantin'. She knows when things are rough. And she knows we're givin' her our home too. But your mamma and daddy—you ast them fer money, and y' jest know what they're gonna think even if they don't say it. They're gonna think they're right and I cain't take care of y'!''

"It'll just be a loan, Billy. Once I get out of school I'd be making money . . .''

"Sure. Prob'ly makin' more money'n I will.''

"No. You'll be doing much better by then," she assured him, knowing she hadn't managed to find that fine line between being convincing and overselling. "And none of that matters anyway. Why should it? If we're really married we should both be doing everything we can to help. And it isn't just helping . . ." Why was she getting so muddled when she'd planned her dialogue so intelligently? "It's something I really want to do. Please say you'll support me."

"I'd love to say I'd support y', girl. 'Cause if'n I could say that an' have you believe me, we wouldn't even be gettin' into this."

He gave her one long hard stare, and then wrenched the door open.

"Don't get cones," she yelled after him as he slammed the door and walked toward the ice-cream store. "Get a pint of black walnut. That's Ma's favorite."

She started to reach into her purse to take out some change, and then snapped the purse shut and bit her lip, hoping he'd have money on him. *So damned stubborn,* she thought to herself. *No, he's not—it's that I put it wrong. Should have waited until we were in bed. No, I couldn't have. That would be like blackmail. I couldn't do that.* She watched him through the window of the store. He had stuffed his hands into the pockets of his dungarees, his right hand feeling around for change. "Oh, please, let him have some money," she whispered. He found some coins, smiled deferentially to the girl behind the counter, and stared at the floor, oblivious to the fact that the girl was smiling back flirtatiously and had started to pack the ice cream extra hard into the container to give him a good deal. *He doesn't even realize how handsome he is. He doesn't even notice that girl's looking at him, because he's busy worrying about me. And I've made him feel inadequate,* she thought. *What was it Ma said? 'Women are stronger 'cause we know how to give way.' I know what she means. But I can't give way on this. If he could only see . . .*

He came back, closed the door without slamming it, and put the carton of ice cream between them. Neither of them spoke until they were almost back to the house. Then his voice came so soft that at first she thought he was talking to himself and didn't catch the first words.

". . . so I don't think they'll even let y' in. But if'n yer heart's set on it . . ."

She reached out and touched his cheek with a gesture of total adoration, wanting to tell him that she knew how much it meant for him to give way to her, wanting to assure him that she appreciated it.

"I'm takin' this here ice cream in 'fore it melts. Y' comin'?"

"In a little while, Billy."

As he went into the house, she rested her forehead on the dash-board, cupped her hands between her legs and closed her eyes. Three years wasn't such a long time. Not when you really thought about it. Not when you could imagine a little name plate that said Sheila Hickock, R.N. She would have dignity. A real salary. A crisp white uniform. People would rely on her judgement and endurance, her kindness. Like Sister Kenny . . .

CHAPTER
XV

THE BELLBOY put down the suitcase, crossed to the window, raised the shade, and backed up to the door to wait for his tip. He watched the woman's derriere as she threw her purse on the bed and hurried over to the window. Half the fun of the job was sizing up the guests and this one was a real peach. She'd registered as Mrs. Collins, though there was no Mr. Collins in sight. He'd heard her say to the guy on the desk that she'd been in New York before, but here she was, hanging out the window and rubbernecking the view of Central Park like any first-time tourist. Maybe she was a high-class call girl. No, the clothes were too understatedly classy for that—damn those French fairies and their "New Look," you could hardly get a decent gander at a pretty leg anymore—besides, she'd brought a suitcase and she'd checked in for three nights. There was something about the way she carried her body that suggested she might be a performer. More than likely she was some actress he'd never heard of having a hot weekend tryst with a producer. He'd check it out with the other bellboys. They could usually figure out who was sleeping with whom by checking the register for adjoining suites, and verifying their suppositions with the guys from room service.

"I'm sorry to keep you waiting," she said, twirling away from the window and surprising him with an ingenuous smile. "The view from here . . . it always overwhelms me."

"Yeah. New York: 'Stream of the living world where dash the billows of strife! One plunge in the mighty torrent is a year of a tamer life!'"

His fifth-grade teacher, a spinster from Arkansas, had forced him to memorize the verse. It had turned out to be the most profitable part of his education. He usually reserved it for dowagers who needed an incentive to cough up a twenty-five-cent tip, but sometimes he tried it out on more sophisticated types. This one was listening raptly, eyes dreamy, lips slightly parted. He went on:

> City of glorious days,
> Of hope and labour and mirth,
> With room and to spare on the splendid bays,
> For the ships of all the earth!

"That's quite lovely," she said in that funny accent, reaching for her purse. When she slipped the dollar bill into his hand he knew it must be an affair.

"Thank you very much, Mrs. Collins. I hope you'll enjoy your stay at the Plaza. Will there be anything else?"

"Yes. I'd like a bottle of the best champagne. Oh, and that florist shop in the lobby: I'd like them to send up some gardenias. Gardenias always give a room such a lovely fragrance, don't you think?"

"Yes, ma'am, I do. I'll take care of it right away."

Gaynor shut the door, kicked off her shoes, and ran back to the window. Three whole days together in Manhattan. She'd never actually thought that they'd be able to arrange it. Right after Joey was born, Richard had promised that he would find a way to take her to New York for a holiday. For four months she'd been waiting, not just for the trip, but for a chance to be alone with him, a real opportunity to figure out what she was supposed to do about her future.

It hadn't been easy to stay on at the big house. Etna and Faustina had been busy fussing over Joey, but it was more difficult to placate Ricky. She had the excuse of Joey's health, which was in truth very frail; and she'd played up her own depressions, though now that she was over the pregnancy she felt remarkably well. She had made two trips to visit Ricky in Princeton and he had flown back once to see Joey, but it was only a matter of time before compliant Ricky would blow his stack and demand that she and the baby return to him. She'd convinced him that a major obstacle to being reunited, apart from Joey's delicate condition, was finding a suitable place for all of them to live. But only last week he'd telephoned to say that he thought he'd found a larger apartment.

Well, she wasn't going to worry about how she'd cope with that problem now, she told herself as she hoisted up her skirt and took off the garter belt and nylons. They had pulled it off. They were going to have a wonderful three days in New York. It was a holiday, a celebration. From the time Richard had told her about his business trip to New York, the plotting had been frantic. She'd called Ricky and told him that she was coming to visit, but since she was wary of the off-chance phone call from Etna to make sure that she'd arrived safely in Princeton, she'd had to come up with a detour that he wouldn't be able to check on. She was longing for some contact with someone from Australia, she told him, and planned a three-day visit to her friend Sheila in Virginia before coming on to Princeton. He said that a side trip to see an old girlfriend was just the sort of thing she needed. He was sorry that he couldn't drive down there and pick her up, but he was hard at work on his dissertation. She understood about his work, she answered sympathetically, she didn't mind making the detour alone. It all fell into place. The only moment of panic was when Jackson had driven her to the airport and wanted to wait around to help her with the bag and make sure that she departed on time. She'd sounded very imperious when she'd ordered him to leave her at the curb. She didn't want to hurt Jackson's feelings but . . . what the hell. None of that mattered now.

The champagne and flowers arrived. She took off her dress, tucked a gardenia into the lace bodice of her slip, pulled up the champagne bucket, and sat at the window, staring out at the skyline. An Indian summer breeze stirred the curtains. Directly in front of her was the lush green expanse of the park, while off to the right, the facades of Fifth Avenue buildings caught the last rays of the sun. Looking down, she could see people hurrying home from their day's activities. The sound of traffic was too distant to be grating; instead it seemed to beckon, promising the excitement of a great city at night. There would be music and fine food, plush watering holes where powerful men and glamorous women enjoyed the rewards of their frantic work days. She sipped the champagne, one hand absently fondling her breast, and watched the lights flicker on in a million windows. There was a tap at the door.

"Mrs. Collins?"

She walked slowly over to the door, opened it with a dignified "Won't you please come in," and shut it behind him. He held her at arm's length, looking at her until the bright gleam of possession in his eyes became almost pensive. Then he pulled her to him, kissing the top of her head and moving her toward the bed.

"No, Richard," she teased, struggling to break free. "I insist on a proper courtship for a change. You'll have to take me to dinner first."

"If you want to be taken out, why are you sitting around in your underpants?"

"I was going to get dressed, but then I just sat here looking out the window and drinking champagne. I know it's cliché, but being high up does give one a very special feeling, doesn't it? I think I'm tipsy already. Would you like some?"

"Champagne? No. I hate the stuff. I'll send down for some scotch."

"You have to have champagne. At least one glass. Our first holiday together demands a celebration."

"You are a demanding little girl tonight, aren't you," he smiled, slapping her behind as she moved away from him. "All right. Just to please you I'll have a glass. Then you'd better get some clothes on because I'm taking you out to dinner. Afterwards we'll go to a couple of nightclubs—though I won't promise to dance with you—after that, we'll go to a bar and see some television."

"Television? Oh, I forgot to ask, how did your meetings go?"

"Great. I put out a wad but I feel good about it. It's going to be big, Gaynor, very big. It'll replace radio, movies, books . . . it'll probably even replace conversation. Fifteen years from now when people don't know what to do in their bedrooms they'll turn on the TV set. Every home in America will have one—maybe even two or three."

"Come on! Do you really think people will be such drongos that they'll stay at home and watch wrestling matches on a little box?"

"The box won't stay little. And there'll be more than wrestling. We're already up to thirty hours a week in programming and it'll improve. Another couple of years the sets won't just be in the bars. It's going to be very big—one of the best investments I've ever made."

He raised the glass and touched it to hers. "But what the hell. Money isn't everything. How are you? Trip okay? Come down here and give the old man a kiss."

She backed off from him, doing a parody of a Mae West walk. When he grabbed for her, she ran toward the bathroom door, dropped her shoulder strap, and laughed, "No. A proper courtship this time."

They dined at the Plaza, and then took a cab to the floorshow at the

Copa. The covetous looks she attracted from other men only increased his desire for her. They walked up Fifth Avenue holding hands. Gaynor oohed and aahed into the shop windows. He didn't give a damn for all the expensive geegaws, that had never been the reason that he'd wanted money; but her enthusiasm, the drive of her acquisitiveness, amused him and filled him with surprising tenderness.

"Let's head back to the room."

"But I thought you wanted to go to a bar and watch television."

"Not now. Not now."

In the elevator going up to the room, they both stared ahead without speaking. They made love without bothering to take off all their clothes. Afterwards, when they'd undressed and lay together in a woozy, blissful lassitude, Richard told her she was great in bed and promised to buy her a special present. As he dropped off to sleep, she touched his back, brought her feet next to his, and curled her body around him. It was the first time they had been able to spend the night together. In a way she wanted him to stay awake, relish these stolen moments of intimacy. But that wasn't Richard's style. He'd probably just think she was sentimental. And it really didn't matter if they felt the same things after they'd had sex. She knew they felt the same things during. That was more than she'd had with any of the others.

Some time later she woke up, dehydrated by the alcohol. She staggered into the bathroom and scooped handfuls of water into her parched mouth. A clock somewhere struck three. *I'm like Cinderella at the ball,* she thought as she walked back to the bed and stared down at the hulk of his sleeping body. *Why kid myself? He's not going to put any glass slipper on my foot.* She fumbled around in the dark and located her pack of cigarettes, resentful that he was dead to the world while she was already feeling the queasy remorse of a hangover. Anger building, she crossed to the window and sat, smoking and looking out at the sky that was still illuminated by the glow of a million lights.

She didn't hear him get up, but suddenly he was behind her, folding his arms across her breast, nuzzling into her ear. She drew away and crushed out the cigarette. Why bother to tell him how she felt. She might just as well keep her mouth shut, go back to bed and get some sleep. But when she rose and he turned her around in his arms, stroking her head, she burst into uncontrollable sobs.

"Hey, little girl, what's the matter? I thought you were happy tonight."

"I was. I was happy. It was one of the only things I've looked forward to that lived up to my expectations. But, I know . . . I *know,*" she cried, "I'll just have to go back to everything the way it was. This weekend is just something out of time. It's not real, Richard. Nothing between us can ever be real. It's some kind of a dream that can't touch anything else in my life."

"What about Joey? He's real. He's something in both of our lives."

"How the bloody hell can you say that to me," she demanded, jerking away from him.

"He's our son. That means a lot to me, Gaynor. I admit when I first went to bed with you I never had anything like that in mind but . . ."

"You don't have to tell me your reasons for screwing me, Richard. I know your bloody reasons."

"And I know your bloody reasons for doing it so willingly," he snarled back, his voice instantly hard. "That doesn't matter. There's no percentage in thinking about that now. Goddamn it, you'll be like Etna soon, moping around with your brain in a bottle, mourning the past."

"Don't you dare mention her to me. I don't want to talk about her. Ever!"

"Listen kid, if you're going to survive, you live in the present and the future. I thought you knew that."

"I do," she spat out, pacing the darkened room, "don't you think I know that? It's all very well for you to talk about the future. Yours isn't quite as muddled as mine, is it? You've got your business and your deals. You've got another son to push around. What about me?"

"You'll be taken care of. I'll see that Joey is taken care of. I've already told you that."

"All right for you, great man of commerce, all right for you to make it sound like a business deal. You can dispose of me with a quick telephone call to your lawyer. How the hell do you propose to take care of me? I couldn't even go out and spend the little tips you'd give me for my services, because I'd have to hide whatever I bought from that goddamned hawk-eyed housekeeper. If I really were your daughter," she sneered, knowing she was speaking the unspeakable but needing to push the confrontation to the point of violence, "instead of just your son's wife . . ."

Her eyes, now accustomed to the darkened room, saw his hand clench and jerk into the air. He lowered his fist with a slow-motion gesture, and then walked back to the bed and took a cigarette, gathering the sheets around him. "Shut up," he ordered sharply. "I've never been in any situation that I couldn't get myself out of, this isn't going to be an exception."

"Yourself. Always talking about yourself. What about me?"

"Let's not try to outdo each other in selfishness, Gaynor. That contest would surely be a draw."

"I can't keep on like this. I can't go back to Ricky."

"Jesus, why did you marry him?" he muttered to himself.

"If I hadn't married him I wouldn't have met you."

"I know that, you silly bitch."

"Don't you dare call me that! Don't you dare!"

"I've called you that before. I've called you that in bed and you even seemed to like it."

"I hate you, Richard. Have I ever told you how much I really hate you?" she hissed, kicking the pile of clothes at the foot of the bed. She grabbed her slip and heard the silk rip as she tugged it over her head. "I'm leaving."

"And where are you going?" he asked softly, with a little laugh. Cornered. Trapped. She sank down into the chair and reached for the half-empty champagne bottle, glupped a mouthful and shuddered as the sweet, warm liquid went down her throat.

"You're funny, Gaynor," he said at last. She had quieted now, staring out of the window, taking occasional swigs from the bottle and putting it back between her legs. "No, actually you're not funny. You're dangerous. Because you're so intelligent and yet so stupid. Why did you marry him? There must have been other men with money. Why the kid?"

"Because . . . because . . . and if you laugh I swear I'll break this bottle and grind the glass into your heart . . . because he treated me with respect."

"Oh, baby," he said in a husky voice, "respect is the last thing you want in bed."

"I didn't care about bed," she went on slowly, as though understanding it herself for the first time. "I've had men panting after me ever since I started to get bumps on my chest. I wanted protection and money. But mostly I wanted respect. And I thought . . . I thought Ricky was a way out. You don't know what I came from. You'll never know."

"I think I do know. I think I knew the first time I ever saw you."

"Yes, I suppose you did," she said, her voice flat, devoid of feeling.

"I suppose that was what petrified me at the same time it made me want you. Because it's lonely not having anyone who really knows. That was why I wanted you—apart from any disappointment with Ricky. That was the real reason."

"I know. I told you that first night that we were alike."

"Yes . . . And I've never asked you what you came from."

"That doesn't matter anymore. It's what I am now, what I've made of myself that's important. My past is so far away that it doesn't have any reality for me. If I read my own life story I'd think it was the stupidest kind of fiction. But I'm fifty-six." He put out the cigarette, hoisted the sheet around him, and walked over to the window, sitting in the chair opposite her, and then motioning for her to come to him. She stumbled into his lap. He stroked her hair, then lowered her onto the floor. "Tell me. Tell Daddy what it's all about."

She told him. From the earliest memories, through the years when the development of her own womanhood was a promise and a terrible curse. She told him as she had never told anyone—not Ricky or Evan or even her first love and betrayer, Lela Waddington. Laughing and crying, lacerating herself with the pain of dreams deferred, desires thwarted, trust destroyed, she poured it all out, right up to the point where she had hoarded the cash her mother's lover had given to keep their dirty little secrets and she had been able to strike out on her own. And then she stopped.

"But there must have been a lot of men before Ricky," Richard urged her on. The gush of memories and recollections dried up as she sensed the danger of her position. She had told him the truth thus far, but would it be wise to admit to all the lovers that had preceded her marriage? There might be some time in the future when Richard could punish her for such admissions. He was a man, and men, no matter how sympathetic, judged women by another standard. And he was her lover. Possessiveness was an integral part of sexual passion, especially to a man like Richard. Might he not use her past against her, throw it up to her, call her a whore, claim that she was unfit to mother the child that had finally bound him to her?

"Of course there were a few men. You know that. But never, never like it is with you. I wasn't a whore, you know. It wasn't until I went to bed with you that I really wanted it."

She twisted her body around so that she was kneeling before him, her arms around his legs, her upturned face on his knees. She watched his chest expand as he turned from her supplicating face and stared out the window. She had made the right choice. She had said what he wanted to believe.

"We have to think about this clearly, Gaynor," he said finally, in his board-of-directors voice. "I don't want you to have to go back to Ricky. When you see him, you'll tell him you want a divorce. I'll set you and the boy up in your own house in Kansas City."

"Wouldn't that look suspicious?"

"I don't see why. You're away from your own country and family. It's only natural that you'd want to be near the grandparents of your child. I'll come and visit you as often as I can. I'll provide you with an allowance. It's not ideal, but I don't see any other way around this. Apart from seeing you I want to see Joey. He's the son I've always hoped for. I didn't think that would ever happen again, but it has. You've made me feel young again, little girl. You've brought it all back. I love you."

The words she'd wanted so long. More than the words, the feeling behind them. It didn't matter that she'd had to go through that horrible pregnancy, didn't matter that she'd borne a child she could barely stand to look at or touch, didn't matter what anyone in the whole world thought about her. Through accident, fate, she didn't know what to call it, she had secured his love. Knowing what he knew—all of her sordid past, well, most of it—he still found her worthy. More than worthy: desirable. Lovable.

"I love you too, Richard. I love you more than anything in the world. I've wanted to tell you so many times. Even the first time I went to bed with you, and then, before I found out that I was pregnant—I swear, I loved you so much I could have killed you. It was the worst pain I'd ever had, to think that you didn't need me, that you were just using me. I hated you for that. God, how I hated you," she cried, tears welling up in her already puffy eyes, clinging to her lashes and dropping onto her breast. "Oh Richard. Why weren't you always there? Why didn't we fall in love before I met Ricky?"

"See what I mean?" he said somberly, picking her up and holding her next to him. "You're smart but you're dumb. Don't question it anymore. Take what you can get."

"That's all right as long as I've got you," she said, shuddering in the chilly predawn air. "I do have you, don't I? Say it again. Say you love me again."

They sank to the floor, kneeling. He pushed her back, fingers slowly inching from knees, raising the hem of her slip, tickling, and probing the mound of flesh between her legs until she went moist, expanded under his touch. He was loving her. Not with words, but with hands, and eyes and a mouth that left the bruising sucks and bites of possession on her thighs, her shoulders, her neck. Her nipples stood up, hard and ticklish as he pulled the slip over her head. As he threw the sheet from his own legs, she knew the pride he felt at seeing himself erect and powerful. Now. Easing. Slowly. Holding back lest it engulf one and leave the other behind. Ah. Groans rippled from her throat. She knew it would be together this time. Not the satisfaction of two separate bodies demanding individual release, but the unity of split-second, artful, aching triumph. Clearing the hurdle together for the first time.

She was only dimly aware when he left in the morning. She opened her eyes long enough to see him putting on the vest of his suit, vaguely remembered his hand on her forehead and some whispered reminder of the time they were to meet. Then she saw the slit of light from the hallway as he opened and closed the door.

She woke up inhaling the strong, penetrating fragrance of the wilting gardenias. It was almost noon. She reached for the phone to dial room service, slowly drawing on her robe. Richard really did have the constitution of a billy goat. She was quite exhausted from the drinking and lovemaking of the previous evening, not to mention the emotional catharsis.

She stretched luxuriantly on the mussed-up bed, turning her head to see the bright blue of the autumn sky from the window. High contrast photos of the night before flashed through her brain, bringing a shiver to her flesh. The cute bellboy who had helped her with her bags held back the door as an older waiter wheeled the breakfast cart into the room. While the waiter poured her coffee and fussed over the chafing dishes, the young one picked up the glasses and empty champagne bottle and watched her out of the corner of his eye. She settled on one of the brocade chairs and sipped her coffee, looking back at him with a removed but insouciant smile. How wonderful to be desirable and yet be powerful enough to pretend that you were oblivious to the admiring glance. That must be how men felt.

After breakfast, she dressed and went for a walk, exploring the shops near the hotel, Bergdorf's, Bonwit's and Tiffany's. Here she was at last with money in her purse. This time she wouldn't use the hundred-dollar bills that Richard had left on the night table. This time she would only look and fondle. But soon . . . after she'd divorced

Ricky and been set up in her own place with no one to spy on her, she would be able to leave stores like these with armfuls of beautiful things. That frothy peach-colored negligee with the ecru lace trim, wouldn't she beguile Richard in that? Or that glittering emerald choker. Whose neck could show it off to better advantage? Her life had only been window shopping until now. Soon she would be able to own all the things she wanted. And she wouldn't just buy clothes and jewelry, she decided as she peered into gallery windows and passed the foyers of theaters. She would learn about painting and sculpture. She would go to concerts, cultivate her mind, enjoy a charmed and exciting life.

Around three in the afternoon, she strolled back to her suite. She bathed, and put some witch hazel on cotton pads, pressed them to her eyes, which were still a bit puffy from last night, and lay down to rest. Richard called around five o'clock as promised, and said he'd been delayed at meetings. Would she come up to his room while he showered and shaved? Her impulse was to rush upstairs to him. But after she'd hung up the phone, she felt a twinge of anxiety. So she took her time getting into the plum-colored moire cocktail dress and painting her face before she took the elevator to the next floor.

He yelled out for her to come in when she tapped on the door. She fixed herself a drink from the cart and poured a scotch for him. He came out of the bathroom slapping some aftershave on his face, a towel wrapped around a waist that was still trim even if it wasn't as firm as the flesh she'd imagined under the bellboy's uniform.

"My, don't we look like Tarzan?"

"No, we don't look like Tarzan. Don't get fresh with the old man, otherwise he won't come and save you the next time the crocodiles are snapping at your pretty legs."

"Someone's bound to come if I yell. I'll just let out a 'coo-ee'— that's the cry you give when you're lost in the bush." As they clinked their glasses, his eyes shone with satisfaction and, she thought, a softer glimmer of affection. Her trepidation disappeared. "You know," she continued, smiling back at him, "I haven't thought about Australia in ages, but just today I was imagining how nice it would be to go back. I don't mean permanently, I just mean I'd like to go and parade around and watch all the people who were cruel to me drool all over themselves."

"That's a mistake, my darling. The people who didn't approve of you then wouldn't approve of you now. I've tried to explain about going back into the past. You don't need their acceptance anymore. You've gone beyond that."

She raised her glass in a toast. "You mean 'it's you and me against the world, baby'?"

"Something like that." He sat down, gulped his drink and held out his glass for her to replenish. "I'm just gonna take a couple of swift belts, then I'll let you drag me out for another night on the town. It's been a helluva day."

"Poor baby," she teased, walking back to the drink cart.

"You 'spose Joey's okay?"

"Of course he's okay, darling," she replied lightly. "Do you like my new dress?"

"All right, you vain thing, show it off."

She put down the glass and strolled to the farthest corner of the room, turning this way and that and finally posing with her back to him and her head turned seductively over her shoulder.

"The dress is fine, but I think I like what's under it a lot more."

"Aren't we vulgar!" she gasped, putting on thick English accent and crossing her hands protectively over her decolletage.

"Come over here and I'll show you just how vulgar we can be," he grinned, pleased with her little show.

She started slowly across the room. When she had almost reached him, he slumped forward slightly, his hand going up to his temple.

"Something the matter?"

"Headache. Terrific sharp headache. Didn't feel anything a minute ago but . . . " The blood drained from his face.

"Should I call room service and get them to send up some aspirin?"

"No. I . . . "

"Please don't tell me you're going to manufacture some excuse to stay in bed," she teased, kneeling beside him.

"Strong as an ox. I'll outlive you all. I . . ."

His eyes clenched shut. His arm fell from the armrest. His head jerked forward, and then drooped.

"What is it? What's the matter?" She shook his arm. His breathing seemed to stop, then rattled out of his throat with a harsh strangled sound. She took his head in her hands. His neck was rigid, his right eye dilating wildly. Dropping his head, staring into the eyes that were no longer looking back at her, she crawled backwards and fumbled for the phone.

"Send a doctor up to Mr. Cunningham's suite. Sixteen-twelve.

No. I mean twelve-sixteen. Hurry. I said hurry, damn you!"

She dropped the receiver and stared at him. His entire body was stiff as a mannequin's except for the crazy jerk in his right eye and a slight twitching of his right hand. "Richard?" she whispered. Her voice seemed to come from far away. "Richard?" A freezing panic swept through her. When she tried to crawl toward him, she found she couldn't move. It was like a childish nightmare in which something stalked and transfixed her so that she wanted to run but couldn't. She crouched on the floor, numbly staring at him as the minutes ticked by. It took some time before she could respond to the knock at the door.

"I'm Dr. Goodwin," the man in the dark suit said as he rushed past her to Richard's side. "What happened? When did he get like this?"

"I don't know. I mean . . . about ten minutes ago. He was just sitting there having a drink and then he suddenly slumped forward and started to twitch and I . . ."

"All right. All right," he muttered quickly, opening his medical bag and reaching for a hypodermic. She inched a few steps closer, and then backed off. Richard's breathing was audible again. The same gently snoring sound of air coming through slightly congested passages that she'd heard last night. She couldn't see what the doctor was doing but the breathing was there. Eezh—ahh. Eezh—ahh.

Then it stopped.

"He's unconscious. Call an ambulance. Call the front desk and tell 'em to get an ambulance here fast."

She moved back to the phone and called the desk, then stood, zombielike, watching him inject something into Richard's limp arm.

"You're Mrs. Cunningham?" He talked as he worked on his syringes and bottles.

"Yes."

"I can't be sure but I think it's a massive cerebral hemorrhage. Can you tell me anything about his past medical history? Anything . . ."

"I know he has high blood pressure . . . but he's strong as an ox . . . I think . . ."

The impact of her presence in this room struck her. She was Mrs. Cunningham, but she wasn't the right Mrs. Cunningham. She would have to leave. Get out. Somehow. She couldn't be found here. But if he were really dying? But he couldn't be. Richard was alive. Thirteen, fifteen hours ago he had been making violent love to her. He was the most alive man she had ever known.

She watched as his face went ashen.

"Try to stay calm, Mrs. Cunningham. The ambulance should be here any minute. I've given him a dose of papaverine and amyl nitrite."

She backed toward the door. This man hovering over Richard's body. He thought she was Mrs. Cunningham. *Richard? Richard, I love you. Richard?* Then, without any word from the doctor, she knew that he was dead.

"Mrs. Cunningham, I'm afraid . . ." Turning, he saw her figure disappearing down the hallway. He stood up, staring at the seminude elderly man whose body he was preventing from falling forward, and then swiveled his head back toward the open door.

"Hey, Doc," the bellboy who had appeared at the threshold was asking, "is there anything I can do? The ambulance is on its way."

"Get his wife back. She just ran out of here. I don't know what in the hell's going on, but we've got a corpse here. You'd better go after her."

"I saw, what's her name—that Mrs. Collins—running down the hall. Hey, you mean . . . ?" The boy turned around in astonishment and looked down the vacant hallway. "Jesus! And I had a five-dollar bet that she was sleepin' with the guy in eleven-thirty."

SHE SLAMMED the door of her room and threw the suitcase on the bed, snapping the clasps shut without bothering to put in any of the things she'd taken out. Grabbing up her purse, she yanked the door open again and ran to the elevator. Why wouldn't it come faster? Doors opened. No one else there. Good. Through the lobby and into the street, ignoring the doorman, her arm already raised in supplication. A cab swerved to the curb. The doorman tried to help her with the suitcase but she brushed him aside.

"Where to?"

"Just go. I'll tell you later."

The cabbie circled the park for twenty minutes, checking her out in the rear-view mirror. Terrific-lookin' dame. Thought she was late for a plane, the way she hailed him down. She was shaking like crazy. Maybe she'd been thinkin' about running out on her old man and was gettin' cold feet. Crazy the way she was shakin' like that, as though it was fuggin' December already. A real nut case. Well, you got at least one every day. Now she was brushin' her hair like she was afraid that a bunch of bugs had nested in it and laughin' like she'd heard the best joke in the world. What a crazy dame. If she didn't tell where she wanted to go in the next five minutes, he'd just pull over and ask her what the hell was goin' on. Now she was taking out her compact and puttin' powder on her face. She'd probably be all right in a minute. That was one thing about dames: soon as they got their face together they were usually all right. Now she's calmin' down. Sittin' back all pale and wide-eyed like she was going to a fuggin' funeral or somethin'.

"Where to, Miss?"

"Princeton, New Jersey," she said, phony English accent and all. Like she was the queen mother goin' on a tour of the provinces. Then she let out a wail and started sobbin' in that jerky, quiet way a little kid does when you spank it and it starts to get hysterical. If she hadn't leaned forward and thrown a twenty-dollar bill on the seat, he would have driven her straight to the nut house.

SHE LEANED on the buzzer for a long time before Ricky opened the door and stood before her blinking in amazement.

"Honey, what are you doing here? I didn't expect to see you until Sunday afternoon."

"I had to come earlier. Sheila has that little baby and I couldn't get any rest down there, so . . ."

"Why didn't you telephone? I would have picked you up at the station," he said as he took her arm, picked up the suitcase, and guided her into the apartment. He kissed her cheek, feeling the coldness of her flesh through a thin film of perspiration. Even in the dim circle of light coming from the single lamp above the kitchen table, he could see that her lashes were matted and a streak of inky mascara smudged her cheek.

"You've been crying. What's the matter?"

"I'd like a drink."

"Sure. I guess there's some left around here. I was going to go out shopping before you came but . . ." He scouted around under the sink while she slumped into a chair at the kitchen table. "Yeah, there's about a third of a bottle left. Hope there's enough ice cubes. The refrigerator's been on the fritz again. God, I'm glad to see you. I've been working day and night. I've showed the rough draft of the dissertation to Lukas. He's already talking to people about getting me a job. Christ, I've got so many things I want to talk to you about. Are you sure you're feeling all right?"

"I'm just tired from the trip."

He pushed aside the books on the table and set the glass down. She held it in both hands like an infant who has just learned to hold a cup, and then drained it.

"Are you really okay?"

She pushed the glass toward him.

"I was hoping that you'd enjoy your little side trip to see Sheila what's-her-name. Did anything happen down there?"

"I told you. Her baby was sick. That's why I left sooner than I'd expected to."

"Mother called last night. She says Joey's doing fine." He poured the remains of the whiskey into her glass. She wrapped her hands across her breasts, stroking them and staring around the room.

"Gaynor, what is it? What's happened?"

"Sheila's baby got the croup or something so I decided to come up sooner. I would have called, but she doesn't have a phone. I really don't want to talk now. I'm glad to be here. I just want to have another drink and go to bed."

Her hands went back to the bodice of her dress, touching her breasts as though reassuring herself that they were still there.

"Is that a new dress?" he asked, thinking that it looked more like something she'd wear to a dinner party than a traveling outfit. Her hands stilled, she looked around the room again with a trapped expression.

"Hey, honey, relax. I'm not going to start in on any nonsense about you spending money. The dress looks pretty on you," he said casually, forcing his eyes away from the arousing sight of her fondling herself. "God, I'm glad to see you. Can't you tell me why you're upset?"

She looked down at her hands. The muscles in her throat strained and she seemed about to burst into tears.

"All right. No questions now. I'm just so glad to have you here."

She closed her eyes, then opened them with an imploring look. He reached toward her tentatively, afraid of a repeat of the rejection that had marked all of their contact since she had found out she was pregnant. But instead of pulling away, she clutched at him, burying her head in his chest. "Gaynor?"

"Please, let's not talk now . . . darling."

The tone was crooning, helpless, the little-girl voice he hadn't heard since the first days of their marriage. The closeness of her body swept away everything but the pounding of his own blood.

"I don't want to talk either. You know I'd rather make love. It was just that you seemed so upset. I didn't think you'd want to."

Anything was better than having him pry into her feelings. If he questioned her one more time she wouldn't be able to control herself, she would scream that Richard was dead. It was better to cut off her mind completely, go through the act with him. She had before and she could do it again. If she didn't collapse first, she would just fake it. The ability to fake it was one of the few advantages that nature had given to women. He took her hand and started to lead her toward the bedroom. She held back long enough to drain the rest of her drink.

After it was over, Ricky lay beside her whispering inane endearments. She pretended to drop off to sleep. He put on his robe and padded out to the kitchen, closing the door behind him. Her eyes opened and her hearing became almost painfully acute. He was puttering around fixing coffee. She lay perfectly still, rigid with expectation, feeling as though her mind had left her body and was floating somewhere above her. Someone in New York would contact Etna about Richard. Etna would call Ricky. Then it would be a fact, not just a horrible hallucination. She could hear him turning the pages of his book. When the telephone finally rang, she didn't even start. She couldn't make out his words, but she heard the tone of greeting. Then his voice inflected upward, questioning. A pause. More questioning. A mumbled assent. After a time the door opened. She turned in the shaft of light, rubbing her eyes.

"Gaynor? I'm sorry to wake you, but something has happened to Richard. Faustina just called. It seems he was on a business trip to New York and he's had an attack or something."

"An attack?"

"Maybe it's his blood pressure. I'm going to drive into the city and go to the hospital."

"Is it bad?"

"I don't know," he lied. Faustina had said the call had come from the medical examiner's mortuary. She had instructed him to contact her as soon as he got there, saying she would not tell Etna anything until they were absolutely sure.

"What did they tell Faustina?"

"Just what I said. He's had some sort of an attack."

"Oh my God, that's awful! I'd better get dressed and come with you," she cried, but made no attempt to move.

"No. You just rest. I'd really rather handle it alone. I'll call when I find out what's going on."

"Are you sure you don't want me to come?"

"No. I don't. I just want you to let me hold you for a minute." He embraced her with a strained intensity. When he released her suddenly and reached for his pants, his hands were shaking. She knew that he had already learned the truth.

At Bellevue, after identifying the body, he talked to the doctor. He could see the "you're a cold bird" appraisal in the man's eyes as he asked questions and filled in forms. He felt quite numb as he drove through the deserted predawn streets. Suddenly, he felt very hungry. He stopped off at a diner, ordered the biggest breakfast he'd ever eaten, and listened to the conversations of cabbies and truck drivers. He tipped the waitress and asked for some change. The sausage, eggs and three slices of toast felt heavy in his gut as he walked to the phone booth. His hands were sweating so much that he dropped the dime. When Betty's voice came through the receiver, he apologized in his best prep-school manner for waking her and asked if he might come over to her apartment. He sat in the car watching a street-sweeper clean an entire block before he turned on the motor and headed for 110th Street.

Betty was waiting at the door of her apartment. He stared at her yellow seersucker pajamas and the kerchief tied around her pin curls.

"What's happened?"

"My father's dead," he announced, looking past her to the window. The sky was quickening into the pale, milky blue of early morning. "The doctor told me he was with some call girl at the Plaza. He seemed like a decent sort of guy—the doctor I mean. So I don't think any of that will get into the papers. I think I can keep Mother from finding out."

"Oh, Ricky . . ."

"Apparently it was very fast. Massive cerebral hemorrhage. No one could have saved him," he continued as though he were delivering the weather report.

"Oh, Ricky . . ." She put her arms around him. A terrible rasping sound came from his throat.

"I think I'm going to be sick," he gagged, pulling away from her and staggering down the hallway toward the bathroom.

CHAPTER
XVI

DAWN PULLED ASIDE the blue curtains she'd cut down to fit the small windows of the Quonset hut. The weather looked ominous. There had been a frost during the night and the diapers and shirts hanging on the clothesline that divided the huts bounced stiffly in the morning breeze.

"Better put on a cardigan for school today," she told Faye as she left the window and knelt beside her, starting to tie her shoes.

"Mummy, I can tie my own shoes now."

"Then hurry up. Be in that bathroom in five minutes so I can fix your plaits, otherwise I won't have time to walk you to school."

"They're not plaits, they're pigtails. Please don't nag at me," Faye scowled. Her tongue twisted to the side of her mouth and her brow furrowed in intense concentration as she pulled at the laces of her Buster Browns.

"All right, missy, five minutes."

She hoisted Nita onto one hip, walked out into the kitchenette, took the bowls of soggy cornflakes from the table, and deposited them in the sink.

"We're going out now. Going bye-bye, taking Faye to school," she told Nita as she sat her on the countertop and reached for a washrag. "Now let's have a go at that milky face of yours."

"Noooo. Nooo," Nita gurgled, twisting away from the washcloth and reaching for the faucet.

"Not a bath, pet. Just a lick and a promise. Now sit still like a good girl and Mummy will tell you all the things we're going to do today.

Are you listening?" The baby threw her chubby arms around Dawn's neck and looked up attentively. "First we'll do our shopping. Then while you're taking your nap, Mummy is going to write some letters and do the wash. If it doesn't rain, we'll go to the park and you can . . ."

Talking to a baby didn't do much for one's mind or vocabulary. Still, it was better than talking to yourself, though she'd found herself doing quite a bit of that lately too. Zac was gone for weeks at a time, Faye was off to school. Even when Faye was home she didn't seem to listen the way she used to. She had her playmates and her books. Her six-year-old character was already strong-willed and outspoken, traits she had apparently inherited from her grandfather Charlie. Much as Dawn was pleased by Faye's displays of independence, they also made her feel the sting of rejection. Now she always wanted to do everything for herself, even when Dawn offered to help.

With Zac, Faye was much more compliant. She adored him, wept when he went away, bounced around with delight when he returned. On the rare occasions when he showed her how to do something, she was attentive. When he gave an order, she might bristle, but she obeyed. Whenever Dawn told her to do something, she dawdled and told her not to nag—an expression she'd picked up from Zac. Well, the father's job was always easier. He could disappear and come home with gifts. The daily discipline, the scolding and cajoling, the wiping of noses, ministering to cuts and bruises, checking bathroom habits, fighting over bedtime and the cleaning of teeth was always left to the mother. She couldn't expect the girl to understand the difference until she'd grown up and had children of her own.

After she put Nita in the stroller, she braided Faye's hair, checked her appearance, and hurried to the door. As they went down the step, she saw Toshi McFadden struggling to take the wash down from the line.

"Ohio gozimas, Toshi."

"Good morning to you, Dawn," the girl bowed, her straight black hair falling forward, curtaining her delicate face.

"It's cold this morning, isn't it? Never see a sky like this on all those sunny southern California posters."

"Velly cold," Toshi repeated, bowing again.

"I'm just walking Faye up to school. Can I get you anything from the PX?"

"Maybe wice cwispies," Toshi said, wrapping her slender arms around her body. "You come back, we have tea."

"Good. I'll see you in a while."

She pushed the stroller up the concrete path toward the barbed-wire fence that encircled the huts. Faye skipped in front of her, stomach thrust forward, hands brushing the skirt of her dress. When they'd almost reached the shops of the main street, she slowed down and walked back to clutch at Dawn's dress.

"It looks funny when Toshi bobs up and down like that, doesn't it?"

"That's because she's from Japan. There are different customs in different countries. When people meet each other here they shake hands . . ."

"Men shake hands, ladies kiss."

". . . in Toshi's country it's polite for people to bow to each other."

"Toshi's a Jap, isn't she? A boy at school told me Japs are bad."

"I don't want to hear you calling her a Jap, Faye. That is not a polite thing to say."

"But are they bad people?"

"No. Well . . . Toshi isn't bad. Use your intelligence, you know her. She's a very nice lady." How could she explain the war, international relations, cultural differences, when she didn't even understand them herself? It was such a responsibility. Whenever Faye opened her mouth these days it was either to challenge or to question. How could she give the child truthful answers and not frighten her? "The Japs . . . the Japanese, were our enemy in the war . . ." She remembered the propaganda posters of the snarling Yellow Peril, remembered her own discomfort when Toshi had moved in next door. Zac had said that Jeff McFadden had probably picked Toshi up in a bar. Even after knowing her for months, she still had no notion of her past. But there was nothing about the polite, shy girl that suggested low life. She only knew that Toshi was a war bride like herself, and that she must feel loneliness and homesickness too.

"Didn't the Japanese kill Uncle Kevin?"

"No. The Germans killed Uncle Kevin." Impossibly complex.

"But why did they do it? Are they bad too?"

"Men on both sides were killed. People in Toshi's family were probably killed too. That's what happens in a war."

"But if they weren't bad, why did they kill each other?"

"The governments of their countries were bad. They wanted to go to war."

"And all the people let them?"

"When a government of a country decides a thing, sometimes the people who live in that country don't have any choice. They have to do what the government says."

"You mean the government is like a daddy."

"I suppose . . . yes, in a way it is."

"But what happens to all the people who get killed?"

"They go to heaven." What else could she say to a six-year-old?

"Are they up in the sky and they can see us but we can't see them?" Faye squinted at the rain clouds.

"I really don't know," Dawn said wearily.

"Suds said almost everyone goes to hell. And it's dark and hot there and you get punished all the time."

"Forget about what Suds says. She doesn't know anything. Oh, look at these turtles," she said, approaching the window of the pet store, grateful for something that might divert the child's attention.

"I want a turtle, Mummy! Please can I have a turtle? You said I can't have a dog because the hut's too little, but a turtle wouldn't take up any room. He could sleep under my bed."

"We'll see. Now come on or we'll be late."

Faye lingered, pressing her nose against the window of the pet store, as Dawn pushed the stroller up the street. When she stopped at the crosswalk, Faye ran up to her side.

"Do turtles go to heaven when they die?"

"Oh, dear, do stop asking so many bloody questions!"

When she'd seen Faye into the schoolyard, she went to the PX and then pushed back to the huts. After dumping her own things, she picked up Nita and the Rice Crispies and trotted over to Toshi's hut. They were sipping tea under a picture of General MacArthur and a hand-painted view of Mount Fuji when she heard the distant ring of her phone.

"I'd better catch that, Toshi. You'll watch Nita for a moment, won't you?"

"Sure. She precious baby," Toshi said as she scooped Nita onto her lap.

Dawn raced into her living room and grabbed the telephone, but the party at the other end had already hung up. Just as well, she thought as she stacked some cookies she had baked the previous day onto a plate and started back out the door. It couldn't be Zac. He was going to be at sea on maneuvers for another two weeks. More than likely it was Suds calling to tell her to confess her sins because the apocalypse was definitely scheduled for next Tuesday. The phone rang again.

"Dawn? Is this Dawn Mueller?" The voice strained through the crackling on the line.

"Yes, this is Dawn Mueller."

"Dawn, I'm so glad I reached you. This is Sheila."

"My God, Sheila! Fancy hearing from you. I didn't recognize your voice. I think you've started to lose your accent . . ."

"Dawn, I don't know how to tell you about this, but I'm in terrible trouble."

"What kind of trouble?"

"I can't explain it all now. I'm in nursing school . . ."

"Yes. You wrote me about that. But you said you were doing well. Has anything happened?"

"The fact is . . . I'm pregnant again."

"Oh, Sheila, congratulations!"

There was a long pause at the other end of the line.

"Sheila? Are you there?"

"I'm here. I've decided not to have the baby."

"But . . ."

"I can't tell you about it now. I'm only calling to let you know that I'm coming to California. Actually, I'm going to be in Mexico. I have a friend here, a woman doctor, and she's gotten me the name of someone in Tijuana . . ."

Dawn sank down on the couch, trying to make sense of what Sheila was saying. There was another long pause at the other end of the line and she thought she could hear Sheila crying.

"Are you coming alone, or with Billy?"

"Billy doesn't know. Helen tried to find somebody for me in New York, but it fell through. The only doctor we can find is in Tijuana, so I'm coming there. I know you're only a couple of hours from the Mexican border and I thought . . . Please, Dawn, can I come and see you?"

"Of course. Of course you can. But are you sure you want to . . ." She couldn't bring herself to say the word.

"I'll be there a week from today. I'm coming into San Diego, so if you'll give me the directions I'll take a bus out to your house. I'm going to tell Billy that you're very sick and that I must come and visit you. I've never lied to him before. I don't even know if he'll believe me . . ."

Dawn could hear her sobbing. "Sheila, please . . ."

"Don't think I'm awful, Dawn. Please don't. I have to do it. There are all sorts of things I can only explain when I see you. Please don't think I'm awful. I just don't know what else to do."

"Of course I don't think you're awful. Don't cry. Don't cry. I'll help you in any way I can."

"Thank you. I always knew you were my dearest friend. Oh, thank you, Dawn. I'll let you know when I'm arriving. I have to hang up now because I'm using the phone in my friend's clinic. I'll see you next week."

THE BUS rumbled past squat pastel-colored buildings, billboards bleached by the sun, and scraggly palm trees that were nothing like the lush tropical variety she'd seen in the Dorothy Lamour movies. Sheila opened her purse to check the contents of the large brown envelope again: passport, seventy-five crisp dollars, and the piece of paper with an address and telephone number but no name. She clipped the purse shut and closed her eyes. In a little while she would see Dawn again. She would make the phone call to confirm her "appointment." Tomorrow she would cross the border and go to 4 Calle Obregon. She would give them the money. And then . . . Her imagination recoiled from everything that was to follow. But what else could she do? If she had the baby . . . no, she corrected herself, if she carried the pregnancy to term—if she thought of "the baby" she wouldn't be able to go through with it—it would mean dropping out of school, writing to Da that the tuition money had gone down the drain. Worse than that, it would mean relinquishing any hope of changing her life. She would be sentencing not only herself but also Spencer and Billy to a future of meanness, dirt and deprivation. And this time she was responsible. She could even pinpoint the moment of conception.

On Friday nights it was Billy's habit to cash his paycheck and spend a couple of hours drinking in a local bar with his factory buddies before coming home. That particular Friday night they had waited supper until after eight, but Billy hadn't shown up. After they'd eaten, Ma had cleared away the dishes while Sheila gave Spencer his bath. It was the one daily ritual that she always looked forward to. She soaped and rinsed him, patted him dry, and carried him into the big bed. Sprinkling him with talc, she rubbed her nose into his sweet-smelling little belly and crooned childhood songs that had been lost to her memory until Spencer was born. When he'd fallen asleep, she lifted him into his crib and tiptoed into the kitchen.

Ma had already dozed off in the old rocker she'd insisted on bringing from the other house. During the day she went about with slow, steady movements, as though she had an invisible internal gauge capable of measuring out her energy. But in repose—her head nodding to one side and showing the deep folds in her neck, her jaw slack, her hands curled, arthritic—the weight of her years showed. "She can't keep up the pace much longer," Sheila thought. As she touched her arm, she imagined all the things she would be able to do to make Ma's life more comfortable once she'd graduated and could bring in more money.

"I musta dropped off."

"Why don't you go in to bed?"

"Guess a mattress is all I'm fit to tussle with these days," she yawned, getting to her feet. "Billy's real late tonight."

"I'll wait up. I have some studying to do anyway."

"Goodnight, daughter."

She fixed herself a pot of tea and opened her books. She was doing better in her classes than she'd thought she would, but there was a constant pressure to keep up. With Ma's help, the household ran smoothly, so she was able to devote a good deal of time to Spencer. It was Billy who was most neglected. Their time together was mostly confined to meals, groggy predawn sex and occasional Sunday afternoon drives in the hills. Perhaps when Easter vacation rolled around they would be able to go off for a night together, stay at a hotel, make love and talk till dawn as they had on their honeymoon. She'd tell him then how much she loved him, let him know that she cared about his struggles as well as her own. They might even drive to Richmond and she'd see all those lovely antebellum houses and . . . "No more daydreaming," she said out loud, underlining a passage of her biology text.

Her head jerked up from the table when she heard the familiar sound of the pickup. Clock said twelve-thirty. She must've dropped off. She stretched and walked over to the stove to put the kettle on. From the sound of the fumbling with the door handle, she guessed he must be pretty drunk. But she wasn't going to say anything about it. Circumstance might have forced her into being a leader, but she wasn't going to be a nag.

"Cup of tea?" she asked without turning around.

"I don't want no damned tea."

She stopped shaking the tea leaves into the pot and glanced over her shoulder. He was steadying himself against the table. An ugly swelling puffed out the flesh of his right eye, and a cut crusted with dried blood slashed through his eyebrow.

"Billy! My God, what happened to you?"

"I got in a fight."

"Your eye," she cried, rushing over to him. He waved her aside and staggered to the other end of the table.

"Did you have a fight in the bar?"

"Worse'n that."

"What do you mean? Tell me what happened."

She grabbed a clean towel and pulled open the refrigerator door to get some ice.

"Worse'n that," he said with a slow, silly grin. "I finally slugged that son-of-a-bitch foreman. He's been ridin' me ever since they locked me up in that rat cage. He wouldn'ta even got a poke at me if'n some o' his goons weren't holdin' my arms. I woulda licked him sure."

"You hit the foreman? Oh, Billy, why? Why?"

"I tolt you he's been ridin' me. Tolt me to speed up the line. Cain't speed up the goddamn line any more lessen I wanna get mangled in the machinery. I tolt him to leave me alone, but he jest . . ."

"Okay. Okay," she said quickly, trying to keep her voice calm. "Don't worry about it. Monday morning you can apologize. You told me yourself you're one of the best workers, so surely . . ."

"Ain't gonna be no more Monday mornin's. I'm fired. Or I quit. Cain't remember which right now."

"If you apologize . . ." She started toward him with the ice.

"You ain't listenin' to me, Sheila. I'm not goin' back. Man's got to have some pride or he ain't a man anymore. That s.o.b. called me down fronta the whole line. I ain't Rockefeller, but if'n I let someone treat me like that I might as well be dead."

He slicked back the hair that had fallen over his forehead, accidentally brushed the cut, and winced.

"Why did you have to hit him? How will we get by if you don't have a job?"

"I knowed that would be the one thing that'd bother you. Not my pride. Not my goddamned eye. Jest . . ."

"Shhh. You'll wake Spencer. Now let me have a look at your eye. I'll fix it."

"Why, that's what I tolt the boys," he said sarcastically. "I tolt 'em my wife could fix anything up. She knows everythin'."

"Billy, you're drunk. I'm not going to listen to anything now."

"I told 'em my wife's a real brain. She can find out anythin' she needs to know from them books o' hers. She jest loves them books. Loves 'em more'n she does her li'l baby. Sure loves 'em more'n she does her dumb hillbilly husband."

"You know that's not true," she protested, stung by the bitterness in his voice. "I'm going to school because . . ."

"I know why yer goin' to school. Yer goin' because you know I ain't never gonna be worth a good goddamn. I jest think you'd better pack up and run back to that daddy of yers and yer fancy li'l house. That's what y' wanna do, i'nt it? That's what y've wanted to do since the first mornin' y' woke up in m' bed. I'm dumb, Sheila, but I'm not as dumb as y' think."

"I never thought you were dumb. I never thought that. Please, Billy . . ."

"I knowed y' didn't at first. Y' thought I was some sort of big Yank hero. I got news fer y', girl: the war's over and this hero don't amount to more'n a handful of coal dust. An' don't tell me y' don't want to leave, 'cause I know y' do."

"Yes, I have. I have wanted to leave. What of it? I'm here, aren't I? That's what counts."

"What counts is I don't have a job no more."

"You'll get another one."

"Where? Y' think they're gonna give me references? Y' gonna find me a job by lookin' in those books of yers?" he cried desperately, staring at the books as though they were a nest of tarantulas. With one powerful sweep, he sent them hurtling to the floor. She moved backwards toward the sink, startled by the force of the crash, afraid that he might lunge and strike her.

"Spare me your self-pity, Billy," she said angrily, her face turning a bright red. "I can put up with anything but that. I'm not the one who hit the foreman. I'm not the one who got us into this mess! I'm here and I'm trying to cope. You might give me a little credit instead of attacking me!"

His shoulders sagged and his fists uncurled. He made an abortive gesture to reach down for a book, then straightened up. His mouth twisted into a cynical, quivering grin that threatened to give way to a sob. He looked so miserable that her rage disappeared. "You'd better let me look at that eye now," she said in a firm, practical voice.

"Don't bother, Sheila. Jest don't bother." He gave her one weary, disgusted look and moved unsteadily into the bedroom.

The ice was melting through the cloth in her hand and dripping onto the floor. She threw it into the sink, slowly knelt down to pick up the books, and then sank into a chair. It was too much to think about what would happen to them now. She stared at the linoleum— it was called "Confetti" and wasn't supposed to show the dirt—until the little blobs of color began to merge. Finally she went to the medicine cabinet, got out some Mercurochrome, wrapped another piece of ice in the cloth, and crept to the bedroom.

"Can I turn on the light?"

"No. Don't turn it on."

In the shaft of light from the doorway, she could see him, flat on his back with his clothes still on, the wounded eye shut, the other eye glistening, marooned in his tight, miserable face.

"I don't know if it'll do much good to put the ice on since the swelling has already come up, but it might make it feel a little better." She shut the door and felt her way over to the bed.

"That foreman was ridin' me, Sheila. I know I was wrong to hit him like that, but . . ."

"I know. He's a son-of-a-bitch."

"Do y' know it? It's important fer a man to know that when he comes home his wife's gonna believe what he says is true."

"I know what you say is true."

She sat down on the side of the bed and put the compress on his eye. He sucked his breath in through his teeth and said nothing, then put the ice on the floor and lay back, staring at the ceiling.

"And I didn't mean what I said to you. I know you love Spencer."

"I love you too."

"I sure as hell don't see how."

"We'll figure out a way to handle this, Billy."

"Shit, I don't know how we're gonna."

"I don't either, but we will."

"This is the first bad fight we've ever had."

She leaned forward and put her fingers to his lips.

"I know. I'm sorry too."

He raised himself up, his arms encircling her, pulling her down with him. They clung together, trembling. It wasn't enough, she thought as she heard him whisper, "Girl, I want you," into her hair. It wasn't enough. But it was all they had to keep them going.

CHAPTER
XVII

A HEFTY WOMAN struggling with an untidy bundle was the first passenger off the bus. Then a frail old man, and a bedraggled girl with a suitcase and an armful of books. "Excuse me, please," Dawn said, moving in front of the man who was obscuring her view, and searching for a glimpse of Sheila's blond curls. When the last passenger, a teenage boy with a bad case of acne, stepped down and the doors of the bus closed, Dawn did a double take. The girl with the books was wearing a pair of worn red high heels just like the shoes Sheila had called her Wizard of Oz specials. Dawn's eyes travelled quickly up the length of the slim body. It was Sheila. The eyes, once so full of mischief, were filled with anxiety as they searched the depot, and the wide mouth with the slightly protruding teeth was drawn down at the edges.

"Dawn! Oh, I'm so glad to see you," she cried, dropping the suitcase and throwing her arm around her.

"Sheila. I didn't recognize you at first . . . Your hair is different."

"That's a polite way of putting it," she smiled, patting the barrette that held the straggly hair at the nape of her neck. "I know I was the one who always said a girl didn't have to let herself go just because she was married, but I never have time to set it anymore. But you look wonderful, you really do."

"I look a damned sight better than I did on the ship anyway. Here, let me take your suitcase. The car's parked outside. I've learned to drive, but I'm waiting for Zac to get back from maneuvers so that he can take me for my license. So just pray we don't get stopped by any coppers."

"I'm glad Zac's not home," Sheila said quickly, scanning her friend's face with relief.

"He probably is too. If he ever gets out of the Navy I'm sure he'll want to get a job as a traveling salesman."

"It's not that I don't want to meet him. It's just that . . ."

"I know what you meant. It's better this way. We'll have a chance to talk by ourselves. Faye's at school and my neighbor is taking care of Nita."

"I do want to see the kiddies."

"You'll see them tonight. You are going to stay the night, aren't you? It wasn't really clear from your note."

"Yes. I'll stay the night. I'll have to start out early tomorrow morning . . ."

She stopped, glancing around the station as though afraid that someone might overhear her and guess the nature of her trip.

"C'mon. Let's get out of here."

She picked up the suitcase, took Sheila by the arm, and guided her to the car. In the glare of the noonday sun, Sheila's face looked pale, her eyelids puffy from crying and her nose red at the tip. Dawn wanted to ask her all sorts of questions, but as she looked at her clasping the schoolbooks to her chest, staring blankly out the windshield, she decided to wait.

"Is it sunny here all the time?"

"Most of the time. The climate's rather like Perth."

"I did appreciate your sending that snowsuit to Spencer. It's still too big for him, but I suppose by next year . . ."

"I don't think I'll be needing it anymore. Nita's outgrown it and Zac has said that he doesn't want to have any other children."

"Were you just kidding when you said he doesn't like to be home?"

"It's hard to know how he feels about it. Like most men he doesn't seem to be able to talk about his feelings. He's happy enough when he first gets back. But after a day or two he starts to get restless. Then he starts pacing around looking miserable and I have to keep the children out of his way. I think he likes the *idea* of having a home, but the reality of it just makes him feel caged in."

"It must be hard for you having him gone so much of the time."

"I used to miss him dreadfully. Now . . . to tell you the truth, it only seems to disrupt things when he's around. I used to think it was natural for everyone to get married, but some people just aren't cut out for it. Zac's really much happier when he's with his cobbers on the ship.

I'm not sure he could have made a go of it with any woman, but with me being such a homebody, it's particularly hard for him."

"And what about you? Do you like it here?"

"I've never gotten over being homesick. If anything, I miss the family more than I ever did. I don't mean there aren't other things in life. I really enjoy the children. That's probably the closest bond anyway; the one between mother and child." Her face flushed. What a clumsy thing to say under the circumstances. "I don't mean there aren't other things that are equally important," she fumbled, hoping that she didn't sound insensitive. She was trying not to judge what Sheila was about to do, but ever since the phone call she'd been in a terrible state of confusion. Try as she might to understand, the idea of an abortion was unacceptable. Her revulsion came from a deeper place than any religious or social prohibition. It came from her own experience, from her very flesh. During the war she had lain awake nights, felt the child move inside her, and wondered whether or not its father would live to see its face. But the child was there. She was responsible for it. And what was her vulnerability compared to the growing embryo that depended on her for its very existence? It had never occurred to her, even in her most fearful imaginings of the future, to try to end her pregnancies. "And how are your parents doing?" she asked quickly. "Did I tell you that my sister Patsy's engaged to be married? Charlie thinks she's still too young but . . ."

When they arrived at the hut, Sheila put her books on the couch and looked around the room. "You do have a talent for fixing things up. You've made this place look very cheery."

"I've done what I can, but a hut is a hut. On the hot days when the sun hits this corrugated tin roof, I feel a bit like a missionary in the tropics. It's a far cry from the split-level dream house with the landscaped lawns that dear old Mavis keeps writing to me about."

"Yes," Sheila laughed. "Old Stickybeak. Those mimeographed letters of hers just drive me crackers. I don't know how she manages to have her nose in everyone's business at a distance of thousands of miles, but she does."

"Come and sit down at the table. I'll put the kettle on. Or would you like something stronger? I'm sure there's a bottle of Zac's whiskey hidden in one of the cabinets. He always squirrels it away behind something. Force of habit from all those years with his mother. Blimey, Sheila, you should have seen her. She was a cross between Carrie Nation and Attila the Hun. My happiest moments at that house were when I daydreamed about boiling her in oil. I wrote to you about that blue I had with her, didn't I? . . . Just listen to me rattling on. But it's so good to see you again. So what'll it be? Tea or whiskey?"

"Tea will be lovely, thanks."

"Good, I've made some things to go with it," she said, taking plates of food out of the refrigerator. "My mum sent a Christmas package with plum pudding, Marmite and some tins of passion fruit, and I've been saving them for a special occasion."

"Sponge cake with passion-fruit icing. I haven't had that since I left home."

"Know what I miss the most? Fish and chips wrapped in newspaper."

"Me too. That was the thing I wanted most when I was pregnant with Spencer: a good feed of fish and chips."

"Now tell me all about going back to school," Dawn said as she cut into the cake and put a piece on Sheila's plate. "I think it's bloody brave of you to do that."

"I like it a lot. I think next year I might even try for a scholarship if I can keep my marks up. But I'm always worried about falling behind. I even brought my books with me so I could study on the bus, but needless to say I haven't looked at them." She turned and looked distractedly toward the pile of books, cut into the cake, and took a deep breath. "What was I saying? Oh, yes. Nursing school. It's been a bit of a problem financially. I quit my job at the restaurant, and I had to write and ask Da for tuition money. My biggest concern was about Spencer, but he seems to be doing all right. Billy's mother is very good with him. Spencer . . ." She looked around the room again as though she were hoping to find Spencer there. "So, I actually thought that things were improving until Billy lost his job . . ."

"You didn't tell me that. When did that happen?"

"About six weeks ago. That was when I . . ." She raised the fork to her lips, and then lowered it again. "You see, I had been taking precautions after Spencer was born, but when Billy was fired we had this awful fight and . . ." the fork moved upward again, but stayed poised in midair as she bit her lip. ". . . that was when I got pregnant. I'm sorry. I know you've gone to a lot of trouble to prepare this food, but I just can't . . ." The fork clattered to the plate.

"That's all right, Sheila. Really."

"It just couldn't happen at a worse time." The tears welled in her eyes. "I'm so unprepared for it. But that's the trouble with me. I've been unprepared for everything. From the very first night I arrived in Blacksburg . . ."

Dawn pushed her own plate away, rested her elbows on the table, and asked Sheila to tell her all about it. The letters had given her part of the story, but they couldn't come close to the impact of Sheila's own quavering voice. She told of her shock at finding herself in the shack in the hills, described her pregnancy with Spencer, her move into town and her job at Della Mae's. Dawn got up slowly, found Zac's bottle, and poured two shots into some jelly glasses. Without making a toast, they automatically clinked the glasses together. Sheila dabbed her eyes with the table napkin.

"I was so ashamed to go to Helen and tell her that I might be pregnant again. She's been so encouraging to me. She's always tried to help me to think things through instead of just diving in and then having to live with the consequences. But she's rather judgmental, and I was afraid she'd think I was impossibly stupid."

"But it wasn't your fault, Sheila. You can't take it all on yourself. No matter how intelligent you are or how much you try to plan, you can't control everything."

Sheila gulped a mouthful from the jelly glass. "That's what Helen said too. When I told her Billy had lost his job and all, she suggested that I think about an abortion. At first I said a flat no. I was just horrified by the idea of it. I knew other women did it, but I just couldn't imagine that I ever could. I went through a whole month just pushing it out of my mind. When I'd walk by the delivery room in the hospital I'd just go to pieces. Then I came home one night after school—I'd made up my mind that I was finally going to tell Billy—and as I pulled the car into the street I saw all these grubby kids playing in the yards. One of the littlest ones was sitting on the fender of this old wreck and eating a dirty cracker. I thought about Spencer. I could just see him in a couple of years. I could see *me* in a couple of years too. I'd be ground down into nothing. I'd be like those women in those terrible photos from the Depression. I said 'No. I won't let it happen to me. I just won't let it happen.' "

There was a ring of defiance in her voice; and, for a moment, she looked like the confused but spirited girl Dawn had first met. Dawn nodded and touched her fingertips to her temples, feeling the beginning of a pounding headache.

"So I decided not to tell Billy. And I didn't want to tell Ma. It wasn't that I thought she might try to talk me out of it. It's just that she's getting so old and tired. It would only be one more burden she couldn't do anything about. When I think about the resentment I used to feel against my parents because they tried to protect me from things." She shook her head. "I used to think the only honorable thing to do was to come straight out with it, no matter how ugly or unacceptable a thing was. Now I've developed the same old protective attitude toward the people I love. Though perhaps it isn't just a desire to protect them," she shrugged helplessly. "Perhaps I also want to protect myself from having to deal with their feelings."

"Are you sure you're doing the right thing, not telling Billy? It's his child too."

"Right now his opinion of himself is, as they would say in Blacksburg, lower than a snake's belly. If I told him I didn't want to have the baby, I know it would just be another blow to his self-esteem. He loves me, Dawn. I know he does. And he's crazy about Spencer. He does the best he can, but he just isn't equipped. He doesn't have the faintest prospect of another job. If we were forced back to living in the hills, I actually think he'd feel relieved. The only thing that would make him unhappy is if I were unhappy. And I would be. I can't live like that anymore."

Dawn smoothed the tablecloth and stared at the wall. She could think of nothing to refute Sheila's arguments. Her headache was getting worse.

"But are you sure you'll be safe?" she asked finally. "I don't know much about these things, but I've heard some grisly stories. Aren't you afraid that it might be dangerous?"

"That's why Helen went to such trouble to find me an M.D. She made lots of phone calls. We thought we'd found someone in New York, but it fell through. At one point I was so desperate I even thought of asking her to do it. But that wouldn't be right. In the first place she's come under a lot of criticism from people down there because of her clinic. If there were any complications it could ruin her career. Besides, she's more like a relative than a doctor to me now—it wouldn't be right. It's awful that I'll have to go out of the country, but she's reasonably sure that this chap in Tijuana is a doctor. Of course it's not legal there either, so it won't be in a hospital. I have no idea what to expect. I'll have to telephone down there in a while and let them know I'm coming tomorrow. Then I'll have to call up and find out about the bus schedules.''

Dawn sipped her whiskey. She still wanted to say something to dissuade Sheila, but the pounding in her temple seemed to have destroyed her ability to think. They sat silently until they heard the shouts of children coming home from school. Dawn got up and walked to the screen door. She wanted no part of any of it. She didn't want to be involved. But she couldn't bear to turn around and see her friend's face contorted with grief and fear.

"I'm going to drive you down there.''

"No. You can't do that. I'm not asking you to do that. I only came because I wanted to see you and talk. Besides, I know you think I'm doing the wrong thing.''

"I can't say that, Sheila. I don't know what to say. I truthfully don't know what I would do if I were in your place. But I do know that I'm coming with you. I'll ask Toshi to look after the girls.''

"I wouldn't want anyone else to know about it.''

"Toshi won't ask for any explanations. She's not like that. You need someone with you, Sheila. It's for my sake as well as yours. I couldn't just sit here worrying about what might happen to you.'' She crossed back to the table and put her arms around her. Sheila's mouth gaped open, trying to form an objection. "Now just button your lip. I'm coming with you.''

She could feel the narrow shoulders trembling against her breasts. The screen door slammed. Faye ran in shouting, "Auntie Sheila from the boat.'' The women pulled away from each other abruptly. The child stopped as she saw the looks of guilty complicity on their faces. Rubbing one shoe on the back of the other, she pulled the ribbon in her braids, staring from Dawn to Sheila.

"Faye! Lovey-ducks. I'm so glad to see you.'' Sheila wiped her cheeks and extended her arms. "You've grown so much. You're such a big girl now.''

"I know. Mummy says I'm growing up too fast. She wants me to be a little girl always, but *I* want to be a teenager.''

Dawn pulled the child to her, hugging her fiercely. Faye wiggled uncomfortably, looking over her shoulder at the food on the table.

"Can I have some of that cake now?''

"Kiss Auntie Sheila first. Then I'll go and get Nita and we'll all have a tea party.''

THEY LEFT the next morning after Faye had gone off to school. Toshi didn't ask any questions. Dawn was so jittery when she started the car that she backed into the metal barrier in the parking lot and scraped the rear fender.

"Shouldn't we get out and check the damage?" Sheila asked, as the car pulled forward.

"No. Let's just get a move on. I'll drive until we're close to the border. Then I'll have to let you take over because the guards might want to check my license."

"I hadn't thought of that."

"I have. I may look like a bloomin' idiot, but I'm thinking."

They drove for at least an hour, sharing only trivial and desultory conversation. Then, to break the tension, Dawn began to sing. Sheila picked up the tune. They went through an entire repertoire of popular songs—"Do you remember this one . . . ?" "You sing the verse, I'll harmonize on the chorus . . ." "Hey, matey, you were flat, how about . . ."

When they were within a few miles of the border, Dawn pulled to the side of the road. They changed seats, put their passports on the dashboard, and fell silent. As they pulled into the line approaching the stucco facade marked "Welcome to Mexico," they both put matter-of-fact expressions on their faces. The car inched toward the immigration booth. A swarthy man wearing a sweat-soaked khaki uniform, sunglasses hiding his eyes, shoved his head into the window and asked why they were coming to Tijuana.

"Shopping," Sheila answered in a barely audible voice.

"We've heard we could get imported perfume here very cheaply."

"Surely, *senoritas*. All the ladies come to buy their perfume." Dawn thought she could hear a knowing derision in his voice. "And where are you born?"

"Australia."

"Ah, you come a long way to buy perfume," he grinned, exposing a set of large white teeth. Dawn gathered up the passports and started to thrust them toward him, but he shook his head. He lowered his glasses long enough to give them the once over, then pushed them back onto the bridge of his nose.

"No, *senoritas*. Show the passports to the officer when you want to reenter."

He bared the teeth again, waved them forward, and sauntered off to the next car. They moved across the border into another snarl of traffic. Off to the side of the road there were clusters of single-story buildings advertising car insurance. Dawn was already wondering how she would explain the fender scrape to Zac. She thought of asking Sheila to stop, but as she saw her, hunched forward, hands gripping the wheel, eyes squinting at the signs directing them toward the main part of town, she decided to keep quiet. They bumped onto another road. Whenever they slowed to check the signs, swarms of barefoot children and men in battered sombreros rushed up to the car trying to sell piñatas and brightly painted plaster bulls. They rolled up the windows and stared straight ahead until they found the Hotel Imperial.

Dawn put the suitcase on the bed and looked around the room: turquoise walls, a wooden table with a crepe-paper flower stuck into a Coke bottle, a 1946 calendar from Goodyear tires. Sheila took the white card from her purse and dialed the number. Yes. She should come to 4 Calle Obregon at two o'clock. Dawn checked her watch: twelve-thirty.

"Are you hungry?"

"They told me not to eat for twelve hours before. That's why I didn't have any breakfast."

"Oh."

They stared at each other.

"Speaking of food," Dawn said, desperately trying to fill the silence, "you should have seen us at Thanksgiving. Zac was away as usual. I asked Toshi over because she was alone too. I got out *The Betty Crocker Cookbook* and made everything listed under 'Traditional Thanksgiving Dinner.' So there we were—two foreigners—Toshi looking down at the pumpkin pie as though it might jump up and bite her, while Faye lectured us on the meaning of the feast. Of course she got it all mixed up. According to her the Pilgrims made friends with the Indians because they gave them marshmallows to put on their sweet potatoes . . . God, it's hot in here. Would you like me to open these shutters?"

At one-thirty, Sheila got up and started to comb her hair. She asked Dawn if she could borrow a lipstick. Dawn picked up her purse, tried to stop her hands from shaking, and waited at the door. As she reached for the knob, Sheila backed away from the mirror and sat down on the bed. She squeezed her eyes shut and mentally started to count to ten. *One, two three . . . I can still turn around . . . four, five . . . I don't have to go through with this . . . six . . . I can't . . . seven . . . please, no, don't let this happen to me . . . eight . . .* A long, painful breath. "I'm ready."

They walked out into the sweltering street. Tourist shops full of hats, dolls, leather sandals, perfume and gewgaws. Heavy dark-skinned women, their heads covered with serapes, stood by carts hawking tacos and sticky candies. A sorry-looking donkey, straw hat bashed down over its ears, flies clustered around its eyes, shook its head while its keeper lifted the gringo child onto its back and snapped a picture for the smiling parents. Dawn darted into the road to ask a traffic policeman for directions to Calle Obregon. She took Sheila's arm. Left onto another narrow street. Raucous music blasted from the caverns of bars. Smells of sour liquor and hot sauce. Neon signs bleached into nothingness by the blazing sun flashed around photos of seminude women. Turn right again. A bakery. A funeral parlor. Then sudden quiet as the street became residential. Rows of pink stucco buildings. High cement walls with chips of glass embedded in the top to discourage intruders. 4 Calle Obregon. A wooden door with an iron bell next to the fading number.

Dawn looked at Sheila. Great beads of perspiration had broken out on her face, yet she was shivering. She reached up and pulled the bell rope.

The door was opened a crack. An elderly woman with high Indian cheekbones peered out at them, the wilted greenery of a courtyard visible behind her head.

"Buenos tardes, senoritas."

"I'm Mrs. Hickock. I have an appointment with the doctor."

"But she . . . ?" The woman eyed Dawn.

"She's a friend."

"She go away. Wait for you some other place. She come, we send you away." The mouth puckered, the dark eyes searched the street behind them.

"But I just . . ."

"No. It's all right, Dawn. Go back to the hotel."

"How long . . . ?"

The woman moved aside just enough to let Sheila squeeze past her.

"Two hour maybe."

The door was shut.

Dawn turned around and leaned against the wall. Three men across the street whispered to each other. One made a sucking noise, and they all broke into laughter. She turned the corner into a dirt road, then, realizing that she had gone in the wrong direction, doubled back. She crossed the street, walking quickly past the men, her eyes on the pavement. When she found herself on another street lined with automobile-upholstery shops, she knew she had taken another wrong turn. She kept walking, afraid to ask any of the workmen for directions. Around another corner. The spire of the church. She could ask directions there.

It was gloomy and fetid inside. She felt her way up the aisle, groping the rough wood of the pews, adjusting her eyes to the gilt altar where banks of candles were burning. Kneeling down at the rail, she put her head in her hands. When she looked up she saw the massive cross with a wooden Christ hanging from it. The statue was painted. Drops of carmine-colored blood dripping from the head, hands, feet and side. It had glass eyes and a wig. She had never seen anything like it before in her life. She got to her feet and started back down the aisle. Over to the side an altar in soft blue light, the Virgin and Child. She dropped a coin into the poorbox, took a taper, and lit one of the candles that sat in the row of tinted glasses.

"Help her. It's not in her heart to do anything wrong. Please make her safe."

She turned to see a small boy in a baggy shirt and pants that looked like pajamas.

"You wanna buy a charm, lady?" he asked as he thrust under her nose a piece of cardboard on which tiny silver ornaments were pinned. "Eef you sick, your mother sick, you buy. Give to the Virgin."

"No, thank you. I'm afraid that I'm lost," she said, hearing their whispers echo through the darkness.

"Where you wanna go?"

"Hotel Imperial."

"Okay. For one dime I take you."

He turned and scuffled toward the doors without waiting for her to catch up with him. Once on the street, he raced ahead of her, the cardboard box of religious charms tucked under one arm, shoeshine equipment clutched in the other. She cursed her high heels as she struggled to keep up. Down the street, through an alleyway and up another street lined with tourist shops. She had almost caught up with him when he started across another street, and then leaped back, almost knocking her over as a car careened around the corner and blasted its horn.

"Are you all right?"

"*Sí.*"

"You won't get lost, will you?"

"No. I go every day. I know all places. My uncle drive a taxi. You want a taxi, lady?"

"No, thank you."

"You want a shoeshine?"

"No. Why aren't you in school?"

He trotted off. As they came to the entrance of the hotel, he turned to her again. "Sure you don't want no shoeshine?"

When she shook her head he looked angry and dejected. She felt in her purse for some change.

"Here . . . What is your name?"

"Hey-sus."

"Hey-sus?"

"Hey-sus. In the church," he demonstrated, stretching his arms out at shoulder height.

"Well . . . thank you, Jesus. Here's . . ."

The fingers of the outstretched hand closed over the fifty-cent piece. His eyes shot a quick suspicious look, as though fearing she might want to reclaim the coin; then he darted off into the crowd.

She walked swiftly through the lobby, ran upstairs to the room, and shut the door, her body bathed in perspiration. She undid the buttons of her dress and looked at the tile stall with the single spigot protruding from the wall in the bathroom. If she took a shower she might not hear the phone ring or the knock on the door. She slipped off her shoes and sat, motionless, on the bed. If only she had brought her knitting or some embroidery. If her hands were busy, she might be able to ignore her fearful imaginings. She checked her watch, then called the desk to ask the time. Three-thirty. Sheila must be on her way back now.

At four-thirty she was frantic. What if there had been complications? What if Sheila had gotten lost on the way back? She got up, opened the shutters, and paced the room. She couldn't go back to the wooden door. That might cause Sheila further trouble. But she must do something.

At six o'clock she went downstairs and stood at the desk. A chubby clerk, shirt buttons pulled taut exposing the flesh of his belly, was asleep with his head on a radio. The Spanish version of a cereal

commercial bleated out. She cleared her throat, looked around for a
bell she might ring to rouse him, and then stupidly began to sing the
commercial in English.

> Ask your mother in the morning
> To serve you up a steaming plate.
> It's a grand, hot whole wheat cereal
> And the cowboys think it's great.

The clerk wiped his hand over his eyes and blinked at her.

"I'm sorry to disturb you. I'm not feeling very well. I wonder if
there's a doctor—an American doctor—in town. One who would
speak English?"

"Don't know. Other guy come to work at seven o'clock. Maybe you
wait. He help you. You got . . . ?" He rubbed his hand over his belly
and grimaced as though he were throwing up.

"No, my stomach isn't upset. That is . . . I'm just not feeling well.
I'd like to contact an American doctor," she answered, articulating
each syllable:

"Seven. Maybe seven-thirty, Juan come. He tell you."

He put his head back onto the radio, raised his arm to protect his
exposed ear, and drifted back to sleep.

She looked around helplessly, hoping to spot a telephone book, and
then trudged back upstairs. She would wait until the next desk clerk
came on. If he could provide her with the name of an American doctor
she would just call, explain the situation, and ask for help. If he turned
her down, she would find out where the American embassy was
located. But would there be an embassy in a sleazy border town? She
could always try to find her way back to 4 Calle Obregon. If they
wouldn't answer the door, she would drive back to the border and ask
for help.

She stood by the window and watched the light fade from the sky.
The steady, frenetic beat of a mariachi band drifted through the
casement. Footsteps in the hallway, followed by some laughter and
muffled voices in Spanish. She ran to the door and pressed her
ear against it. The voices receded. She went back to the window,
gulping great drafts of the humid air and watching the neon lights
flashing on the bars. Finally, there was a scratching sound on the
door. She started, turned on the bedside lamp, and stumbled over.

"Dawn. It's me. Open the door," a husky, drained voice whispered.

"My God, Sheila, I've been so worried. Are you all right?"

"There were so many women. They didn't take me for hours," she breathed as Dawn helped her toward the bed.

"But are you all right?"

"I think so. I can't talk now. Just let me rest for a minute, then I want to get out of here. They told me at the doctor's that the border guards ask to see things you've bought. Do you think you could go downstairs and get something? I'm afraid that it might look suspicious if we don't have anything to declare."

"Of course. Just let me . . ."

She took off Sheila's shoes and helped her to lie down. "Are you in pain?" she asked softly, reaching out to smooth the hair back from her forehead. Sheila waved her hand away and stared past her, eyes lost in a private world. Dawn sat beside her for several minutes, wanting to comfort, but realizing that any gesture might unbalance the hard-won control Sheila was fighting to maintain. It was dark now but the room was still sweltering. She opened the shutters some more. The discordant blare of the mariachi band filled the room. After wringing out a washcloth and sponging Sheila's face and neck, she left.

When she got back with the bottle of Tabu and the sombrero she'd bought with her housekeeping money, Sheila was sitting up trying to rub some rouge into her colorless cheeks. "I think I can move now. I'm ready to go."

MILES AFTER they were safely back across the border, Sheila pulled onto the shoulder of the road. Dawn put the bottle of perfume and the hat by the roadside, slid into the driver's seat, and pulled back onto the highway. Sheila rested her head on the back of the seat and shut her eyes. Dawn could see that she was wincing and breathing heavily.

"How do you feel?" Dawn asked. Sheila said nothing. "Are you all right?"

"I feel . . . very, very old."

"You're only twenty-one," Dawn answered gently, knowing that wasn't what Sheila meant. "And I've thought about it a lot," she added after a long pause, "and I think you did the right thing. You did the only thing you could under the circumstances." She wasn't entirely convinced that she meant it, but comfort, not judgment, was the only human response to another person's pain.

"But it isn't really about how old you are, is it," Sheila went on, following her own thoughts, seemingly oblivious to her friend's attempt at absolution. "It's when you take a certain turn and you know there's no going back. You've taken that particular turn. None of the others. The others aren't possible anymore. No matter what the circumstances, you've made the choice. It wasn't made for you by your mother or your da or your husband. It was your choice. It feels . . . lonely."

"Yes."

"I used to think that if you loved someone, really loved him, that you wouldn't ever feel lonely. But this is something that being in love doesn't even touch. When I was waiting there I kept looking at the other women. Some of them were much younger than I am. Some were much older. I tried to imagine what their husbands or boyfriends were like, and I just couldn't imagine them. Each of those women was there all by herself. I know it doesn't make any sense, because I was the one who decided not to tell Billy, but suddenly I was very angry because he wasn't there with me. That's crazy, isn't it?"

"No. When I went into labor I felt the same way. I knew it wasn't Zac's fault that he wasn't there, but I still felt deserted."

"But you've never lied to Zac. I've broken trust with Billy. Even if I look at him again and want him—and right now it seems as though I couldn't ever want him again—but even if I did, it would all be different."

"You did what you had to do, Sheila. Don't make it worse by blaming yourself," Dawn said firmly, trying to give the reassurance she knew was needed.

"Have you ever lied to Zac?"

"Not about anything important. Though I don't think he really pays enough attention to me to know what I'm doing. Sometimes I feel more lonely when he's there. I'm just the person who takes care of the kids and worries him about the housekeeping money. I don't think he looks at me as a woman anymore. I'm going to be thirty next year, but I feel that part of my life is over. So I know what you mean about feeling old. If I put on a new dress or do my hair now, I know I'm doing it for myself and for the children. Zac doesn't seem to notice. With us it's not that the honeymoon is over; it's that it never really began. The funny part is that I didn't even know how much I wanted him until I realized that we would never really be intimate."

"Have you thought of leaving him?"

"Oh yes. I've thought about it. One night after we'd had a real bang-up fight—dishes smashed, the whole thing—I dressed the girls and just left the hut. I got about three blocks. Then I realized I didn't have anywhere to go. Didn't even have any family or friends I could call to go to."

"What did you do?"

"I sat on the curb and cried. Then I noticed how upset the kids were so I turned around and went back."

"I didn't know things were that bad with you."

"I don't like to talk about it. Silly, isn't it," she laughed, "but I still feel that somehow I'm being disloyal if I let anyone know how things really are. But I don't want to make it sound too hopeless; I still get a lot of pleasure out of life. The kids amaze me all the time and I guess I'm simple-minded enough to enjoy things that don't seem important to other people. I get a lot of satisfaction out of turning out a really good dinner, or sewing a pretty dress. I like to walk down to the pier and watch the sunset. Peace, even those everyday things about peace, means a lot to me. I mean, I'm the sort who feels good just because the weather's fine."

Sheila reached across and put her hand on Dawn's arm. They drove on, listening to the swoosh of the cars passing, staring into the oncoming headlights, comforted by each other's presence.

The next morning Sheila boarded the bus to go back to the train station. As she clutched her textbooks with one hand and waved out the window to the woman with the lovely auburn hair and the sad gray eyes she felt the tears she had suppressed well up. When she had first met Dawn they had been friends because they were thrown together, needed companionship, and found each other acceptable. Now the bond between them was permanent. Each knew things about the other that required trust to tell and affection to accept. Their lives were truly linked.

CHAPTER
XVIII

THOUGH SHE WOULD never have put it that way, even to herself, Mrs. Everett Meade, the Episcopal bishop's wife, knew that Richard Cunningham's funeral would be the social event of the fall season. Even so, she was surprised when she arrived at the church a full hour before the ceremony to find a large crowd in front of the building. Judging from their appearance and demeanor, very few of them had any personal relation to the deceased. They had come out of curiosity, to see the famous and near-famous mourners who were bound to attend. There were several reporter types milling about. A young photographer had perched himself in a tree and now sat, camera slung across his chest, smoking and grinning down at the mob who were elbowing each other for the best positions and spilling over onto the lawns. Lord only knew what the gardener would say when he saw what they'd done to the flower beds!

She trotted around to the side entrance, colliding with a spotty-faced acolyte who was struggling with a huge wreath—"With Bereavement and Respect, United Real Estate Association"—and popped into the sacristy to remind Everett to take his indigestion pills. She raced up to the choir loft. Miss Cotler, the organist, like all artistic types, was highly strung and needed a few words of encouragement when she was about to perform for an important audience. After bolstering Miss Cotler, Mrs. Meade hurried back downstairs to caution the ushers about admitting unauthorized persons into the pews cordoned with black and gold ribbons. She checked the tilt of her new black toque in a brass memorial plaque, and settled down, third row center, to watch the proceedings.

Miss Cotler pumped out a traditional dirge as the first mourners took their places. There was Harrison Phelps—it was rumored he had gone from being a moderately successful small-parts manufacturer to millionaire status as a result of government contracts during the war. J. T. Grant, president of the meat-packing company that bore his name, and Mrs. Grant. The papers said she had plans to sponsor a new opera company in the city. The junior and senior state senators, minus their wives. Mrs. Zoe Hamlyn and that poor unfortunate son of hers who had lost his leg somewhere in Germany on the very day the peace treaty was signed. A trio of men who *looked* important, though she couldn't place the faces . . . probably from out of town. Fred and Mabel Richardson with their son, Jimmy, and daughter, Betty. Apparently living in New York hadn't improved Betty one bit. She still looked about as exciting as a rice pudding and she was wearing a singularly unbecoming hat. Of course she was supposed to be a brain, but what else could she choose to be after Ricky Cunningham came back from overseas with his stunning new wife?

Everyone said that Donald Manchester was on the verge of divorcing Kay, but here they were holding hands and looking the very picture of marital devotion. Robert "Bobs" Carpenter—no one could ever pin down exactly *what* he did, but whatever it was, it was lucrative. Esther Lewellyn Smith and that young man she *said* was her second cousin from Chicago. Yes, everyone was here, except the deceased's family. Finally Ricky Cunningham walked past her, holding his mother by the elbow. Ricky was more handsome than ever, though looks weren't enough to overcome the rumors that he was a bit odd. And poor Etna Cunningham! She looked as though she might faint dead away. Of course everyone knew that she overindulged, so it was impossible to tell if her faltering step was a manifestation of widow's grief or she'd had a nip before she'd come. That tall Negro woman walking behind them carrying the baby—she must be the housekeeper. Surely they weren't going to let her . . . yes, they were! Ricky moved aside and ushered her past him into the front pew. Mrs. Meade clutched her hymnal and stared down at the floor as the crowd focused on that spectacle.

Then there was a shift in the collective attention: the younger Mrs. Cunningham had arrived. She was as spectacularly attractive as she was reported to be, though her features were so impassive she might have been at the ceremony to model the broad-brimmed hat that partially hid her face. It would be hard for Everett to command the attention of the audience with Gaynor Cunningham sitting in the front pew. The acolytes came onto the altar. That pathetic Lonnie Diamond honked his nose into his handkerchief and stifled a sob. Once Everett had started the invocation and she could tell he was in good voice, Mrs. Meade allowed her gaze to wander back to Ricky and his wife. No one knew anything about the woman, though it was generally accepted that he must have married her because of physical attraction. Physical attraction of a very high order, of course. And they were such an exemplary couple: looks, poise, education and now, all that incredible wealth. Old Cunningham must have left millions.

". . . to honor the passing of one of the great men of this state, nay, of this nation. A man whose industry and patriotism, whose foresight and strength have led us all in . . ."

Such a lovely turnout! The banks of flowers, the somber, well-groomed mourners, Miss Cotler pedaling out the Bach, and perhaps, in a few months, the commission of a commemorative stained-glass window. . . .

As SOON AS they reached the house, Gaynor took Joey from Faustina and excused herself to go upstairs. Joey had been quiet during the funeral service; but as soon as she took him, he started whimpering through his stuffy little nose. When she hugged and rocked him, he only cried louder. She put him into the cradle near the bed and rushed into the bathroom, shutting the door behind her. The sedatives the doctor had prescribed were sitting on the sink. She took off her hat and gloves, placed two pills on her tongue, and scooped a handful of water into her mouth. Her throat constricted. She gagged and tried again, this time coughing the pills into the sink and retching with their bitter taste. She'd lived on little more than brandy and sedatives since Richard's death. And now she couldn't swallow.

As she looked at the pills disintegrating in the basin, she wondered if she would have the guts to renew the prescription and take the whole lot at once. That would be fast and courageous.

Not that she gave herself many points for courage. But perhaps that was a better way out than returning with Ricky and Joey to Princeton. She could hear Joey crying in the other room. If he didn't shut up soon, she'd have to go downstairs and ask Faustina to take care of him. Then she could pour herself another brandy and go to sleep. But no, the house was full of people, people who had come to honor Richard's memory. Or so they thought. Bloody hell, she did need a drink. But she had to go easy on that. Her mother had been a beauty too, and look what the drink had done to her. If you were going to be a lush you should at least have the cushion of money, as Etna did. She could probably get some money yet. Unless Richard had cut Ricky out of the will entirely, which wasn't likely. But it would mean having to put up with Ricky, intolerable thought. Ironic that it had been her plan to try to get Ricky to accept his father's money. That was before she fell in love with Richard. She shook her head, washed the remains of the pills down the sink, and picked up another two. This time they went down.

"Darling?"

"I'm in the bathroom."

"I could hear Joey crying so I came up."

"I just wanted to take a sedative," she said wearily as she opened the door.

"Are you feeling all right? Well enough to come downstairs? Lots of people are asking where you are."

"In answer to your first question, I feel bloody awful. In answer to your second, I don't want to come downstairs. And as far as the correct protocol of greeting the guests: I thought you were the rebel who didn't care about social form."

"I don't. I was thinking of Mother. I guess that's difficult for you to grasp since you rarely think of anyone but yourself."

"As opposed to whom? I think you spend a great deal of time thinking about yourself too, but you're an intellectual, aren't you? You wrap your self-involvement in a nice protective blanket of ideas and good works."

"Oh for God's sake, Gaynor. I didn't come up here to fight with you. Let's just admit that we're both under a lot of strain and at least try to be decent."

"I was being decent. I was closeted away helping myself to a lovely little pill when you barged in on me."

"I came in because I heard Joey cry. Do you want me to get Faustina?" he sighed, picking the baby up and trying to calm him.

"No. Don't take my baby. Give him to me. I want to rock him."

"Okay. Okay. Here he is."

He went out quickly, starting to slam the door, remembering the guests downstairs and pulling it to him with restraint. He'd better get

Faustina. Lonnie Diamond stopped him in the hallway, put his arm around him, and led him to a corner.

"It's time for some straight talk, Ricky. Hell, I've known you since you were just a kid. 'Member how I used to play catch with you in the backyard of the old house?"

"Yeah, Lonnie, I remember," he nodded, trying to duck away from the beefy, sorrowful face.

"I knew your dad pretty well. I won't say we were intimates. I wasn't in Richard's league. He knew it and I knew it. I'm talking to you straight now, Ricky. I know you and the old man didn't always see eye to eye. Because of that, I know that you're probably in a lot worse shape than you're lettin' on. And I want you to know that if you need me for anything, I'll be right there."

"Thanks, Lonnie. Thanks."

He could see that Lonnie was genuinely moved, genuinely trying to express some inarticulate male loyalty. He wanted to punch him in the mouth. "Excuse me, I have to get Faustina."

"Sure, kid. You keep the household goin'. You're the head of it now."

When he'd found Faustina and whispered to her that Gaynor might need some help with Joey, he slipped out the back door and walked as fast as he could toward the tennis courts. Betty was sitting on the bench smoothing the feathers on her hat.

"Were you looking for me, or did you come out here to be alone?"

"I came out to be alone."

"Oh."

"But you're the next best thing."

"If you mean you don't want to talk I certainly won't be the one to force you into it."

"I've got nothing to say." He kicked at the gravel and stuffed his hands into his suit pockets.

"If you want to laugh I could put this hat back on my head. I know it makes me look like something out of the Our Gang comedies, but I didn't have one of my own so mother insisted I put this on. She told me it was stunning." She plopped it back onto her head and looked at him cock-eyed.

"Sorry. I know I'm not very amusing. I'll go back in and leave you alone if you like."

"Actually you are pretty amusing. Or the hat is."

He sat down on the bench, let out a deep sigh, and looked up through the trees at the bright cloudless sky. "I just had to get out of there and breathe for a bit. It was enough listening to that pompous funeral oration, I don't want to hear it regurgitated by those homo boobiens sitting in the living room like a flock of well-fed crows."

"Yes, the Reverend Meade did outdo himself today, didn't he: 'Friends, Romans, countrymen, lend me your purse. I come not to bury Caesar but to get a new stained-glass window.' See, I knew I could make you laugh. Is your mother all right?"

"She seems calm enough. It's hard to tell. I haven't seen her shed a tear in public, but last night on my way up to bed I passed her room, and thought I could hear her crying. Christ, after the way he treated her!"

"She loved him, Ricky."

"Yeah. I always knew she did. I just couldn't figure out why . . . Say, it was good of you to fly back here. I know how busy you are at school."

"You knew I'd come."

"Sure, I knew it. Does that mean I shouldn't be grateful?"

"No. I guess not. How long are you planning to stay?"

"Couple more days. Manchester's supposed to come over and read the will on Friday."

"Ah yes, the will. Another scene of high drama."

"Please. Let's not even talk about it."

She tucked her hands into the sleeves of her jacket, watched the afternoon breeze move the tops of the trees, and waited for him to speak. Without looking at her, he ran his hand along her arm, got up, and straightened his shoulders.

"Guess I'll go back in, look mournful and shake a few hands."

"Did you take that apartment you'd found?"

"Hell no. Spent months looking for the damned thing, then with all this . . . I'm sure someone else has it by now."

"That's too bad. It'll be cramped with the baby."

"I might just be there alone. Gaynor hasn't manifested any burning desire to come back with me. She's not that good with Joey, either. Maybe it would be better for his sake if they stayed on. That way Faustina can give her a hand."

"She's probably upset about the funeral."

"C'mon, Betty. How many excuses are there?"

She turned her head away and smoothed the feathers on her hat. It was indisputable now: Gaynor wasn't in love with him, or if she was, she wasn't willing to really stick by him. But that was not a subject that she wanted to get into. At least not at a time like this.

"Hey, did I tell you that they've okayed my thesis?" she asked brightly, getting up and linking her arm through his.

"So what's it to be?"

"The Matriarchal Family Structure in Rural America. Sound impressive?"

"Very."

"Actually one of my professors wants to do it. If I agree to travel all through southern Appalachia, do the interviews, and collect the data, he'll compile it and put his name at the top of the paper."

"Congratulations. For God's sake don't wear that hat when you interview anyone; they'll think you're a human artichoke."

"I see your humor has been sufficiently restored for you to make snide remarks about my fashion sense," she laughed. "Ready to face the lions?"

"And the Christians as well," he smiled cynically. "If I can find Mrs. Meade I'll tell her that we want to put in the biggest stained-glass window she's ever seen. That way, someone will have a good time today."

BY FRIDAY morning the weather had turned around. The reprieve of Indian summer was over, the skies chill and threatening. Ricky woke up from a fitful sleep as the rain gusted against the window. As soon as he'd come to consciousness he remembered that this was the day they were to hear the will, the day he was to fly back to the heap of neglected work in his lonely apartment. He wanted to pull the covers up over his head and ignore all of it, but now that his mind was working, he knew that was impossible. Throwing back the comforter, he shuffled into the bathroom, relieved himself, and then came back and raised the shade. Steady sheets of rain were coming down on the garden furniture that had been left out on the terrace. The sight of it made him feel unaccountably hopeless.

Shivering, he looked across at Gaynor. She had turned onto her side, and her dark hair fell across her face. Her arms were crossed over her chest, hugging her shoulders, pushing her breasts out of the nightdress. One small foot, with funny-looking lacquered toenails, peeked out from the blankets. He had once heard someone say that even an enemy could inspire tenderness if you saw him sleeping.

Despite the distance between them, despite the arguments of the last few days, his heart went out to her. He longed to crawl back into bed, snuggle into the warmth of her body, kiss her until the lovely eyes flickered open and then closed again as she gave in to a drowsy waking embrace.

He sat on the edge of the bed and touched her hair. He could see the eyes moving behind the moist-looking lids. *Come back with me. Can't we start again? Can't we just . . . start again? Without apology or blame, without analysis. Can't we put our bodies together; seal the truce? Give up on personal wars?*

"Gaynor?"

She pushed his hand away and rose up, panting.

"Where am . . . what time is it?"

"Shhh, baby. It's early."

"Why did you wake me up?"

"I couldn't sleep myself. I wanted to talk to you. Manchester's coming over at eleven. My plane leaves at five and I haven't packed yet."

"All right. I'll get up."

"You don't have to get up. I just wanted to . . ."

"Yes. I know."

She flung her head back onto the pillow and pulled the covers aside with the pained tolerance of someone who has just let a stranger push ahead of her in line.

"Not if you don't want to."

"Ricky, please. If you want to we can."

He slipped in beside her, hating himself as he felt desire overwhelm judgment. *Yes, goddamnit, I want to.* He pulled her toward him roughly, giving her no chance to withdraw. As he ran his hands over her body and pressed his mouth onto hers, he felt a new sensation twisting in his gut: the power of assertion, the satisfaction of taking what he wanted without bothering about her needs. He pinned her down and pulled the nightdress up over her stomach, marveling at the dexterity of his movements. Lunging into her, he heard a groan of pleasure break from her throat. She was yielding, coming to meet his desire with her own. Her responsiveness calmed him, brought him back to the realization that this was his wife, a woman he loved. He wanted to please her, really make love to her instead of just using her as a receptacle for his lust. But as he moved away, controlling himself, touching her to make sure she was ready for him, she grew icy and passive again. His hands stopped. The film of perspiration that had come over his body turned cold. She lay perfectly still, her legs flung wide, open, uninvolved. What had seemed excruciatingly desirable to him minutes before now seemed obscene. He drew the covers over her and sat up, swinging his feet down onto the carpet.

"I thought you wanted to."

I did. I do. I don't know what happened just then. "Not like this, Gaynor. Not if you're going to feel like some sacrificial animal."

"Do you want to make a speech or do you want to get laid?"

"Why are you talking like that?"

"Like what?"

"Why are you talking like a whore?"

"Don't you dare call me that!"

"I'm sorry," he said wearily, looking down at his legs and finding them incredibly ugly. *Hopeless. It's hopeless. Why am I bothering to talk? Am I some lap-dog husband begging for bed privileges? Hopeless.*

"I said don't call me that," she yelled. But he had already started to walk away from her into the bathroom.

DONALD MANCHESTER arrived promptly at eleven o'clock. He'd been a guest in the house many times before, but now he handed his raincoat and umbrella to Faustina without the usual pleasantries and stood in the hallway wiping the raindrops from his briefcase while she went to summon the family. He shook hands with Ricky without looking him in the eye, nodded briefly in Gaynor's direction, then stood back politely, indicating that Etna was to precede him into Richard's study. He put the papers on the desk, moving around to sit in the leather chair. When Etna saw him in the chair that had been Richard's exclusive property, she knotted her handkerchief and turned to stare out the window.

"This heavy rain won't be good for the chrysanthemums, will it? I noticed the other day at the church that the soil was so dry it was cracked, so with a downpour the seeds could be flooded out and . . ."

Ricky pulled his chair closer to hers and patted her hand. She stared around distractedly, and then straightened her spine. Gaynor drew a cigarette out of her case and looked down at the carpet. Manchester cleared his throat.

"I shall read the will in its entirety. Afterwards, I shall be glad to explain any of the provisions that you feel require further clarification." He looked at each of them in turn, smoothed the papers in front of him, and cleared his throat again. "The will is dated April 20, 1947. 'I, Richard Cunningham, being of . . .'"

Gaynor's head jerked up involuntarily. The will had been made a week after Joey's birth. She tried to remember the conversation she'd had with Richard after she'd come home from the hospital. He had been cryptic, but very pleased with himself. He had said that he would take care of her. She could see Manchester's mouth opening and closing, but she couldn't make sense of the words. "Discretionary trust . . . corpus of the estate . . . to my beloved wife Etna, a one-million-dollar trust, plus all property . . ." How much money was there, really? If Etna got $1,000,000, what did that mean? "The corpus to my beloved grandson Joseph upon her death . . . To my daughter-in-law, Gaynor Cunningham . . ." She drew on the cigarette, turned her eyes to the carpet again. "To my daughter-in-law, Gaynor Cunningham, a trust fund for life at fifty thousand dollars per year . . ." *Richard! My darling, darling Richard!*

"All other property to trust for Joseph to be administered by my lawyers, the firm of Potter, Manchester and Little, for educational expenses at the Westfield Military Academy, where Joseph shall be registered upon his seventh birthday . . . medical expenses, a modest spending allowance. Upon the twenty-fifth birthday of Joseph, he is to receive a twenty-five-thousand-dollar annual allowance . . . To my son Richard Cunningham the Second: the sum of twenty-five thousand dollars, given in the expectation that he will learn to assume a respect for and ability to manage his financial affairs."

Manchester's voice droned on, outlining bequests to this civic organization, that academy and university. When he had finished reading, he shuffled the papers again and asked if there were any questions. Gaynor stubbed out her cigarette and lit another, never raising her eyes. The only sound was the persistent slashing of the rain on the windowpane.

"If you don't mind," Manchester smiled, reaching over to turn on a lamp. Gaynor shifted her eyes without raising her head and saw Ricky's face twisted in a sardonic smile.

"So it means that Joey . . ." Etna faltered.

"Joseph is the principal beneficiary, yes."

"But does it mean that Richard can force Joey to go to military school? I've never liked the idea of children being sent away. My cousin was sent to a military school and I know that he was quite miserable."

"Mother," Ricky cut in with soft laughter, "you didn't suppose that Richard would allow his influence over our lives to stop just because he died, did you? He still wants to run the show. He wants to make sure that one male Cunningham can be created in his own image. Since he failed so miserably in his first attempt, he's determined that I'll be punished and that Joey will be a general in the next world war. Now listen to me, Manchester, I want to tell you right now that no son of mine . . ."

"I'm very sorry," Manchester said, the stolid features clouding with embarrassment. "I'm very sorry, but I have an important meeting at the office. If you wish to discuss the details of the will at a further meeting, I will, of course, be at your disposal."

Ricky's jaw set. His mouth set into a hard, determined line. His eyes were cold, staring Manchester down. As Gaynor stared at him she thought he had never looked so much like his father in his life. Then the determined expression fragmented, bewilderment and anguish softening the eyes, slackening the lips. The mask began to crumble. He turned and rushed out of the room.

"Ricky darling . . ." Etna was on her feet. "Please excuse us, Donald." She ran out after him.

Manchester averted his eyes, stacked up the papers and returned them to his briefcase. "I really *do* have an important meeting," he said to himself, starting out the door. He stopped and looked down at Gaynor's head.

"Naturally, Mrs. Cunningham, as a trustee of the estate, I am available to you at any time."

"Thank you so much, Mr. Manchester," she whispered without getting up. "And now, if you'll excuse me . . ."

"Of course. Don't get up. I know the way out."

The ash on the end of her cigarette dropped onto the carpet. She looked at it for a moment, inhaled again, and then got up and slowly closed the door. Running her hands along Richard's desk, she settled into his chair. How lovely to be in this warm room. The rain beating on the windows only increased her sense of protection. She rubbed herself against the chair like a small animal settling into a burrow. So cold and nasty outside. Here, inside, beautiful furniture, carpets, cognac and silverware, flowers, clothes, jewelry, light and shelter.

"Thank you, Richard. Thank you, my darling. Oh, thank you."

CHAPTER
XIX

"I WONDER HOW it is that Zac always manages to pull duty on moving days," Dawn laughed, knotting the twine around another cardboard box. "This time I don't even think I'll bother to unpack; we'll just live out of boxes and suitcases. Oh, I do feel like a bloody gypsy. I have no idea what San Francisco will be like."

"Lotsa hills. Cable cars. Earthquakes," Toshi answered as she yanked down the blue curtains and collapsed the rod.

"Have you been there?"

"No. *National Geographic.*"

"I already know about the earthquakes. Zac's mother sent me a clipping from the newspaper about the earthquakes."

Toshi ducked her head and covered her mouth.

"She one crazy lady, that Suds. My mother-in-law, she not so crazy. First she think I'm Tokyo Rose, then she think Madame Butterfly. Now she see I'm regular girl, she be okay. But Suds, she don't like you no how."

"Tolerance isn't her long suit. I guess as long as I don't have to be around her I can laugh at it, but she really did make our lives miserable while we were there."

"Same as my Aunt Tamiko. When my mother get scared and send me to Kyoto, I'm so sad all the time."

Dawn filled the kettle. She watched Toshi lumber down from the couch and fold the curtains against her pregnant belly. She smoothed the cloth, turning it gently, as though it were a costly tapestry. It always delighted Dawn to see the delicacy with which Toshi performed the most mundane tasks.

"Oh, Toshi, I'm going to miss you."

"Me too. Nobody to knock on the wall to when I get scared. Nobody to talk to. If I say homesick to other girl, she get mad, think I don't like U.S.A. Just I think of my mother, my brothers all times. Always sadness."

"I know. When I got my sister's wedding pictures and then when I heard my mum was sick, I was just a wreck. It's hard for Zac to understand because he feels happier when he's away from his family, but I still have this frightful longing to go home. Come on now, you've helped enough for an expectant mother. Let's sit down and have a cuppa."

She poured the scalding water into the pot, covered it with a tea cosy, and crossed to open the front door. The children had come down with head colds last week and there was still a lingering odor of fruit peels and cough syrup hanging about the hut. She was more worried about the disruption another move would cause in their lives than about the extra work and anxiety another relocation meant to her. Faye had made a good adjustment to school, found a "best friend," and been asked to join the Brownies. By taking some money she'd set aside to have some work done on her own teeth, Dawn had been able to enroll her in ballet class. The dancing teacher had said she was naturally talented and it had given Dawn pleasure to watch Faye, brow furrowed with intense concentration, rehearsing her ballet positions. When she'd told her that they would be moving before the first recital, Faye had cried for hours.

"Here's to you," Dawn said, raising her teacup in a toast as Toshi eased herself onto the floor. "I'd hoped I would be here when your baby was born."

"Me too. Older woman always help. Now I have to read Dr. Spock."

Dawn tucked her legs beneath her and faced her friend. As they touched their teacups they both started to laugh. Their bodies rocked to and fro until, propelled forward, they wrapped arms around each other and pressed their cheeks together.

Over the course of many months, sharing recipes, borrowing food or sanitary napkins, planting a communal garden of string beans, tomatoes and sunflowers that had never quite flourished in the arid earth between the huts, they had overcome their shyness with each other. Despite their strange names, Toshi's Aunt Tamiko and her brothers Soji and Toshiro had taken on personalities and idiosyncrasies as real as those of her own Patsy, Charlie and Marge.

"Bloody hell," Dawn sighed, wiping the tears from her cheeks. "My whole life seems to be packing and saying goodbye."

"You be okay. You one warrior woman."

"I think you mean 'war bride.' "

"No. Warrior woman. Fight for children. Fight for home."

"You too, Toshi. Listen, can you use those blue curtains? I've cut them down once and I think that's enough."

CHAPTER
XX

HELLO CHUMS:

Hard to believe that it's been over three years since we stepped off that ship in San Francisco, isn't it? By now the accents and the memories are starting to fade (though Herbie has promised me a trip Down Under once we've paid off the new television and the rumpus room).

It's a pair of twins to Winnifred Thomas—that brings the total to five—Catholic or careless, Winnie? But seriously, we all wish you congratulations.

Violet McCracken entered that old-time recipe for steak and kidney pie at the county fair in Laramie, Wyoming. She got honorable mention and hubby Jake got a blue ribbon for a prize bull. Never thought Violet would become a real cowgirl!

Moina Meheil is head of her local tennis club in Arlington, Virginia. She says she doesn't know a serve from a backhand, but the local ladies just wouldn't believe that an Aussie couldn't play tennis.

Dawn Mueller has moved again—this time to San Francisco. What a lucky girl you are, Dawn. You've seen more of the country than a roving ambassador.

I'm involved in so many activities that it's a struggle to get the Courier out on time. Not that I suppose any of you mind—you probably have more interesting reading. I know there's a three-month waiting list at our library for the Kinsey Report. All I can say is, I'm glad I'm not Mrs. Kinsey!

Cheerio till next time,

Your faithful friend,
Mavis

JACKSON PUT Gaynor's bags into the trunk and hurried around to open the door of the limousine. Since she'd been to Reno to divorce Mr. Ricky, he didn't think it would be right to ask if she'd enjoyed her trip. He told her what the weather had been like while she'd been gone, and then spun off one of his best Jackie Robinson stories. When that got no response, he asked if he might turn on the baseball game. She grunted permission, turning her face to the window.

He flipped the dial and watched her reflection in the rear-view mirror. Her fancy, beaded hat only made her face look more sullen. It was hard to figure out why a lady so rich and so pretty could be so miserable so much of the time. It sure wasn't because of Mr. Ricky. Faustina had said, and he'd agreed, that Miss Gaynor didn't care about Mr. Ricky any more than she cared about yesterday's newspapers. She was just one of those creatures who suffered from an affliction of the heart that was as real as a humpback or a walleye even though you couldn't see it. She was a gal of constant sorrow, with secrets that only her mama could know.

"Here you are, Miss Gaynor. Home, sweet home."

"Thank you, Jackson. Is there gas in the convertible? I thought I might go for a drive later."

"I know how you love that car, Miss. It's always ready to go."

Etna was waiting at the front door. She kissed her daughter-in-law on both cheeks, trying to think of a polite way to ask her about the divorce proceedings. It was hard for her to understand just how a marriage could be severed. She could only picture a Jehovah-like figure bringing down a sword with a resounding whack on a ream of papers. Reason told her such a vision was absurd, but it made more sense than words like incompatible or irreconcilable. What did such words have to do with marriage?

Gaynor squeezed her arms and called her Mother, and started into the bar. Etna followed her, pausing in mid-step as though she had forgotten something. It was so difficult to hold all the threads of her life together. Because Richard had died away from home, she still kept thinking that he was on an extended business trip. And now there was this horrible split between Gaynor and Ricky that she was power-less to understand. She could overcome the social embarrassment, though it was the first divorce on either side of the family, but she was plagued by a deep sense of personal failure: her only son had not fulfilled her hopes for a happy married life. Gaynor refused to discuss their problems and suggested that she talk to Ricky. But Ricky didn't want to talk to her anymore. The last time he'd come home, he'd tried to persuade her to join him in contesting Richard's will. It had torn her apart to refuse his request, but she had followed Richard's orders during his life and felt that it would be sacrilegious to challenge any directives that came from the grave. She'd tried to console Ricky by offering him a large allowance out of her own money, but he'd re-jected the offer roundly, shouting that she didn't understand anything. Faustina had counseled her not to interfere, so she'd sought the com-fort of her seed catalogue, her bottle and her beloved grandson, and tried to push the unpleasantness out of her mind.

"Faustina," she called up the stairs, "Gaynor's home. Bring Joey down. I know he's anxious to see his mother."

She drifted into the living room, accepted the drink Gaynor handed to her, raised the glass in a toast, but could think of nothing to say. The housekeeper appeared, carrying the little boy. She put him on the floor, smoothed his velveteen rompers, and took his hands, guiding his uncertain steps toward the couch.

"He's been a cranky little dickens, haven't oo, baby Joe," Etna cooed between sips of her drink. "If you can persuade him to take the pacifier out of his mouth, you'll see that he's cutting a new tooth. We've had to take turns sleeping in the nursery, haven't we, Faustina. I suppose he's missed his mommy."

"Mmmm," Faustina replied, standing at attention by the couch, her eyes alert to the child's every movement, her lips turned up tolerantly.

"I don't think we need this silly dummy in our mouth, do we?" Gaynor asked, pulling the pacifier away and embracing the child.

He let out a howl as loud as a police siren, jerking his body away from her and reaching out for Faustina.

"I think he might just as well have it until he's finished teething, if you don't mind," Faustina suggested.

"Of course I don't mind," Gaynor said stiffly, hoisting him onto her knee and reaching for her drink.

"You've had lots of phone calls and letters. Faustina's put them all on the silver tray on your dressing table. Your friend Kay Manchester telephoned almost every day. She is a pretty woman, isn't she? I never thought she'd end up marrying anyone as staid as Donald. I remember going to her coming-out party . . ."

The child sucked away on his pacifier while Etna started a scattered account of Kay's debut. He reached up to grab the glittering beads on the hat, knocking the drink out of Gaynor's hand.

"Oh bugger all," she cried as Faustina reached over and took the child from her, "I just had this suit cleaned!"

"He didn't mean to, did oo, precious boy? He's just attracted to pretty things. Perhaps you'd better take him away, Faustina. He can say hello to his mommy when she's had a chance to rest."

"I do think I'd like to go up and have a lie-down before tea," Gaynor answered tiredly.

Closing the bedroom door behind her, she stripped off her clothes and tossed them on the floor. She slipped into a robe and shuffled through the papers on the silver tray: a reminder about a meeting of the Preservation of Historic Buildings Society, a request to join Mrs. Grant's committee to improve the cultural life of the city, an invitation to a fashion show and another to a garden party. She had taken great pains to ingratiate herself into Kansas City society and her efforts had been well received. She was, after all, an heiress, and an impeccable dresser. There was no reason to doubt that she was well born, and she had such colorful stories to tell about her English ancestors and her Australian uncle with the sheep ranches and the opal mines.

She had understood that she would have to have a female ally if she were to crash the inner circle. Kay Manchester seemed the best candidate. She was about Gaynor's age, confident enough of her physical endowments not to be easily threatened by another beauty, and so utterly bored with her marriage that she was always available for shopping tours, parties and tennis. Because she had education as well as means, she provided Gaynor with tips on what was *de rigueur* in the arts. The other reason she had selected Kay was to ensure that Donald Manchester would have a personal obligation, as well as the incentive of a hefty legal fee, should Ricky be foolish enough to contest Richard's will.

Gaynor had let hints of her dissatisfaction with Ricky trickle out for several months. Then, one afternoon, after she'd thrown a tennis game to Kay and they sat on the veranda of the clubhouse sipping Sea Breezes, she sadly announced that she was at the end of her rope. She hadn't heard from Ricky in ages. She was dreadfully lonely. If she was forced back into that squalid apartment filled with Ricky's university cronies, she was sure she would lose her mental balance. Kay, too, fearful to sever her own marriage, but taking a voyeuristic delight in witnessing the dissolution of another, commiserated and encouraged her to get a divorce. In one of her rare pillow talks with Donald, she related Gaynor's plight. Lunching with Gladys Grant, she reiterated the story and begged Gladys not to repeat it.

Within a week, news of the unfortunate war bride and the impending divorce had circulated through the "in group." Collective sympathy was overwhelmingly on Gaynor's side. People had not forgotten that Ricky had always held himself aloof, scorning both their values and their company. Memories reached far back into the past: Mabel Richardson recalled that he had never wanted to play sports and had rejected invitations to join fraternities; Iris Phelps remembered that he had courted (and probably seduced) Betty Richardson and then abandoned her. Mrs. Meade said she was sure it was Ricky who had encouraged the old Negress to sit in the family pew at Richard Cunningham's funeral. It was common knowledge that he had turned down his father's offer of partnership, which indicated to the men that he was strangely antibusiness and probably anti-American. And everyone knew that he'd come back from the war, dumped his foreign bride into the lap of his poor, alcoholic mother, and taken off to the East Coast to become a professor. It was obvious that he was an egghead, a social pariah and probably a pinko. Thank God old Richard has been smart enough to put paternal sentiment aside and provide for his daughter-in-law. It was apparent that Ricky would never make a dime.

"Gaynor darling, was it too, too dreadful," Kay asked over the phone. "You'll have to tell me all about it because the way Donald's been acting lately I just may have to take the plunge myself."

"It wasn't too bad. I was bored out of my bloody mind sitting in the hotel and I probably drank too much."

"My dear, who wouldn't? It must've been so traumatic. You know I was dying to come along and give you moral support, but I just couldn't leave because of that silly cotillion."

"I understand, Kay. I know they couldn't have gotten it on without one sensible head."

"It was just as dreary as I'd anticipated, but we did raise about five thousand dollars for the polio fund. Thanks so much for your check. But let me tell you, you really missed a wild party at the Hamlyns'. I'd always thought that Donald was the only man who was tasteless enough to get drunk and have domestic brawls in public, but Bobbie Hamlyn proved me wrong . . . listen, an old college friend just sent me a copy of *Memoirs of Hecate County*—it's really hot stuff, positively pornographic —of course it has considerable literary merit . . . but what was I telling you? Ah yes, the Hamlyns. Well, we were just about to sit down to dinner—that is if we could find a place—you know how Virginia always overdoes the decor. She had the entire place rigged up like an underwater grotto. Even had the poor waiters dressed as sailors and some very cheap-looking girl propped up in a shell with a mermaid's costume on. Virginia stole the whole idea from some big Hollywood party because I remember seeing it in *Life* magazine just a couple of months ago. Anyway . . . Bobbie got caught up in one of the fishnets, brought the whole blessed thing down on himself, and started bellowing at Virginia that she'd chosen the underwater theme because she'd read that male sea horses were the ones who had the babies. . . ."

She paused long enough to elicit the expected laugh from Gaynor, yelled at her maid to take the dogs out of the room, and went on. "Then he, Bobby I mean, got really boorish and wanted to know how much the whole thing had cost. I tell you, if they weren't Donald's clients I promise you I'd never lower myself to see either of them again. Say, can you play golf tomorrow?"

Gaynor lit a cigarette and coughed.

"You're not crying, are you, dear? You really mustn't allow yourself to be upset. You did everything you could do to keep that marriage together."

"Oh, Kay . . . I just feel that I have to do something to get a different perspective on things. Etna is terribly sweet. You know how good she's been to me. . . ."

"I know, dear. But it's the interference. Donald's mother is much worse, believe me. She keeps insisting that Betsy needs braces on her teeth, and I know she doesn't, because she's got my bite and it'll just correct itself with time. . . ."

"And then there's Faustina."

"I know. I know. They don't say anything. They don't even show you on their faces, but you *know* they're whispering about you in the kitchen."

"Yes. It's just that it's another woman's house and I feel so constrained."

"Of course you do. You're young and beautiful and you deserve some life of your own. I don't mean you'd want to remarry immediately—not that there's anything to choose from in our set—but I know what you mean: *A Room of One's Own.* I read that in college and whenever I think about it I just get tears in my eyes. Now say, the Covingtons are going to Europe for a year. They're always poor-mouthing, so I'm sure they'd jump at the chance to lease their place. Why don't you let me put out a feeler for you?"

"That would be terribly kind."

"What are friends for? And listen, if you don't turn up for golf tomorrow at two I'm just going to slit my wrists."

ETNA WAS predictably tearful when she heard of Gaynor's plans to lease the Covington place, though Gaynor assured her that she would let Joey stay at his grandmother's several nights each week. During the first months of her occupancy, when she was hiring a staff and throwing dinner parties, she enjoyed herself immensely. But as the summer drew to an end, she began to feel restless. Knowing Ricky was coming to town to visit Joey, she accepted an invitation to go to Chicago with Kay. But they stayed with Kay's relatives and she was bored before the week was out. Coming back to the Covingtons', she began to feel dissatisfied with the house. The tennis court needed to be rolled. The ceiling was starting to peel in the foyer. The arrangement of the garden displeased her.

She lay in bed wondering why she'd bothered to put on the sleek black nightdress when there was no male eye to appreciate it. The same obsessive memories of Richard that signaled another bout of insomnia ran through her head. She dropped off to sleep around one, but woke again at four. Shivering, she went downstairs, poured herself a brandy, and turned up the heat. She mounted the stairs and crept into Joey's room. The Donald Duck nightlight showed a crumpled little form, arms and legs thrown every which way as though his body had been hurled from a car in an accident. She crouched down and looked through the bars of his bed, vowing, if only for Richard's sake, to be a better mother. She would get up early tomorrow morning. She would feed him breakfast instead of letting the housekeeper do it. But how could she get up early if she hadn't had enough sleep? Perhaps just one more brandy would calm her.

Feeling her way back downstairs, she remembered a rare childhood outing with her own mother. It had been Thelma's day off. They were to go to the fair. She stood by the dressing table with the kewpie dolls and photographs of departed uncles struck around the mirror and watched Thelma spit into her mascara. When Uncle Reggie didn't show up, she was sure that Thelma would be angry and cancel the promised trip. But Thelma fortified herself with a cup of gin, announced that it was ladies' day out, and trotted her off to the tram. She bought her toffees and licorice whips, stroked her head proudly when the merry-go-round ticket taker commented on what a pretty little girl she had. Then she took her into a tent. It was dark and malodorous inside, smelling of kerosene, rosewater, and fish and chips. They sat down on canvas chairs. A woman with a scarf around her head and clawlike, bejeweled hands shuffled some cards. Gaynor was amazed and frightened when the woman talked to Thelma about a tall dark man and a thin red-headed one. How could this stranger possibly know about Uncle Reggie or Uncle Ian? Thelma drew another sixpence out of her purse and asked to hear her daughter's fortune too. The woman played with the cards again, and then fixed Gaynor with a gaze so mysterious and yet so certain that goosebumps popped out on her arms. "She'll 'ave more money than Mr. Smith and 'is brother 'ave cough drops," the fortune teller croaked. "She'll travel the world."

She took the brandy with her and went into Victor Covington's library, turned on all the lights, and spun the globe around. Why had she ever been so impressed with Kansas City? It had been so easy to manipulate these people, so simple to gain their acceptance, that she began to feel contempt for them. And what was the glory of being a big frog if you knew the size of the pond anyway? If she'd managed to get from a town in Western Australia to the middle of America, how much farther might she go? She could live in a great city with style and culture. A place where she might meet another man of Richard's stature. San Francisco? New York? Paris? She twirled the globe again, watching it spin until she began to feel giddy.

CHAPTER

XXI

GREETINGS KANGAROO COBBERS:

Just had the most exciting week of my life: Herbie took me to Philadelphia (that's where they keep the Liberty Bell) for the G.O.P. convention. There was a 31-minute demonstration for Mr. Dewey—who, we all know, will soon be President Dewey. I was moved to get my naturalization papers after all that excitement. When I finally said "I do" to being Mavis Slocum, U.S. citizen, Herbie presented me with a bonzer beagle puppy. I've christened him Truman because he looks so sad!

As you may remember, Jeanette Rigley's husband is a sports commentator. He managed to get ringside seats to a Gorgeous George wrestling match. She says it's too bad we don't have colored television to see George in his chartreuse satin shorts.

Joanie Muleski offers to send old maternity clothes to anyone who needs them.

Eleanor Thomas's twins tap danced their way to first prize in a Denver talent contest. Remember what a beaut accompanist Eleanor was on those sing-alongs on the ship?

Janet Eagleton went back to Aussie for a trip and smuggled in slips of Donkey Orchids and other native flora when she returned to her home in Marin County, California.

Hating to close on a sad note, but wanting to let you in on the news: Kathleen Webster is divorced but plans to stick it out in the States. Not all marriages are made in heaven, so remember, Kathleen, your Kangaroo Cobber is still available if you need support.

All love,
Mavis

Billy pushed back the curtains at the kitchen window and looked out at his wife. She was sitting on the running board of the pickup next to Spencer's new sandbox, pouring sand from one hand to the other. Her hair fell forward onto her face. Her expression reminded him of guys who had suffered shell shock. When Spencer filled his bucket, dumped it onto her foot, and crawled back to wait for a reprimand, she kicked the sand from her shoe and continued to sift the sand without even looking up.

It didn't make a goddamn bit of sense. When things were really rough—when they'd lived up in the hills or when he'd lost his job—she'd been like a rock, always talking about ways to improve their lives. But now that things were going better than he'd ever hoped they could, she'd slipped into a sort of fog he just couldn't penetrate.

She still got up before the alarm went off, went to school, and did her chores. But the bounce had gone from her step. She took care to put up her hair and groom herself, but she didn't seem to notice his compliments. She still accepted his embraces, but with a passivity that let him know he didn't touch her deepest secrets. And whenever she wasn't aware of being looked at, her face would sag into a hangdog expression that drove him crazy. He had worried for years that she might leave him, and now she had left in a way he hadn't even imagined.

He had been so desperate to find out the reason for her withdrawal that he'd stooped to spying on her; he had gone through her purse, read her mail, rifled her school notebooks. Even now, as he sipped his beer and stared out the window, hoping to pick up some clue to her feelings, he felt ashamed. He turned away in disgust. "Shit, I done everythin' I know how an' I still cain't make her happy," he muttered resentfully. "I even got a real good job an' it still don't make no never mind."

Right after she'd gotten back from taking care of her friend Dawn,

277

they'd had a stroke of luck. Dr. Helen had told Sheila there was an opening at the college for a horticultural technician. He didn't know what kind of a job that would be, but he was sure he wouldn't be qualified. Sheila told him it just meant taking care of plants, but he was still reluctant. He knew that going up to the college and seeing all those rich kids in bobby sox traipsing around the lawns carrying books would just make him feel like a jackass. But Sheila had insisted, so he'd slicked back his hair and put on his good jacket.

He'd found the area of fields, greenhouses and pre-fab huts behind the big brick buildings, but when he went into the office with Professor George Suttam's name on the door, and saw the old man in dungarees behind the desk, he thought he was a handyman who'd gotten in by mistake. The man passed his thick hand over his shiny scalp, blew his nose on a square of cotton, and introduced himself: "George Suttam, Ph.D. Call me George." He asked Billy where he had been stationed during the war, blew his nose again, and started into a lengthy speech about the beauty of apples.

". . . which brings me to that famous quotation from the Song of Solomon," he concluded. "You know it, don't you?" Without waiting for a response, which Billy wouldn't have been able to provide in any case, he boomed on. "I don't mean that I'm religious. I'm a man of science. Just an illustration of the point I've been making. 'Comfort me with apples': that's the quote. People love apples, you know. Even the damned federal government knows that people love apples. That's why they've given me this money to study them. We're going to find the very best way to grow them and transport them. Why should the American public be victimized by our paucity of knowledge? Why should our fellow citizens have to pay too much and get a mushy apple when science can give them a nice, firm apple at a lower cost? You see what I'm talking about, Mr. Hickock?"

"Yeah. I like apples a lot m'self. Cousin of mine use 't have an apple tree. I remember climbin' it when . . ."

"I'm going to start you on Monday, Mr. Hickock." He studied Billy with sharp, intelligent eyes and wiped the square of cotton across his nose again. "I think this is a propitious meeting. You're just the sort of young man I've been looking for. The job is mostly physical labor —caring for the orchards, harvesting and such. But that doesn't mean you won't have to use your brain. I want a man who has the sense to follow instructions as well as making a few decisions of his own. We test for temperature at storage, the effect of various climatic conditions and different types of fertilizers. We test for sweetness and firmness. You'll be using your brain as well as your brawn. All right? See you on Monday. Now go on over to the administration building and try not to let them spoil your day with all their damned paperwork.''

Billy almost laughed out loud as George got up to shake his hand. This character was going to be unlike any boss he'd ever had. Sheila didn't seem nearly as pleased as he thought she'd be. She congratulated him, but then she got sad again.

Initially, her lack of enthusiasm didn't bother him. He loved the work. He was outdoors most of the day. He didn't have to punch a time clock. The increased salary meant he could buy Sheila some of the things she needed and, for the first time in his life, he began to think of himself as a man with a future. He started to save for a new car, looked forward to the time when he'd be able to move the family into a nicer house. He didn't even mind when his buddies at the bar kidded him about his fancy title. He'd curse and take fake punches at them when they teased, but it seemed appropriate, since his wife was going to be a nurse, that he should have a job at the university, a job that even George Suttam said required brawn *and* brains. But none of it meant very much when he realized he'd lost his sweetheart. Whenever he looked at Sheila now he had the physical sensation that the clouds had blocked out the sun and a chill wind prickled his flesh.

He went out into the yard, letting the screen door slam to announce his presence. Sheila looked up, wiped the sand from her hands, and pushed her hair back behind her ears. He sat down beside her, putting his arm around her shoulders.

"How y' doin', girl?"

"I'm all right."

"But watcha thinkin' 'bout?"

"Life."

"Aw, c'mon."

"I was thinking about my mother. Thinking about how unkind I was to her when I left."

"I figure she sort of deserved it."

"That's not the point. She just tried to warn me about what a momentous decision I was making. I remember her saying, 'Marriage changes everything in a woman's life. For a man it's different, but for a woman, there's no going back.' ''

"What's the point of goin' back? Goin' back's fer old people. We're livin' in the here and now."

"I didn't have any notion of the decision I—we were really making."

"I didn't twist yer arm, sweet thing," he smiled ingenuously.

She sighed with the same patient hopelessness she displayed when she'd wipe up spilled baby food for the third time. "Forget the . . . I don't know . . . the *principle* of what I'm saying. I guess I'm just sad because now I live halfway across the world from her. I'll never be able to really tell her any of this."

"Y' never know. We might strike it rich someday and go on back fer a visit."

"That's unrealistic. There isn't any going back. Not ever. I've only made one real decision in my life and . . ."

"You mean marryin' me?"

She sighed again, picking up another handful of sand, sifting it back and forth between her hands. "No, honey. That's not really what I meant."

"Dad-dy," Spencer shrieked, frustrated that his parents had ignored him for so long. When they kept looking at each other, he hurled a fistful of sand into the air.

"Okay. I see y'. I see y', son." He picked the boy up and threw him onto his shoulders. Spencer howled with delight, kicking his legs against Billy's chest and rubbing his face into his hair.

"I'm gonna run a washcloth over this varmit's face and put him down fer a nap. How's about we take a li'l rest fer ourselves too?"

When he'd wiped the grimy face and put the child into his crib, he walked to the bedroom and silently closed the door. Sheila was standing by the window. The afternoon sunlight highlighted her hair and made the cloth of her housedress almost transparent, so that he could see the outline of her body underneath. He shivered with longing.

"Cain't you tell me what's botherin' you, honey?"

"Nothing's bothering me."

"Hell, Sheila, you must think I'm blind in one eye and cain't see outta the other. You've been mopin' 'round like a grass widow fer 'bout six months now."

"It'll pass. It's just life."

"I swear I don't know what yer talkin' 'bout."

"Life," she said wearily. "It's not fancy dress balls or walking into the sunset. It's just shirts without buttons and head colds and tests and getting older."

"It's dancin' and makin' love and a new car and . . ." He struggled to find the things that might convey some of his enthusiasm to her. ". . . and apples . . . and babies."

She broke into a fearful sobbing. He pulled her to him, stroking her hair, patting her back, trying to calm her.

"How's about I take you to a movie tonight, girl?"

"No," she gulped, sucking in her breath and twisting away from him. "I don't ever want to go to the movies again."

CHAPTER

XXII

THERE WAS NOTHING like a long, solitary trip to give you time to think about the direction of your life, Ricky told himself as he tossed his duffle bag into the back seat. He'd been moping around too much lately—sleeping late, eating poorly, worrying about what he should do next, but too mired in self-pity to take any positive action. This trip to visit Betty for a week and then driving her back to New York would be a real shot in the arm.

Gassing up, checking the tires, and choosing a route on the map gave him a sense of purpose he hadn't felt since the days when he'd organized the General's chalk talks. The illusion of confidence and order lasted for several hours. He didn't even mind the snarls in late-afternoon traffic as he drove through the capital. Once out on the highway again he contemplated the sunset, feeling resolute and peaceful. After a meal of plain, heavy food at a roadside diner, he decided against looking for a hotel, feeling he had enough energy to drive straight through to Virginia.

By three in the morning, the steady swoosh of passing trucks and the glare of the headlights on the dividing line started to have a hypnotic effect on him. He rolled down the window and turned on the radio. The report of the day's news—continuing poverty in Europe, rumblings from the Soviets, the House Un-American Activities Committee hearings—sent him into a slump. It seemed as though conditions in the country paralleled the downhill slide of his own life. Just four years ago the nation had felt a great surge of optimism: the war was over, the peace was won, Americans were walking into a future as golden and promising as the sunset in the last reel of a Hollywood movie.

Then there had been inflation, wage disputes, a tangle of overseas commitments. The euphoria of victory began to dissolve under the pressure of complex decisions and responsibilities. Confidence gave way to uncertainty. Paranoia began to eat away at trust. People didn't talk about the glories of peace anymore. Now they speculated about where and when the next conflict would begin.

He reached forward and switched the dial.

> Some enchanted evening,
> You will see a stranger,
> You will see a stranger,
> Across a crowded room . . .

That first date with Gaynor. How lovely and lithe she'd looked. How she'd clung to him on the dance floor, the mirrored ball above their heads dappling her face with light. She'd tucked a gardenia into her hair and its heady fragrance mingled with the scent of perspiration and face powder. He could feel the incredible softness of her breasts against his uniform. He had lowered his head to kiss her when the painful wail of sirens interrupted the music. The bandleader had made a joke about an encore after the air raid and told the crowd to evacuate the building. Ricky had taken her arm protectively, guiding her through the crush of bodies onto the street. Lights were doused in quick succession. A sliver of a moon illuminated the rain-drenched streets. When she'd suggested walking to her flat instead of going to an air-raid shelter, he'd thought her incredibly brave.

As they crept to her door and she fumbled in the darkness for her keys, his heart had knocked against his ribs. They'd groped their way to the couch near the window and there, the moonlight shining on her face, she'd asked him to tell her about his life in America. Tonguetied, he'd quoted Frost and Whitman. He asked her about her life. She'd moved closer to him, lips parted. "What is there to tell that could possibly matter under the circumstances?" He'd seized her then, amazed at his courage, even more amazed when her mouth opened to welcome his tongue. He'd tried to French kiss girls before, but she was the first nice girl who seemed to enjoy the intimacy. Emboldened by her acceptance, he pushed her backwards onto the couch. There was a yowl and a hiss as the cat who had been curled there unnoticed leaped up and darted across the room. He was afraid the magic of the moment had been shattered, but she laughed softly, lolling back into the cushions and drawing him to her. Here was the sort of woman he had always hoped to find: sensitive but courageous, capable of rising above petty social conventions. Premonitions of untold pleasure shot through him as he felt her fingernails dig into his back. He knew, as he kissed her again, that they could be one in body and spirit. She understood, as he did, that the war had made their lives more precious, that love was the power that would enable them to survive.

His head started to ache. He reached over, impatiently switching the dial again.

> Chickery chick, cha-la cha-la
> Check-a-laromey-in a ban-nan-ika . . .

He'd tried to sing that to Joey the last time he'd visited Kansas City. The child had looked at him suspiciously, then stumbled across the room to hide his face in Faustina's skirts. Coaxed to come to Daddy, he'd started to whimper. "It's not that he doesn't like you, Ricky," Faustina had explained. "Just he hasn't seen you for months, so he's shy." He'd nodded, saying that of course he understood. But in the three days of his visit, Joey had never come to him of his own will. The rejection cut deeply. Etna became the target of his frustration. He criticized her for being too indulgent with the boy, belittled her choice of toys and clothes. The night before he was to leave, he was in a particularly bad temper, accusing her of taking Gaynor's side in the divorce, though he knew that wasn't true. His mother didn't have enough confidence in her judgement to be able to take sides. She was just an unhappy fence-sitter, caring deeply but lacking the courage of involvement.

He snapped off the radio, pushed down on the accelerator, and drove as though the Furies were chasing him. When the pale sunlight filtered onto the tops of the mountains, he felt chilled and fatigued. Gaynor had always made fun of his introspection and of course she was right. It had been foolish to believe that the long drive could help him to think things through. This dredging up had only given him a pounding headache and a sense that he was out of control.

The sun rose to its zenith. There was a warm, sultry feeling to the air. He pulled to the side of the road, shuffling through the glove compartment to find Betty's map. "Pass the train station . . ." That must be the old-fashioned cupola next to the tracks. "Go down two blocks to the Main Street of Blacksburg . . ." He blinked several times to clear his vision, watched two barefoot kids playing stick ball, and then eased the gears into first. His head was throbbing. His body ached. He drove slowly past the rows of shops looking for Lee Avenue. When he'd located the address, he shut off the motor, leaned against the steering wheel, and chuckled, "Just gimme a coupla aspirin. I already got a Purple Heart." He'd heard that line from a wounded G.I. and the memory of the man's toughness warmed him. He walked up the path where the crabgrass pushed through the cracks in the pavement, opened the door to the screened-in porch, and stood near the rusty glider.

"Betty Richardson, renowned sociologist, does she live here?"

The tapping of a typewriter stopped. He heard a cry of "Oh my God." Betty, wearing a pair of dark slacks and a sloppy man's shirt printed with tropical fruit, ran to the door.

"Ricky! I wasn't expecting you until tonight. I was planning to have cool drinks, hot hors d'oeuvres and a terrific hairdo by the time you got here. Oh, I'm so glad to see you. Come on in."

"I've brought the hors d'oeuvres—that Polish sausage you like." He tossed a shopping bag onto the divan.

"You got that specially for me?"

"There's also some pumpernickel, which is probably stale by now, a bottle of champagne and some back issues of the *New York Times.*"

"You do know how to turn a girl's head, don't you? Gee, I've missed you."

"It's great to see you too," he smiled, draping his arms around her shoulders. At times like this, when she had a high color in her cheeks and her eyes crinkled up in that affectionate smile, she really looked pretty. "How long has it been?"

"'Bout six months, I think."

She knew it had been seven months and a couple of weeks since their Dutch treat dinner and the ride on the Staten Island ferry. She'd even kept the prize he'd given her out of his Cracker Jack box.

"Guess I was still a married man then, wasn't I?"

"Let's not talk in here," she said quickly. "As you might guess from looking at that line of plaster ducks flying across the mantelpiece, the living room isn't exactly my style. Fact is, the lady I rented this from is visiting relatives in Richmond, so I've more or less been camping out in the kitchen and the bedroom. 'Course I was glad to get it. When I first got into town I didn't know where I was going to stay. Then I called up this classmate of one of my professors. Well, Helen Abromovitz has turned out to be a real fairy godmother. Not only did she find me this house, she also persuaded some of the women who come to her clinic to let me interview them. That cut down on a lot of legwork. I'll let you take a look at some of my interviews if you're interested. Oh Ricky, the stories I've heard! They sure make me see how sheltered I've always been. The incredible hardships that these women have to endure . . .''

"Big-hearted Betty."

"Go ahead and scoff, Professor. The real-life stuff makes your novels of social criticism look like comedy. Why, just yesterday I interviewed this little girl who's going to have a baby. She's only thirteen. Can you imagine . . .''

"Big-hearted, *talkative* Betty."

"I am sorry. You've been driving all night and I stand here in the doorway blabbing my head off. Come on."

She led him through a musty-smelling hallway into a roomy kitchen lined with windows that opened onto an overgrown backyard. The table was covered with notebooks, three-by-five index cards and a typewriter.

"This place isn't so bad," he said, straddling one of the chairs and looking around. "At least you have room to move. My place feels like a monk's cell."

"Compared to the shack I was living in in Goose Neck, Kentucky, it's a veritable Versailles. Do you know there are forty-one thousand, six hundred thirty-three homes without toilets in Kentucky?"

"I know it now," he smirked, tipping back and forth in the chair as he watched her fill the coffee pot. "You'd better watch out, Bet. Quoting statistics is an occupational disease for sociologists."

"That's not the worst part. I've started to dream about graphs and footnotes. During the day I'm all keyed up about the work, but at night I go into awful slumps. I suppose it's not having anyone to talk to. I just can't wait to get back to New York. 'Course it'll take me about another week to wind up things here, but then we can start off. We can even take a detour, see old battlefields of the Civil War, if you'd like. It really was kind of you to offer to come down and drive me back."

"What else do the unemployed have to do but drive around the country?"

"Still no job offers?"

"One nibble from a cow college in Montana. I don't expect it'll come through. Even if it did, I'd feel rotten about taking it. Not just because it doesn't fit into my grandiose career plans. It would mean I couldn't visit Joey as much."

"How is he?"

"Spoiled, precocious, scared—reminds me of myself as a kid. In other words, he's the opposite of what I'd like him to be. I didn't see Gaynor the last time I was there, but I don't suppose her capacity for mothering has improved much. If the kid had any sense he'd pack his rubber duck in a knapsack and grab the first train out of town. Thank Christ Faustina's around."

"And your mother?"

"She's no help. Well-intentioned of course. But if you haven't formed an opinion or made a decision in thirty years it's bound to affect your mental capacity. You know she let Gaynor just pick up the kid and move across town without so much as an objection."

"What could she say? I mean, if Gaynor wanted to move it certainly wasn't Etna's place to try to stop her."

"No. It's Etna's place to sit in the solarium like a goddamned hothouse flower, guzzle booze and watch the world crumble around her."

"You're being awfully hard on her, Ricky. You used to be so fond of her. Now you just sound bitter."

"I'm bitter about what she let him do to her."

"She loved him, Ricky. Difficult as that is to understand; she loved him. She just didn't have the strength to stand up to him. Besides, that's all in the past. If you're going to let yourself get stuck in the past, it'll make it even more difficult for you to go forward. Just speaking for myself, it wasn't until I learned to forgive my parents that I really started to become an adult."

"I see you've taken Basic Psychology as well as statistics."

"I just don't understand why you haven't been offered a job," she went on, ignoring his sarcasm. "A brilliant young Ph.D. fresh out of Princeton . . ."

"Who knows? I might be blacklisted."

"Blacklisted?"

The coffee boiled over onto the gas jet. She switched off the flame and then turned back to him, her mouth hanging open.

"I did join the American Veteran's Committee. I did write all those asinine editorials. You know: 'Live up to the great ideals of American society, fight the moneybags before they take over the economy . . .' All that crap."

"It wasn't crap. Anyway, you couldn't possibly think anything you've said or done could be construed as subversive. What evidence do you . . ."

"I don't have any evidence. Blacklisting is like infidelity: the injured party is usually the last to know. But if a fancy guy like Alger Hiss can be indicted because some idiot congressmen want publicity, if solid citizens want to burn *The Grapes of Wrath* because they think it's pinko propaganda, if movie stars are spilling their guts about who said what at whose swimming pool, why then I tell you, sister, 'The times are out of joint.' Anything can happen. And a bozo like me who's published a thesis about themes of social injustice in the American novel might not be too popular."

"I've never even thought of blacklisting as being a reason for your not getting a job," she said slowly, her eyes clouding with confusion. "It just can't be true."

She sat next to him, reaching for his hand. He got up swiftly, almost knocking over the chair, and walked to the window without looking at her.

"Ah, who the hell knows. Maybe it's a paranoid delusion. I mean, if your father cuts you out of the will and your wife divorces you as soon as she gets her hands on some money and your kid makes a face every time you try to touch him, I guess you're entitled to a few paranoid delusions. What would your psychology books have to say about *that*?"

"You don't have to be snotty with me. I'm on your side, remember?"

This certainly wasn't the reunion she'd hoped for. They'd been together for less than an hour and he seemed intent on picking a fight. But why was she, who had nothing but sympathy for him, the target of his sarcasm? She set the cups on the table and tried to take the edge out of her voice.

"I know the last couple of years have been horrendous for you. And I'm sorry. I just don't understand when you became so bitter about everything."

"Let me try to pinpoint it," he went on, in the same derisive tone. "When did I become bitter? I know it was sometime between VJ Day and the beginning of the Cold War. Was it when the Russians got the bomb?"

"Ricky . . ."

"No, no, you will say. That's putting a cosmic construction on purely personal problems. Okay. Back to me. Perhaps it was when my dearly beloved kicked me out of bed. Then again it could've been when I found out I couldn't find a job. Or maybe it was when I realized my old man was right about me: I'm a whining idealist who's unfit for dealing with the world or the people in it."

She stared at him for a long time. "I'm your friend so I'm going to give it to you straight. You have had a hard time. But you're wallowing in self-pity, and apart from being addictive, it's not going to help you out of the mess you're in."

A crushing retort sprang to his lips, but then remorse overcame hostility. He turned away from her, looking into the backyard. He could see the loveliness of springtime there, but it had no power to touch him. He was isolated, cold and alone. He knew damned well that he would never expose his best male friend to this self-indulgent tirade. Yet he was inflicting it on this caring, intelligent woman who was trying to offer him the affection and concern he'd missed so much. He remembered when he had first fallen in love with Gaynor. He had told her that all women were more beautiful to him because of her. But those tender feelings were gone. Perhaps the sense of betrayal he felt because of her had poisoned all of his relations with women. Perhaps trust and hope were irretrievably lost to him.

"I loved her so much," he cried.

Betty turned away. How could she tell him now, when he was experiencing so much grief, that he had been a fool? He had been infatuated with his vision of a goddess and Gaynor's only claim to divinity was her extraordinary good looks. Had his judgment not been misted by romance and overwhelmed by plain old lust, he would have known after a couple of dates that Gaynor was a selfish, neurotic woman. But it would be useless to point out his self-delusion.

The silence lagged on. Embarrassed, she sat down and started to straighten the index cards on the table.

"You don't look well," she said at last.

"I feel like hell."

"Why don't you go in and rest? You must be exhausted from the drive. I've got some work to do out here. I'll wake you when it's supper time. The bedroom's the second door to your right."

He left the room without looking at her. She took a swallow of the coffee, rinsed the cup and rested her elbows on the sink. Who was she to judge his ridiculous marriage? She'd persisted in a crazy, unrewarded devotion to him ever since he'd chosen her for his doubles partner in the seventh grade. And she had the gall to accuse *him* of living in the past? She'd tagged after him like a puppy, willing to be part of his life on any terms he wished to dictate, hoping that one day he would recognize the possibilities for happiness that were so obvious to her. Even her two affairs with other men had only been attempts to exorcise her desire for him. Her obsession was just as strong as his for Gaynor. Of course, it took a more benign form, but that was only because she had such a low opinion of herself that she was willing to settle for the crumbs of "friendship."

She pulled the typewriter back to the edge of the table and shuffled through her notes.

"My name is Della Mae Watson. I had m' first baby when I was 'bout seventeen. When m' husband took to drinkin', I took m' babies —I had three by then—an' I figured since cookin' was alls I could do, I'd best make m'self a nickel by slingin' hash . . ."

At times like these, when she was tempted to give way to the self-pity she'd cautioned him against, she was glad of her Mid-western background. She'd gone beyond much of its conventionality and denial of emotion, but the strong work ethic kept her steady. And while the recognition that there were people with problems greater than her own did not eradicate her unhappiness, it did help to keep it in perspective. She rolled a sheet of paper into the typewriter and hammered away transcribing her notes until the fading light began to change the colors of the backyard into deeper greens and blues.

Pushing her chair back from the table, she turned on the light and tiptoed down the hall. The bedroom door was slightly ajar. Ricky was on the bed, legs drawn up, arms hugging himself. *Classic fetal position,* she thought in disgust. Returning to the kitchen, she started to scrape some carrots and immediately nicked her finger on the knife. "Damn him," she cursed as she washed off the cut. It just wasn't fair that a pair of gorgeous legs could outweigh loyalty, laughter and trust. It wasn't fair; but it seemed to be true.

When she'd peeled the vegetables and put the roast in the oven, she rushed into the bathroom to put on some lipstick. Rummaging in the hall closet, she found a good linen tablecloth and a pair of candles.

One of the candles was bent, but she figured it wouldn't be noticed once she'd turned out the lights. As she set the table, the warmth and order of the kitchen began to restore some of her optimism. It was possible that a quiet meal and a bottle of champagne might salvage the evening. She was about to go out into the garden to pick a few flowers for a centerpiece when Ricky appeared at the kitchen door. His teeth were chattering, his face bathed in a drenching sweat.

"If there's a hospital in this burg I think you'd better drive me there. Feels like I've got a recurrence of malaria."

HE OPENED one eye to see the group of white uniforms clustered around the foot of his bed.

"We're not getting as many of these cases as we did when the boys were first comin' home, but y'all know about the possibilities of relapses," the doctor drawled, slapping the edge of the bed with a chart. "This one seems to be resistant to chloroquine so we're treating him with pyrimethamine. The fever has declined, but still isn't within normal range." He acknowledged Ricky for the first time by shaking his foot. "Hiya, fella. What unit were y' with?"

Ricky shut his eyes, pretending not to hear. The group moved on to another bed. As he looked after them, a pretty blond nurse hesitated, turned back, and gave him a compassionate smile.

"Not to worry, you'll feel better before next Christmas," she whispered before she hurried off to join the others.

There was something about her pronunciation that unnerved him, but he was too racked with fever to give it any thought. He snorted and turned his face to the wall.

She was back later in the afternoon. He watched her from beneath half-closed lids as she checked the charts and arranged things on the bed table. Her gestures were quick and efficient, yet there was a delicacy in the way she touched things that was pleasing to watch. The starched uniform flattened whatever breasts she might have had, her face was smooth and unlined, but there was a seriousness about the eyes that belied the youthful appearance.

"Bet you were never an Army nurse."

"Excuse me, I thought you were asleep. Feeling better?"

"Sure. Now this bug is my chief concern. Sometimes being physically sick is almost a relief, know what I mean?"

"May I take your temperature?"

When he opened his mouth to reply, she instantly popped in the thermometer, checking her watch with self-conscious professionalism. He guessed she was a novice and had been insulted by his remark about being an Army nurse. Her eyes darted from the watch to his face, and a furrow creased her forehead.

"I do know what you mean about being physically ill," she said gently.

"Mmmmm." *I'll just bet you do. But I can see by looking into those big brown eyes that you wouldn't be the type to let yourself get sick just because you were unhappy.*

"But you'll have to face the other problems soon," she said brightly, withdrawing the thermometer, "because you're getting better. See, only a hundred and two degrees."

He ignored the thermometer to look at the nameplate attached to her uniform.

"Well, Hickock, S., if you keep giving me this tender loving care I expect I'll progress very quickly."

A slight flush suffused her face. She straightened her back, resumed her professional manner, and started away from the bed with a curt, "I'm sure you will."

He shifted around to watch her leave the room.

"Ain't she a daisy?" the man in the next bed called out. "Did you see those legs? I tell y' if she'd crawl into bed with me, I'd know soon enough if I was sick."

He laughed so much at his own joke that he brought on a coughing fit. Ricky slumped back in the bed, wishing that he'd been given a more companionable roommate. This one had apparently spent his entire stretch in the Army memorizing dirty stories about nurses. Still, it was understandable. Guys had fantasies about nurses that ran the gamut from smutty jokes to images of ministering angels. No matter how rotten you felt, if you were stuck in a bed and there was a hovering female presence it was bound to stir the erotic imagination.

He rearranged the sweat-drenched pillow and looked at the bedside table, remembering the cowboy lamp he'd had next to his bed when he was a kid. Oh, that cozy childhood world of blankets, cherry-flavored cough syrup and story books He'd contracted the usual list of childhood diseases, but sometimes he had taken advantage of his mother's protectiveness and manufactured an upset stomach. The shades would be drawn. The doctor with the fat bag full of wonderful instruments would visit. Faustina would sit beside him for hours whispering long beautiful stories. Not the fables of naughty rabbits who learned the virtues of obedience after misadventures in the cabbage patch or moral lessons about little-engines-who-could that were Etna's stock in trade, but meandering sagas of her Great-uncle Thaddeus's escape through the Underground Railroad or idylls of the house in Louisiana where she had spent her girlhood. Lovely, wise Faustina.

He floated off into a blissful sleep, awakened hours later by racking chills that brought back visions of jungles, tent infirmaries and groaning men. Betty sat with him until she was informed for the second time that visiting hours were over.

The next morning, when it was time for his sponge bath, he was relieved to see the pretty blonde wasn't on duty. The fever had broken. He was no longer in such a state of physical misery that he could tolerate being bathed by an attractive woman without feeling desire and embarrassment. He made a casual inquiry about Hickock, S., and found out it was her day off.

The following day, as he was sitting up and jotting some notes in his journal, he heard the squeak of rubber soles on the polished floor and looked up to see her.

"Nice to see you looking so well, Mr. Cunningham."

"Yes. I'll consider myself a real goldbrick if they don't let me out of here tomorrow."

"You'll have to ask the head nurse or the doctor about that. To tell the truth, I'm just a third-year student getting some experience on the wards."

"I know I'm going to be released tomorrow. I was just making conversation."

His flirting apparently made her uncomfortable. She turned away, straightening the books on his night table.

"Do you like Theodore Dreiser?" he asked.

"I like to read."

"Have you read that one?"

"No. I don't actually have time to read anymore."

"That particular writer isn't much in vogue these days anyway."

"What does he write about?"

"Oh, the failure of the American Dream, social values, the taboos of gentility . . ."

"No. I mean, what's the story?"

"The story?"

"Isn't that why people read books? For the story?"

"Yes. I suppose that's why," he chuckled. "Of course that's why. That's why I started reading books. I'm pretty far afield of that now."

She smoothed the cover of the book, and then looked down at him, waiting for a further explanation.

"I'm a literature professor. No. That's not exactly true. I have a Ph.D. in literature, and I'm looking for a teaching job."

"I see. It must be wonderful to read for a living."

"I trust it will be, Hickock, S. I trust it will be. Say, why don't you take the book. I have another copy of it."

"I'm not sure if I'd understand it."

" 'Course you would. I was just being pompous and making it sound difficult. Actually it's the story of a poor girl who runs away with a rich married man and ruins his life."

"Dear me, she sounds rather evil."

"She's not evil. She's just a victim of social circumstance."

"I'm not awfully fond of victims."

"Then you may be in the wrong profession." They laughed together, their eyes holding after their smiles had faded.

"Well, thanks awfully," she said, replacing the book. "I can't accept it, but I'll remember the title. It's been nice talking to you, Mr. Cunningham, and I hope you don't have any more go-ins with malaria."

"Hey, where are you from?" he called, when she was almost out of the room.

"Western Australia."

"I knew I recognized the accent. But you've picked up some of the Southern dialect and that threw me off. My wife . . . or more properly, my ex-wife is from Western Australia."

She moved back toward the bed. "Mr. Cunningham . . . you're not . . . I mean I knew a girl named Gaynor Cunningham. We came over on the same ship."

"I'll be goddamned. Excuse me. I meant small world or some other cliché. You must be Sheila in Virginia. Gaynor came down to visit you once."

She shook her head in confusion, barely hearing the remark. They started to speak simultaneously, then stopped.

"I'm sorry to hear about your divorce," she went on in a lower tone, aware that the patient in the next bed was feigning sleep and straining to hear their conversation. "And I do feel a proper fool not to have recognized you. Gaynor showed me your photo several times, but I thought you lived in another part of the country so I just never made the connection."

"Sure. Ah . . ." he tried to arrange his features into a less shocked expression and find something to talk about that would keep her at his side. "How are you adjusting to life in the States?"

"Oh, life in the U.S. That's a very long story."

"You just told me you liked stories."

"I'm afraid I'd rather read them than tell them. Besides, there are other patients I should attend to."

"Could I talk to you sometime?"

"I knock off at two in the afternoon. I don't suppose you'll feel much like coming back to the hospital tomorrow after your release, but if you'd like I could meet you for a cup of coffee in the cafeteria."

"I'll see you then."

She backed off a few steps, and then turned quickly and hurried out of the room. The man in the next bed propped himself up and leered across at Ricky.

"You lucky bastard. Looks like you've got yourself a hot date."

CHAPTER
XXIII

HE TOOK a table near the entrance to the cafeteria, propped up a book, and pretended to be reading. Every time a white uniform came through the swinging doors his head popped up. By quarter after two he was checking his watch every few minutes and feeling anxious that Sheila wouldn't turn up. He still wasn't sure why he wanted to see her so badly. Of course she had known Gaynor; he'd be able to indulge his compulsion to talk about her. He might even find out something he didn't know—some clue to her character or behavior that had eluded him. But apart from her association with Gaynor, he wanted to be with Sheila again. There was something about her presence that was simultaneously invigorating and comforting, a womanliness that was intelligent without being overbearing.

At twenty after two, when he was beginning to give up hope, she pushed through the doors, moving toward him with a light, hurried step. Her hair was drawn back beneath her nurse's cap and there were circles underneath her wide-set brown eyes, but she still looked very young—like one of his students who had stayed up all night cramming for an exam.

"I do apologize for being late," she sighed, taking a seat opposite him. "There was an emergency surgery I wanted to look in on. Nurse Wohlford was assisting and she's absolutely the best."

"May I get you a coffee?"

"No thanks. I've already adopted your American habit of drinking too much coffee. But I wouldn't mind a lemonade. What are you reading?" she asked, her tired expression changing to one of curiosity

as she picked up the book. *"Principles of Statistical Analysis.* My goodness, you do have a broad range of interests."

"The book's not mine. It belongs to my friend Betty. She left it on
the seat of my car so I picked it up. It's always good to have a book
with you when you're waiting for someone or eating alone. It's a sort
of protective covering that says to the world, 'I don't mind being alone
because my mind is on higher things.' "

"I'd never thought of that. I assumed people carried books because
they were reading them."

"No, they use them as props. See that skinny girl over there? The
one with the cottage cheese and the book with the blue jacket? She's
been here as long as I have and she hasn't even turned a page."

"Perhaps she's visiting a patient and she's too worried to be able
to concentrate," Sheila whispered, sneaking a look at the girl. "Or
maybe she's a slow reader."

"Nope. It's protective covering. Another thing I've been thinking
about while I've been sitting here: why do all cafeterias smell the
same? Every cafeteria I've ever been in, from the lunch room in grade
school to mess halls in the Army—they all have that steamy amalgam
of overcooked vegetables, gravy and coffee grounds." Hell, here he
was being cute, trying to impress her with his trivial observations as
though they were freshmen on their first date. Next thing he knew
he'd be telling her that he'd read *War and Peace* when he was fourteen
years old. "Hey, I'll get us those lemonades."

She watched other women's heads turn to look at him as he sauntered over to the counter. When he'd first been admitted to the ward
the other nurses were all atwitter over the handsome new patient. But
she'd refused to gossip about him, feeling that it was her professional
responsibility to give equal attention to patients regardless of whether
they were physically attractive or downright repulsive. Besides, she
was married, while most of the other nurses her age were still going
out to parties and dances and had a right to be interested in eligible
men. Yet once she had started to talk to him it was more difficult to
ignore his appeal. He was articulate and quickwitted; what her parents
would have called a cultured gentleman. And he looked so unhappy.

She had been jittery all morning, rationalizing that a cafeteria meeting with the ex-husband of an old acquaintance could in no way be
considered a date. At lunchtime she had found herself in front of the
mirror in the locker room, pinching her cheeks and wishing she'd
taken more trouble with her hair. She remembered something Helen

had said during one of their far-ranging conversations. "A man can be a veritable humpback, but if he has enough sadness in his eyes, he can be infinitely attractive to most women. Because when men look unhappy, women are seduced into the notion that they can comfort. They're flattered by the idea of being a source, or a cure. It's one of the few ways society allows women to exercise power. Of course it can also get them into a helluva lot of trouble. Not many men consciously realize that their misery is appealing—but the smarter ones do." And Ricky had elicited all of those feelings in her. His attention flattered her, made her feel pretty and important.

"So here we are, two lemonades. You said you were assisting in surgery?"

"Not assisting, just observing," she answered quietly. Her attendance in the operating room had been entirely voluntary. If she hadn't been in such a stew about seeing him again she wouldn't have bothered to attend. "I'm thinking of taking some more classes so that I can assist."

"You must be very busy."

"I am a bit bushed," she confessed, sipping the lemonade. "I used to think all I'd have to do was waltz up and down the halls showering sick people with sympathy."

"And then you saw your first patient die."

"No. The first time I saw a patient die he was in such terrible shape that I looked upon it as a blessing. It's actually the dirty work that gets me down—bedpans, mopping up, that sort of thing. Spencer, my little boy, has broken me into mopping up . . . he's three and a half now, so I think the worst of it is over. But I really don't know how the girls who haven't had children manage to cope."

"So you have a little boy?"

"Yes. Didn't I hear you had a boy too? I still get silly newsletters from this woman called Mavis Slocum and I thought she'd written that Gaynor had a child."

There. She'd mentioned dirty work and children, two subjects that would certainly dispel any hint of flirtation. She reached for her purse.

"Would you like to see Spencer's picture?"

"Sure."

"And do you have a photo of . . . ?"

"Joey. Yes, I think I do."

A glow of maternal pride crossed her face as she pushed the snap-shot across the table. It showed a rugged-looking young man, naked to the waist, with a tow-haired boy straddling his shoulders. The child held onto his father's head, an expression of exuberant, devilish excitement on his face. Ricky felt almost ashamed as he handed her the photograph of Joey dressed in embroidered rompers, looking forlorn as he sat beneath a Christmas tree surrounded by piles of presents.

"Spencer looks like a sturdy little cuss," he said, passing the picture back to her.

"He's a handful all right. Incredible energy and a very strong will. Just like his daddy. Your Joey is very . . . beautiful. I suppose 'beautiful' is the wrong word for a boy, isn't it? I meant that I can see Gaynor's looks in him."

"Yes. He resembles her," he said quietly, returning the snapshot to his wallet. He turned the wallet in his hands, as though uncertain what to do with it. Their silence seemed to create an invisible circle around them, cutting them off from the clatter of dishes and the snatches of conversation from the other tables. She pulled her eyes away and turned in her chair.

"You're right about the girl with the cottage cheese not reading. I've been watching her and . . ."

"So you were friends with Gaynor on the ship," he cut in. "You didn't know her before that, did you?"

"No, I didn't. But life is full of strange coincidence, isn't it? For all we know we might have been jitterbugging on the same dance floor six years ago. Did you go to those servicemen's parties that the Working Girls' War Effort put on?"

"I might have gone to one or two. I'm sorry I didn't meet you then."

"Yes . . . well . . . I can't really say that I was friends with Gaynor on the ship. I did talk to her a lot. But we were too unequal to be real friends then."

"Does friendship require equality?"

"I don't know. I haven't ever thought about it. I suppose not." These turns in the conversation where the personal was suddenly changed into the theoretical made her nervous. She couldn't tell if he was genuinely interested in her ideas about the nature of friendship or if the question was designed to test her in some way. She supposed it had something to do with his being an intellectual, and while part of her was impressed, another part wanted to ask him to speak simply, just come out with whatever it was he wanted to say. "One of my best friends is an older woman who's a doctor. I don't think of myself as her equal, she's more like a loving relative. I suppose a friend is someone you enjoy who's willing to stand by you. It wasn't like that with Gaynor. She seemed so much more mature than I, so beautiful and sophisticated. She was the first real woman of the world I'd ever met. At least that was my perception of her at the time. But I was very naive. I used to watch her, hoping to pick up hints on how to present myself.''

"I don't think Gaynor would have much to teach you that you couldn't pick up from a fashion magazine.'' He pushed his glass aside and leaned toward her, one side of his mouth twitching into a crooked smile. "But as you say, you were very young. Youth entitles one to a certain amount of naivete, doesn't it?''

"But I was really a case—green as grass, addicted to movies and daydreaming. I had all these romantic notions about what my life in the States would be. I was totally unprepared for any of it.''

"Don't you like America?''

"It isn't that. It's just that at first . . .'' she stopped herself, unsure of how much she wanted to reveal.

"Well, Hickock, S.—or may I call you Sheila now?—you don't strike me as naive. You seem to have a pretty firm grip on reality. There aren't many girls who would go back to school when they've already got a husband and a child.''

"You're making me sound like Florence Nightingale. The fact was that we didn't have any money. I had to find something to do and the doctor I told you about encouraged me to go into nursing. I didn't do it alone. I borrowed money from my Da, and my mother-in-law was good enough to take care of Spencer. Even Billy came around when he saw how important it was to me.''

There. She'd blabbed out all of their private business. Just because he seemed intelligent and solicitous and . . . yes, because he was handsome. It was one thing to admit her deprivations to female friends, but to tell another man that her husband hadn't been able to provide for her was something else again. It would wound Billy to know that she'd made such a confession. But why did she always feel that she had to protect Billy? She grabbed her glass and sucked on the straw. It made a dreadful slurping sound.

"All gone,'' he smiled, looking at her with the same delighted, indulgent expression she'd seen on Da's face so many times. "Can I get you some more?''

She could tell he was trying to smooth over her embarrassment. He *was* a gentleman.

"No. No, thank you. Oh, I do talk on, don't I? That's why my teeth stick out like this," she laughed.

"Your teeth stick out because you talk too much? I've been told some pretty colorful examples of local folklore, but I didn't know loquacity was punished with dental problems hereabouts."

"I didn't mean that . . . When I was a little girl I was supposed to have braces to correct my overbite. Mother took me to the dentist. He put all those instruments in my mouth and started talking *at* me and I couldn't talk back, so I just refused to have the braces. Mother warned me that I'd regret it once I grew up. She thought I was too vain to have a mouthful of tin, so I just let her go on thinking that. But the real reason I didn't want to go to the dentist was because I just couldn't bear not being able to answer back."

"I felt the same way when you'd put that thermometer in my mouth."

"You can't imagine what an evil sense of power that thermometer gives me."

"I shouldn't worry about it. I don't think you're the sadistic type. I'm sure you're going to be a terrific nurse."

"I hope so. Wanting a steady salary was part of going back to school, but it's much more than that. I could never have gone through with it if I hadn't had a dream about doing something worthwhile and doing it well."

"Yeah. Idealism is a powerful motivation. We can add that to naivete as one of the entitlements of youth."

"You say that as though you were a hundred years old. Don't you want to be a professor because you want to help your students to understand and appreciate books?"

"I used to think so. Now I'm not so sure. Now I'm beginning to think the only reason I wanted to do anything was because my old man didn't want me to."

"I know what you mean," she answered, eased by his exchange of a personal confidence. "I used to be so rebellious. It's funny, because now that Spencer's gotten to the stage where he says 'no' to absolutely everything, he drives me crazy because he reminds me of myself. Of course he's just a toddler. I was still like that when I left Australia."

"And now you're sorry for it?"

"I can't really say I'm sorry. I just wish I could have been more understanding toward my parents at the same time. But then, if I had been, it would have made it very easy for me to turn tail and go back home when I hit the rough spots. At the time their concern only seemed selfish and meddlesome. Now that I have a child of my own, I know that protectiveness is an inescapable part of love. But you're a parent, you must know what I mean."

"I'm not much of a father. My protectiveness fritters into ineffectual anxiety. I don't see Joey very often because I still live in Princeton."

She nodded. His need to charm, to interrogate, to protect himself had dissipated now, and they opened themselves to a conversation that flowed effortlessly from remembrances of childhood to present concerns. When they started a discussion of books, she took a pencil out of her purse and wrote down his list of favorites. As she folded the paper napkin, she looked up and noticed that the women behind the serving counter had removed the food and were scrubbing down the tables in preparation for the evening meal.

"My gracious, it's quarter to five," she exclaimed, looking at his watch. "I should have been home ages ago."

He walked her to the parking lot, slowing his pace so that he might prolong their talk. She hurried a few steps ahead of him, stopping beside a pickup truck.

"You drive that?"

"I'm the terror of the backroads," she giggled. "If I'd been around during Prohibition I would have delivered white lightnin' door to door. Billy gets a ride to work with some other fellows now, but we're going to be able to buy a new car as soon as I graduate. He can have it. I'm going to keep the truck. Oh, we've had some times in this ol' wreck."

He opened the door and helped her up into the cab, amused at the sight of her perched on a pillow so that she could see through the windshield.

"I hate to see you leave, Sheila. I've really enjoyed being with you."

"I have too. Billy's the strong, silent type and I really miss talking."

"I am going to be down here for another few days before Betty and I drive back to New York. Do you think we could see each other again?"

"I don't know." She hesitated, averting her eyes. He had listened to her. He had been interested in what she thought and felt. He had made her feel intelligent and attractive. Since he was going away and there was no possibility of the relationship going any further, would it really be wrong of her to see him one more time?

"You're really so pleasant to be with," he persisted. "I can see why Gaynor wanted to come down and visit you."

"I didn't know that she did. I'd written to her a few times when we first came over, but she never answered my letters."

"I meant the time she came down to stay with you a couple of years ago. It was right after Joey was born and she was depressed and needed to get away."

She shook her head in confusion. "Gaynor has never been down to visit me. It must've been someone else."

He opened his mouth as though to question her further. Then a look of shocked recognition blanched his face. She stared at him, too bewildered to speak, realizing that she must have uncovered some horrible lie of Gaynor's. He turned his head abruptly, composed his features and looked back at her with an overly bright smile.

"I must've made some mistake. Must have been some other friend. It's been a pleasure to meet you, Sheila. Best of luck."

She reached out to shake his hand, but he turned away, stuffed his hands into his pockets, and walked off without a backward glance. She watched his retreating figure with its shoulders pulled stiffly back in an unconvincing swagger, knowing that she had unmasked the evidence of Gaynor's infidelity. There was no way in the world that she could have known that her chance remark would hurt him so deeply, yet she felt a sickening sense of guilt.

Sheila was unusually quiet throughout dinner. She wanted to confide in Billy, but knew he wouldn't take kindly to the idea of her meeting another man without telling him about it beforehand. Ma watched her pick at her food. After Sheila had helped her with the dishes, she mentioned that they'd changed the double bill at the Paradise and urged them to go off to the movies.

In the protective darkness of the theater, Billy's arm draped around her shoulders, she watched Olivia DeHavilland lock the door on her faithless lover and imprison herself in self-righteous spinsterhood. She wept silently into her handkerchief, her sorrow at having caused Ricky pain merging with her sympathy for the heiress's blighted life. When the Woody Woodpecker cartoon came on, she whispered to Billy that she didn't want to see the next feature.

"Girl, you take these damn movies too serious," he chided her as he took her hand and walked her toward the pickup. "Now if'n we'd gone to see a good action movie you wouldn't be mopin' 'round like this. It's jest a made-up story, you know."

"But it's true," she insisted. "People betray each other all the time. It isn't just the good guys and the bad guys. People hurt each other accidentally. I . . . I mean, they . . ."

"C'mon. We don't betray each other. That there woman in the movie was jest foolish. If he treated her bad she should'a jest gone on to someone else. You know the ol' sayin': lovers are like streetcars; there'll be 'nother one along in ten minutes."

She stopped and stared up into his face. "Do you really believe that," she demanded. "What would you do if I betrayed you?"

"Why, I'd get m'self a jug o' whiskey 'n two good-lookin' women an' I'd . . ." He put his hands on her shoulders and pulled her head into his chest. ". . . and I'd wanta die."

CHAPTER
XXIV

THE OLD MEN lolling on the courthouse steps eyed Ricky as he walked into the hardware store. He didn't have to open his mouth for them to know he was an outsider. When he placed the sleeping bags and the Coleman lantern on the counter, the grizzled clerk looked him over with the same barely veiled suspicion.

"Y' travelin' through?" the man drawled.

"Yep." He put his money on the counter and shrugged. When he was in Kansas City or Princeton, he knew he should feel at home, but never did. Here, at least, there was a reason to feel alienated. He gathered up the supplies and walked back toward the library, where he had parked his car.

It was Betty's idea that they should take their time driving back to New York. She suggested buying some camping equipment and stopping along the way. Ricky wasn't particularly enamored of the idea of roughing it in the woods, but he felt he owed her something. He'd been a burden during his illness, and since Sheila's revelation he'd been struggling unsuccessfully against a new tide of depression. Of course he had known that Gaynor had lied to him about everything from her family background to the price of a dress, but the confirmation of another deception weighed heavily on him.

Slamming down the trunk, he moved toward the car door and was stopped by the sight of a pretty girl coming down the library steps. Squinting his eyes against the sun, he watched as she crossed the lawn and paused at the water fountain, rolling her head from side to side to relieve the tension in her shoulders. Her cheap cotton dress had been washed so many times that it looked soft and filmy and her pale blond hair fell past her shoulders. Since he had never seen her out of uniform or with her hair down, it took him a minute to realize that it was Sheila. He hurried across the lawn.

"Beautiful day, isn't it?"

"Oh." She started, standing up straight and wiping the water from her mouth. "I didn't see you. How are you feeling?"

"I'm feeling fine, thanks. We're leaving the day after tomorrow. I wanted to call and say goodbye, but I didn't know how to get in touch with you."

"We don't have a phone." She clutched the books closer to her chest and smiled, trying to think of something to say. "I usually come to the library on Saturdays because it's hard to study at the house."

"Could we go somewhere and talk for a bit?"

"There really isn't any place to go; besides, I have to get home."

"You always have to get home, don't you?"

She knew the question wasn't intended to bait her. If anything there was a note of pleading beneath his casual tone. Yet it annoyed her, made her realize how constrained her life was. The limits of what she could and could not do, though mainly self-imposed, were more binding than the restrictions that had been put upon her by her parents and teachers. She was so tired of studying, and it was a lovely day. Besides, she reasoned, she owed him some sort of apology.

"You're leading me astray, but I suppose I could consent to playing truant for a few hours. We could go for a drive. I'll show you the hill where we used to live."

"Fine. Want to give me a spin in that pickup of yours?"

"No." She shook her head, smiling. "I'd prefer the luxury of a sedan."

"Comparative luxury only. It's over ten years old."

"That's still luxurious to me."

They drove into the hills, conversing with the easy give and take of their afternoon in the cafeteria. He told her about his thesis and, after turning the radio on, interrupted the news broadcast to give her his political opinions. She was impressed by the breadth of his knowledge and his easy way with words. He asked her about Blacksburg, and when she peppered her answers with Ma's anecdotes as well as her own impressions, he laughed appreciatively, as though she were the brightest, most entertaining woman in the world. As they turned off highway to the dirt road that led to the shack, she could feel the excitement between them. The unspoken acknowledgement that their time together was limited and precious, the keen awareness of waiting for the real conversation to begin.

"Turn right. Here by the big tree."

He bumped into the clearing, turned off the motor and looked around him in disbelief.

"Yes, I know. It was a bit of a rude awakening for me when I first saw it. We'd come in the middle of the night, you see, and it wasn't 'til the next morning that I really got a look at it. Oh, did I pack on a turn! Now we don't have to live here anymore, I actually think it's rather picturesque . . . well, not so much that I want to venture into the house again," she added with a rueful smile. "Come on, I'll show you the woods. There's a really lovely view from the top of that hill."

She slipped off her shoes and clambered out of the car.

"Will you be okay going barefoot?"

"Now aren't you jest the city mouse! Why, the soles of my feet are as tough as nails. And would you believe I'd never even heard of hillbillies 'til I came here," she laughed, motioning him forward. "Get a move on, slicker. And watch out for yer pants, there's a lot of brambles."

He followed her up the steep pathway through the woods. The sun beat down, warming the earth, and there was an incessant hum of insects. When they were halfway up the hill, she took some bobby pins from the pocket of her dress and fastened her hair onto the top of her head without slackening her pace. She paused to point out a rabbit. He focused on the delicate shape of her exposed neck. She was such a strange combination—an unselfconscious, almost tomboy assertiveness, yet finely formed, tender. He was sure that if he kissed her neck it would smell of sunshine and leaves. She moved on, tripped and fell backward. He caught her and steadied her, wanting to hold her fast. "I'm right, mate," she laughed, moving away and putting all her energy into the final ascent.

"Whew! That takes it out of you, doesn't it?" she panted, as they reached the summit. "But it's good to be up here. It was Billy who really taught me how to love the woods. I used to be afraid to go into the bush because I thought it was full of snakes, but Billy taught me that there's nothing to be afraid of."

She flung herself down on the grass, her small breasts heaving. There were beads of perspiration on her upper lip and tendrils of hair stuck to her forehead. He sat down at a little distance, watching her stomach muscles relax under the thin cloth of the dress; then, lying back, catching his breath, he shut his eyes. *Christ, I can't imagine what she had to go through, living in that shack. And she doesn't even seem bitter. Gaynor would take one look at that and be on the next train out of here. No. Gaynor would never be here in the first place. I wonder where she is now. Probably sitting on the veranda of the country club complaining that there's not enough ice in her drink.* "About the other day . . ."

"Yes. I was trying to find the right moment to bring it up myself. I know that without meaning to I'd made you unhappy. I'm really very sorry. You see, I didn't know anything about it."

"That's okay. Of course I can't help wondering where she was. I'm sorry I brought it up. It's none of your concern. Shouldn't be any of my concern anymore."

"I don't mind your talking about it. It's just that there's nothing more I can say. But you mustn't think the worst, because it may not be true." She paused, embarrassed. "I suppose you think . . ." She turned toward him, rested her head on her arm, and let her eyes complete the question.

"That she was with another man? I don't know. That's the most obvious reason she'd have to lie."

"But it's not the only one. After all, you've been divorced for some time now and she hasn't remarried, has she?"

"No. I haven't heard any rumors to that effect." *How the hell would I know? For all I understood about Gaynor's sexuality she might be attracted to mating with goats at a witches' Sabbath.* "I didn't understand her in many ways. Especially that way. I wasn't very experienced with women. I'd been in schools with other males all my life and I didn't know . . . of course I'd read about . . ." *That's right, stupid. Yammer away and admit that you were a virgin.*

"You were smarter than I was," she smiled gently. "I hadn't even read the books." She rolled onto her back again and looked up at the sky, feeling that to watch his confession was to inflict unnecessary pain.

"So I suppose I disappointed her. But then, I disappointed her in so many ways. We always had rows about money. And that was ironic, because one of the reasons I was attracted to her was because I didn't think it meant much to her."

"I didn't think it meant much to me. Until I found myself without, that is. I've thought about it a great deal since then."

"Gaynor's always thinking about it. For all I know she might have been on a clandestine shopping spree instead of being with someone else. I remember she had a new dress on when she came to visit me that time." *I can still see it in almost perfect detail—a sort of purplish shiney stuff. She was upset because she thought I was going to criticize her for it. And then . . .*

"Go on," she urged. He bit his thumbnail and squinted his eyes, as though he were reaching for some important connection that had eluded him. He shook his head.

"But it wasn't as though we were ever in dire want. Just that nothing was ever *enough.* For her anyway. She wanted me to take money from my father, but that was the last thing I could do, I guess because we'd hated each other ever since I was a kid. I don't know. I tried to encourage her to do things. Not necessarily go out and get a job, but take classes or something."

"You wanted her to go to school?"

"Yes. She has a really good mind, you know, but somehow . . . I know this sounds funny, but she doesn't have any real confidence in anything but her looks. 'Course that bit of insight didn't hit me until after we were separated. Then I realized I didn't know a damned thing about her."

"I didn't know much about Billy either. Not that he was ever dishonest with me—it was just a combination of misunderstanding and ignorance."

"Ah, yes. 'Ignorance is like a delicate, exotic fruit; touch it, and the bloom is gone.' "

"What's that?" she asked, her eyes crinkling with amusement.

"It's not original. It's a quote from Oscar Wilde. Since I haven't been able to find lucrative employment, I now consider the chief benefit of my education to be a supply of quotations expressing other people's thoughts. It helps me not to be tongue-tied when I'm too confused to come up with my own."

He reached over and covered her hand. He was afraid she would pull away, but she remained perfectly still. "I'm sorry about Gaynor," she said at last, disengaging her hand.

"I know you wouldn't hurt anyone on purpose. And it isn't that I didn't already know Gaynor had broken trust with me. She couldn't have broken trust, because we never had it, not even at the beginning. At least I never lied to her."

He threw his arms behind his head, took a blade of grass and chewed it meditatively, watching her face change into a wistful, far-away expression.

"I don't mean to take her side, Ricky, but sometimes it isn't possible to tell the truth, even to someone you love."

"I know you're just saying that to make me feel better, but I deluded myself. People who are in love should never hold back. It's unforgivable that they should lie to each other."

She tilted her head to one side, her eyes vacant and sorrowful. "I've lied to Billy."

"I can't imagine you lying about anything. You're one of the most honest people I've ever met."

"Do you think people are just one thing?" she asked impatiently. "Do you think they can be judged by a single act? I'm not educated like you, but I know that none of us is simple. I think of myself as honest, but I've lied to my husband . . ." Her breath came fast and her upper lip quivered. ". . . And about something very important."

She put her arm over her eyes, gulping the air. There was no heaving of her breast, no wracking sobs; he could not see her eyes, but twin rivulets began to trickle down her cheeks. He instinctively turned away and then reached out, his hand stopping before he touched her.

"Do you want to tell me about it?"

"No."

"Whatever it was, I'm sure you had a good reason."

A tiny helpless laugh choked in her throat; but when she spoke after a long pause, her voice was quiet, almost colorless. "It is something that I take responsibility for. It will be with me for the rest of my life. But it is my responsibility."

The sun had started to sink, its radiance firing the leaves and grass with luminous, autumnal light. The first chill breeze trembled through the trees. He shivered, feeling the thinness of his shirt, drawing closer to her. She had stopped crying now. One of her arms lay across her breast, the other on her stomach. Her large brown eyes looked up, unblinking, into the darkening sky.

"Oh, my dear, dear, Sheila."

He gathered her into his arms. She stiffened, but then relaxed, turning her face to his.

"I hope you can find a way to forgive her," she whispered.

"I don't know if I have the character to face forgiveness. I don't know if I have the character to take responsibility for my own life."

"You will," she said simply. "I know you will."

They huddled together in a sweet, rocking intimacy. Neither of them spoke. "It's funny," he whispered hoarsely, wiping the tears from her cheek. "I know it's a cliché, but I do feel as though I've known you for a long, long time. Something you said the other day has stuck with me. Remember when you said we might have been on the same dance floor six years ago?"

"Mmmm."

"I started to imagine that we were. I've thought about it so much that I can even recall seeing you. Did you ever have a long blue dress?" She shook her head. "And I started to imagine what our lives might have been like if we had met. And I wish . . . I wish I'd asked you to dance."

She felt the trembling clumsiness of his hands on her arms and back and arched into him, squeezing her eyes shut, so that all she could see was the pulsing, hot glow of a sun inside her head. His lips fluttered over her face and neck, covering her with kisses. His legs were tight against her own. And now her hands were moving, knowing nothing but the desire to explore. They ran over his back, kneading his flesh, then rising, felt the texture of fine, silky hair unlike any other she had touched. He guided her head toward him and their mouths met— creating a sensation like the rosy warmth behind her eyes. He ground into her, hard and insistent. But then a thought intruded in her mind, *She couldn't break trust with me because we never had it.* She blinked, saw his blond lashes, and, as she pulled away, the gray irises of his eyes. Billy's eyes were green.

She wrenched herself free and sat up, pulling her skirt down, clasping her arms around her knees to stop her hands from shaking.

"I'm sorry, Ricky. But I can't."

She looked into his face until she was sure he understood.

They got up, brushed the grass from each other and started down the path.

She stood beside him as he opened the car door. As she started to get in, he noticed a smudge of dirt on her face, took her arm and turned her toward him. He wet his finger and wiped the smudge away, and then cupped her chin in his hands.

" 'Shall I compare thee to a summer's day? Thou art more lovely and more temperate . . .' "

"You said you only quoted other people's lines when you couldn't figure out what to say yourself," she challenged.

"Well . . . You're a lovely woman, Sheila. You're rare and fine. I only know one other woman I like as much as you."

"YOU'RE NOT EXACTLY the reincarnation of Daniel Boone, are you?" Betty griped, watching him fiddling with the kindling.

"You were there when I flunked out of Boy Scouts, Bet. I'd never have risked this camping thing if you hadn't wanted to do it."

"Okay. So it wasn't such a great idea. I'll take the rap."

"Nope. This is a partnership. We'll both take the rap. Can you feel that?" he asked, turning his palm upward. "It's starting to drizzle. That's why this fire won't light."

"Then again," she said through clenched teeth, snatching the box of matches from him, "it may have something to do with the fact that the kindling goes *under* the logs. Do me a favor, Ricky, just go and sit down somewhere 'til I get this started."

"I'll put up the tent before it gets dark. At least they taught me how to do that in basic training."

"Good. You do that."

He got up from his haunches and ambled toward the car. She poked at the twigs, burned her finger on another match, and blew on a tiny curl of flame. A few drops of rain fell. She cursed under her breath. The fire wouldn't catch and she was about to lose her temper. He'd been moping about like a condemned man ever since he'd been released from the hospital. Then, yesterday, when he'd come back to the house looking as though he'd been pulled through the wringer of a washing machine, his mood had inexplicably changed. He was calm and affectionate, thanking her for her kindness and offering to help her pack. When she'd waved him aside, he had sat on the bed and watched her, saying cryptic, philosophical things that apparently had great meaning to him but only succeeded in driving her to the outer limits of patience. Knowing how taciturn he was in most social situations, she had intended to go by herself to the farewell dinner party Helen Abromovitz had arranged. But he had insisted on accompanying her, and surprised her again. He was courteous without being over-polite, so genuinely attentive to everything his hostess had to say that the critical gleam had disappeared from Helen's eyes before they got to the after-dinner drinks. Now he was bungling around with the tent poles, singing "You're the top, You're the coliseum" and grinning like an idiot.

"You are a schizophrenic!"

"Maybe I am! You know me better than anyone else, so I'm not going to argue with you. Could you throw those potatoes in and leave them, but fix the hot dogs now? I'm really hungry."

"And you're a bastard," she went on, angrily skewering the hot dogs.

"Anything else?" he called back amiably.

The fire caught. She stuffed the fork into the flames, pulled her plaid jacket around her, and went over to him, determined to have her say.

"I've got news for you, Cunningham. You think you're a man of ideas, but you're just opinionated. You think you're above money, but you're obsessed with it. In your own way you're just as obsessed as your father ever was. I don't mean you're materialistic—that would be too obvious for a man of your ideals—but you're still twisted about it. That's why you couldn't see you'd picked a gold-digger for a wife. But that's not surprising either, because when it comes to women, you only see what you want to see. You think you prize honesty but you rarely say what's on your mind—I suppose your inner monologue is more illuminating than conversation with the rest of us mere mortals. You are one of the most chronically self-involved people I've ever met."

"That's quite a tirade," he smiled, raising his hands and backing off in a gesture of surrender.

"Yeah, well, don't bother to listen to any of it. Just put it down to the fact that I'm getting my period."

"You're right, Bet. Sorry to take the wind out of your sails, but I concede."

"You're not taking the wind out of my sails. I'm not spoiling for a fight and believe it or not I don't think being right is the grand prize. I just think it's time you know how I feel."

"And?"

She put her hands on her hips, looked upward, and marched back to the fire. "And now that I've had my say, we can have supper."

There was a clap of thunder. He shrugged, gave a grunt of self-congratulation as he shook the tent pole, and then walked over and hunched down next to her. "I'm sorry. I know I've put you through a lot. I know I won't change overnight, but I'm working on it. I've been mulling things over for a helluva long time—chronically self-involved, as you pointed out, but I think I've turned the corner." She wrapped her arms around herself, too disgusted to reply. "If you're really uncomfortable out here," he went on, "maybe we could drive to the next town and get a hotel room."

"The next town is fifty miles and we don't know if there's a hotel there," she grumbled.

"So we're stuck."

"I'm not stuck. I said I was going to camp out, and I'm going to camp out."

"You've always been like that, haven't you? Okay. When we get back to the city I'm going to treat you to two days in the fanciest hotel we can find. You can put aside your interviews and graphs and books and have room service morning 'til night."

"Why are you talking that crap? You know I'll have to get right back to work. This was supposed to be the vacation. Besides . . ."

Another great roll of thunder boomed across the sky. Sheets of rain swept through the trees. He dashed for the tent, holding the flap open for her. "C'mon. C'mon." She stopped long enough to look down at the mess of food, and then ran over.

"Cozy in here, isn't it?" he asked, wrapping a blanket around her shoulders.

"God, what a disaster," she laughed. "What a disaster."

"Here, give me the matches and I'll light the Coleman so we can see each other."

"This wool coat of mine smells like hell now it's wet," she sniffed, handing him the matches.

"Here, light one so I can see what I'm doing. Fine. Now I'll adjust the filament . . . there, now we can see each other." He set the lamp in front of them and draped his arm around her shoulders. "Boy, it's really coming down out there, isn't it?"

"Let's not talk about the weather, Ricky. Let's talk about you. What the hell's been going on with you? Why this sudden mood change?"

"I don't really know. It's what I was trying to say a while ago. It's as though I was working on a mosaic—working very close up—and now I've stepped back; or, more properly, I've been knocked back, and I think I can see the whole thing. I know getting malaria again was some kind of regression and . . . well, a lot of other things happened—I'm not going to tell you about them now, but I will tell you some other time. Anyhow, I know it sounds melodramatic, but I think I've gone through some kind of catharsis. I feel hopeful. When we get back I'm going to apply for some other kinds of jobs. I've got a few friends in publishing, so I thought I'd nose around and . . ."

"You haven't mentioned Gaynor in forty-eight hours, so I guess you must've gone through some kind of metamorphosis," she said wryly.

"I know. I feel as though I'm free of it."

"You don't want her back."

"No."

"You don't want to get back *at* her? No regrets? No obsession?"

"Regrets? Sure, I have regrets. But obsession, no."

"It sounds a bit too much like a magic spell to convince me."

"You're a hard-headed woman, Bet."

She turned away from him, curling her body up on the canvas floor. He put his hand on her back, shifted it tentatively to her arm. "Another thing I realized is that I'm the sort of guy who needs to be married."

"Yet another candidate for serial monogamy? Since you're feeling so positive I suppose it's only natural that you'd succumb to the triumph of hope over experience."

"Now don't get sarcastic. Just listen to the rain. It's good to lie here like this, isn't it? Makes you feel protected."

"The pole will probably collapse during the night, and we'll drown. Dammit, the food's all spoiled, and I'm hungry."

"Remember when we were kids and I put my hand under your sweater and you cried?"

"Now you want to fill me with nostalgia. I'd settle for a hot dog."

He paused. "I want to ask you if it's all right to do that now. I also want to ask you if you'll marry me."

"Sweet Lord in heaven." She turned to look at him, struggling with the blanket between them. "You really *are* schizophrenic," she laughed helplessly.

"Shush. Don't laugh."

His face was stern, his voice unredeemably serious. She raised her hand to cover her mouth, shaking her head. He brought his finger up, tracing the outline of her face until she grew silent and grave.

"Ricky . . . The answer to the second question is, we'll have to wait and see."

"And the answer to the first? It's going to be cold tonight, you know."

"The answer is yes."

315

CHAPTER
XXV

"Darling, I'm just pea green with envy," Kay Manchester's voice cooed through the phone. "When I think of you in New York for three whole days, I feel so sorry for myself I just want to slash my wrists. But if I don't get Betsy settled into camp I'll be sentenced to an entire summer of chaperoning swimming lessons and picnics."

"I wouldn't have accepted Grace's invitation if I'd known you were going to back out," Gaynor sighed, tucking the receiver between her ear and shoulder and reaching for the nail-polish remover. She glanced at Joey, who was sprawled on his belly at the foot of her bed, a red Crayola clutched in his left fist, a heap of coloring books scattered around him. "Of course I'll have to go through with the trip now," she said, returning to her nails. "How is the cultural committee going to book our next season if we don't see what's happening in New York? But I *am* disappointed. I'd thought we'd be able to combine business with pleasure—go on a shopping spree, take in some nightclubs."

"Unless you're going to venture out alone, you'll have to abandon the idea of having any fun. I've traveled with Grace before. She's strictly tours, tea rooms and tedium. She thinks she's in the know but she's absolutely middle-brow. The last time we went to a dinner party at her place I was so bored my head was nodding into the turtle soup. And after dinner she had that anemic-looking niece of hers entertain us by singing Schubert lieder and accompanying herself on the piano. I mean really! Even Donald knows that domestic recitals went out at the turn of the century. But enough of Grace and her fuddy-duddy clique. You really don't have any choice about going with them this time, do you? I mean, you absolutely can't be here in town when Ricky and his bride-to-be come to visit, can you?"

"That doesn't bother me. I've managed to avoid him whenever he's visited before. I'm completely neutral on the subject of what Ricky does."

At the mention of Ricky's name, Joey raised his eyes from the coloring book, then started to press down on the page with violent, slashing lines.

"Didn't I hear that Ricky's finally gotten some sort of a job? I thought Etna told Grace that he was going to be an editor of some silly leftist magazine."

"Yes, I guess I heard that. It's no concern of mine."

"I think you're being very noble about it. And I can't say the rest of the community shares your charitable feelings toward him. I mean, it's only been a little over a year since the divorce. You don't suppose he and Betty were carrying on with each other before you started the proceedings, do you?"

"If they were, I don't give a damn. If it weren't for the complication of Joey, I'd never bother to speak to Ricky again."

Joey threw aside his Crayola and wiggled across the floor toward her.

"Well, they're perfectly matched. That Betty Richardson has always been an oddball. She dropped out of her sorority in her second year of college, you know. Said she was too busy with her studies, but we all knew it was because she wasn't getting any dates."

"Stop that!" Gaynor shouted angrily, as Joey threw his arms around her legs. "No, Kay, I wasn't talking to you. Joey just grabbed me and —*bloody hell*—he's upset the polish remover."

She threw the receiver on the dressing table, yanked Joey up by one arm, and yelled for Faustina.

"Now look what you've done! You'll do anything to get attention, won't you," she yelled, mopping up the spill with a wad of cotton.

"I didn't! I didn't!" he cried defiantly. "You spill it."

"F-a-u-s-t-i-n-a!"

The housekeeper walked calmly through the door, wiping her hands on her apron. "I'm right here."

"Sorry. I never hear you come in. Will you take him downstairs? He's about to drive me mad."

"I didn't do it," Joey protested. "I didn't . . ."

"Everything's all right," Faustina whispered, easing her bulk to the carpet and picking up the Crayolas. "Let's pick up your things and go downstairs."

Gaynor watched the two of them crawling around the floor like a big, black mother bear and her albino cub. She grabbed the phone again, sighing into the receiver.

"Kay? Sorry for the interruption. Now what was I saying? Yes, about the trip to New York. I do plan to escape from Grace and Emily long enough to look around. I told you last week that I'm seriously thinking of moving to New York, and I want to see what the market in apartments is like."

"You just *can't* think of moving, Gaynor. I'd be so bored if I didn't have you to talk to."

"I wouldn't be moving for months. You can come back with me and help me find a place when I really decide to take action. But while I'm there, I would like to get a look around. And don't feel bad about my moving. At least you'll have a place to escape to."

"Just hold on a minute and let me check my address book. I'm sure Donald knows some guy there who's in real estate. I'll give you his number. As I recall, Donald says he's a terrible wolf."

"Well, I'm not exactly Little Red Riding Hood. I can't imagine the wolves have sharper teeth on Fifth Avenue than they do at the country club. Listen, I'm in a terrible rush to finish packing. You look up that number, and I'll call you back later. Okay?"

She plopped the receiver back into the cradle and capped the bottle of polish remover. Joey had climbed up onto her bed and was sitting there examining a scab on his knee as though nothing had happened. Faustina sat back on her haunches, holding the coloring books and the packet of crayons, her eyes fixed on the carpet.

"Anything wrong, Faustina?"

"No'm."

"Then please take him downstairs. I should be finished in about twenty minutes, then you can call Jackson and ask him to pick us up. If that new girl you got for me had been about her business she would have had the ironing done earlier, and I could have packed this morning." She held her arms out to Joey, motioning him to come to her. "Mummy's sorry she yelled, but you must learn not to prance about when she's on the telephone. Now you run along with Faustina. Mummy will be ready soon, then we'll go to grandma's house for tea.

You can take your suitcase, because Mummy's going bye-bye, and you're going to stay in your old room at grandma's. Won't that be fun?"

Joey looked to Faustina for confirmation of his mother's statement. She nodded at him, lumbered to her feet, and lifted him from the bed.

"Kiss and make up." Gaynor pursed her lips seductively.

He leaned from Faustina's arms and clasped his hands on either side of her face.

"Moo-moo needs to go to."

"Moo-moo can go if Faustina's willing to set an extra place at the table for him. But Moo-moo will have to be going on a trip himself soon." She winked at Faustina.

"No. No," he shouted furiously.

"Please take him downstairs. I'll be ready soon," she groaned, ushering them toward the door. She finished touching up her nails and moved to the closet to look at her mink stole. It had been an unseasonably chilly spring and, she reasoned, if she did meet that friend of Kay's and he asked her out for the evening, she might need a fur. But was it fashionable to wear furs in May? She'd looked over all the copies of *Vogue* and *Bazaar,* but she supposed the only reliable index of what was stylish would be to see what other women were wearing. Grace would probably try to rope her into matinees and a guided tour of St. John the Divine, but she was determined to set out on her own. She trusted her instincts enough to know that she could adapt to any social situation with chameleonlike ease. She would sniff out the best spots in the city, so that when she did move, the transition could be accomplished smoothly.

It was good to know that she was finally plotting her escape. Not that she hadn't been superficially satisfied with her role as the modish young divorcee. She still enjoyed the golf lessons, the parties and the clubs. But whenever she'd had a bit too much to drink or was left alone for more than a day, life in Kansas City depressed her. Now that the Covingtons were coming back from Europe to reclaim their house, she had a reason to put her dreams into action. It was time to move on. She wrapped the stole around her shoulders, turning this way and that to appraise herself in the mirror, feeling excited about her decision to conquer more glamorous territory. Laying the fur next to the suitcase, she started to select the jewelry she would take with her. There was a tap on the door.

"Come," she called out happily; then, seeing Faustina, she dropped the pearls back into the jewelry box. "I told you at least half an hour, Faustina."

Faustina closed the door without a sound. She advanced a few steps, her shoulders held back in a deliberate, upright posture that looked as though she were walking down the aisle of a church. "I have to talk to you."

"If it's about Moo-moo I just don't have the time now. Besides, there's nothing to worry about. I spoke to Kay Manchester and she says that Betsy wandered around talking to an imaginary playmate for years. It's perfectly normal. Goes to show that even though Joey's a troublesome child, he is highly intelligent and has an active . . ."

"I couldn't help overhearing what you were saying to Mrs. Manchester," Faustina interrupted in a deeply sorrowful voice.

Gaynor examined a pair of earrings, her mouth curling upward on one side. "Surely you didn't come in here to confess to eavesdropping. I'm in rather a hurry, so please get to what it is you want to say."

"I heard what you were saying 'bout going away. I think you must know how much it would hurt Miss Etna if you took the little boy from her. Joey is 'bout all she has to keep her going."

"Faustina, I know you love Joey. I know Mrs. Cunningham loves Joey. And you may rest assured that when I make a decision to leave I will discuss it with Mrs. Cunningham. In the meantime, I'd appreciate it if you didn't alarm her by carrying tales about conversations you may have overheard in this house."

"Then you won't move away?" she asked in a half-pleading, half-threatening voice. "You know how she dotes on him and . . ."

"I shall run my life as I see fit," Gaynor replied impatiently, returning to an inspection of her jewelry. "In all probability we shall be moving. And now, if you'll excuse me."

". . . and I wouldn't want her to lose that little boy," Faustina droned on as though she hadn't heard her. "I want to make sure that his grandma and his daddy—I mean Mr. Ricky—will be able to be with him."

There was something about the pause she took between "his daddy" and "I mean Mr. Ricky" that halted Gaynor's perusal of the jewels. "You've been immensely helpful to me, Faustina," she said with cool forbearance. "I know Joey is fond of you, and I understand that, to Miss Etna at least, you are almost a part of the family. But I will not put up with this interference. I think you'd best know that as soon as I get back from New York I will make it a priority to find a full-time nanny for Joey."

She snapped the jewelry case shut and swung around to look her in the face, hoping that her tone had been sufficiently intimidating to hide the fact that her hands were beginning to shake. But Faustina continued to stand there, massive, composed, her arms folded loosely in front of her belly, her sloe eyes sorrowful but determined. "If you do try to move away, I'm afraid I'll have to speak to Mr. Ricky and Miss Etna."

"Speak to them by all means, though I have no idea what you'd have to say."

"You know Mr. Ricky is unhappy about the will. And Miss Etna is sure upset about those orders 'bout sending Joey away to military school. If they do decide to fight the will and if you try to move away, I just may have to tell them what I know."

"Aren't you a little out of your depth, Faustina? I wasn't aware that servants were conversant with the law."

"I do know about undue influence, Miss Gaynor."

"I have no idea what you're talking about," Gaynor said in an icy tone.

"Lotsa times folks don't see things. It's not because they're stupid. It's just that the heart protects the brain. Brain won't let you see things if it's too much for the heart to bear. I think you know what I'm talking about," she went on, a low compassionate resonance in her voice. "But once somebody pulls back the curtain, why, the brain has to admit what it's known all along. I grant you Miss Etna's a foolish woman in some ways; but she has righteousness, even when it goes against herself. And Mr. Ricky's not really weak, he just don't show his courage in any usual ways. Once they see the truth, they won't deny it."

It was only with supreme effort that Gaynor stopped her legs from buckling beneath her. A rage so potent that it made her entire body feel as though it were burning seared through her.

"You may fancy yourself some sort of backwoods preacher, Faustina, but let me remind you that you are a housekeeper in the employ of this family. You may carry whatever evil tales your voodoo imagination has manufactured; but I seriously doubt if you will be believed, and your vicious meddling just may cost you your home."

"Etna and I been together since before her daddy sent her off to college. I was with her when her baby was born. I changed his diapers and cared for him when he was sick. I have never lied to them. They know I have never lied to them. When I show them the evidence of what I know . . ."

"What evidence?" Gaynor snarled.

"Ricky told me there was a woman with Mr. Richard when he died. I cleaned Mr. Richard's desk. I 'spose there are blood tests an' all that could be done on the boy . . ." She swayed slightly on her feet, her right hand shooting up as though bearing witness, her head bowed like a penitent's. "I know Mr. Richard was your baby's daddy."

The spring breeze moved the curtains, bringing a fragrance of rotting wood, damp earth and lilac into the room. Gaynor sank back into the chair by the dressing table, her fingers moving back and forth across the jewelry box, her eyes glazed.

"You are an insane and vicious woman," she said quietly. "You will leave my room this instant."

"None of it has to come out. It's just that it would cause Miss Etna a lot of pain if you took the boy away."

Faustina moved quietly from the space she had occupied and dominated, pulling the door shut behind her. In the hallway she leaned against the wall, feeling in her apron pocket for the packet of blood-pressure pills. She swallowed one and gasped, her lips moving in prayer.

"Lord, forgive me if I gave false witness. I told her that I have evidence when You know that all the evidence I have is what I know in my heart. I told it to help the people I have to look out for. Forgive me."

She stood still until she felt the benediction she had asked for had been given, and then turned on the hall lights and slowly descended the stairs.

"WON'T YOU CHILDREN join me in a nightcap?" Etna called over her shoulder. Humming contentedly to herself, she turned on a lamp near the coffee table and settled onto the couch.

Betty stifled a yawn. "I'm afraid I've already had too much champagne. Besides, we have to catch that early plane in the morning."

"I promise not to rob you of too much beauty sleep, dear; but I'm in such a lighthearted mood. Son, will you do the honors?"

"Just wait until I get the first layer of this armor off," Ricky answered, taking off his tuxedo jacket. "I didn't want to risk too many drinks at the party, but I could do with a stiff belt myself."

"You looked so handsome in your tux, dear. And you looked very sweet too, Betty. That pale blue chiffon with the tiny pearl buttons is most becoming. Oh, seeing you together tonight made me feel young again. I don't know when I've been so happy. It was such a lovely party, wasn't it."

"Did you really think so, Mother? I couldn't wait for it to end. I haven't answered so damned many questions since I went into the Army."

"Don't be cantankerous, dear. People ask questions because they're interested in you. It's such a shame you won't be able to come back and have the wedding here."

"I'd rather turn myself over to the Spanish Inquisition."

"Yes, it is a shame," Betty cut in. "But since we're both working we can't take any more time off. Besides, we want a simple ceremony, and if we came back, you know we'd end up with a guest list a mile long. When you come to New York it will be a vacation for you, and you'll have an opportunity to see our new apartment."

"You've always been such a sensible girl," Etna beamed again, accepting her drink. "Now, tell me all about the wedding. Where is it to be and what will you wear?"

"St. Thomas's. Ricky's friend Evan will be best man. One of my friends from the Sociology Department will be matron of honor, and I haven't chosen the dress yet."

"Evan. Isn't he that psychiatrist fellow?" she asked.

"Yeah," Ricky smiled, easing into the leather chair and sipping his scotch. "He's got a Park Avenue practice now. Makes money hand over fist by helping divorcees and high-class call girls to understand their angst, but he's a decent guy underneath it all. He introduced me to the editor of my magazine, you know. The way he went to bat you'd think he owed me something."

"Loyalty in friendship is a lovely thing," Etna said with dreamy-eyed sentimentality. "Now Betty, do tell me all about the apartment."

Betty took off her shoes, tucked her feet under her long skirt, and answered Etna's questions. Ricky finished his drink and stretched.

"All right, I get the hint," his mother smiled at him. "I'm just going to put this lovely orchid corsage in the refrigerator, then I'll trot off to bed and leave you two alone."

As soon as she'd left the room, Ricky unhooked his tie and moved to the couch. "Christ, I hope this takes care of the family obligations until next Christmas."

"I know it was awful, but we had to do it."

"We didn't have to do it."

"Yes we did. My parents would never have forgiven me if we hadn't let them make a splash, and you can see how happy Etna is. Their pleasure outweighed our discomfort."

"Speak for yourself, darling. I'm feeling very uncomfortable at the moment."

"Poor baby," she teased, poking him in the ribs. "How is it that your liberal compassion doesn't extend to your family?"

Etna tottered back into the foyer. "Sweet dreams," she called, waving her handkerchief.

When they were sure she'd made it up the stairs, Ricky stretched out, putting his head in Betty's lap. "I guess you're right. It did seem to make her happy. She didn't even notice that most of the guests were looking at us as though we were mounted under glass at the Smithsonian. The only person who was pleasant to me was old Lonnie Diamond, but he was so pie-eyed I'm not sure he knew who I was."

"At least you weren't stuck in the ladies' room with Kay Manchester," Betty giggled. "She came in while I was still on the john. Before I could even flush, she'd sailed over and kissed me on both cheeks. Then she said, 'I'm so happy for you, Betty—you're *finally* getting married.' The way she said 'finally' made me feel as though I'd made it into the last lifeboat on the *Titanic.*"

"She buttonholed me at the bar, but she only kissed me on *one* cheek. Then she said she was so glad I'd *finally* found a job."

"What a night!" She covered her mouth, her shoulders shaking with laughter. "Thank God you were there."

"Even someone who doesn't read Emily Post knows it's customary for the groom to be at the engagement party."

"Don't get smart. I meant I couldn't have made it through if I hadn't been able to look across the room and make faces at you once in a while."

"That didn't help me much. But I did appreciate the way you felt my leg under the table."

He reached up and kissed her lightly, and then leaned back, his hand playing with the pearl buttons at the front of her evening gown. "Dammit, I wish we could sleep together tonight."

"So do I, darling. Do you really think your mother doesn't know?"

"She knows; but she doesn't want to know, so she doesn't know—if you get my drift."

"Oh, I do. When I was getting dressed tonight, my mother came in looking so solemn and nervous I knew she was going to talk about sex. I know she thinks I'm still a virgin, so I took her off the hook by telling her that I'd read all sorts of biology books. . ."

"With illustrated texts."

"With illustrated texts. She looked vastly relieved and started talking about silverware. Gosh, I'm tired."

"Then let's go up. We'll have a lifetime to do post-mortems on rotten parties."

He put his hands on her hips as they mounted the stairs. When they reached the room he'd shared with Gaynor, she started to flip on the light. He took her hand and pulled her to him. "Don't turn it on."

"You seem very glum," she said softly, after they'd held each other for a moment. "The worst is over now. We'll be home tomorrow afternoon."

"It wasn't just the party. You know being back here always depresses me and tonight, just as I was coming over to pick you up, Faustina came in to talk to me."

"Why should that upset you?"

" 'Cause she seemed pretty upset herself. She told me she'd overheard Gaynor saying she was planning to move to New York."

"That's not so awful," Betty said, after pondering for a minute. "New York's a big city. We shouldn't have to run into her more than we want to, and we can see more of Joey."

"I know, but Faustina was worried that it would upset Etna."

"I'm sure it will. But she can come and visit. Gaynor's never given you any trouble about visitation rights."

"Faustina seemed really worried. She's the one who really sees how Gaynor is with the kid, you know. And I've got to admit I'm concerned when I think about Faustina not being around."

"I know how you feel," she sighed, seeing his troubled face in the shadowy light. "But legally there's nothing you can do to stop Gaynor. I've thought perhaps, if you didn't mind, I might approach her. She'd never think of me as a threat and since she doesn't really want Joey, perhaps she'd let us have him. If that doesn't work, we could go into a custody fight."

"That's what I told Faustina. Though I'm not about to get into any legal battles just yet. I want to have an extended honeymoon and increase the circulation of the magazine. I figure those two things should keep me occupied for awhile. Then, if Gaynor won't comply, we'll talk to some lawyers. I figure our chances in court will be better if we've been married for awhile."

"Yes." She tilted her head, offering her lips to him, but he didn't move.

"I'll just look in on Joey, then I'm going to try to get some shuteye," he said stiffly.

"It's the room, isn't it? That's why you didn't want me to turn on the light."

"I'm beginning to have second thoughts about marrying a woman who's so intuitive," he smiled. "Yeah . . . the room bothers me."

"It bothers me too. It still feels like her territory. But I'm so tired, I'm just going to ignore it." She moved away from him, slowly unbuttoning her gown. "I remember the first time I saw her . . . she made me feel so intimidated. It wasn't just her beauty. It was the way she had of occupying space. When she comes into a room she seems to create an illusion that she's the center of the world."

"She *is* the center of the world to herself."

"I can't really understand that sort of narcissism," she went on contemplatively, taking off her dress and holding it to her breast. "I expect she must be very lonely."

He turned her around, putting his hands on her shoulders and looking into her eyes. "I'll make a bargain with you, Bet. You don't waste your pity, and I won't waste my regrets."

And she rested her head against his shoulder, as he looked past her, scanning the room, trying to formulate a thought. " 'Leave her to heaven,' " he murmured at last. " 'And to those thorns that in her bosom lodge, to prick and sting her.' "

CHAPTER
XXVI

"DON'T BOTHER to raise the shades," Gaynor snapped. "I have a splitting headache."

"Would madam like room service to bring some aspirin?" the aged bellhop inquired solicitously, hobbling toward the door.

"Yes. A packet of aspirin and a bottle of Johnny Walker," she ordered, putting a fifty-cent piece into his hand.

She pressed her fingertips to her left temple and threw herself on the bed without unbuttoning her traveling suit. She'd smoked over a pack of cigarettes on the flight, and her mouth was dry and evil-tasting. She knew she'd been bitchy and irritable during the trip, but just didn't have the energy to rise to the occasion. When they'd checked in at the desk and she'd excused herself to take a nap, the elevator doors had not even closed in front of her before Grace Grant and Emily Taylor put their heads together clucking with disapproval. To hell with them, she thought, squeezing her eyes shut. She didn't give a good goddamn if they took an ad in the *Kansas City Star* accusing her of conduct unbecoming to a lady. Their nattering was the least of her worries.

She dragged herself up to answer the door and took the tray from the waiter. Rummaging in her purse for the little gold pill case, she placed a sleeping tablet on her tongue, chasing it with a belt of scotch. She hadn't been able to sleep the previous night and now the stabbing pain in her left eye was causing her real agony. A full-blown vision of Faustina, laid out in a wooden coffin surrounded by flowers, sprang into her mind.

"Don't waste time on such childish thoughts," she said aloud. "Try to think intelligently."

Sinking back onto the bed, she opened her jacket, fondling her breasts and wondering what Richard would do in this situation. Money. Richard would buy the housekeeper off. But that wouldn't work. First of all, an offer would constitute an admission of guilt; and she had been cogent enough to deny all guilt. And Faustina was the least likely person to be interested in blackmail.

No. Money was out. Besides, her intuition told her the whole thing must be a bluff. The woman would never go to Etna and Ricky. She wouldn't take the risk of shattering their lives. But what if she did? Ricky and that dumpy girlfriend of his might just be perverse enough to thumb their noses at the community and bring the scandal out into the open. She'd talked about evidence. What evidence? Richard wouldn't have been stupid enough to put anything into writing, but had the woman spied on them? Could she have had them followed when they were meeting downtown at the hotel? And what about the airline ticket to New York? Had she destroyed it, as she was almost certain she had, or had Faustina discovered it in one of her bags?

She reached for the glass and took another swallow. She must call a lawyer. Not Donald Richardson, of course. Some outsider. She would find out about—what was it Faustina had called it?—"undue influence" on a will. But if she did broach that subject to a lawyer, wouldn't she have to give him the facts of the case?

No. It was all quite ridiculous, she assured herself, as the silver dots dancing before her eyes started to fade. Faustina had tried to intimidate her and she had been caught off guard. The woman couldn't be in possession of any real evidence. She had just stated her suspicions with such confidence and unexpected menace that she'd managed to frighten her. The best thing to do was to do nothing at all. She tossed around on the bed until the pills and the liquor eased her into oblivion.

Grace Grant called some hours later. Gaynor answered in a groggy voice, explaining that she was suffering from a migraine and would not be able to join them for the evening. She turned down another invitation for breakfast, but promised to meet them at the theater for a matinee of *South Pacific* the next day. Swallowing another pill, she undressed, took the phone off the hook, and curled up in the bed.

She spent the morning at a salon on Fifth Avenue being pummeled, stroked and massaged by attendants in pink uniforms whose voices never rose above a whisper. She had her hair shampooed and coiffed. A fussy young man who sputtered self-congratulations whenever he'd achieved his desired effect dabbed and painted her face while another attendant knelt at her feet doing a pedicure. Turning this way and that before the full-length mirrors, she perceived an image of flawless glamor. The elaborate pampering session had cost more than she could have earned in an entire week during her working days, but it was worth it. Her self-possession had been restored.

She glided into the sunny street, head high, aware of every admiring glance. Seeing a coral necklace in a shop window, she decided to indulge herself in another treat. She felt it might demean her attractiveness if she appeared to be buying jewelry for herself, so she told the salesman that she was selecting a gift for her mother. She waited until she was back on the street to unwrap the silver paper, tuck the gift card into her wallet, and hook the necklace around her throat. As she walked on, she imagined a movie camera moving in front of her recording her loveliness, capturing her every gesture. She had a perfect sense of what she looked like: white linen suit and pumps, full-brimmed peach-colored hat casting rosy shadows on her face, the coral necklace emphasizing the ivory smoothness of her neck. The picture made her feel buoyant and incredibly happy until she approached the marquee of the theater. Grace greeted her with strained tolerance, but Emily looked as ruffled as a chicken who had just got the worst of a barnyard squabble.

"Nice to see you've recuperated," Emily said archly.

"Now, Emily, the show's almost ready to start; don't upset yourself," Grace cautioned.

Gaynor smiled sweetly. "I am sorry. I only get these migraines twice a year, but when I do I'm incapacitated."

"Then I suppose we're safe in assuming that you will be able to use the ticket for Carnegie Hall tonight," Emily snapped. "You know last night's ticket was wasted. The cultural committee paid for them and . . ."

"I'll be happy to reimburse the committee," Gaynor said over her shoulder as she started into the lobby. "I think the curtain's about to go up. We don't want to miss the overture, do we?"

The show was so delightful that it managed to erase all troublesome thoughts from her mind and banished her companions' sour moods.

Emily was atwitter when they left the theater, pausing on the sidewalk to praise Mary Martin's performance and blocking the stream of theatergoers who were coming out behind them.

"Gaynor! G-a-y-n-o-r Cunningham!"

"I think someone's calling you," Grace said, turning back to look at the crowd.

"It couldn't be. I don't know anyone here."

"Coo-ee! Coo-ee, G-a-y-n-o-r," the voice rang out again.

"Yes, she's calling you. That woman in the funny yellow hat."

Gaynor viewed the sea of millinery bobbing out of the lobby, settling her glance on the yellow hat. It was such a ridiculous affair, looking like a velveteen crepe that had been flipped out of a frying pan, that at first she couldn't recognize the face over which it drooped.

"Don't you recognize me?" the woman with the popping eyes demanded as she pushed her way toward them. "It's your Kangaroo Cobber! It's Mavis!"

"Oh, dear, yes. I am sorry, Mavis. I wasn't expecting . . ."

"But you *know* I live on Long Island," Mavis insisted, plucking at her arm. "I've told all the girls that if they're coming to New York they must contact me."

"It must've slipped my mind. Mavis, these are my friends . . ."

"Mavis Slocum. So pleased to meet you. Gaynor and I came over on the ship together. I don't see how she could ever forget that voyage. There we were, scared as rabbits and seasick to boot. Oh Gaynor, do come and have a drink with me."

"I'd love to, Mavis. But unfortunately, we have a rather tight schedule. We have to be getting back to the Waldorf."

"Nonsense," Grace cut in, glad for an opportunity to punish Gaynor's behavior. "You just run along with your Australian friend. We'll meet you in the lobby at seven. Don't be late. So pleased to meet you Mrs. er . . . such an original hat . . . come along, Emily."

"Blimey, this is a surprise," Mavis laughed, hooking her arm through Gaynor's and leading her down the street. "You've been so naughty about contributing to the newsletter that I was afraid you might have gone back to Australia."

"Not a chance."

"I feel the same way myself. 'Course I get homesick once in a blue moon—don't we all—but I'm a real Yank now. I even go to baseball games! How's about this bar? I know it doesn't look like much but it's an actors' hang-out, so we might see some celebrities. It's just wonderful being near the city. Of course we wouldn't live here. The whole country is moving into the suburbs, isn't it? That's the wave of the future, Herbie says. Oh, you do look well, Gaynor! But then you were always the best-looking woman on the ship. You and Claire Johnson. Remember her? Tall girl, lovely auburn hair . . ." She managed to push open the door, find a table, and hail a waiter without interrupting the gush of chatter. ". . . Anyway, Claire doesn't look so lovely now. She's had three kiddies—pop, one, two, three like scones coming out of an oven. Sent me one of those Christmas card photos and my dear, you wouldn't recognize her she's put on so much weight. And you were friends with that terribly young girl, Sheila Hickock, weren't you? Ever hear from her? What'll you have? . . . Scotch? One scotch and one Manhattan, waiter. The last I heard from Sheila she was going to nursing school. Reading between the lines—not that she actually *said* anything—I'd guess the boy hero she married hasn't been able to support her. Otherwise, why would she be going to school? Still there are worse things than a tight budget. Remember Ruby Keller? Her hubby . . ."

Gaynor sipped her drink, taking in the checkered table cloths and the autographed photos on the walls, giving only minimal attention to the litany of gossip. She guessed that Mavis's neurotic interest in other people's lives must supplement the utter sterility of her own existence. On the second round of drinks, the yellow monstrosity now drooping over both eyes, Mavis's backbiting took a more salacious turn into madness, homosexuality, and the ever-popular subject of adultery.

". . . so Chris had no idea that David was mentally ill until he tried to commit suicide. Then it came out that he'd been in an Army hospital for months after Salerno."

"I think I'd like another," Gaynor said softly as the waiter passed their table. "And you, Mavis?"

"No. I never drink. I just like the cherries in the Manhattans. Besides I have to pick Herbie up at six." Gaynor's eyes flitted to the clock on the wall. "Don't worry, Gaynor, we have another half an hour. I'll just run off to the loo, but when I come back you must tell me all about yourself."

She slid out of the booth, picking her way between the tables and rubbernecking the customers. *She'll probably be able to tell me the dirty secrets of the couple in the back booth by the time she gets back,* Gaynor thought.

Mavis had made her unaccountably nervous. She took another swallow, hoping that it would soothe her jangled nerves, but reminding herself that she mustn't drink so much that she would be tempted to let down her guard. Conscious of someone looking at her, she turned to see a strikingly good-looking young man sitting across the room. His companion, an effete fellow about his own age, was hunched over his drink talking frantically. The good-looking one smiled and raised his glass, acknowledging that they were both trapped by talkative bores. She lifted her own glass.

"Now what was I saying?" Mavis inquired as she plopped down into the booth. "Ah yes . . . about you: I think I heard through the grapevine that you'd gotten a divorce."

"That's right," Gaynor answered slowly, wondering how she'd come by the information.

"Was it dreadful, dear? Do you feel terribly alone?"

"Everybody's alone when you come down to it."

"I do hope you don't believe that," Mavis cried, her face stricken. "Another man on the horizon?"

"Not at the moment."

"With your looks you shouldn't worry. Someone will turn up soon. I can't imagine what I'd do if . . ."

An expression close to panic crossed her face. She motioned for the waiter, who was beginning to bring hors d'oeuvres to the tables, and ordered a plate.

"Herbie's always saying that he couldn't afford to divorce me," she laughed loudly. "Not that he would ever really think of it. We're almost an ideal couple. Besides, he's very religious. Oh, that little drink has gone right to my head! Won't you share these cocktail sausages with me? Do you have a picture of your little boy?"

"No. I'm sorry, I don't carry it with me."

"Then let me show you a snap of our family," she said proudly, popping another sausage into her mouth and reaching for her bag.

Gaynor looked away. The young man was still eyeing her. She returned his seductive glance. Mavis, oblivious, piled the table with keys, makeup and other items before she found the snapshot.

"There! Aren't they too precious for words? My babies." It was a photo of Mavis sitting on the front steps of a tract house surrounded by five beagles. She had one puppy in her lap, holding his floppy ears out to full length, while the other four dogs crouched around her in mournful obedience.

"There's my family. Truman is the oldest—I think I wrote to you when I got him. Then we had Mrs. Windsor—they're all named after celebrities, you see. That's Winchell and Kinsey and the youngest, the one on my lap, is Ike. Aren't they darling?"

Gaynor ordered another drink, trying not to laugh. Mavis kissed the picture, and then placed it in her bag, her eyes meeting Gaynor's with a pleading expression.

"I'm very organized. I have my housework done by ten in the morning and I'm not the sort who likes to loll about. In fact, I feel crook unless I'm busy. I thought of getting a job—not that I need to, Herbie's a wonderful provider—but he put his foot down. Said it would look bad to have his wife working. So the dogs are my answer to it all! I've trained them myself, you know; had to take all sorts of obedience classes. But they really are man's best friend. They're obedient *and* affectionate . . ."

"But they can't talk," Gaynor said archly, turning her eyes back to the young man.

"Too right. You've put your finger on it. But if you're good to them, they're good to you. They really love me. Where could you find that kind of simplicity in human relationships? Have you ever thought of getting a pet?"

"I had a boa constrictor once."

"You wha . . . Oh, Gaynor, what a sly sense of humor you have. You almost had me on for a minute. I guess those Manhattans have gone to my head. And look at the time! Herbie will be furious with me," she laughed, spearing the last sausage. "Can I give you a lift to your hotel?"

"No, thanks. I have to drop by the box office up the street to pick up some tickets."

"It's been smashing running into you like this! You'll be the star attraction in the next newsletter, I promise you. Now where's the check?"

"I'll shout you," Gaynor said quickly, as Mavis started to pile the contents of her purse on the table again.

"Thanks awfully. And do keep in touch. No matter how much we change, we are what we came from, aren't we?"

She adjusted the yellow monstrosity and almost knocked over the glasses as she bent across the table to kiss Gaynor's cheek. She bustled away, pausing at the door to call out "Ta-ta! Cheerio!" in a voice that made Gaynor want to melt into the booth.

She leaned back, feeling giddy and a little annoyed that she'd allowed Mavis to upset her. The bar was almost empty now. She turned to see the young man and his friend get up and walk toward the door. She thought he was going to leave without a backward glance, but he patted his companion on the shoulder, ushered him out, and sauntered toward her with a cockiness well in advance of his years. Placing his hands on her table, he leaned forward, his heavy-lidded eyes fixing her with a blatant seductiveness. His mouth, so softly sensuous that it was almost feminine, curled in a knowing smile.

"I hope my friend catches up with your friend. And I hope they give each other an earache. Can I buy you a drink to help you recuperate?"

"Yes," she said slowly. "I think you may."

An hour later, when the place had started to fill up with the pretheater crowd, he excused himself to go to the men's room. Leaning against the green tile wall, he stroked his hair into place and examined the contents of his wallet. There was no denying she was the classiest piece he had come across in a long time, but she had ordered three more scotches to his one beer and he was afraid he was about to run out of funds. Ironic that the dames who had money always ended up costing you the most. She had said very little about herself, but she seemed to be interested when he'd told her about his acting credits. Yet there was something behind her come-hither looks that suggested she might be a mean drunk. He stuffed the bills back into the wallet and made a decision: he would put it to her now, but if she acted coy he'd give up on it.

"It's getting late," he whispered, pointing out at the streets, where neon lights had now started to flash. "How's about we go back to your place for another drink?"

"No, no, no. You can't come with me," she laughed, tossing her head and exposing her teeth. "You wouldn't fit in. I'm a proper lady with proper friends. How can I put it, darling? My set doesn't look kindly on ladies picking up jackaroos. You may flirt with your friends' husbands as long as it's on the sly and everyone is playing by the rules, but you mustn't pick up boy actors in strange pubs. No, no." She wagged her finger at him. "V-e-r-y déclassé."

"Then how about going to my place in the Village?" he countered, annoyed that she had referred to him as a boy but not wanting his investment to go to waste. "My roommate's out of town with a show. I'd even fix us some supper. You'd better eat something or you'll get sick."

She leaned forward, eyes downcast, fingernails scratching zigzag patterns on the tablecloth. He thought she was playing at demure indecision, but when she looked up she stared past him as though she'd forgotten his presence.

"Well, it's getting late," he grunted, reaching into his back pocket. "It's been nice talking to you, but I think I'd better be moving on."

As he rose from the table, she lunged for him, grabbing his arm and pulling him back down beside her.

"Don't go," she pleaded, guiding his hand under the table.

"I'm sorry but . . ."

He moved his fingers slightly, feeling the slippery texture of a satin petticoat underneath her skirt. She stared straight in front of her as his hand advanced to her thigh and fondled the rubber nipple where her garter belt hooked her stocking.

"Another drink?" he asked, feeling his palms perspire.

"You know, Captain Putney was right," she said after some deliberation. "Even if you do become a pike, there are lots of minnows swimming about. They try to nibble away at you because they know you're powerful. They nibble and nibble—little pieces—right down to the bone."

She was sure a crazy broad. Captains and fish. Next thing he knew she'd probably be telling him she was a gypsy orphan who'd been raped by pirates.

"I really have to be getting home. I've got an audition tomorrow and I haven't done any homework on the script."

He pulled his hand away and threw some bills down. She steadied herself against the table, hooked her arm through his, and followed him out the door. He hailed a taxi, shoving her into the back seat before she could change her mind again. He took off her hat and wrapped his jacket around her shivering shoulders. She cuddled up next to him, letting his hands stray over her breasts. When he kissed her throat, she put her hand up to touch her necklace.

"This is mine. I bought it with my own money. People could say that it's really Richard's money. But it's mine. I earned it. I did earn it, you know."

She leaned forward, straightening her back with a drunken self-righteousness, as though he had accused her of shoplifting.

"Sure it's yours. It's pretty," he moaned, pulling her hand into his crotch. "Anything you want is yours."

They necked all the way to the Village, so that he had trouble straightening up when he got out of the cab.

"I know it's not much," he apologized, kicking a bag of laundry out of the way and flicking the wall switch. She moved past the pool of light from the overhead lamp and fell onto the couch, doubled up with laughter.

"No, it's not much," she wheezed, giving way to a coughing fit. "But when I was a kid, I would have thought it was bleedin' Buckingham Palace. You're a great galah, aren't you?"

He shrugged defensively. "Want another drink?"

"Galah. Galah. It's a bloody parrot from the islands."

"I think there might be some wine around somewhere." He gestured toward the pullman kitchen, where dishes were piled in the sink.

"I can send down to room service if it's a drink I want," she slurred, stretching back on the couch. "Hey, my hat. Where's my hat?"

"I guess you must've left it on the seat of the cab."

"So what? Plenty more where that came from."

She jerked her zipper around to the middle of her belly, tugging at it helplessly. The skirt wiggled up, exposing the hooks of her garter belt and the white flesh of her thighs. He crossed the room noiselessly, pushing her backward and trying to ease the zipper down.

"Back off, Romeo." She jerked away, almost toppling him to the floor as she staggered up. He thought perhaps she was going to leave, but when she reached the center of the room where the light was brightest, she stopped dead.

"You an actress?" he panted, watching her sway beneath the light.

"What?"

"I said are you an actress? I'm very good at observing people. One of the tricks of the trade, you might say. When I saw you in the bar I figured you were either married to some rich old coot or else you were a British starlet. And just now . . . hey, nobody but an actor reacts to lights that way. I think it's an instinct. I'm studying the Method right now. Method people think it's cheap to care about stuff like lights. They say if you notice that kinda shit it means you're not emotionally involved with the scene. But I think it's an instinct, at least with the old pros. I did a show with Lureen Tuttle. Blindfolded she could find the light. Gravitated to it like a moth to a flame."

"Is that so," she leered, unbuttoning her jacket. "So you judge me to be an actress. And are you a hung jury?"

"If you come over here and do a love scene with me you'll find out."

She ignored him, humming softly to herself as she slipped out of the high heels, yanked the zipper open and slithered the skirt to the floor. "I'm very good," she crooned in a sing-song voice, almost tumbling over as she rolled down the stockings and kicked them aside. "I've been told I'm very good. As an actor—you did say you were an actor, didn't you?—as an actor you will appreciate my performance. My reviews say I'm very good."

"If you weren't boozed up you could probably beat Gypsy Rose Lee," he grinned as she pulled the fancy slip over her head. "Are you really a stripper?"

"I am not a stripper," she hissed. "Don't you understand anything?" She pulled off the brassiere and panties and stood naked in the circle of light. Sweat glistened on her face, but goosebumps were forming all over her flesh. Yanking her hair back with both hands, she stared up into the light. "I will *not* be beaten down. I've always gotten out of trouble and I'll get out of this. She's lying. I will not be beaten down."

"Sure you won't," he whispered, unnerved by her private incantation. "Long as you've got the bucks you're gonna be all right." He inched toward her, reaching out. She stood perfectly still as his hands moved over her breasts and hips, but when he grabbed her buttocks and pulled her toward him, she wrenched away, staggering to the couch.

Just his luck, he thought bitterly. On top of the fact that he'd blown an audition yesterday, he had to get all excited over some schizo nymphomaniac and waste his unemployment check getting sloshed. It didn't matter that she was the most beautiful thing he'd ever come close to having; she was just too crazy to deal with.

"Listen, lady, you're outta control. I think maybe I'd better get you back into your clothes and call you a cab."

And now she became docile, folding her hands across her pubic hair protectively. Her eyes were great dark things, wide with fear but expectant in some horrible way, like a child who's waiting to be punished. "Don't you want me?" she implored in a soft little voice, as though his rejection had cut her to the quick.

Dammit, she was something. Lying there all vulnerable and sad as if she were offering him a home-made gift he might not want. Very Tennessee Williams. He'd never met a real woman who was this neurotic. Some of the girls in acting class really worked hard on the wild, unpredictable look, but this one was the genuine article. And she wasn't really dangerous, he decided now. She was really kind of pathetic. He could learn a lot from having sex with a woman like this. He might go through six months of his life without this kind of an opportunity. And if he stored it up, remembered every detail, consciously recorded every single sensation, why, he could use it in class next week. He'd really impress Strasberg then.

He unbuckled his belt, moving toward her with slow, sinuous movements. He was really beginning to feel hot.

"Please hurry," she moaned. "I'm cold. I'm so very, very cold."

CHAPTER
XXVII

IT WAS the first hot spell of the year. The sun had been up for only a few hours, but heat waves already shimmered off the pavement, and no breeze moved the humid air. Dawn walked slowly up the hill toward St. Timothy's, pulling Nita along behind her. Her panty girdle was chafing her legs and the nylon dress was already sticking to her back. She would have preferred to spend the morning dressed in shorts, tending the patch of earth in front of the apartment; but Faye was going to parochial school now and, whether out of religious fervor or fear of the nuns, insisted on attending early Mass. She walked ahead of her mother and sister, waving her arms wildly and staggering from side to side.

"Why are you walking like that, Faye?"

"Because we're lost in the desert. Our camels have all run away and we are dying of thirst. Oh, water, water," she groaned, giggling and running back to Dawn. "Can I go to *Treasure Island* this afternoon? Can I?"

"We'll see."

"Come on, Mummy. Just because Nita's too little to sit through a movie I don't see why I can't go. Peggy's mother lets her go alone."

"I want to go too, Mummy. Let me go too," Nita whined, pulling the elastic band under her chin and pushing her hat askew.

Dawn bent down to straighten Nita's hat. Faye pulled her face into an agonized expression resembling the holycard martyrs who decorated her bedstead along with photos of Rita Hayworth and Jennifer Jones.

"Let's get a move on, kids. We've already heard the first bells, and we're going to be late. And Faye, I've asked you a million times not to chew your gloves. I bought that pair at Easter and they're already ratty looking."

"I'm hungry."

"You'll have a big breakfast as soon as we get home. You said you wanted to go to communion, and you know you can't eat before communion. The nuns have explained that to you, haven't they?"

"Yes, but I forget why."

"So do I, but you can't."

The second warning bells pealed. Dawn hurried them on past the modest houses where a few sleepy-eyed inhabitants had already come out to dampen their lawns. They cut through the school yard, passed the rectory, and turned the corner near the church. She was surprised to see that there was quite a large crowd still loitering on the steps. Mrs. Stebbins, who was always trying to involve her in the Sodality, stepped aside from her husband and acne-faced son and touched her on the arm.

"So glad to see you again, Mrs. Mueller. My, don't your girls look cute. Isn't it just awful—about Korea, I mean. Does it mean your husband will have to go?"

"I'm sorry, I don't know what you mean."

"Why, haven't you heard? The North Koreans crossed the border . . ."

"The Thirty-eighth Parallel, Mom," her son corrected her.

". . . Anyhow, they crossed it during the night. It seems as though we're at war."

"Don't be an alarmist, dear," Mr. Stebbins put in. "We don't know yet if it's a war. It may just be an incursion instead of an invasion." Gary Stebbins had been the principal of the local high school for years and tended to address everyone as though he were calling an assembly to order.

"I'm sure I don't understand the difference," Mrs. Stebbins said impatiently. "If people are shooting each other, I'd call it a war. And if it's a war, it means they could call Christopher up, couldn't they?"

"Not for another six months, Mom. Hell, I don't even know where Korea is."

"Watch your language, Christopher. It's near Burma."

"Don't be ridiculous, dear. It's right next to Japan. MacArthur's in Japan so we've got men there already, don't we?"

"I don't know if we do or not. I didn't know anything about it until this morning's news report."

"North Korea has probably invaded South Korea," Mr. Stebbins explained. "It's part of our containment policy to back the government of South Korea, so if it is a war it means we'll go to their defense. Not just us. The whole United Nations, I guess."

"But you just said it wasn't a war," Mrs. Stebbins said testily.

"I wouldn't give you a plug nickel for the United Nations," Christopher fumed. "Who the hell is the United Nations?"

"Christopher, *please.* You're standing on the church steps, you know. You never used to curse until you started running around with those boys from . . ."

The last ringing of the bells cut short the debate about international events and Christopher Stebbins's language. The Stebbinses excused themselves and started into the church. Dawn stood rooted to the spot, blinking her eyes against the sun. "Mummy, is Daddy going to go away again?" Faye asked, tugging at Dawn's arm as she moved mechanically up the steps.

"I don't know, dear. I don't understand what's happened. We'll find out later."

"Later, later, everything's later," Faye sighed, dipping her fingers into the holy water without taking off her gloves. "I'm going to sit up front with my friends. I'll see you after Mass."

Dawn slid into a back pew, lifting Nita onto the seat beside her. She felt completely numb during the first part of the service, rising and kneeling a full beat after the rest of the congregation. When it was time for the sermon, the young Jesuit who was so popular for his sense of humor mounted the pulpit looking grave. He announced he was putting aside his prepared text, and then intoned: "Oh, Lord, we beseech Thee in this time of trial, to give your heavenly guidance to our leaders and, if need be, courage to our fighting men. Brethren, let us pause and offer a silent prayer for peace." Dawn bowed her head, feeling so sick to her stomach that she thought she might have to leave the church.

After Mass she bought a newspaper and hurried home. The children ate their waffles while she read the reports. "At 4 A.M. Korean time, artillery split the night just above the 38th Parallel . . . still not determined if this is a full-scale invasion . . . emergency meeting of the U.N. Security Council . . . President Truman is expected to fly back to Washington from Independence . . . the checkered history of the Republic of South Korea . . . ."

She gave in to Faye's request and took them to the matinee. Sitting amid squealing kids and flying popcorn, she tried to reason it through. If this did turn into another war, it would surely take Zac. He would be shipped out and she would be left alone with the children. Not just left alone—she was used to that and no longer felt doubts about her ability to cope or make decisions—but left alone with the added burden of constant anxiety. The nightmares of disaster would start again. She would be fearful when she opened the mail, tense whenever she listened to the news.

After supper she put the children to bed and re-read the newspapers. She felt a bone-aching weariness, but knew she wouldn't be able to sleep. She baked a coffee cake and scrubbed the kitchen floor, and then fell into bed. Zac was due home early the next morning. She lay awake listening to passing cars until after midnight. At five o'clock she woke with a start. Knowing she wouldn't be able to go back to sleep, she got up, showered, and sat on the couch waiting for him to arrive. He came in just before sunrise, his jacket slung over his shoulder; great patches of sweat stained his khaki shirt.

"You're up already. I guess you've heard the news."

"Yes. Someone told me at church yesterday. I've read the papers and listened to the radio, but I'm still not sure I understand what's happening."

"You and the rest of the American public, honey."

"Have you got any orders yet?"

"Not yet. Is there any beer in the refrigerator?"

She brought him a bottle and sat, twisting her wedding ring, while he loosened his tie and took off his shoes. "Well, we've been caught with our pants down again," he said disgustedly, taking a long swig of the beer. He got to his feet and began pacing about, cursing the administration and asserting that he and most of his shipmates had seen this coming. Waving the bottle, he went into a harangue about military preparedness, giving statistics on weapons and troop locations that bewildered her. Finally, his fury spent, he rested his arm on the doorjamb and stared out at the sunrise.

"I hope it doesn't mean another war. It's such a tragedy," she muttered.

"Yeah. Yeah, it is," he agreed; but she noticed the excitement in his eyes and the tensile energy in his movements. In some way she simply couldn't fathom, she knew that he welcomed it.

He drained the bottle and sat down next to her, putting his arm around her. "And how are you, Mom? I'm sorry this had to happen now. I know you've been worried about Marge being sick and now it looks as though I'll be shipping out."

"Do you really think so?"

"Don't talk foolish, honey. As soon as those bums in Washington look at a map and figure out where the hell Korea is, I'll get my orders. How are the kids?"

"They're fine."

"Dammit, I'm tired."

"Why don't you go off to bed? I'll keep the kids quiet when they wake up."

"Okay." He pecked her on the cheek and got up. "Try not to get all worked up about it, Dawn. Christ, it's gonna be another scorcher today, isn't it?"

She went outside and turned on the hose. It was still too early for anyone to be about and in spite of the blazing sun, the street had an eerie feeling. The apartments had been constructed—or more accurately, thrown up—just a few years before. In order to maximize profits the developers had razed the trees and crowded the buildings into close, uniform rows that went on for miles. They had called the place New Village, perhaps hoping to give it an aura of community, though it had no church, library or school. The only meeting places were an equally new supermarket, a laundromat, and the Toddle Inn, a bar where the men and some of the more free-wheeling wives congregated.

When she had first seen the two-storied stucco boxes with the numbered doors—advertised as "Modern Living with a Homey Touch"—they had reminded her of a stage set, so insubstantial-looking that she was afraid to open a door lest she find nothing on the other side. She couldn't decide if the architecture affected the inhabitants or vice versa; but her neighbors seemed to have an impermanent, rootless quality. Most were new to the area but had no plans to stay on, and consequently took little interest in caring for property or nurturing friendships. She had gone to a few Fuller Brush parties given by other women, but hadn't found anyone she really wanted to talk to. She had seeded the patch of ground in front of her door, planted flowers, and painted the mailbox, but her attempts at beautification seemed paltry and out of place in the sterile environment. As she got down on her knees to weed the clump of marigolds, she realized with a sinking feeling that no matter what she tried to do, New Village would remain for her what it was for the other inhabitants: a dwelling place, but not a home.

She remembered the almond tree in her parents' backyard. It had been planted by her great-grandfather shortly after he'd arrived from Ireland, and it was still referred to as "Pop Devlin's tree." She, Kevin and Patsy had swung from its branches, sending showers of glorious white blossoms onto the lawn. Marge had used the almonds to make sweets and Charlie would sit underneath it on an afternoon, reading his paper and railing against Liberal Members of Parliament and cricket players who hadn't given their all in the last match. During her childhood she had never thought about the tree. It was just there. But when Pop Devlin died on her thirteenth birthday she had gone into the yard and put her arms around the trunk. Without understanding why, she had felt proud and comforted.

She sat back on her haunches and closed her eyes. She had held on in America out of a sense of loyalty to Zac; but if he were going away, if the illusion of making a home for him was taken from her, what purpose would it serve for her to stay on? She wanted—she had the right to—some happiness. She had never pressed him before, but now she was determined to ask and, if need be, to demand to go home. Washing the dirt from her hands, she rose with slow deliberation and went into the house. The shades in the bedroom were drawn. Zac lay on his side, his back to her, stripped down to his undershirt and shorts. Hearing her come into the room, he drew the sheet up over his legs.

"Are you asleep yet?"

"Nope. Just lying here thinking."

"I've been thinking too. How soon do you suppose they'll let you know about your orders?"

"Coupla days at the most."

"I hope you don't have to go . . ."

"C'mon, Dawn."

". . . but if you do have to go and if you think it's going to be for a long time, I'd like to take the girls and go back to Australia."

He turned around and looked at her in amazement. "I know it would be expensive," she went on calmly. "I know it would take everything we have in savings and then some, but I want to go home. You know Marge has been sick, and I'm longing to see Patsy's new baby . . . And I don't have any real friends here in New Village, so if you're not going to be coming home . . . I just don't see the point of it anymore."

"I know it'd be tough for you. That's one of the things I've been thinking about. Maybe you could go back to Ohio and stay with Suds and Homer."

She let out a soft, incredulous laugh, and then became serious again, commanding him to look into her eyes. "Oh, Zac, how could you possibly suggest that? That woman—I don't mean to talk unkindly about her, but . . . bloody hell, I'm going to say what I feel! I would never, ever be in her house again. I want to go home. I mean it. So if you'd think about it and let me know how you feel, then we could discuss it and . . ."

"Would you mind getting me a glass of water?"

She stood up, glad to be relieved of her self-imposed obligation not to let her glance waver from his face. Her knees felt weak as she walked to the kitchen. When she returned, he had put on his pants and was sitting on the edge of the bed. He took the glass and sat it on the night table.

"I hope you don't think that my wanting to go home means that I'm deserting you," she said softly. He waved her to be silent.

"No, Dawn. I don't think that." He felt, in fact, that it would be a salve to his conscience to have her back with her family. The journey would impose financial problems, but that would be easier to cope with than worrying about her well-being. If he were going off to war again it was only decent that he should get her settled in a place where she would be happier. "If I get orders to leave, I think you should go back to your folks."

She felt as if the effort of confronting him had reduced her powers of concentration. Had he actually agreed to let her go without so much as a discussion? And was his acceptance based on concern or a lack of it? She tried to study his face, but he picked up the glass and drank the water, turning his head away from her. After all these years she still didn't understand how his mind worked. The old pain of her failure to be intimate with him came back, almost making her renege on the decision. She reached for his hand and held it tight. The roughness of the calluses stirred a tenderness she rarely felt anymore.

"I guess we'll just wait and see what happens when your orders come through," she said finally.

"Sure. But there's not really much to talk about, is there?"

There was everything to talk about, she thought. Everything, and nothing. She heard the children in the next room.

"I guess the kids are up," she sighed, releasing his hand. "Do you want to see them now?"

"Sure. Let 'em come in."

HIS ORDERS CAME through two days later: he was to ship out in ten days. He took their savings and booked the airline tickets. She cabled her family that they would be coming home, flying out of San Francisco the following Sunday morning. By a stroke of luck, he found a guy at the base who was willing to take over the apartment and buy all their furniture. Zac offered to take her to dinner at the base on Saturday night if she could find a babysitter.

Saturday night, the apartment scrubbed, the packing almost done, the knick-knacks she hated to leave but didn't have room for distributed to neighbors, she stood before the mirror over the chest of drawers. The bedroom, stripped of photos, doilies, vases and the white table radio he had given her for their fifth anniversary, was as barren as a hotel room. She struggled to open the jar of foundation cream.

"I haven't used this in so long I think the lid's stuck."

"Here, let me have it."

He finished tying his shoe, moved to the bureau, and twisted off the lid with a quick jerk.

"Thanks."

Hoisting up his pants, he stood near the open window, bouncing on the balls of his feet and whistling the same tuneless phrase over and over until she wanted to throw the jar at him. She leaned closer to the mirror, patted the cream onto her cheeks, and examined the pores near her nose. She'd just read an article warning that a glamorous appearance couldn't be achieved in a single evening, but required a daily regimen of beauty care. "Too bloody right," she whispered, reaching for the powder.

"You say something to me?"

"No. Talking to myself. I do it a lot lately. I shudder to think what I'll be like in my old age."

"You about ready?"

"Five minutes. If you want to hurry things up you could go next door and bring the kids home. I do hope this girl we've hired will be all right."

"You said what's-her-name next door has used her before."

"I know. It's just that we go out so rarely, I'm not used to leaving them."

"Dammit, I can't help it if I've pulled extra duty all the time," he answered gruffly.

She drew in her breath and counted to five. "I didn't mean it as a criticism, Zac. I was only talking about how I felt leaving the girls."

"Yeah. Those kids are your whole life, aren't they?"

It was hard to tell whether he meant it as a reproach or a simple statement of fact. She turned around to look at his expression, but he moved past her to the door.

"Okay. I'll go over and get them."

"And thank Barbara for letting them visit," she yelled after him.

The screen door slammed. She closed her eyes, burying her face in her hands. Whenever they exchanged words, even in the most trivial conversation, she felt as though she were walking in a mine field; one wrong move could result in an explosion. She was so tired from the packing that all she wanted to do was stand under a cool shower, and then crawl into bed. She'd tried her best to be pleasant to Zac today, yet they were on the verge of another argument. The frustrating part was that she could tell he had been making an effort at getting along with her. He had even offered to help with the lunch dishes and he'd played with the children for hours. But good will, even mutual good will, didn't seem to be enough to overcome all the pent-up tensions between them.

She screwed on the earrings her parents had given her for her twenty-first birthday and stepped back to look at herself. The lime-colored sundress had been purchased when she was thinner and now the skirt didn't hang well. After a disastrous attempt at a home permanent she'd cut off most of her hair, and the short curls were too boyish to be really becoming. Still . . . she backed up another step, allowing herself a more generous appraisal. Green was her color. The few dabs of makeup did give her a smoother complexion. She didn't look too bad.

"Mummy, you look like a movie star," Faye cried as she ran into the room. "The babysitter's outside with Daddy. And don't worry, I'll show her where everything is. Have a good time on your date."

DAWN WAS a bit disappointed when she saw the outside of the club. It was like all the other buildings on the base: squat and institutional. But once Zac had opened the door and let her inside, she was pleased by the soft lighting, the spotless napery, the aquarium above the bar. She ordered the chicken with mushroom sauce from the mimeographed menu and said she would have a cocktail. The chicken was overcooked, but Zac seemed to be enjoying his T-bone, so she said it was all right. They had three rounds of drinks, grasshoppers for her, scotch and sodas for him. When they'd finished their ice cream, he led her through the bar into another room where a jukebox was playing and tables circled a dance floor. He ordered another scotch and reached for her hand.

"Okay, chicken, let's see if you remember how to cut a rug."

"I'm a bit wobbly on these heels, and I have dishpan hands; but I'm game if you are."

By the third dance, her hesitancy was gone. She didn't feel shy that people were watching them, because she knew they were the best couple on the floor. He led her with smooth confidence, whirling, dipping, cueing her with "remember this one," executing turns she thought she had forgotten. His eyes were bright as he pulled her to him, led her back to the table, and excused himself to go to the men's room. They were having a good time, she thought in amazement. She was feeling lightheaded and full of fun, smiling back at any eyes that caught hers. A tall, good-looking man got up from a nearby table and asked her to dance. Feeling very flattered, but slightly flustered, she declined his offer. Zac returned to the room in time to see the man leave their table.

"He somebody I know?" he asked, peering through the dim light.

"I don't think so."

"Then what did he want?"

"He asked me to dance."

He tipped back in his chair, raising his hand for the waiter and looking at her with a critical but not unappreciative glance.

"Your hair looks kinda nice cut like that."

It was the first time in recent memory that he had offered a compliment on her appearance. She touched her short curls, grateful that he had noticed her in "that way," but feeling a little sad that it had taken the attention of another man to stimulate his interest.

"You could have danced with him if you wanted to, you know."

"I'd rather dance with you."

"So what are we waiting for?" he grinned with that winning Yank aggressiveness she hadn't seen since their courtship. She held both hands out to him. He helped her up and whirled her onto the floor.

WHILE HE WAS taking the babysitter home, she looked in on the children, washed, and brushed her teeth. She was packing the green dress in the suitcase when she saw the satin nightgown she'd worn on her honeymoon. The lace around the neckline had frayed and been mended, but it was still her best gown. Her next-door neighbor, Barbara, a rowdy, free-spoken girl who neglected her housekeeping to sit and drink beer in the afternoons, had once said, "The only thing that keeps me from having an extramarital affair is the shabby state of my underwear." Dawn had laughed along with the other women sitting at Barbara's kitchen table, wondering if there was any truth in the jest. Barbara noticed her embarrassment and hooted, "I mean it, Dawn. You know, you're like the Marines: Semper Fidelis; but I share the motto of the Boy Scouts: Be Prepared." Of course Barbara had guessed the truth about her.

Even as she looked ahead to the months and possibly years without Zac, Dawn knew that she would never violate her marriage oath. But there would be all sorts of things to compensate for her deprivation. She would be with her loved ones again. There would be kidding, affection, closeness. There would be picnics in the bush, tram rides to the beach, energetic debates at the dinner table. The children would be settled in a real family.

She heard the lock in the door. She slipped into bed, turning off the light. Zac usually undressed in the bathroom; but tonight, probably because he was a little drunk, he came into the bedroom without speaking and began stripping off his clothes.

"You awake?"

"Yes, I'm awake."

The curtains were thrown back because of the heat. She could see him clearly in the moonlight. When he came close to the bed, she threw back the single sheet and moved into his arms, hoping to prolong the joyous mood of the evening. He made love to her quickly and wordlessly. She wanted to whisper to him to slow down and let her relish this last night together, but it was already too late. Afterwards he got up, went into the bathroom, and put on his pajamas.

They lay together silently. She neither sobbed nor choked, but a wetness came from her eyes and rolled down her cheeks.

"We've gotta get a head start for the airport. I don't want to get caught in traffic."

"We've never been on a plane before. Faye's so excited about it I'm surprised she was able to sleep. But I'm scared to death."

The ticking of the clock and the sound of crickets seemed unnaturally loud. Someone had once told her why crickets rubbed their legs together to make that constant, pleasing noise; but she'd forgotten the explanation. Zac cleared his throat and doubled the pillow beneath his head.

"When I get to Japan, I'll send you some things. They have that kind of fabric you like. What's it called?"

"Oh, it will be good to see everyone again," she murmured, wiping her eyes and pulling the damp, predawn air into her lungs. "Patsy says that Mum has aged a lot since she's been sick, but I expect that once I'm there to help out she'll come 'round again."

"Look Dawn, I could be wrong about this Korean thing. We might have it mopped up in a couple of months."

They listened as a car went down the street, its headlights flashing on the ceiling.

"Brocade."

"What?"

"That material you were asking about. It's called brocade."

He turned on his side, and then abruptly rolled back, pulling her head into the crook of his neck.

"What's that thing you say to the kids when they go to sleep?"

"Goodnight, sleep tight, don't let the bugs bite," she answered.

"I'm going to miss you."

"I'll miss . . . oh, God . . . I'll miss you too, Zac."

"It'll be okay. Goodnight, Honey."

BECAUSE OF ZAC's caution, they arrived at the airport a good hour ahead of flight time. He checked the baggage and hurried into the waiting room to see the three of them sitting on the low-slung, uncomfortable couch. The girls were outfitted in their Sunday best: matching print dresses, white gloves and shoes, hats Dawn had bought from the dime store and decorated with daisies and ribbons. He felt the same surge of pride that prickled his flesh when the flag was raised. They were his family. And they were good kids, really. Sure they were a pain in the ass sometimes; but then, he guessed all kids must be. Now that they were older it was even fun to be with them sometimes. Faye was a sassy little thing, but her mind was quick as a whip. He looked at her and her stringbean legs made him feel protective and somehow melancholy. And Nita. If she'd only been a boy he wouldn't have had to look at a photograph album to see a replica of himself as a child. When he came home and she'd leaped up onto him, her plump arms circling his neck, he had an almost embarrassing sense of importance. She perspired profusely when she slept, exuding that sweet, baby smell; and her hair—which was the same color and texture as his own —curled into delicate tendrils. Yes, they were good kids. Everyone except Suds commented on how pretty and well behaved they were. It had never really struck him before just how much labor went into molding them. And Dawn wasn't like Suds. She never seemed to begrudge what she did for them. Ironing clothes, helping with home-work, arranging birthday parties seemed to give her pleasure. Well, maybe not the ironing. She did bitch about that once in awhile, but that was just because she had some spirit underneath all her calmness. Still, she was an exceptional mother. If anything, she was too devoted to the kids. But he couldn't really blame her, since he was gone so much of the time.

They sat for another twenty minutes. Dawn rummaged in her purse to make sure the passports were there and fidgeted with the children's clothes. Faye ambled off to introduce herself to the other passengers. Nita crawled over the couch and then began to investigate the con-tents of the ashtrays. Dawn had no sooner pulled her back to the couch than she announced she had to go to the bathroom. Zac called Faye back from her socializing, and when Dawn and Nita returned from the ladies' room, he commanded both girls to stand in front of him. He warned them that if they didn't settle down they wouldn't be allowed to go on the plane. Nita looked confused, but Faye smiled disbelievingly and did a little dance step. Dawn took them by the hands and guided them to the bay window, whispering furiously. He checked the clock over the departure ramp: ten minutes to go.

Turning back to the window, he watched Dawn crouch down, tie Nita's shoe, and issue another warning about their behavior. As she straightened up and walked back toward him, he noticed how inviting her arms looked in the summer dress. Hell, he'd left her alone for five minutes last night and that masher had tried to pick her up. He should have told her then how pretty she was. Some guys said that the only faithful women were the homely ones, but when they were grumbling about their wives cheating, he would tease them brutally, saying that if they didn't have the sense to pick a decent woman they deserved whatever punishment they got. He'd never had to worry about finding another man in his bed. Even when he returned home unexpectedly, his house was always in order, and Dawn was waiting with a smile on her face. She was a helluva good wife.

She took a place next to him, tense and upright, her eyes still on the children. "Now listen, Dawn . . ." His voice had that self-important, no-nonsense tone of an officer dressing down a first-class seaman. It was the tone he took whenever he was about to say something emotional: the voice he'd used when he'd asked her to marry him. She turned, her gray eyes expectant, wanting to cry out: "Why can't you just talk in a normal voice? Why do you have to sound pompous and protective when you try to express a feeling?" She folded her hands in her lap and gave him her full attention.

"Now, Dawn . . . I know it hasn't been easy for you sometimes. I've had to move you around a lot and you've missed your folks. We . . . you and I . . ." And now the voice cracked, losing authority. "You wanted to have a home, furniture and all that. I haven't been able to give you what you wanted. I guess if I'd known I couldn't give you . . . well, I shouldn't have taken you away from Australia where you were set and . . . So I just want to tell you that . . ."

He looked away, stretching his neck as though his collar were too tight, inspecting the room, watching the clock. She waited, nodding ever so slightly to encourage him.

"Flight number four-seven-six for Hawaii now boarding at Gate Six," the voice squawked over the speaker.

She lifted her hand, signaling him to ignore the interruption, but he shifted and straightened his tie, eager to move. And she knew that he couldn't say it. He couldn't say "I love you" or "I'm sorry." Not now. Not ever. Yet she believed he felt it, knew he would feel so deeply lonely that he would lie awake in his bunk as his ship crossed the immense, mysterious ocean; knew that he would send packages and checks but no letters. Her own anguish and disappointment seemed to evaporate. She felt sorry for him, and even though she knew that pity was the most miserable aspect of love, she felt none of the contempt that comes with pity.

"Oh, Zac," she said tenderly. "It hasn't been so bad. I liked America. I really did. Why, I got to see the Arizona desert and Fourth of July parades and supermarkets and . . . I've made some wonderful friends. If I hadn't come over I wouldn't have met Mr. DeLongini and Toshi. I couldn't have been with Sheila when she needed me. And you shouldn't worry about us being on our own. Being alone used to frighten me, but I've learned that I can cope with all sorts of things. I'm really very independent. Besides, I'll be back with Mum and Charlie and Patsy, and they'll help me with the girls. You're the one I'm worried about. You won't take any unnecessary risks, will you?"

"Flight Four-seven-six for Hawaii now boarding at Gate Six."

Passengers had gathered up their belongings and were pushing toward the gate. She motioned for the children. He scooped Nita up into his arms, holding her so tightly that she twisted away, casting an imploring glance at her mother. Faye wrapped her arms around his legs, whimpering, "Daddy, Daddy, I need you to come too."

"Now just calm down. Your mother's going with you so you'll be okay. Have you got everything, Dawn?" he asked, the authoritarian tone returning to his voice. "Okay troops, let's move out. In order now. Faye, you take your sister's hand and lead the way. Your mother and I will bring up the rear. Ready, march."

Dawn hesitated at the entrance to the ramp, turning to him open-mouthed, anguished.

"Come on, old girl." He patted her back. "You're blocking traffic. No tears now. You're going home."

He stood at the window for a long time after the plane had disappeared into the sky. A sharp, insistent pain constricted his throat. He ground his teeth, set his cap more firmly on his head, threw back his shoulders with dress-parade stiffness. Then, turning sharply, he moved through the crowd of strangers.

CHAPTER
XXVIII

"YER CRAZIER'n a bed bug, Sheila. You been wantin' to take a vacation fer years and now we're ready to go, yer screwin' up yer face an' actin' like y' don't wanna leave. An' I know why. You think 'cause y' passed the state boards with such a high score the hospital walls are gonna fall down if'n yer not there to hold 'em up."

"That's not it," she sighed, bending her arms behind her to struggle with the clasp of her brassiere. "I'm glad to be away from work for a while. I just hate to leave Spencer."

"Didn't y' see his face when Ma walked him outta here? It prob'ly hurts y' to realize it, but he's happy to be rid of us. Ever since y' took that nutrition class the poor li'l guy cain't beg but one Popsicle a week, and he knows Ma's gonna let him sneak candy an' stay up late." He pushed her hands aside, hooked up the bra, and rubbed his chin on her shoulder. "Now hurry on and get dressed 'fer I get all hot 'n bothered 'n don't wanna travel no further'n the bed."

She zipped the mauve floral dress, picked up a matching cardigan, and turned in front of him. "How do I look?"

"Y' hair's as yella as a Pippin, y' got lips like a Winesap, but yer tart as a Granny Smith."

"Working outdoors so much has given you sunstroke, Billy."

"Made me more poetic is all," he winked. "Or maybe bein' 'round ol' man Suttam is makin' me nutty. I swear he's the craziest ol' guy I ever met outside o' m' first sergeant. Y' know last week when we's workin' late 'cause of the frost? I go by his office an' I hear him talkin' to this apple on his desk. Really havin' a conversation with it. I jest wanted to ask him bout m' overtime, but he starts chewin' on my ear 'bout what a shame it is that this company we're workin' fer wants to put a picture of Adam an' Eve an' a snake on their advertisin'. Sez it's a mean myth—slur on apples and womankind. Sez we'd still be livin' in caves if women hadn't brought us into a agricultural society. An' he's not even married. I tell y', Sheila, too much education's a dangerous thing." He grinned, snapped the clasps on the suitcase, and hoisted it from the bed. "Got everythin' y' want? Hell, Sheila, don't be straight'n up the dresser table now. Let's get goin'."

She stood, preoccupied, looking around the room; then she followed him through the kitchen and out into the muddy yard. The little girl from next door was squatting in Spencer's sandbox picking her nose. Her older brother lolled in the driveway, transfixed by the glory of their bright new Plymouth.

"Y' kids run on home now," Billy said. "Spencer's gone with Ma an' I'm takin' Miz Hickock to Richmond. Y'all stay outta that pickup while I'm gone."

The boy nodded mutely, yanked his sister up, and struggled across the driveway. As Sheila got into the car and spread her skirts on the bright upholstery, she could feel their mother's eyes from behind the torn screen door. She felt very grand as Billy backed out and drove slowly through the neighborhood, as though they were the lead car in a parade.

"We got a radio, we might as well use it," he said importantly as they drove through the main part of town. They were silent for most of the Hit Parade, mesmerized by the luxury of having music in the car. The news came on, announcing MacArthur's landing at Inchon. Billy flipped off the radio, shaking his head from side to side.

"But that sounded hopeful," Sheila ventured. "Now they'll recapture Seoul, won't they?"

"I don't know. I think this one's gonna be a real mess."

"You know when I first heard about Korea I got very frightened. I thought perhaps you'd want to join up again."

"Not hardly."

"But you were such a hero during the war. I know you never talk about it, but I thought perhaps you missed it." He snorted, looked both ways, and pulled out onto the highway. "Dawn says Zac was straining at the bit. I don't suppose she'd ever have gone back home if he hadn't been shipped out again. But you know, I'm glad she did. You can tell from her letters how much happier she is now. But you know when I think about the war—our war, I mean—I realize how little I really know about it. It makes me want to go back, read about it, try to understand the causes and the reasons."

"When yer a li'l ol' lady you'll still be pesterin' around lookin' fer causes and reasons, won't y'? 'Course even a hound dog like me starts thinkin' 'bout things once he slows down. Hell, I was only eighteen when they took me inta the Marines. Didn't understand anythin'. I'm not sayin' I'm sorry 'bout m' time in the Corps, but I sure feel different now. An' when I think 'bout those poor bastards in Korea—an' nobody's wavin' any flags fer them—well, it jest makes me angry. I hope to God nothin' like this is goin' on when Spencer grows up. I'm gonna teach him to be good with a rifle an I want him to be able to hunt, but shootin' guys y' don't even know? I still get sick thinkin' bout that. Didn't see their faces, but I still think 'bout it."

"I know. You don't have nearly as many nightmares as you used to, but I still hear you talking in your sleep sometimes. It's combat trauma. Sometimes, if you can talk about it, it helps to bring it to the surface of consciousness . . ."

"Don't be comin' at me with any of yer book conversations, girl. Jest look on up that big ol' highway . . . miles and miles takin' us to a fancy hotel in Richmond. This here car moves like a dream, don't she? Don't know why y' don't wanna trade and let me drive the pickup. Bet them doctors at the hospital think yer a real sorry gal drivin' that ol' thing. Y' know, you cain't look too ladylike tearin' 'round in that."

"Look who's acting as though he cares what other people think! I like the truck. It's sort of like an old friend who likes to complain: it creaks and it whines but it still keeps going. So don't you be payin' me an' m' truck no never mind."

"Y' know how crazy y' sound when y' say somethin' like that? Every time I hear y' mix up yer accents like that I get a kick outta it," he chuckled, slapping his own knee and then reaching for hers.

"You'd better stop feeling ladies' knees and keep your mind on the road, ducky. You've just turned off the highway."

"I know it. There's somethin' I wanna show y'."

"What?"

"Y'll see."

He squeezed her hand so hard that his wedding ring cut into her fingers, and then released it. His eyes were full of anticipation, his chin jutting forward as though pointing to some goal. *He's headed for some orchard he's particularly proud of,* she thought. *Or maybe he's plotting a seduction in the woods.* She wasn't sure her desire was still impetuous enough to relish bedding down on the damp ground and ruining her new dress. She smoothed the fabric and loosened the belt. Silly vanity to think she could still fit into a size 7. She'd never been able to shed the two extra inches that had come onto her waist after Spencer was born. But Billy had changed too. Fine lines now crinkled the flesh around his eyes and indentations ran from his nose to the corners of his mouth. His chest, which had been flat and smooth as sanded wood when they'd first met, now had the musculature of a mature man and crisp brown hair showed above the neck of his open shirt. She watched him, imagining how the lines would deepen, how the flesh would change and remold itself, thinking that he would still be handsome when he was an old man.

They splashed up the dirt road through puddles left by the previous night's rain. White pine, sugar maple, mountain laurel and celandine grew in profusion along the rutted road. Drops of water shaken from the overhanging trees fell on the windshield. The September sun shone with a clear mellow light. Being together on such a blessed day made her feel as though they had recaptured the adventure of their first meetings. As they reached the crest of a hill a rolling, protected valley lay before them. The land looked as though it had once been under cultivation; but now the grass had grown waist high, and the natural vegetation encroached on the fields. There was a small pond where two brooks converged. He turned off the motor, draped his arms over the steering wheel, and gazed out.

"It's fer sale. I happened on it last week an' the minute I saw it I wanted it so bad I could taste it."

"It's beautiful."

"That's why I wanted to show it to y'. I know we ain't got much saved up yet, an' I know every time y' get a letter from Dawn or yer folks y' get that faraway look an' y' start talkin' 'bout a trip back to Australia. So's I figured whatever money we're puttin' together should be fer that trip. But I jest wanted to show it to y'."

She nodded. She had been dreaming of a trip back home for years now, recalling the people and places of her childhood with a clarity and nostalgia that amazed her. But there was something deeper that Billy didn't guess: a belief that the trip would mark a turning point in her life. She had no intention of talking about her struggles; but if she could step off a plane, proud and pretty, holding Spencer's hand, if Da and Mother and all the relatives she thought she didn't care about, but now wrote to, would rush forward with tears and flowers to greet her . . . why, then she could say "Look, I've come through" to herself. She could give secret witness to her own victory.

She brought her attention back to Billy. He was saying something about mortgage rates and soil composition. ". . . So I'm not sayin' it wouldn't take a helluva lot of work, but if I took that weekend job working produce over to the supermarket in Radford that would bring in an extra . . ."

"Billy, your jaw's gonna get sore if you keep talking so much. Let's get out and take a look at it."

He came around and opened the door for her—a gesture of politeness that had disappeared years back. She smiled ruefully, offering her hand. They walked through the overgrown path toward the pond.

"Now look up yonder on that hill. See how there's a kinda contour in the land there where that ol' walnut tree stands? Y' could build a real fine house there. Right next t' that tree. Earth's kinda hollowed out so's y'd be sheltered. Winds wouldn't be raw on y' but y'd still have the lookout on the mountains 'n the pond."

A bird cawed hoarsely through the still air. She paused, sniffing, wishing he'd stop talking. "'Course we wouldn't have the cash to start buildin' till next year. But this could be a place fer us to be proud of, Sheila. We could put down real roots here. An' I know y' want some place pretty, some place with more room. Specially if we decided to have another baby. 'Member how y' used to say y' hated bein' an only child? 'Member how y' said y' wanted Spencer to have brothers and sisters?"

"Of course I remember."

"Do y' still feel that way?" From the way he scanned her face she knew that many other questions were embodied in one.

"It would mean more than you can know for me to have another baby."

"So, what do y' say?"

"I'd like to be alone for a bit. Do you mind?"

"Nope," he lied. "I'll jest walk 'round. I wanta see how deep that pond is anyway. Y' go on an' look by yerself."

She climbed the hill toward the big tree, found a patch of dry ground, and sat down, tucking her skirts beneath her. She watched Billy take off his shoes and socks and walk around the pond. Why had he chosen today—when they were finally on their way to a specific destination—to detour them into a fantastic dream they couldn't afford? She picked up a twig and began to scratch in the dirt, feeling vaguely annoyed. Then the part of her imagination that still leaped forward began to envision the lines of a house. A grand house, nestled beside this majestic tree. There would be a vegetable garden in the rear and a flower garden in the front. Bay windows to take advantage of the view. On summer evenings they would sit on the sloping lawn, sipping iced tea, entertaining their guests and watching the kids. Spencer could play in the woods, learn all the things Billy knew and wanted to teach him. Upstairs there would be a room for Ma, and a nursery. And downstairs . . . perhaps she could have a room all to herself. A kind of office, like Helen's. The master bedroom would be private, opening onto the veranda so they'd be awakened by the light filtering through the tree. At Christmastime the children would play around a fireplace, singing songs and opening their presents. She would look matronly, but still very desirable and . . .

"And the roads will be so rotten in the winter that it'll take a half hour to dig yourself out," another voice said. "And it will be a longer drive to the hospital. And it's all very well to think about Christmas parties, but another child will mean more washing and ironing, another two inches around the waist, and putting off the advanced training in surgery for another two years. You won't be awakened by dancing sunbeams: you'll have to set the alarm the way you always do. And you'll still be grouchy in the mornings and look like hell and you'll never learn to turn an egg without breaking the yolk and . . ." She could see him coming up the hill toward her, his shoes in his hand. ". . . and the money will be tight, tight for years to come . . ."

"Sheila, y' wanna go now?"

"How do you mean?"

"I mean shall we drive on to Richmond. I'm gettin' kinda hungry an I can see yer all confused about this. We don't have to talk about it. I jest wanted to show it to you."

"Well, I like it," she said simply, getting to her feet. "I like it fine. Let's go ahead and buy it."

"Do you mean it? Y' don't want to think 'bout it some more?"

"Not if you're sure you want it too. I've thought about it and y' know, some of my best decisions have been made on impulse."

"It would mean you couldn't go home fer years and years."

"I *am* home, Billy. I'm home free."